"THE GODDESS
HA:

D0357443

Simply wonderful reviews for

Miss Wonderful

"*Miss Wonderful* is Loretta Chase at her magical best as she spins a deliciously witty tale of an overworked woman, an underchallenged man, and a romance that shimmers with passion, humor, and tenderness." —*Mary Jo Putney

"Wonderfully funny, romantic, and sexy—a classic Loretta Chase tale with a wonderful hero." —Patricia Rice

"Chase takes a delightfully romantic story, filled with wit and unforgettable characters, and sets it against a rich historical backdrop with some marvelously heated love scenes for a joyous reading experience. *Miss Wonderful* is a delicious pleasure; we can welcome Chase back with a rousing cheer and heartfelt thanks for a superior read."
—*Romantic Times* (Top Pick)

"A splendidly written tale . . . Chase's beguiling blend of deliciously complex characters, potent sexual chemistry, and sparkling wit give this superb romance a richness and depth readers will treasure." —*Booklist* (starred review)

continued . . .

Mr. Impossible

LORETTA CHASE

BERKLEY SENSATION, NEW YORK

THE BERKLEY PUBLISHING GROUP
Published by the Penguin Group
Penguin Group (USA) Inc.
375 Hudson Street, New York, New York 10014, USA
Penguin Group (Canada), 10 Alcorn Avenue, Toronto, Ontario M4V 3B2, Canada
(a division of Pearson Penguin Canada Inc.)
Penguin Books Ltd., 80 Strand, London WC2R 0RL, England
Penguin Group Ireland, 25 St. Stephen's Green, Dublin 2, Ireland (a division of Penguin Books Ltd.)
Penguin Group (Australia), 250 Camberwell Road, Camberwell, Victoria 3124, Australia
(a division of Pearson Australia Group Pty. Ltd.)
Penguin Books India Pvt. Ltd., 11 Community Centre, Panchsheel Park, New Delhi—110 017, India
Penguin Group (NZ), Cnr. Airborne and Rosedale Roads, Albany, Auckland 1310, New Zealand
(a division of Pearson New Zealand Ltd.)
Penguin Books (South Africa) (Pty.) Ltd., 24 Sturdee Avenue, Rosebank, Johannesburg 2196,
South Africa

Penguin Books Ltd., Registered Offices: 80 Strand, London WC2R 0RL, England

This is a work of fiction. Names, characters, places, and incidents either are the product of the author's imagination or are used fictitiously, and any resemblance to actual persons, living or dead, business establishments, events, or locales is entirely coincidental.

MR. IMPOSSIBLE

A Berkley Sensation Book / published by arrangement with the author

PRINTING HISTORY
Berkley Sensation edition / March 2005

Copyright © 2005 by Loretta Chekani.
Cover art by Dan O'Leary.
Cover design by George Long.
Interior text design by Stacy Irwin.

ISBN: 0-425-20150-3

BERKLEY® SENSATION
Berkley Sensation Books are published by The Berkley Publishing Group,
a division of Penguin Group (USA) Inc.,
375 Hudson Street, New York, New York 10014.
BERKLEY SENSATION and the "B" design are trademarks belonging to Penguin Group (USA) Inc.

PRINTED IN THE UNITED STATES OF AMERICA

10 9 8 7 6 5 4 3 2 1

A Note on Spelling

An 1898 edition of Baedeker's guide to Egypt laments the difficulties of rendering Arabic into English spelling. "It is greatly to be wished that the Arabs would adopt a simpler alphabet," says the author, "with a regular use of the vowel-signs, and that they would agree to write the ordinary spoken language." In the ordinary spoken language, furthermore, he complains, not everyone pronounces vowels the same way. The consonants are consistent, but some have no equivalent English sound.

More than a century later, we still encounter a mad variety of ways for spelling Arabic and Egyptian words using the English alphabet. I ended up choosing one approach for place names (familiar modern spellings) and one for words and phrases (easiest to read). A number of these words and phrases, like customs—and many monuments—have changed or disappeared since the early 1800s.

Chapter 1

THANKS TO HIS MOTHER, RUPERT CARSINGTON had hair and eyes as dark as any Egyptian's. This did not mean he blended in with the crowd on the bridge. In the first place, he was easily the tallest man there. In the second, both his manner and attire marked him as an Englishman. The Egyptians and Turks, who judged men by the quality of their dress, noticed, too, that he was not a man of low birth.

The locals had the advantage of the Earl of Hargate's fourth son.

Having arrived in Egypt only six weeks ago, Rupert was not yet able to distinguish among the numerous tribes and nationalities. Certainly he couldn't size up social status at a glance.

He could, however, recognize an unequal match when he saw one.

The soldier was large—a few inches shy of Rupert's six-plus feet—and armed like a man-of-war. Three knives, a pair of swords, a pair of pistols, and ammunition protruded or hung from his wide belt. Oh, yes, he brandished a heavy staff, too—in an unfriendly way at the moment, at a bruised, limping, filthy fellow in front of him.

The poor devil's crime, as far as Rupert could see, was being too slow. The soldier roared some foreign threat or curse. Stumbling away, the terrified peasant fell. The soldier swung his staff at the man's legs. The wretch rolled to one side, and the staff struck the bridge, inches away. Enraged, the soldier raised the weapon and aimed for the unfortunate's head.

Rupert broke through the gathering crowd, shoved the soldier, and yanked the staff from his hand. The soldier reached for a knife, and Rupert swung, knocking the blade to the ground. Before his adversary could draw another weapon from his arsenal, Rupert swung the staff at him. The man dodged, but the edge of the weapon caught him in the hip, and over he went. He reached for his pistol as he fell, and Rupert again swung the staff. His opponent howled in pain, dropping the pistol.

"Go!" Rupert told the dirty cripple, who must have understood the accompanying gesture if not the English word, because he scrambled to his feet and limped away. The crowd parted to let him through.

Rupert started after him a moment too late. Soldiers were forcing their way through the growing mob. In an instant, they'd surrounded him.

NEWS OF THE altercation, greatly embroidered, traveled swiftly from the bridge to el-Esbekiya. This quarter of Cairo, about half a mile away, was where European visitors usually lodged.

During the inundation, in late summer, the overflowing Nile turned the square of the Esbekiya into a lake where boats plied to and fro. The river being low at present, the area was merely a stretch of ground enclosed with buildings.

In one of the larger houses, a mildly anxious Daphne Pembroke awaited her brother Miles. The day was fading. If he did not arrive soon, he would not get in, because the gates were locked after dark. They were also kept locked during times of plague or insurrection, both regular occurrences in Cairo.

Daphne was only half-listening for her brother's arrival,

though. She gave the better part of her attention to the documents in front of her.

Among them was a lithographic copy of the Rosetta Stone, a recently acquired papyrus, and a pen-and-ink copy of the latter. She was nearly nine and twenty years old, and had been trying to solve the mystery of Egyptian writing for the last ten years.

The first time she'd seen Egyptian hieroglyphs, Daphne had fallen madly, desperately, and hopelessly in love with them. All her youthful studies had aimed at unlocking their secretive little hearts. She had become infatuated with and wed a man nearly thrice her age because he was (a) poetically handsome, (b) a language scholar, and (c) the owner of a collection of books and documents for which she lusted.

At the time, she'd believed they were ideally suited.

At the time, she'd been nineteen years old, her vision obscured by the stars in her eyes.

She soon learnt, among other painful lessons, that her brilliant scholar husband, exactly like stupider men, believed that intellectual endeavors put too great a strain on the inferior female brain.

Claiming to have her best interests at heart, Virgil Pembroke forbade her studying Egyptian writing. He said that even male scholars familiar with Arabic, Coptic, Greek, Persian, and Hebrew had no hope of deciphering it in her lifetime. This he deemed no great loss: Egyptian civilization being primitive—greatly inferior to that of classical Greece—decipherment would contribute little to the store of human knowledge.

Daphne was a clergyman's daughter. She'd made a sacred vow to love, honor, and obey her husband, and she did try. But when it became clear that she must pursue her studies or go mad with boredom and frustration, she chose to risk perdition and disobey her husband. Thereafter, she continued her work in secret.

Virgil had died five years ago. Sadly, prejudice against women scholars did not die with him. This was why, even now, only her indulgent brother and a select group of friends knew the secret. Everyone else believed her brother Miles was the linguistic genius of the family.

Had he been, he might have known better than to pay two thousand pounds for the papyrus she was studying. However, a merchant named Vanni Anaz had claimed it described the final resting place of a young pharaoh, name unknown—as was the case at present for most Egyptian royalty. The story was clearly the product of the romantic Eastern imagination. No educated person could possibly believe it. Nonetheless, it had apparently captivated Miles, much to her surprise.

He had even gone to Giza again to study the interior of the second pyramid, because, he said, it would help him understand the thinking of ancient tomb builders and aid in locating the young king's tomb and its treasures.

Though Daphne was certain the pyramids could tell him nothing, she held her tongue. He delighted in exploring Egypt's monuments. Why spoil his fun? She merely made sure he took sufficient supplies for the overnight stay he planned.

She declined to accompany him. She'd gone with him once to Giza and explored the two pyramids it was possible to enter. Neither contained any hieroglyphic writing, although various visitors had scratched their profound thoughts upon the stones, e.g., "Suverinus loves Claudia." Equally important, she was not eager for another squeeze through the pyramids' long, small, hot, smelly passageways.

At the moment, however, the pyramids were far from Daphne's thoughts. She was deciding that Dr. Young had incorrectly interpreted the hook and the three tails signs when her maidservant Leena burst through the door.

"A bloodbath!" Leena cried. "Stupid, stupid English hothead! Now the streets will run with blood!"

She tore off the head and face veils she despised but must wear in public, revealing the dark hair and hazel eyes of an older woman of mixed Mediterranean origins. Daphne had hired her in Malta, after her English maid proved unequal to the rigors of foreign travel.

Leena not only spoke English, Greek, Turkish, and Arabic, but could read and write a little in these languages—unheard-of accomplishments for a woman in this part of the world. She was, on the other hand, deeply superstitious and fatalistic, with a tendency to discern the dark cloud attached to every silver lining.

Accustomed to Leena's histrionics, Daphne merely raised her eyebrows and said, "What Englishman? What has happened?"

"A crazy Englishman has been fighting with one of the pasha's men and broke the pig's head. They say it took a hundred soldiers to capture him. The Turks will cut off the Englishman's head and put it on a pike, but that will not be enough. The soldiers will make war on all the Franks, especially the English."

Unlike most of Leena's Impending Doom announcements, this sounded all too plausible.

Egypt's Ottoman rulers would have been right at home in the Dark Ages. Beatings, torture, and beheading were their methods of maintaining order. Egyptian and Turk alike had no great regard for "Franks," the despised Europeans. The military—comprising a homicidal assortment of Egyptians, Turks, and Albanian mercenaries—took a hostile view of everybody, including at times their leader Muhammad Ali, Pasha of Egypt. They made Genghis Khan's Mongol hordes look like giggling schoolgirls.

And Daphne was alone, but for her servants, all of whom were, most intelligently, terrified of the soldiery.

She was aware of alarm stirring within, of a chill and a welter of thoughts tumbling one over another. Outwardly she remained calm. Her marriage had taught her how to hide her true feelings.

"This is difficult to believe," she said. "Who would be so foolish as to fight one of the pasha's men?"

"They say the man is new to Cairo," Leena said. "Only this week he has come from Alexandria to work for the English consul general. They say he is very tall and dark and beautiful. But I think he will not look so beautiful when they carry his head through the town on a pike."

The revolting image rose in Daphne's mind. She hastily banished it and said briskly, "The man must be fatally stupid. Which ought not surprise us in the least. The consulate has too much to do with persons of dubious character." This was because the English consul general,

Mr. Salt, was here mainly to collect as many antiquities as he could, and he was not overscrupulous about how the task was accomplished.

Now, thanks to his adding a violent imbecile to his staff, the military had an excuse to run amok. No European in Cairo would be safe.

And *Miles*—on his way back—blond, blue-eyed, tall, and unmistakably English—was all too tempting a target. As was she, a green-eyed redhead like their late mother.

She looked down and saw her hands shaking. *Calm down,* she commanded herself. *Nothing's happened yet. Think.*

She had a brain, a formidable brain. It must be able to formulate a solution.

She stared at the lines of Greek characters praising Ptolemy while she debated what to do.

Sarah, the wife of the famous explorer Giovanni Belzoni, had a few years earlier donned the dress of an Arab merchant and safely visited a mosque forbidden to women and infidels. With any luck, Daphne could escape Cairo in such a disguise and meet her brother en route. Then they could hire a boat and head upriver, out of danger.

She opened her mouth to tell Leena the plan. At that moment, the courtyard erupted in shouts.

An anguished wail rose above the other voices.

Daphne bounded up from the divan and hurried to the latticed window, Leena beside her. Coming up the stairs from the courtyard was a group of Egyptian men.

They bore the inert body of Miles's servant Akmed.

The following morning

IN A MANSION in another part of the Esbekiya, His Majesty's consul general was reflecting with mixed emotions upon the prospect of Rupert Carsington's head parading on a pike through the city streets.

In the month and a half since the Earl of Hargate's fourth son had arrived in Egypt, he had broken twenty-three separate laws and been jailed nine times. For what Mr. Carsington had cost the consulate in fines and bribes,

Mr. Salt might have dismantled and shipped to England one of the smaller temples on the island of Philae.

He now knew exactly why Lord Hargate had sent his twenty-nine-year-old offspring to Egypt. It was not, as his lordship had written, "to assist the consul general in his services on behalf of the nation."

It was to saddle someone else with the responsibility and expense.

Mr. Salt brushed sand from the document before him on the desk. "One ought to be grateful, I suppose," he told his secretary Beechey. "The soldiery might have used this as an excuse for slaughtering the lot of us. Instead they merely demand an extortionate fine and twice the usual assorted bribes."

Amazingly enough, the injured soldier's comrades had not hacked Carsington to pieces and let their superiors make up a law to explain it later. He'd certainly tested their patience on the way to the city. Though outnumbered twenty to one, he attempted escape three times, inflicting many injuries in the process.

Yet the city remained quiet, and Lord Hargate's troublesome son was alive and in possession of all his limbs, confined to a rat-ridden hellhole of a dungeon in Cairo's Citadel.

Though this conveniently kept him out of trouble, one could not leave him in the cesspit indefinitely.

The Earl of Hargate was a very powerful man who could easily arrange for Mr. Salt's exile to some godforsaken, antiquity-less corner of the globe.

But getting Carsington out—Good God! The consul reviewed the figures on the document in front of him. "Must we pay all these people?" he said plaintively.

"I'm afraid so, sir," his secretary said. "The pasha has discovered that Mr. Carsington's father is a great English lord."

Muhammad Ali was an ignorant, illiterate man, but he was not stupid. After someone had read to him Machiavelli's *The Prince*, the pasha of Egypt had said, "I could teach him some things."

One thing Muhammad Ali could do to admiration—besides lead an army of deranged killers repeatedly to victory—was count, and he had counted up a ludicrous sum to free the great English lord's son.

If Mr. Salt paid the sum, his rapidly dwindling funds wouldn't cover his excavation expenses—and the instant he abandoned a site, his French competitors would move in.

If, on the other hand, he did not arrange for Carsington's release, Mr. Salt might easily end up as British ambassador to the Antarctic Peninsula.

"Let me think," said the consul.

The secretary went out.

Five minutes later, he came in again.

"Now what?" said Mr. Salt. "Has Carsington blown up the Citadel? Made off with the pasha's favorite wife?"

"Mrs. Pembroke is here, sir," said the secretary. "A matter of great urgency, she says."

"Ah, yes, Archdale's widowed sister," said the consul. "Something of earthshaking importance, no doubt. Perhaps he has discovered a vowel. I can scarcely contain my excitement."

Though Mr. Salt was mainly interested in acquiring impressive Egyptian artifacts, he did have a scholarly interest, and had made his own attempts at deciphering the baffling code. But today he was not in the mood.

He'd returned from a too-short holiday in the suburbs to the Carsington fiasco. Swiftly sinking into the gloom of his perpetual money troubles, he could not view Mrs. Pembroke with scholarly detachment.

The deep mourning she wore, head to toe—and her elderly husband dead more than five years!—did nothing to raise the consul's spirits. She always put him in mind of certain ghostly shadow figures he'd seen on the walls of royal tombs.

On the other hand, the late Mr. Pembroke had left his young wife everything, and *everything* comprised a magnificent property and an even more magnificent fortune.

If Mr. Salt could feign excitement about whatever little squiggle she imagined Archdale had deciphered, she might feel inclined to invest a part of her wealth in an excavation.

As she entered, Mr. Salt arranged his mouth in a smile of welcome and advanced to greet her.

"My dear lady," he said. "How good of you to call! What an honor this is! Please allow me to offer you refreshment."

"No, thank you." She put back her widow's veil, revealing a pale, heart-shaped face. Shadows ringed the unnaturally green eyes. "I have no time for social pleasantries. I need your help. My brother has been kidnapped."

AKMED WAS NOT dead. He had been badly beaten, though, and when at last he reached the Esbekiya, he'd collapsed.

It was long past sunset yesterday by the time he regained sufficient strength to speak, and then he was barely intelligible. By the time Daphne made sense of his tale, it was too late to act. At night the streets of Cairo belonged mainly to the police and the felons they hunted.

In any event, Europeans in difficulties must apply to their consul, not local officials. Mr. Salt and his secretary being away yesterday, Daphne had had to wait through the long night.

Now, body and spirit exhausted, she was on the brink of hysteria. She could not succumb. Men merely humored emotional women. She needed to be listened to. If she wanted men to take action, she must first make them take her seriously.

After her initial shaky declaration, she let Mr. Salt lead her to a shaded portico overlooking the garden. She drank the thick, strong coffee a servant brought. It restored her fortitude.

She told the story from the beginning, as requested.

Her brother, servants, and crew had returned from Giza early yesterday morning. Shortly after Miles disembarked from the ferry at Old Cairo, some men who claimed to be police took him away. When Akmed attempted to follow— to find out where they were taking his master and why—he was taken up, too. The "police" dragged Akmed to a solitary place, beat him senseless, and left him.

"I did not understand why they beat Akmed and abandoned him," Daphne said. "He believes these men were not police, and logic compels me to agree. If they truly were

law officers, why did they not take Akmed to the guardhouse with Miles? Moreover, it is impossible that my
brother committed any crime. No person of sound intelligence would dream of running afoul of the local authorities. Everyone knows that diplomatic conventions mean
little here."

"It will turn out to be a silly misunderstanding, I daresay," said Mr. Salt. "Some of these petty officials are over-
quick to take offense at trifles. They are not all as honest as
one could wish, either. Still, there is no need for alarm. If
Mr. Archdale has been jailed, you may be sure the authorities will inform me before the day is out."

"I do not believe he has been jailed," Daphne said. Her
voice climbed. "I believe he has been kidnapped."

"Now, now, I am sure it is nothing of the kind. Merely
an official looking for a bribe. An all too common occur-
rence," the consul added bitterly. "They seem to think we
are made of money."

"If money was all they wanted, why not send Akmed directly to me with their demands?" Daphne said. "Why beat
him senseless? It is illogical." She waved her hand, impatiently exiling all disorderly thinking from the discussion.
"I believe the servant was beaten to prevent his promptly
reporting the incident. I believe that while you try to humor
me with comfortable explanations, the trail to my brother
grows ever colder."

"The trail?" the consul said, startled. "I hope you do not
seriously consider that Mr. Archdale is the victim of a plot
of some kind. Who would risk torture and beheading to
make off with a harmless scholar?"

"If you, who have been consul general in Egypt for six
years, cannot produce a plausible motive, it is absurd to ask
a woman who has been here scarcely three months," she
said. "It strikes me as illogical as well to debate villains' motives. It would make more sense to find the persons responsible and ascertain their motives by interrogating them, do
you not think? And this ought to be done sooner rather than
later, I believe."

"My dear lady, I beg you to recollect that we are not in
England," he said. "Here we have no Bow Street officers to

undertake an investigation. The local police are no substitute, being for the most part pardoned thieves. I dare not abandon my many other responsibilities to search for missing persons, nor can I spare my secretary. None of my agents is within a hundred miles of Cairo at present. As it is, we are sadly undermanned and underfunded for the work we are expected to do. We are all of us a great deal occupied, with scarcely a minute to collect our thoughts."

He added, after the briefest pause, "All of us, that is to say, except one."

Two hours later

ALTHOUGH DAPHNE WAS covered from head to toe, her face veiled, she'd forgotten how clearly her clothes proclaimed, "European, female." Until she entered the Citadel and became aware of the men staring at her, then looking away and muttering to one another, she hadn't considered she might be unwelcome.

She told herself that (a) women were unwelcome in all too many places, and (b) these men's opinions didn't signify. In addition to her maid Leena and the consul's secretary Mr. Beechey, she had an official escort, one of the district sheiks. They followed the prison guard down a deeply worn stone stairway that grew steadily darker while the air grew increasingly rank and oppressive.

By the time they reached the bottom, the stench was making her sick, and she was wishing she hadn't insisted on coming. She might have left it to Mr. Beechey to arrange matters. She didn't need to be here.

But she hadn't been thinking clearly. She'd been too aware of time passing, every minute taking Miles more deeply into danger.

She needed help, and the only help available, apparently, was being held in a dungeon deep enough to be flooded during the inundation. Was that one of the tortures employed here? she wondered. Would they leave a man chained, to watch the water rise until it drowned him? Was Miles in such a place?

She gave one quick, involuntary shudder, then firmly banished the image from her mind and squared her shoulders.

Beside her, Leena murmured a charm against evil.

The men waved the odd torches that worked like dark lanterns, lightening the gloom a few degrees. They could not lighten the air, which was thick and unspeakably foul.

"Rejoice, *Ingleezi,*" the guard called out. "See who comes. Not one but *two* women."

Chains clanked. A dark figure rose. A very tall, dark figure. Daphne could not make out his features in the gloom. Surrounded by protectors, she had no reason to be alarmed. All the same, her heart picked up speed, her skin prickled, and every nerve ending sprang into quivering awareness.

"Mr. Beechey," she said, her voice not as steady as she could wish, "are you sure this is the man I want?"

An impossibly deep voice, most definitely not Mr. Beechey's, answered with a laugh, "That would depend, madam, on what it is you want me *for.*"

Chapter 2

THE SOUND OF AN ENGLISH VOICE — AN ENGLISH *woman's* voice—was more welcome than Rupert would have guessed.

He had been growing exceedingly bored. The feminine sound instantly revived his good humor.

He knew which of the females had spoken. His eyes had long since grown accustomed to the darkness. Though both women were veiled, the taller wore European dress. He knew she was not only English, but a lady. The cultured accents of her clear, musical voice—a trifle unsteady at present—told him so.

He could not, however, determine whether she was old or young, pretty or not. He knew, too, that one could never be absolutely certain of a woman's figure until she was naked. But looking on the bright side, she must possess all the necessary parts—and if she'd made it down all those hundreds of stairs, she couldn't be decrepit.

"Mrs. Pembroke, may I present Mr. Rupert Carsington," Beechey said. "Mr. Carsington, Mrs. Pembroke has generously agreed to pay for your release."

"Have you, indeed, ma'am? That's deuced charitable of you."

"It is nothing of the kind," she said stiffly. "I'm buying you."

"Really? I'd heard the Turks were severe, but I never guessed they'd sell me into slavery. Well, well, you learn something new every—"

"I am buying your services," she cut in, the musical voice frosty.

"Ah, I stand corrected. And which services would you be requiring?"

Rupert heard her sharp inhalation.

Before she could retort, Beechey said smoothly, "It is an assignment, sir. Mr. Salt has released you from your regular consular duties so that you may assist Mrs. Pembroke in searching for her brother."

"If all you want is a brother, you're welcome to one of mine," Rupert said. "I've four. All saints. Ask anybody."

He was not a saint, and no one had ever mistaken him for one.

The lady turned toward Mr. Beechey. "Are you sure this is the only man available?"

"How did you contrive to lose your brother, by the way?" Rupert said. "In my experience, the feat's impossible. Everywhere I go, there they are. Except here. That was one reason I jumped at the chance when my father offered. It came as a vast relief, I'll admit. When he summoned me to his study, I thought it was going to be one of those devil-and-the-deep-blue-sea choices, like the one he offered Alistair three years ago: 'Get married or suffer a fate worse than death,' or something like that. But it was nothing of the kind. It was, 'Why don't you go to Egypt, there's a good boy, and find your cousin Tryphena some more of those stones with the picture writing on them.' Stones and—What else did she want? Those brown rolled-up thingums. Paper rice or some such."

"*Papyri,*" came the melodious voice, strained through gritted teeth, by the sounds of it. "The singular is *papyrus*. The plural is *papyri*. The Latin word derives from the ancient Greek. It is a paper made, not from rice, sir, but from a reed plant native to these regions. The articles you refer to, furthermore, are not 'thingums,' but valuable ancient documents." She paused, then said in milder, puzzled tones, "Did you say Tryphena? You do not refer to Tryphena Saunders?"

"Yes, my cousin—the one with the hobbyhorse about the comical picture writing."

"*Hieroglyphs*," said the lady. "The decipherment of which—Never mind. Attempting to explain to you their importance would be, I have not the smallest doubt, an expenditure of breath to no purpose."

She turned abruptly, in a delicious rustle of silk, and started away.

Beechey hurried after her. "Madam, I do apologize for detaining you in this disagreeable place. Naturally you are distressed. However, I must beg you to recollect—"

"That man," she said in low but still audible tones, "is an *idiot*."

"Yes, madam, but he's all we've got."

"I may be stupid," Rupert said, "but I'm irresistibly attractive."

"Good grief, conceited, too," she muttered.

"And being a great, dumb ox," he went on, "I'm wonderfully easy to manage."

She paused and turned to Beechey. "Are you sure there's no one else?"

"Not between here and Philae."

Philae must be a good distance from here, else the lady wouldn't be scouring the dungeons of Cairo for help, Rupert thought. "I'm as strong as an ox, too," he said encouragingly. "I could lift you up with one hand and your maid with the other."

"He's cheerful, madam," Beechey said, sounding desperate. "We must give him that. Is it not remarkable how he's kept up his spirits in this vile place?"

Obligingly, Rupert began to whistle.

"Obviously, he doesn't know any better," she said.

"In the present circumstances, fearlessness is a great asset," Beechey said. "The Turks respect it."

The lady said something under her breath. Then she turned to the Turk who'd brought them—someone important, apparently, with an immense turban—and said something in one of those impossible Oriental tongues. The big-turbaned fellow tsk-tsked a good deal. She talked some more. He didn't seem happy. It went on.

"What's she saying?" Rupert called out.

Beechey said they spoke too quickly for him to follow.

The maid drew closer to Rupert. "My mistress bargains for you. I am sorry for you that your wits are so slow. When we came, she was willing to pay almost the full price, but now she says you are not worth so much."

"Really? How much were they asking?"

"With all the bribes, it came to three hundred purses," she said. "A white girl slave—the most expensive slave— is only two hundred purses."

"I don't suppose you know what three hundred purses amounts to in pounds, shillings, and pence?" Rupert said.

"It is more than two thousand English pounds."

Rupert let out a soft whistle. "That does seem steepish," he said.

"This is what she tells the sheik," the maid said. "She says you are of little worth to anybody. She says your head on a pike would be good for entertaining the Cairenes, but this is all the value she sees. She tells him that lords are as common in England as sheiks in Egypt. She says only the oldest son of an English lord is valuable, and you are one of the youngest. She says your father sent you away because you are an imbecile."

"Astonishing," he said with a laugh. "She can tell all that—when we've only just met—and in the dark, too. What an amazingly clever woman."

The turbaned fellow launched into a harangue. The lady shrugged and started to walk away.

The price of release was ridiculous; no one in his right mind would pay it, including Lord Hargate. All the same, Rupert was disappointed to see her depart.

Searching for her brother could be interesting. It had to be more interesting than digging in sand for broken chunks of stone, and a good deal more amusing than prying papyri from the clutches of ancient corpses. Yes, he knew what the correct word was. If he'd heard it once, he'd heard it a thousand times from Tryphena. He'd said it wrong only to hear Mrs. Pembroke's reaction—and that was highly entertaining.

Now he might never find out what she looked like.

The maid left to follow her mistress. Beechey threw up his hands and started after them.

Rupert watched the taller feminine figure until the gloom swallowed her up.

Then the turbaned man called out something.

Mrs. Pembroke emerged from the gloom, and Rupert's heart gave a small but unmistakable leap.

DAPHNE DIDN'T STAY to see Mr. Carsington released. Having settled on the price, she left Mr. Beechey to sort out the details and distribute bribes—the baksheesh that oiled most transactions in the Ottoman Empire.

She couldn't wait to be away from the Citadel. Her skin crawled. She berated herself for bargaining with the sheik for so long. But to discover the sort of blockhead upon whom her hopes were to depend, then to be bullied by an official who very likely couldn't write his own name—

It had made her nearly wild.

Her brother was in trouble—lost, hurt, possibly dead—and all the men she'd encountered so far made light of it, mocked her, or tried to thwart her. She wanted to weep with frustration.

But above all, she wanted to get away—from the Citadel and that stinking pit and all those callous men.

As she emerged at last through one of the fortress's doorways into the light, she drank in gulps of hot late-morning air.

"Do you know why they put him there, mistress, so deep under the ground, in chains?" Leena said as she caught up with her.

"It's obvious," Daphne said. "Mr. Salt said Mr. Carsington is the man who assaulted the Turkish soldier yesterday. The man is a brainless, brawling ruffian."

She walked faster toward the Citadel gate, beyond which their donkeys and donkey drivers waited. "I truly hope the other sons are saints, as this one claims," she continued irritably. "It might compensate Lord and Lady Hargate for the affliction—" She broke off as she discerned the logical conclusion of her own words. "Oh, what have I done?"

Daphne stopped short, and Leena bumped into her.

When they'd disentangled their respective veils, Daphne said, "We must send a message to Mr. Salt, declining Mr. Carsington's services."

"But you bought him," Leena said.

"I wasn't thinking clearly," Daphne said. "The place stank so, and the rats were so bold. Meanwhile, there was the illiterate sheik trying to frighten me—and Mr. Carsington behaving so provokingly with his 'paper rice' and 'thingums.' If I had not been so beset, I should have realized that no man could be more ill suited for my purposes than he. We shall be dealing with villains, I'm sure of it. The task wants a cool, calculating brain. What I need is another Belzoni: a man who knows when to employ persuasion, even guile, and when to use force."

"When first we came here, and Mr. Beechey took you to meet the sheik, I heard the guards talking," Leena said. "They said no guardhouse could hold this Englishman. He is quick and cunning and without fear. This is the reason they chained him in the deepest dungeon of Cairo."

"Anyone who is utterly fearless is either demented or dim-witted," Daphne said.

Leena pointed to her head. "You have enough up here for six men. You do not need a man with a great brain. You need a man with big muscles and great courage."

Daphne didn't know whether Mr. Carsington had big muscles or not. All she'd seen was the tall, dark form. Yet there was nothing shadowy about his presence. She'd been aware of him the entire time she haggled with the sheik. She'd heard the deep voice in the background—a rumble tinged with laughter, when he had nothing to laugh about. She'd heard the scrabbling rats. She'd smelled the filth. And she knew what his captors were like.

While she'd argued with the sheik, her mind had wandered repeatedly to the prisoner. Twenty-four hours he'd spent in that place, in the dark, figurative and literal. He'd no idea what would become of him, whether his captors would whip or torture or mutilate him, whether his friends would ever find him or he'd die there, alone.

Miles might be in the same plight.

A cold knot formed in the pit of her stomach.

"I feel filthy," she said. "I need a bath. We'll have plenty of time. It will be an age before Mr. Beechey and the sheik have completed all their bureaucratic rituals."

THE BATHS WERE a sinful luxury Daphne had discovered early in her stay here. The tiled chambers of the women's bath shut out the outside world and its troubles. Here one need only yield to being pampered and listen to the other women laugh and gossip.

Even today the bath worked its magic. She left with a clearer head and a calmer spirit. She was perfectly capable of working out a method for finding Miles, she told herself as she mounted her donkey. She only needed a man to do what she couldn't. In that case, the bigger the better, as Leena suggested—and Mr. Carsington was taller by a head than most of the men hereabouts. He had to be strong, too, to survive a collision with Muhammad Ali's brutal soldiers. All Mr. Carsington needed was a brain—and Daphne could supply that.

Letting the drivers manage their donkeys and clear the way through the crowded streets, she and Leena proceeded at the usual fast clip—dodging camels, horses, peddlers, and beggars—to the house in the Esbekiya.

Outside its gate they dismounted. Leaving Leena to pay the donkey boys, Daphne entered the shaded passageway bordering the courtyard. She was nearing the stairs when a tall form emerged from the shadows and a deep, instantly recognizable voice said, *"Twenty quid?"*

She stopped short, and her heart skidded to a stop as well, then started again, far less steadily.

The area was well shaded, but it wasn't nearly as dark as the Citadel dungeon.

She had no trouble seeing him now, even through her widow's veil. He was tall and broad-shouldered, as she'd discerned in the darkness. What she had not been able to see was the starkly handsome face.

Black eyebrows arched over dark, laughing eyes that looked down at her over a long, insolent nose. Laughter lurked at the corners of the too-sensuous mouth.

Heat washed through her in waves, burning away her hard-won calm and confidence and leaving her, for a moment, swamped in self-consciousness, like the gawky schoolgirl she'd once been.

But she'd never been as shy as she ought, as Virgil had made clear often enough. She wasn't too shy now to take in the rest: the exquisitely tailored coat, waistcoat, and trousers, the crisp shirt and neckcloth. The instant's glance was enough to sear into her mind a vivid image of the lean, powerful body the close-fitting garments only emphasized.

Her mouth went dry and her brain went away, and for a moment nothing made sense at all. Only for a moment, though. Her brain came back, and "Mr. Carsington," she said as soon as she got her tongue untied.

"Twenty quid," he repeated. "Three purses. That's what you argued Sheik Whatshisname down to. At the baths I learned it's the going rate for a *eunuch.*"

"The more expensive eunuchs, yes," Daphne said, quickly adding, "I did not expect to see you so soon. You've even had time to bathe. Miraculous." Her mind produced an image of the gentleman wearing only a *mahzam*—a Turkish towel—wrapped about his waist.

She told her mind to *stop it*. She should not have smoked at the baths, even to be polite. It left a bad taste and made one dizzy. She should not have listened to the women's lewd talk. It had given her smoke-addled mind all sorts of improper ideas.

Ordinarily she took no notice of men, except as obstacles in her path, which in her experience appeared to be their primary function.

She moved past him and started up the stairs, talking rapidly. "It is amazing, is it not, Leena? The Turks usually take hours and hours for the smallest negotiations. I had thought we'd no hope of getting started before tomorrow."

"I don't doubt the sheik would have liked to drag on negotiations in the usual leisurely style," Mr. Carsington said, "but you wore him out."

"The prison was *disgusting*," Leena informed him as she trailed Daphne up the stairs. "To get rid of the stink, we went to the baths. We smoked, we talked with the other women, we learned some rude jokes, and now we are not so sick in the stomach and crazy in the head."

"Smoking?" he said. "Rude jokes? Excellent. I knew this would be more interesting than collecting stones."

RUPERT WATCHED MRS. Pembroke continue up the stairs and through the door in an angry swish of black silk. She had flounced away from the sheik in much the same fetching way.

Since he'd found her entertaining, Rupert was delighted to learn, shortly after her departure, that she was not, as he'd assumed, of Tryphena's generation—old enough, in other words, to be his mother.

Beechey had told him that Miles Archdale, the missing brother, was an antiquarian scholar in his early thirties, and the sister a widow a few years younger.

Rupert had also learned that the plague, which had kept him confined to Alexandria for weeks, had trapped those in Cairo as well. The quarantine had only recently been lifted. Otherwise, Mr. Archdale and his sister would be in Thebes by now. According to the secretary, Archdale was eager to test his language theories on the temples and tombs of Upper Egypt.

Beechey also said that the brother was bound to turn up sooner or later, perhaps the worse for dissipation. One couldn't tell the sister this, of course, but the consul general was certain the servant Akmed had lied.

Cairo offered entertainment for all tastes, and men "disappeared" for days into brothels and opium dens. Archdale was probably still carousing in such a place. No doubt his servant had smoked too much hashish, and ended up annoying somebody, who paid him with a flogging.

Rupert was on no account to enlighten Mrs. Pembroke. He was to humor her.

"You might inquire at the guardhouses and that sort of thing," Beechey had said. "I'd advise you to question the servant privately. If you do run Archdale to ground, or he turns up on his own, as is more likely, give her whatever version of events he prefers. I cannot stress enough the importance of remaining on cordial terms with them. They are in a position to contribute a great deal to our efforts here, in both the scholarly and financial senses. Mr. Salt relies upon you to exercise the utmost discretion, tact, and delicacy."

Rupert had nodded wisely while privately wondering if Beechey, like Archdale's servant, had been smoking too much hashish lately.

Any sober person would have understood that Rupert Carsington was exactly the wrong man for any assignment requiring discretion, tact, and delicacy. Rupert himself could have said so, and normally would. But he liked the way Mrs. Pembroke twitched her skirts when she was vexed, and he wanted to see what she looked like. And so for once he held his tongue and tried to look tactful and discreet.

It wasn't a pose he could maintain for long, he knew.

He followed the maidservant up the stairs and into the house, through a zigzagging series of halls and rooms— each a step up or a step down from the previous one—and finally into a lofty room.

At one end was a raised area, its floor covered with Turkey carpets. Along its three sides ran a low banquette covered with cushions. A wide, squat table, heaped with books and papers, occupied most of the space in the center of the raised area. A narrow shelf on one side of the room held a great lot of small wooden figures.

The widow looked at the table, then sank to her knees and started shuffling through the heaps.

"Mistress?" said Leena.

"This isn't the way I left it," Mrs. Pembroke said.

"How can you tell?" Rupert said.

"I was working on the new papyrus," she said. "I always arrange the materials in a certain way. The papyrus to the right for reference. The copy in the center. The table of signs below. The Rosetta inscription here. The Coptic lexicon alongside. The grammar notes here. There is an order. There must be. One must work systematically, or it is hopeless." The pitch of her voice climbed. "The papyrus and the copy are gone. All that work . . . all those days unrolling it . . . all my care in making a precise copy . . ."

She rose unsteadily. "Where are the servants? And Akmed. Is he all right?"

"Check on the servants," Rupert told Leena. To Mrs. Pembroke he said, "Calm down. Count to ten."

She looked at him—or appeared to have her head turned in his general direction.

"Do you never take that thing off?" he said impatiently. "He must have been remarkable, the late lamented, to warrant so much grief." He made a sweeping gesture encompassing the heavy veil and the black silk. "It must be as hot as Hades under all that. No wonder you're addled."

She went on looking in his direction for a moment, then abruptly threw the veil back from her face.

And Rupert felt as though someone had given him a sharp thump in the head with a heavy Turkish staff.

"Well," he said, when he'd mustered the wind to speak again. "Well." And he thought that maybe they should have worked up to it more gradually.

He saw green, green, deeply shadowed eyes set above high cheekbones in a creamy heart-shaped face framed with silky, dark red hair. She wasn't pretty at all. Pretty was ordinary. She wasn't beautiful, either, not by any English standard. She was something altogether out of the common run of beauty.

Tryphena owned numerous volumes dealing with Egypt, including all of the French *Description de l'Egypte* that had been published thus far. Rupert had seen this face in somebody's color illustration of a tomb or temple. He remembered it clearly: a red-haired woman, naked but for a golden collar about her neck, her arms stretched toward the heavens.

Naked would be good. His experienced eye told him the mortal lady's figure might well be as extraordinary as her face.

Rather like a temperamental goddess, she pulled off the gloomy headdress and flung it down.

Leena hurried in. "They have disappeared!" she cried. "All of them!"

"Really?" Rupert said. "That's interesting."

He turned to the widow. Her face was chalk white. Devil take it, was she going to faint? The only feminine habit he feared and hated more than weeping was fainting.

"We all thought your brother was lost in a brothel," he said. "But this news makes me think, maybe not."

A flush overspread her too-pale countenance, and her green eyes sparked. "A brothel?"

"A house of ill repute," he explained. "Where men hire women to do what most women won't do unless you marry them, and oftentimes not even then."

"I know what a brothel is," she said.

"Apparently, the Cairo brothels make the Paris ones look like Quaker nurseries," he said. "Not that I speak with absolute certainty. The truth is, my recollections of Paris are hazy at best."

Her eyes narrowed. "What you do or do not remember of Paris is of no relevance whatsoever at present," she said.

"I only wanted to point out how immense a temptation it is," he said. "Only a saint—like one of my brothers—could resist it. So naturally, not knowing how saintly your own brother was—"

"You and your associates simply assumed that Miles was cavorting with prostitutes and dancing girls."

"And what with the hashish and opium and whatnot, we supposed he'd lost all sense of time."

"I see," she said. "And so you were assigned to keep me occupied until Miles came or was carried home."

"Yes, that's how it was all explained to me," he said. "It seemed simple enough. A brother missing—we can put it down to drugs and women. But now we've lost a papyrus, not to mention the servants. Matters grow complicated."

"I do not understand how bad people could come here," Leena said. "The doorkeeper Wadid was in his place when we came. He said nothing of any disturbance."

"That fellow sitting on the stone bench near the gate?"

Rupert said. "He seemed to be praying. He certainly paid me no heed."

The mistress and the maid exchanged glances.

"I will go to Wadid," Leena said.

She went out.

The widow turned away from Rupert and returned to the ransacked table. She knelt and moved a book to the left. She shook sand off a paper and set it under the book. She picked up pens from the floor and set them back on the inkstand. The angry spark was gone from her eyes, and the flush had faded, leaving her face dead white, which made the smudges under her eyes appear darker than ever.

Rupert wasn't sure what made him think of it, but he had a vivid picture in his mind of a long-ago time: his little cousin Maria weeping over her dolls after Rupert and her brothers had used them for target practice.

He didn't have any sisters, and wasn't used to girls crying, and it made him frantic. When he offered to try to glue the dolls' mangled parts back together, little Maria whacked him with one of the larger mutilated corpses and blackened his eye. What a relief that was! He vastly preferred physical punishment to the other thing: the nasty stew of emotion.

The dark smudges under Mrs. Pembroke's eyes and the cold white of her face affected him much as his cousin's tears had done. But he hadn't broken any dolls. He hadn't hurt this lady's brother—wasn't sure, in fact, he'd ever clapped eyes on the fellow. Rupert certainly hadn't touched her precious papyrus. There was no reason for him to feel . . . wrong.

Maybe it was something he'd eaten. The prison swill, perhaps. Or maybe it was a touch of plague.

"The thing's definitely gone, then?" he said lightly. "Not misplaced, or mixed in with the other papers?"

"I should hardly confuse an ancient papyrus with ordinary papers," she said.

"Well, I'm dashed if I can make out why anyone would go to so much bother for a papyrus," he said. "On the way here, I was accosted at least six times by Egyptians waving so-called artifacts in my face. You can hardly pass a coffee shop without some cheery fellow popping out to offer you handfuls of papyri—not to mention his sisters, daughters, and extra wives. Virgins, all of them, certified and guaranteed."

She sank back on her heels and looked up at him. "Mr. Carsington," she said, "I believe it is long past time we settled one important matter."

"Not that I'd be interested, if they were the genuine article," he went on. "I could never understand the great to-do about virgins. In my view, a woman of experience—"

"Your view is not solicited, Mr. Carsington," she said. "It is unnecessary for you to 'make out' why this or that. You are not here to think. You are to provide the brawn in this undertaking. I am to provide the brain. Is that clear?"

It was clear to Rupert that irritating her was an excellent way to prevent waterworks. The light was back in her eyes, and her skin, though still pale, was not so taut and corpse-white.

"Clear as a bell," he said.

"Good." She indicated the divan opposite. "Kindly sit down. I have a great deal to say, and it is tiring to look up at you. You needn't take off your shoes first. Eastern custom is inconvenient for those wearing European dress. Not that I am at all sure why people here go to the trouble of taking off their shoes before stepping on the rugs, when the sand easily covers rugs, mats, divans, and everything else with no help from us."

He took the seat she indicated, plumped up a cushion, and leaned back on it. As she settled onto the divan opposite, he noticed that she had shed her shoes. He caught a glimpse of slim, stockinged feet before she tucked her legs under her.

He doubted she'd done it on purpose. She was not that type of female at all. But those nearly naked feet teased all the same, and the usual heat started down low.

The lady opened her mouth to start lecturing, or whatever she had in mind, and he was turning his mind to imagining the view from her ankles up when Leena burst in. She pulled in after her the sturdy, cheerful fellow Rupert had waved to in the courtyard a short while earlier.

"Drugged!" the maid cried. "Look at him!"

Everyone looked at Wadid. He smiled and salaamed.

"All day long he has been smoking hashish—or perhaps it was opium—mixed in his tobacco," Leena said. "I could not tell what it was, because a perfume disguised the smell. But anyone can see that Wadid is in a heavenly place, and looks kindly upon everyone. He can tell us nothing."

Rupert got up, walked up to within inches of the gate-keeper's face, and peered down into his half-closed eyes. Wadid smiled and nodded and said something in singsong.

Rupert grasped him by the upper arms, lifted him off the floor, and held him aloft for a moment. Wadid's eyes opened wide. Rupert gave the man a shake, then set him down.

Wadid stared at him, mouth opening and closing.

"Tell him, the next time I pick him up, I'll pitch him out the window," Rupert said. "Tell him, if he doesn't want to test his flying skills, I recommend he answer a few questions."

Leena spoke rapidly. Wadid stuttered an answer, occasionally darting a frightened look at Rupert.

"He says thank you, kind sir," Leena said. "His head is much clearer now."

"I thought it might be," Rupert said. He looked enquiringly at Mrs. Pembroke.

Her remarkable eyes, too, had opened very wide. Her mouth, previously taut with disapproval, shaped an O. The prim expression had acted, apparently, as a sort of corset. Freed of it, her mouth was soft and full.

He would like to pick her up, too, and bring that amazing face close to his and test the softness of those lips. . . .

But he was not *that* stupid.

"You wished to interrogate him, I believe?" he said.

She blinked, and turning to Wadid, launched into a stream of foreign talk.

Wadid answered haltingly.

While they went back and forth, Rupert departed, in search of coffee.

After a few wrong turns in the maze, he found the stairway, and soon, on the ground floor, what looked like the cooking area.

Its occupants had apparently deserted the place in great haste. He saw evidence of a meal in preparation. A bowl of chickpeas, partly mashed. Wooden implements on the floor. A ball of dough on a stone. A pot on the brazier.

He found the silver coffee service with its tiny, handleless cups, but discerned no signs of coffee.

He stepped into a small, adjoining room, which looked to be a sort of pantry. He started opening jars. Then he became aware of movement. A faint rustling. Rats?

He looked in the direction of the sound. Several tall crockery jars stood in a dark corner. He saw a fragment of blue cloth.

He crossed the room. The lurker attempted to dart past him, but Rupert caught the back of his shirt. "Ah, not so quick, my fine fellow," he said. "First, let's have a friendly chat, shall we?"

Chapter 3

THOUGH ONE COULD NOT TELL BY LOOKING AT her, though she seemed her usual controlled self, it took Daphne a good deal more time than it did Wadid to recover from Mr. Carsington's demonstration of brute strength.

She had felt, for a moment, like a character in *The Thousand and One Nights* who'd inadvertently let a genie out of a bottle. A large, powerful, and uncontrollable genie.

She tried to concentrate on her few clues, but her mind wouldn't cooperate. It produced, too clearly, the look on Mr. Carsington's face when she raised her veil.

She had no name for the look. He was a man far outside the narrow bounds of her experience. She could hardly name her feelings, either: a wild hammering within and a chaos of thoughts and no way to make sense of a single one. There was only a powerful awareness—of the world having turned wild, unpredictable, and unrecognizable— and the sense of something dangerous let loose.

This was irrational, she knew.

But she was too overset to think clearly: Miles gone, the fine papyrus stolen, the house abandoned, the doorkeeper drugged.

When her mind worked in the proper manner, Daphne did not believe in genii, good or bad.

She made herself examine matters logically.

Mr. Carsington was merely an English male of above average but by no means unusual height, she reminded herself. He appeared larger than life because (a) the average Turk or Egyptian was several inches shorter, and (b) he had the muscular physique more commonly associated with certain members of the laboring classes, such as blacksmiths—and boxers, possibly, although she couldn't be certain, never having seen a boxer in the flesh.

Furthermore, the demonstration of brute strength proved how well Mr. Carsington suited her purposes. With him about, no one would dare intimidate her or stand in her way or refuse to cooperate.

True, he was a blockhead, but that, too, was to her advantage. He could not confuse or cow her as her erudite husband had done so often and easily. Mr. Carsington would not assume, as Miles did, that she was too intellectual and unworldly to comprehend everyday life's coarse realities.

Considered calmly and rationally, in short, Mr. Carsington was *perfect*.

Her mind once more in proper order, she focused on Wadid.

He was more than willing to talk now. The trouble was, he didn't know anything.

He didn't know which coffee shop boy had delivered the drugged tobacco. How could he? There were scores of such boys in Cairo, he said. They ran away. They died of plague. They found work elsewhere. Who could keep track of them? He had no idea where the tainted tobacco had come from—assuredly not from Wadid's usual source, one of Cairo's more respectable coffee shops.

As to who had invaded the house and driven the other servants away, Wadid was equally in the dark. He'd been in a beautiful dream, he said. People came and went. Dream people or real people, he could not say.

On learning that someone had stolen the master's beautiful papyrus, he wept and blamed himself. He hoped the master would return soon and beat him, he said.

But please, he begged, would the good lady tell her giant not to tear him limb from limb? The lady was kind and merciful, everyone knew. Had she not brought Akmed back from the dead? The men carry him in, and all the breath is gone from his body. Then she gives him a magic drink, and behold, he breathes again.

Akmed had in fact been breathing, and the "magic drink" was tea from Daphne's precious stores, the sovereign remedy for every ailment, physical, emotional, or moral. But having started talking, Wadid showed no signs of stopping. She let him carry on his monologue while she wondered what had become of her "giant."

He'd been gone rather a while.

Gone back to the consulate, no doubt, she thought grimly. And who could blame him?

She had a man's mind in a woman's body. The feminine arts were a far greater mystery to her than Egyptian writing. She had at least a rational hope of solving the latter. But when it came to femininity, her case was hopeless. Virgil's efforts to change her had only infuriated her—quite as though she *were* a man.

Had she learnt those mysterious arts, had she behaved more prettily with Mr. Salt, he might not have been so quick to dismiss her concerns and fob off on her his aristocratic lummox of an aide.

She had behaved even less prettily with Mr. Carsington. A proper woman would have exercised more tact. Even dumb beasts had feelings, and men could be sensitive about the oddest things.

She rose. She would have to find him. She would return to the consulate, if necessary, and apologize.

"We'll speak more of this later, Wadid," she said. "Go back to your place. Perhaps while you sit quietly, you'll remember more." She hurried across the room and out of the door through which Mr. Carsington had vanished.

"Mistress?" Leena called behind her.

Daphne turned her head to answer.

And collided with something big, hard, and warm. Very big. Very hard. Very warm. Physical sensation knocked out thought, and she tottered, unbalanced.

A large hand clamped on her upper arm and steadied her.

"What a dervish you are, always hurrying this way and that," Mr. Carsington said. "Pray consider the heat and the possibility of a brain fever." He released her arm.

The warmth lingered, and she still felt the impression of long, strong fingers on her skin.

She retreated a pace.

"I came looking for you," she said, her voice strained, as though she'd labored up a pyramid to find him. "I thought you were . . . lost."

"Oh, I never get lost," he said. "Not for long, at any rate. I only went looking for coffee. Turkish coffee is a wondrous beverage, and I thought we all needed a stimulant."

"Coffee," she repeated stupidly.

"Yes. And see what I found." He moved aside. Behind him the twelve-year-old Udail carried the coffee service. "Lucky thing I was in front, eh, Tom, else she might have bowled you over."

"His name is Udail," Daphne said.

"Tom," said the boy, gazing worshipfully up at Mr. Carsington. *"Esmi* Tom."

My name is Tom.

In mere minutes, the man had frightened one servant into submission and cajoled another into idolatry.

And he was tying her mind in knots.

Daphne did not believe in genii. At that moment, however, she had no doubt that her trip to the Citadel dungeon had released a dangerous force.

HER MOUTH, RUPERT noticed, was not only soft and full but mobile: forbiddingly grim at one moment and adorably bewildered in the next. He watched it change from bewildered to grim in the instant it took her to recover from their lovely collision.

He'd seen it coming. He'd also seen no reason to prevent it. Quite the contrary.

Her grim look did not trouble him in the least; neither did her telling him he was not to rechristen her servants.

"How would you like it," she demanded, "if I were to re-name you Omar or Muhammad?"

"A pet name, do you mean?" he said. "I shouldn't object."

After a visible struggle to rein in her temper she said, "What you do or do not object to is not the point. He is an *Egyptian* boy, not English."

"Tom doesn't mind," Rupert said. "In any event, I couldn't tell which part of the earful he gave me was his name."

"He was probably trying to tell you what happened," she said. "I have no idea how you occupied yourself on the voyage to Egypt or during your stay in Alexandria. It is clear, however, that you employed not a minute of the time learning the language."

She turned sharply away and started back into the room she'd just exited: Cairo's version of a salon or drawing room, with the usual unpronounceable name.

"I thought you were to do all the brain work, and I was in charge of the physical side," he said. "Surely you weren't expecting me to interrogate the lad? I had the devil's own time getting him to understand I wanted coffee."

They entered the large room. Wadid had left. Leena was there, though. After Tom set down the coffee service—on top of Mrs. Pembroke's precious papers—Leena grabbed the boy by the shoulders, shook him, then hugged him, talking great guns all the while.

Once Tom had recovered from near suffocation against Leena's ample bosom, he launched into a very long recital.

Several tiny cups of coffee later, Mrs. Pembroke gave Rupert the shorter English version. Apparently, persons calling themselves police had come, saying they must search the house. When Akmed heard their voices, he ran away.

When the lady came to this point of her narration, Tom attracted Rupert's attention. Saying, "Akmed" and something else, the boy did a comical imitation of a man limping.

A green glare from Mrs. Pembroke brought the performance to a halt.

Because Akmed ran away, the widow continued, all the other servants did, too. Tom, who was cautiously sneaking back into the house when Rupert entered the cooking area, had ducked into the nearest hiding place.

Mrs. Pembroke returned her cup to the tray. "Since it's obvious we'll learn nothing more from the other servants, I see no reason to await their return," she said. "The only logical course of action is to retrace my brother's footsteps."

"We ought to check the guardhouses first," Rupert said, recalling Beechey's advice.

"Miles is not in a guardhouse." She rose abruptly from the divan, all impatience and rustling silk. "The men who came here were no more police than I am. And my brother is not in a brothel or an opium den, so you needn't get your hopes up about visiting any of those establishments. We shall talk to those with whom Miles most recently associated. We shall start with his friend Lord Noxley."

"Garnet," Rupert said as she picked up her hat and veil.

She turned and looked at him, her expression wary. "I beg your pardon?"

"Garnet. If someone asked me what color your hair was, I'd say, 'Garnet.' "

She clamped the hat onto her head. "Did you hear a single word I said?"

"My mind wandered," he said. "You're on the tallish side for a woman, I think?" Something over five and a half feet, he estimated.

"I do not see the relevance of my height or hair color," she said.

"That's because you're not a man," he said.

Very much not. The dress seemed designed to play down her assets rather than enhance them. She couldn't disguise her walk, though. She walked like a queen or a goddess, chin high, back straight. But the arrogant sway of her hips bespoke a Cleopatra kind of queen, an Aphrodite kind of goddess. The walk was an invitation. The attire was a Keep Off sign. The combination was fascinating.

"To a man, you see," he continued, "these facts are immensely important."

"Oh, yes, of course," she said. "A woman's looks are

all-important. Her mental capabilities don't signify in the least."

"That would depend," he said, "on what she was thinking."

DAPHNE WAS THINKING it was very hard to think with Mr. Carsington in the vicinity.

She was good at solving puzzles, usually. But the only idea she had about recent events was a ridiculous one, and no more ideas were forthcoming.

She was not easily distracted. One must possess tremendous powers of concentration, not to mention an obstinate and tenacious character, to contend with ancient Egyptian writing.

She might have easily ignored an earthquake or a barrage of artillery fire.

She could not ignore him.

She was aware of his abstracted expression while he calculated her height and decided what color her hair was.

Now, as she sent Udail out to order the donkeys, she was aware of Mr. Carsington's attention drifting away from her person to the table containing her materials.

She recalled her agitated reaction when she first spied the disorder. What had she said? Had she given herself away? But no, she couldn't have. The ruse was a habit by now, practically instinctive. It was Miles who had the more difficult task, pretending to be the brilliant scholar. Luckily, very few people in the world understood enough about decipherment to suspect him—and he took care not to meet those people face-to-face.

Mr. Carsington was frowning down at the copy of the Rosetta Stone. "That papyrus," he said. "I collect it was something out of the ordinary."

She, too, stared at the lithograph, wondering what he saw there. A fragment of hieroglyphic text. Below that another nearly complete section written in the script some scholars called demotic. Then the battered Greek text with its all-important final lines, announcing that all three texts were identical in content.

"Like the Rosetta Stone?" she said. "I wish it had contained some hints in Greek. But it was all in hieroglyphs. . . ." She looked up at him. "Are you asking whether it was valuable?"

He nodded.

"I daresay it was," she said slowly, the truth dawning as she spoke it.

She hadn't thought of the papyrus in that way. She knew it had cost more than most, but then, it was a superior specimen. But that's all it was to her. Perhaps Miles was right, to an extent: She was rather unworldly. It hadn't occurred to her to lock it up, any more than it would occur to her to lock up a book.

"I suppose one could call it valuable," she said. "It was expensive." She related the merchant's tale of the mysterious pharaoh and his presumably untouched tomb.

"I told Miles he encouraged such tall tales and probably set a bad precedent by paying so much," she went on. "Yet it was remarkable. Written entirely in beautifully drawn hieroglyphs. Exquisite illustrations. The others I've seen are not works of art, and most were written in the script form. None was in such good condition. It isn't hard to understand why Miles couldn't resist it."

Mr. Carsington's dark gaze shifted from her study materials to her face. He wore a perplexed expression. "And it didn't occur to you why robbers might want it?" he said. "A guide to buried treasure?"

"No, it didn't," she said. "I couldn't imagine anyone could be so foolish as to believe that story."

"Yet it might seem to others that your brother—a scholar—believed it."

Miles certainly had seemed to believe it—perhaps because he was a little boy in some ways. And he had a romantic streak.

Her romantic streak had shriveled and died years ago. Her marriage had mummified it.

"No educated person could believe that Vanni Anaz or anyone else knew exactly what was written on that papyrus," she said. "No one—I repeat—*no one* can read hieroglyphic writing. But the papyrus did contain symbols associated with royalty. Naturally Miles planned to look for those symbols in Thebes. A number of tombs have been discovered there. More will certainly be discovered. Whether any remain filled with treasure is impossible to know."

"Someone believes it," Mr. Carsington said. "Someone went to a deal of trouble to steal that papyrus."

"But what good will it do them?" she said impatiently. "They *can't read it.*"

"My eldest brother Benedict takes an interest in criminal proceedings," Mr. Carsington said. "He says the average felon is a person of low cunning, not high intelligence."

At that moment the absurd idea she'd kept pushing away stomped to the forefront of her brain.

Miles kidnapped. Papyrus stolen.

"They believe Miles can read it," she said. "Good grief. They must be completely illiterate—or desperately gullible—or—"

"French," said Mr. Carsington.

"French?" she said. She gazed at him in plain incomprehension.

"I hope they're French," he said. "My brother Alistair was at Waterloo."

"Killed?" she said.

"No, though they did their best." He clenched his hands. "He'll be lame for the rest of his life. I've been waiting for a chance to repay the favor."

NOT VERY FAR away, in another corner of Cairo, an elegant middle-aged man stood by one of the windows overlooking his house's courtyard. He did not gaze out of the latticed window but down, reverently, at the object in his hands.

Jean-Claude Duval had come to Egypt with Napoleon's army in 1798. Along with the soldiers had come another army—of scientists, scholars, and artists. These were the people responsible for the monumental *Description de l'Egypte.* To Monsieur Duval, this army of savants was proof of French superiority: unlike the barbaric British, *his* countrymen sought intellectual enlightenment as well as military conquest.

He had been in Egypt when his compatriots found the Rosetta Stone and, being intellectually superior, instantly understood its value. He was here in 1801 when the English defeated the French at Alexandria and took the stone away, claiming it was "honorably acquired by fortune of war."

He was still here, and he still hated the English for a long list of reasons—including, most recently, their employing the infuriatingly lucky Giovanni Belzoni—but their "stealing" the Rosetta Stone constituted Reasons Number One through Five.

Duval had spent twenty years working to even the score.

However, though he had sent to France a great number of fine Egyptian artifacts, he had found nothing approaching the Rosetta Stone's significance.

Until now.

Very cautiously he unrolled the papyrus. Not all the way. Only enough to reassure himself that this was the one. His men had blundered enough already. But it was the one—his chief agent Faruq was no fool—and M. Duval closed the document up again, with the same gentleness, and no small degree of frustration.

The first time he'd seen it, he'd understood it was above the common run of papyri. Even so, he had not believed the story the merchant Vanni Anaz told to justify the insane price he asked. Only the most ignorant persons would believe it. Everyone else knew that no one could read hieroglyphs or any other form of ancient Egyptian writing; therefore no one could tell what this papyrus said.

Still, it was a rare specimen, and Duval had determined to get it.

But before he could arrange to have it stolen, Miles Archdale, one of the world's foremost language scholars, had gone to Anaz's shop, listened soberly to the tale of long-hidden treasure and forgotten pharaoh, and paid the horrendous price. Without a murmur.

One need not be a linguistic genius to comprehend why: Archdale had found the key to deciphering hieroglyphs.

He'd kept it a secret because it would lead to great discoveries, and he wanted all the honor and glory.

He'd seen that this papyrus would lead to the greatest discovery of all, far surpassing anything Belzoni had done and at least equaling the Rosetta Stone in importance: an untouched royal tomb, filled with treasure.

Duval unrolled the foolscap copy of the papyrus. Its margins held numerous notes in English, Greek, and Latin, along with a number of odd symbols and signs, all of it incomprehensible.

"But he will explain it to us," Duval murmured. "Every word of the papyrus. The meaning of every sign."

And once Archdale had given up all his secrets, he would die, and no one would ever find his body. The desert kept secrets even better than he. Jackals, vultures, sun, and sand combined to make corpses vanish with amazing speed.

In the meantime, however. Duval must deal with the infuriating complication. "These must leave Cairo at once," he said. "But I must stay, for a time at least."

The man who'd brought the documents stepped out of the shadows. Though he called himself Faruq, he was Polish. He was educated, one of the more intelligent of the many mercenaries and criminals who found in Egypt a profitable market for their talents.

Duval wished he'd sent Faruq after Archdale. But how could he have guessed he'd need his top agent to carry out a simple kidnapping?

The men sent after Archdale failed to take him in Giza. He was too well-guarded. They could not get to him until he crossed the river again and dispersed his escort in Old Cairo. When the men finally did capture him, they beat his servant and left him for dead, without making *sure*. The servant had somehow crawled back to the sister, who promptly reported the incident to the consulate. By tomorrow, everyone in Cairo would know.

The local authorities did not worry Duval. They were slow, incompetent, and corrupt.

The one who worried him was the Englishman known as the Golden Devil.

He had become Duval's nemesis in the last year. In addition to being cunning, ruthless, and as hungry for glory for England as Duval was for France, the Golden Devil was slightly insane.

Duval hated crazy people. They were too unpredictable.

"The sister will care only to find her brother," Duval said. "She will be easy to divert. The Golden Devil is the graver problem. You must go ahead, to join the others at Minya as we planned. You must take the papyrus. Whatever else happens, it must not fall into his hands."

Though he spoke coolly, Duval was close to weeping with vexation. Everyone dreamt of finding an intact royal tomb. The key was in his hands, in this papyrus. The man who'd finally unlocked the secrets of hieroglyphic writing was Duval's captive, and barely a day's journey away.

But Duval must remain in Cairo to divert suspicion. If he left, his most feared and hated rival would instantly know who was behind the kidnapping and theft. If Duval stayed, he would become merely one of several possible suspects. If he arranged matters well, suspicion would soon shift elsewhere.

And so M. Duval put the two documents into a battered old dispatch bag that wouldn't tempt thieves, gave the bag to Faruq, and told him where and when they would next meet.

RUPERT HAD NOT failed to notice that his comments about the French distracted Mrs. Pembroke from asking the logical question: *What will they do to my brother when they find out he can't read the papyrus?*

It was a question Rupert had rather not answer. He did not count Archdale's life worth a groat once the villains discovered their error. He doubted the man's life would be worth much even if he could read the papyrus.

Still, there was a chance. In Archdale's place, Rupert would pretend and prevaricate, putting off the moment of truth as long as possible. Meanwhile, he'd be looking for a way to escape.

If the villains did discover the truth sooner than was

convenient, one might be able to persuade them to demand
a ransom. That way at least, he would tell them, they
needn't come away empty-handed.

Rupert kept these thoughts to himself and concentrated
on keeping Mrs. Pembroke's mind from dwelling unhap-
pily on her brother.

Fortunately, Rupert Carsington had a natural talent for
driving others distracted.

Because she'd found his renaming the boy Tom so provoking, the first thing Rupert did when they'd mounted
their donkeys was christen his Cleopatra.

"That is not the creature's name," said Mrs. Pembroke.
She told him the Arabic name.

"I can't pronounce it," Rupert said.

"You don't even *try*," she said.

"I don't understand why these people don't speak English," he said. "It's so much simpler."

He could not see her face—she'd put on the evil veil—
but he heard her huff of exasperation.

They set out at a surprisingly fast clip, considering how
narrow, congested, and busy the streets were. He thought it
was wonderful: the donkeys trotting steadily on their way
while carts, horses, and camels came straight at them; the
drivers running alongside and ahead, calling out incompre-
hensibly and waving sticks, trying to clear a path while
everyone appeared to ignore them.

He praised the donkeys to their drivers, congratulated
the beasts on particularly narrow escapes, and told the men
anecdotes about London hackneys.

Mrs. Pembroke bore it for as long as she could, which
was not very long, before she exploded, "They have no
idea what you're saying!"

"Well, they'll never learn, will they, if one doesn't make
an effort," he said.

If the streets hadn't been so noisy, he was sure he'd have
heard her teeth grinding.

She said nothing more, but Rupert was confident she
was too preoccupied with his breathtaking stupidity to fret
overmuch about her brother.

Still, Rupert was not a man to leave anything to chance.

When they reached their destination, he was off his mount even before it had come to a complete halt, and instantly at Mrs. Pembroke's side.

He reached up and grasped the lady firmly at the waist.

"That is not nec—" She broke off as he lifted her up from the elaborate saddle. Instinctively she grasped his shoulders. Smiling into her veiled countenance, Rupert held her in the air at eye level for a moment. Then slowly, slowly, he lowered her to the ground.

She did not immediately let go of his arms.

He did not immediately let go of her waist.

She remained utterly still, looking up at him.

He couldn't see her face, but he could hear the hurried in and out of her breath.

Then she let go and pushed away from him, and turned away in that quick, angry flurry he found so delicious.

"You are absurd," she said. "There is no need to show off your strength."

"That hardly wanted strength," he said. "You weigh far less than I'd have thought. It's the layers and layers of mourning that fooled me." Not completely, though. There was the walk.

"I can only hope that you will be as diligent about finding my brother as you are about ascertaining the dimensions of my person," she said crossly.

By this time the gatekeeper had appeared. He looked to Rupert, but Mrs. Pembroke got in the way and spoke in impatient Arabic.

The gate opened, and they entered the courtyard. Another servant appeared and led them into and through the house.

As they navigated the labyrinth common to Cairo's better houses, Mrs. Pembroke dropped Rupert a few hints.

"Do keep your mind on why we are here," she said in an undertone. "We can't afford to waste time. Please resist the temptation to give Lord Noxley's servants nicknames. I doubt he will appreciate it, and I had rather not spend valuable minutes smoothing matters over. And please try not to wander from the subject. Or tell anecdotes. You are not here to entertain anybody. You are here to obtain information. Is that clear?"

"You're so forgetful," he said. "Don't you remember telling me that you're the brain and I'm the brawn? Naturally I expect you to do all the talking. And naturally I shall knock heads and toss people out of windows as required. Or did I misunderstand? Did you want me to think, too?"

Chapter 4

RUPERT DISLIKED THE VISCOUNT NOXLEY ON
sight.

He was a few inches shorter than Rupert and not so
broad across the shoulders and chest, but he was fit enough.
His hair and eyes were the tawny color properly belonging
to cats. Rupert especially disliked the eyes and their expression when regarding Mrs. Pembroke.

It was the look a hungry lion cast upon the gazelle se-
lected for dinner.

Rupert wished she'd left her veil down.

But she'd thrown it back as soon as she entered the
room, and his lordship's face lighted up, bright as the sun,
at the sight.

And then, as soon as she'd explained what had happened, it was as though a vast thundercloud mounted over
the fellow's head.

Servants hurried in with the obligatory coffee and sweets
and hurried out again at his brusque signal.

"This is incredible," Noxley said. "I can scarcely take it
in. What fool would leap to such a conclusion, let alone act
upon it? But no, it must be a madman. The idea is monstrous. I am sure your brother never gave the smallest indi-

cation of a breakthrough of that magnitude. Quite the contrary. He is exceedingly modest about his work. One can scarcely persuade him to speak of it."

"I agree that it is bizarre," she said. "But the two matters must be connected. Or do you believe it is mere coincidence?"

"No, no, yet I hardly know what to believe." He shook his head. "It is shocking. I need a moment to collect my thoughts. But I am remiss." He indicated the coffee tray with its array of elegant silver dishes. "Do take some refreshment, I beg. Mr. Carsington, you may be unfamiliar with the local delicacies."

He explained the food while lovingly arranging a plate for Mrs. Pembroke. Less lovingly, he prepared one for Rupert. Once this task was done, Noxley forgot about Rupert and devoted his attention to the lady.

Rupert let his attention wander to his surroundings. The room was entirely in the local style. Acres of Turkey carpets. Plastered and whitewashed walls. Elaborately carved and painted wooden ceiling with chandelier suspended therefrom. High, latticed windows. Low banquettes running along three sides of the room, heaped with pillows and cushions. Paneled cupboards above the banquettes. Paneled doors almost but not quite facing each other. The one they'd entered was shut; the other stood partly open. The opening was clearly visible from where Rupert sat. A figure moved past, then returned and hovered there. A veiled face peeked round the edge of the door, and a dark gaze met his.

He pretended to study the design of his coffee cup while covertly watching the woman watching him.

After a moment, she grew bolder and showed more of herself. There was a great deal to show, the veil being the only modest feature of her attire. It must have been too heavy for her, because she dropped it once or twice.

Still, Rupert was attuned to the conversation nearby. Mrs. Pembroke was prodding Noxley to remember something Archdale might have said or done to cause someone to leap to conclusions.

Noxley still seemed bewildered. He described the small

dinner party—merely three guests besides Archdale, all English: one artist and two colonels. "I did wonder," he said, frowning. "Your brother's reason for going to Giza this time seemed odd to me. But I supposed I must have misunderstood him. Either that or he had some private business there he preferred to keep private."

Rupert came to attention. "A woman, do you mean?" he said.

Mrs. Pembroke stared at him.

Noxley looked, too, and his expression chilled. "I had not considered that possibility," he said.

"Really?" Rupert said. "It's the first thing that occurred to me."

"Mr. Archdale would never be so unwise as to become entangled with any of the local women," Lord Noxley said frigidly. "The Muslims have strict notions of propriety, and the consequences of violating them are severe."

"Those notions don't include the dancing girls, I've noticed," said Rupert. "From what I've seen—"

"Mr. Carsington," Mrs. Pembroke said.

He gave her an innocently inquiring look.

"We seem to be straying from the main point," she said. "That point, which may have eluded you, is the possibility of my brother's going to Giza for reasons other than those he gave me."

"Given your theory about the two incidents, Mrs. Pembroke, I find myself wondering whether Mr. Archdale did, after all, make a discovery of some kind at the pyramids," his lordship said. "Or perhaps while at Giza he said or did something to arouse curiosity and speculation. The Egyptians are formidable gossips, as you know. They will endlessly debate the most trivial matters, elaborate on every tale they hear, and pass it on to everyone they meet. News travels up and down the Nile with prodigious speed. Then there are the French and their spies watching everything we do, as though we were still at war. They are so jealous of our accomplishments here—and we all know their agents are not the most savory persons."

"The French?" Rupert said.

"They seem to believe that Egypt and all it contains belong exclusively to them," Noxley said. "They are completely unscrupulous. Bribery, theft, and even violence are nothing to them."

"Now here's something like it," Rupert said. "Violence. Unsavory persons. And *French* besides." He looked at Mrs. Pembroke. "Well, we'd best set out after the scoundrels, hadn't we? By the way, where exactly is Giza, and what's so irresistible about it?"

They both stared at him. Mrs. Pembroke wore a comical look of wondering exasperation.

Rupert was well aware that the Giza plateau lay across the Nile. He must be blind not to be aware. The famous pyramids were plainly visible from any number of places in the metropolis.

He'd asked the stupid questions just to see Mrs. Pembroke's reaction.

"Mrs. Pembroke, I beg you will allow me to assist you," said Noxley. "I am sure the consul general wishes to do all he can to help you, but his resources are limited." He glanced briefly in Rupert's direction. "Please allow me to put my staff at your disposal. And myself, of course. I am sure we shall get to the bottom of this very quickly."

Far more quickly than Hargate's brainless son, was politely left unsaid.

Rupert had to agree about the brainless part. He'd blundered badly. Why should she not discard him in favor of a man presenting clear signs of intelligence?

And how could Rupert blame her?

Noxious obviously knew her brother better than Rupert did. The man had lived several years in Egypt. He seemed to know everybody. He spoke the language.

"Why, thank you," said Mrs. Pembroke. "I shall be very glad to have your help."

Idiot, Rupert berated himself. *Imbecile.* Now Noxious would have all the fun of a search with her, and Rupert would end up in the desert, looking for rocks with writing on them that no one could read.

Then she and Noxley began to talk, as though Rupert didn't exist.

He gave a mental shrug and redirected his attention to the partly open door. The dusky beauty lingered still.

What a hypocrite Noxious was, acting so prim when Rupert spoke of dancing girls, when a member of his lordship's harem stood only a few yards away, half-naked and clearly objecting to her lord and master's attention being diverted elsewhere.

She disappeared and reappeared at intervals, looking more and more vexed at each reappearance.

Watching her, Rupert only half-heard the conversation nearby. Noxley had some people he promised to talk to, starting with the men who'd come to dinner the other night. He'd send some servants out to collect the latest street gossip. He'd call on some district sheiks.

He summoned a servant and gave orders in Arabic. Mrs. Pembroke chimed in.

The servant exited.

Then it was time to leave.

A good deal more subdued than when he set out, Rupert escorted her home. He was vaguely aware of its being later than he'd supposed. He wondered how long they'd been at Noxious's.

"Weren't we going elsewhere?" he said as they reached her street.

"Weren't you paying attention?" she said. "Lord Noxley is going to call on the others. It is very good of him. I had not realized how tired I was until now. But I never slept at all last night. I must have a proper night's rest. I shall be no good at all in Giza otherwise."

"Ah, so you're going to Giza," Rupert said wistfully. He would like to explore the inside of a pyramid, especially with her. He'd heard the passageways were dark and narrow.

"Yes, well, he doesn't know that," she said.

Rupert turned sharply toward her. But there was the hateful veil, hiding her expressive face. "How can he not know?" he said. "He'll see you there."

"Lord Noxley?" she said.

"Who else?" Rupert said.

"But he's not going to Giza," she said.

"He's not?"

"No," she said. "You are."

They arrived at her door. "I am?" Rupert said stupidly.

She let out a long sigh. "Really, Mr. Carsington, I wish you would try to attend. Surely you heard him. He is like Vir—like Miles. They think women—Oh, never mind. It doesn't matter. He doesn't need to know, and you wouldn't understand. But do pay attention now. You are taking me with you to Giza, no matter what he says. You are to come and collect me tomorrow at daybreak. Is that clear?"

"Clear as a bell," Rupert said.

He saw her safely indoors, left the house, and with a wave at Wadid, passed through the gate and set off down the street, whistling.

ONCE MRS. PEMBROKE had gone, all the sunshine went out of his lordship's countenance.

Asheton Noxley liked to have things his way—exactly his way. This wasn't easy anywhere. In Egypt, it was particularly difficult because people here—even, or perhaps especially, Europeans—acted according to no known rules of civilized behavior.

Very early in his stay he had learnt that official documents became increasingly meaningless the farther away one was from the official who'd provided them. For instance, the pasha might give him the exclusive right to excavate at such and such a place or to remove this or that object. But if the site was in, say, Thebes, and the pasha four hundred fifty miles away in Cairo at the time, the one who actually got to excavate was the one who either paid the local officials the largest bribes or produced the largest band of thugs and ruffians to insure his rights.

Lord Noxley had found local officials unreliable. They accepted bribes from rival parties. They were accommodating one day and obstructive the next. They withheld workers, food, and boats when the mood struck them.

Consequently, he had amassed a large band of men he could depend upon to make people behave as they ought.

He now employed agents in most of the major villages between Alexandria and the Second Cataract.

Though Miles Archdale and his handsome sister didn't know about it, his lordship was making arrangements for them, too. His lordship was cultivating the brother, reputed to be one of those nearest to unlocking the secrets of the ancient script. They would make an ideal team, Lord Noxley believed. Together they would unearth a great find, greater than anything Belzoni had discovered.

Equally important, Lord Noxley would make the sister his viscountess. He'd wanted her from the first moment he saw her because she, rather like the papyrus her brother had bought, was a rarity.

Countless beauties in England had thrown themselves at him, and he'd had his pick of their exotic counterparts in Egypt. Mrs. Pembroke had no counterpart.

She was not pretty, not beautiful. He was not sure she was handsome. But her face was striking and her figure magnificent, and she was as rich as Croesus. Moreover, she was conveniently *here*. His lordship need not return to England to renew the tedious search for a suitable bride. He could remain in Egypt for years. When he did return, it would be to great fame and honors.

But someone had disrupted his plans. Archdale, one of the world's great linguists, might be in deadly peril. Meanwhile the Earl of Hargate's hellion son was sniffing about the future Viscountess Noxley's skirts.

Lord Noxley sent for his agent Ghazi, who arrived within the hour.

Ghazi was his lordship's right-hand assassin.

Lord Noxley told him what had happened and asked why he was one of the last to know.

"I will send men to Old Cairo," Ghazi said. "They will discover who took your friend. But it is very strange. One day they steal the man. This I understand. They do it for a ransom. But today they steal a papyrus? This I do not understand. The merchant Vanni Anaz has an endless supply. He has men who make them, too. The peasants sell them in all the villages. Why go to the trouble of stealing?"

Lord Noxley explained.

"Ah," said Ghazi. "But is it true?"

"Someone thinks so," Lord Noxley said.

"It must be the French," Ghazi said. "They grow desperate."

This was because Lord Noxley's agents were steadily driving the French away from the richest sites. He wasn't sure desperation explained it completely, though. Had he erred regarding Archdale, mistaking secrecy for modesty?

"The question is, who possesses the means and is ruthless enough to undertake such villainies?" he said.

Apart from Lord Noxley himself, only one man met the requirements.

"Duval, then," said Ghazi.

"I rather think so."

"I will talk to his people."

The word *talk,* both men knew, was a euphemism for a very broad range of activities.

But Lord Noxley knew Ghazi didn't require specifics. His lordship only added, "And that idiot Carsington." He briefly described Lord Hargate's fourth son. "He'll be in Giza tomorrow. I want him out of the way."

Wednesday 4 April

RUPERT ARRIVED AT the widow's domicile at daybreak as ordered.

He found they would travel with a retinue. All of her cowardly servants but Akmed, it turned out, had skulked back to the house by the time she returned the previous evening. She'd decided they must come along to Giza today.

It took Rupert a while to take this in because he was still trying to digest her appearance.

She'd abandoned the black silk for a costume: a gold-trimmed maroon jacket over full Turkish trousers of a bright blue. And a turban. They would pretend she was a man, his Maltese translator, she said.

She did not in any way resemble a man, Maltese or otherwise. She made Rupert think of harems and concubines and dancing girls. In those thoughts clothing of any kind was not a prominent feature.

He remembered how surprised he was when he lifted her off the donkey: she was smaller than he'd guessed, though quite as generously curved. He could almost feel it still: the inward turn of her waist . . . the flare of her hips where the edge of his hand had rested. A familiar heat, having nothing to do with the morning's temperature, settled into his nether regions. As a consequence, a long moment passed while he tried to get his mind on business.

The ludicrous turban didn't help matters. It begged him to unwind it by spinning her round and round like a top until she was giddy and giggling . . . then pick her up . . .

But he couldn't. Not yet. If he moved too quickly and put his mouth or hands where she thought they didn't belong, she'd send him back to Salt. Rupert would end up toiling in the desert, supervising natives shifting sand and rocks. Lord Noxious would have the fun of a search with her and fights with unsavory, very likely French, persons, while Rupert died of boredom.

Picturing Noxious with his hands on her waist promptly squelched Rupert's lascivious urges.

He turned a skeptical eye upon the cringing servants. He made his expression stern, and adopting the same disdainful tones his father used on such occasions, said, "I should like to know, madam, what good you expect this lot to do, except give you a prime view of their backs the instant trouble threatens."

"We cannot travel unaccompanied," she said. "Not only is it not respectable, it is not at all safe. And we haven't time to apply to the local sheik for replacements."

If they had to apply to a sheik for servants, it would take forever. While Rupert understood almost nothing of Arabic, he knew that phrases such as "make haste" or "we must not lose a minute" or "I mean *now*" were not in the local lexicon.

In short, he must make do with the material at hand.

"Leena," he said, "please be so good as to tell these fellows that there will be no running away today. Tell them that no matter what terrible thing threatens, it will not be half so terrible as what I will do to them if they desert their mistress." He provided a brief, vivid description of what he would do to them, emphasizing with gestures.

Leena rapidly translated.

"For all the good it will do," Rupert said, half to himself. "I should have to catch them first, shouldn't I?"

"They won't run away," Mrs. Pembroke said.

He turned back to her, and his stern demeanor crumbled before the turban and the strange, heart-shaped face that didn't belong under it.

"Won't they?" he said, smiling helplessly.

"Rumors have spread that you are a genie," she said. "Wadid by now has told them what you did to him yesterday, and the feat has been exaggerated beyond all recognition."

"Good," Rupert said. "That saves me deciding which of them to use for the demonstration."

A WHILE LATER, fists on his hips, the long, muscled legs straddling a gap between masses of broken stone blocks, the man who'd brought Daphne to Giza without a murmur of objection stood looking up at Chephren's pyramid.

By swift degrees, Mr. Carsington had discarded his gloves, hat, neckcloth, and coat. Now barely dressed and glowing in the sun's glare, he seemed a bronze colossus.

Daphne was only dimly aware of the pyramid, one of the world's wonders. All she could see was the man, and far too much of him: the shirt taut across the broad shoulders, the thin fabric almost transparent in the harsh light, revealing the contours of muscular arms and back.

It was some comfort to know she wasn't the only one whose gaze he drew. Her servants cast him frequent, wary glances. The men who loitered about the pyramids to help visitors ascend to the top or penetrate its interior also watched him from a respectful distance.

And she might as well have been his shadow. The guides hardly noticed her or seemed to care who or what she was.

They all felt it: the magnetism of that tall figure, the danger crackling in the air about him. All understood that an unpredictable, uncontrollable force had come among them.

Daphne had felt it even before she could see him, when he'd been only a shadowy figure in the dungeon's gloom.

"It's big," he said at last.

"Yes, it is," she said. "I suppose you want to climb it." Men could not resist.

"Not at the moment," he said. "If I climb to the top, it'll only be a prodigious long stairway. No, for the present I like it as it is, immense and impressive." He turned to her. "Unless you think we might find a clue at the top?"

She shook her head. "Miles said he wanted to study the interior. He seemed to think it held clues that would help us find other tombs."

The guides hadn't any useful information about Miles. Yes, they remembered the Englishman with the "white" hair. He had come a few days ago. No one recalled anything unusual about the visit.

Mr. Carsington climbed down from the stones and joined her. He'd unfastened the button at the neck of his shirt, which allowed the garment to hang open in a large V. She directed her gaze away from the expanse of bronzed chest and toward the pyramid.

"Why did Lord Noxious find your brother's reason for coming here so odd?"

"Lord what?"

"You heard me," he said. "I wondered how that insufferable bore could be your brother's—or anyone's—boon companion. But English-speaking fellows are thin on the ground, I notice. Noxious must have won the position by default."

"You didn't like him," she said. Which was about as astute an observation as Mr. Carsington's remarking that the pyramid was big.

There was too much male in view—too much insufficiently clothed male. It was shocking, really. Small wonder she couldn't think. She ought to tell him to put his clothes back on.

"It wasn't *my* liking he was after," he said.

Her gaze shot back to him. The black eyes glinted.

"How concerned he was for you," he said. "So understanding of your predicament. He didn't assume your brother was lolling about in a whorehouse, visiting the Garden of Allah by means of a hashish pipe. No, indeed. His lordship was properly sympathetic and desperately eager to do your bidding."

"I should like to know how this makes him noxious," she said.

"He was so quick to imagine the worst," Mr. Carsington said. "Most men would say, 'There, there now, I'm sure it's nothing to fret about. There'll be a simple explanation—a message gone astray or some such.' Instead, he made a great to-do about it, shoveling on veiled and unveiled suggestions to make you more anxious, rather than less."

"I detest 'there, there now,' " she said. "It is patronizing. And I vastly dislike being made to feel like a child who is imagining things. That is how Mr. Salt behaved toward me. It is exceedingly provoking."

"Maybe the consul general likes the way your eyes flash when you're provoked," said Mr. Carsington. "And the way the pink comes into your cheek, right here." With his forefinger, he drew a line along his cheekbone.

He stood well away from her, yet she felt the touch, as though his long finger grazed her skin instead of his.

She felt the heat climb there, and knew the pink he described must be deepening. She ought to blush—with shame for being so susceptible. "You have a knack for straying from the subject," she said. "You asked what was odd about my brother's reasons for coming here."

"Yes. Why shouldn't your brother find clues here? Why couldn't the mystery tomb be here, in fact? They've still another pyramid to penetrate." He nodded toward the third, unopened pyramid of Mycerinus. "And haven't they uncovered a great lot of mummies somewhere hereabouts?"

Her gaze went to the third pyramid, then shot back to meet his, as innocent as a little boy's. She was not a little girl and was not taken in. "You know all about this place," she said. "You were playing with us, asking those absurd questions about where and what Giza was."

He only smiled and looked away from her toward the

group of guides. "I don't feel like a long climb in the blazing sun today," he said. "But I'm perishing to have a look inside. I should like to see for myself what's so odd about the idea."

"Mr. Carsington," she said. She wanted an explanation.

But he'd already caught the eye of a guide, to whom he signaled. The man quickly joined them. Mr. Carsington pointed to the entrance Belzoni had discovered three years earlier, now a black rectangle on the north face of the pyramid.

The guide summoned another, and the two men led them up through the clearing in the rubble that had for so many centuries concealed the entrance.

Daphne knew it was wiser to save her energies for the ordeal ahead. She reminded herself that she was doing it for Miles's sake, that she loved him dearly and would do whatever she needed to bring him back safe. She told herself that what she felt in the small passageways was irrational, mere emotion. She was a rational being. All she had to do was concentrate on *facts*.

THE ENTRY PASSAGE was four feet high, about three and a half feet wide, a hundred and four feet five inches long, and descended at an angle of twenty-six degrees, Mrs. Pembroke informed Rupert.

Rupert had no trouble estimating the height and width. He'd done that automatically as he entered, and was estimating the angle of descent even while he watched the uneven sway of her handsome backside as she preceded him.

Watching her derrière was no small feat, considering he walked folded almost in half on an uneven surface and had his hands on the walls to maintain his balance and keep track of the passages' features.

In any event, he hadn't as clear a rear view of the lady as he could wish. The guides' torches were fighting a losing battle against the darkness.

They'd gone about fifty feet when Mrs. Pembroke enlightened him about the dimensions.

"You've measured it, then?" he said.

"I quote Mr. Belzoni's calculations," she said. "At the end of this passage, he encountered the portcullis. You can imagine the labor in this constricted space of raising a granite block nearly as tall as you are, five feet wide and fifteen inches thick."

Though Rupert could work out how it might be done, he let her explain how Belzoni had analyzed and solved the problem, using a fulcrum and levers, and stuffing stones in the grooves to support the block as they raised it by slow, slow inches.

When they came to the portcullis, Rupert didn't have to feign admiration. Raising it in this small space was no negligible feat. He paused and ran his hands over the sides of the opening and the bottom of the stone.

Then he huddled under and continued for a few more feet until she stopped to turn toward him.

"We must descend the shaft next," she said. "Belzoni used a rope and later piled some stones to one side, but someone brought a ladder recently, and left it."

"Much more civilized," Rupert said. He noted a hole overhead while watching how gracefully she turned, though she was obliged to move in the same hunched-over style as he.

They descended the shaft in the civilized way, continued down another passage, then up, then straight on. The way grew easier. It was high enough to allow Mrs. Pembroke to walk upright, though Rupert still had to keep his head down.

At last they entered the great central chamber, where he could easily stand straight. The tall room's ceiling tapered to a point, the angle mimicking the pyramid's.

The guides stood by the door, holding their torches aloft. On the south wall, large letters—proper Roman letters, not the curls and squiggles of Arabic nor yet the curious little hieroglyphic figures—proclaimed, *"Scoperta da S. Belzoni 2 Mar. 1818."*

" 'Opened by Signore Belzoni,' " Mrs. Pembroke translated, though even Rupert could deduce the meaning.

"The sarcophagus in Cheops's pyramid stands on the floor," she said, walking toward the west wall of the chamber. "But here, as you see, it is sunk into the ground."

It was not so easy to see. The darkness was so thick one could practically feel it. The torches made little headway against it.

Rupert gazed about the room. "So many secrets," he said.

He knew little more of ancient Egypt than what he recalled from the works of Greeks and Romans. There was the ancient Greek traveler Herodotus, for instance, whose *Histories* comprised a hodgepodge of facts, figures, and myths.

"This tomb may keep its secrets for all eternity," she said. "No hieroglyphs. Do you see why Miles's reasons for coming are so puzzling? Besides, the papyrus allegedly came from Thebes—hundreds of miles away in more mountainous terrain."

Rupert studied the gap between the granite stones surrounding the sarcophagus. What went there? he wondered. An effigy? Treasure chest? Or simply another stone?

"Allegedly," he repeated. "Is there anything about the papyrus we can be sure of?"

"It's truly old," she said. "It took several days to unroll. You can't be impatient with such things or you end up with a lot of charred crumbs—and sick from the fumes of the chlorine gas."

She spoke quickly, her voice a note or two above the usual pitch.

But she'd talked that way since they entered the pyramid, Rupert realized. She'd been exceedingly talkative.

He looked up from the puzzling sarcophagus. She seemed to be looking down into it. He couldn't be sure. It was hard to read her expression in the dim, wavering light.

"Are you all right?" he said.

"Yes, of course," she said.

"Not everyone would be," he said. "Some people have a morbid aversion to closed spaces."

"It is an irrational reaction one must overcome if one hopes to learn anything," she said. "We shall be exploring tombs in Thebes. They do have writing inside. That was the main point of coming to Egypt: to study the hieroglyphs in the temples and royal tombs. To compare names. We know what hieroglyphs form the name Cleopatra. We've deduced some other royal names. With enough pharaohs to compare, we should be able to deduce the alphabet."

We. Rupert noted the choice of pronoun. Not *he* or *Miles.*

"Meanwhile, you'd rather not be here," he said.

"I wouldn't mind so much, but we've wasted our time," she said. "There's nothing. This was a stupid mistake. I should have listened to Lord Noxley. I could have been questioning others in Cairo. What did I think I'd learn from a heap of stones?"

The edgy tone of her voice had softened into despair.

Rupert rose and started toward her, while trying to think of some stupid thing to say to irritate her and rouse her spirits.

From somewhere in the bowels of the pyramid came a bone-chilling scream.

"NO!" Rupert roared, turning toward the door.

Too late.

He had one last, faint glimpse of swiftly retreating light as the guides fled. Then there was nothing. The darkness swallowed them utterly.

Chapter 5

"DON'T FAINT," RUPERT SAID IN AN UNDERTONE.
"I can't see you to catch you, and a concussion would be a
problem."

"Don't be absurd," she said. "I never faint."

If her voice hadn't risen a notch above her normal pitch,
he might have believed she was perfectly composed. But
he was learning the changes in her voice, and he'd noticed
her propensity for hiding things. Her body, for instance.
That wasn't all.

He'd work on the other secrets once they got out of the
present difficulty.

"Stay put and keep talking, but softly," he said. He was
listening. The guides' footsteps had faded. Outside the
chamber silence reigned. He didn't trust it. Someone was
there, he was certain.

Meanwhile he needed to get his bearings. The dark was
prodigious. He'd never experienced anything quite like it.

"I shall not faint," she said. "I freely admit, however,
that our present situation is not conducive to an easy frame
of mind."

Cautiously Rupert inched toward her. He did not want

to stumble over one of the stones ancient tomb robbers had pried loose from the floor, or into any of the holes where the stones had been. Broken limbs or a cracked skull would not only slow their progress but hamper his ability to break villains' heads.

"The circumstances are far from propitious," she went on in the same high-pitched, pedantic tone. "We hear an unearthly scream. The guides instantly decamp with the only source of light. This leaves us to the tender mercies of whoever caused the screaming."

Her voice was very near now. Rupert put out his hand, and it slid over a fabric-covered curve.

With a sharp gasp, she stiffened. Then her cold fingers curled about his and lifted his hand away.

"I cannot see my hand when I hold it an inch from my face," she said, "yet you had no difficulty locating my breast."

"Was that the part I found?" he said. "What amazing luck." *What a splendid bosom!*

"When we get out of this," she said, *"if* we get out of this, I shall box your ears."

"We'll get out of it," he said.

"My mind reverts, repeatedly, to the portcullis," she said. "If they remove the stones holding it up, we'll be trapped here."

"That's too much work," he said. "It would be easier to wait in the dark and stab or shoot us as soon as we come close enough."

"I had not thought of that," she said. "I was preoccupied with the prospect of being buried alive. With you. I could not imagine what we would find to talk about while we died slowly of starvation and thirst."

"Talk?" he said. "Is that what you'd want to do during your last hours? How curious. Come, take my hand. So far, no one appears to be hurrying to cut our throats. I think we might risk setting out."

"Where is your hand?" she said.

There was some fumbling, during which he found the other breast, eliciting another sharp gasp and uncomplimentary muttering under her breath. But at last he had her slim hand in his. It fit perfectly. His spirits rose another few degrees while his heart went faster than before.

"Your hand is warm," she said accusingly. "Does nothing alarm you?"

He was starting toward where he estimated the doorway was. "Not this," he said. "I am armed, you know, and it's simple enough to find the way out."

"It is simple enough if you can see where you're going," she said.

Searching with his free hand, he found the edge of the doorway. "And if you can't?" he said.

"I can think of half a dozen different ways we could die," she said. "With or without villains' assistance."

DAPHNE KNEW SHE was jabbering, but talking helped keep emotion at bay.

Until this moment, she'd allowed herself to cherish a small hope that her alarms about her brother were as silly as the men in Cairo painted them to be. She'd let herself hope, though logic rebelled against it, that Miles was not in trouble, and Akmed had either lied about or misunderstood what had happened in Old Cairo.

The scream and the guides' abrupt departure did not strike her as simple coincidence, and the small, silly hope was breathing its last.

And so she babbled facts.

"The way we came is one of two ways into the pyramid," she said. "Parallel to and below the passage we first entered is another, which leads to a descending passage. This meets the upper one at the shaft. The lower entrance is still blocked, however."

"So there's only one way out," he said.

"Yes, but it is easy to go astray," she said. "We could end up in the wrong passageway. The lower passage has a shaft, too, and a side chamber, if I remember correctly." She wasn't sure. The panic she tried to crush was making a muddle of her mind. She could not clearly picture Belzoni's diagram.

She was not about to let Mr. Carsington know the state she was in, however.

Coolly she went on, "I trust yours is an unerring sense of direction?"

"Yes, actually," he said, the supremely confident male.

"I am glad to hear it," she said, "because it is all too easy, in absolute darkness like this, to become disoriented and wander the few simple passageways endlessly. Or tumble into a shaft."

"If you don't want to become disoriented, I recommend you keep close to me," Mr. Carsington said.

"I ought to remind you as well," she went on testily, "that even if none of these mishaps befall us, it is possible for villainous persons to close the single way out. They've only a small space to block, after all: four feet high, three and a half feet wide. They might roll a few large stones down the passageway without great difficulty."

"I should think the guides would notice if anybody started hauling large stones up to the pyramid entrance," he said. "And I expect they'd strongly object to anyone's trying to block the passage. Taking people into and out of the pyramid is their livelihood, recollect."

Yes, yes, of course. Why hadn't she thought of that?

Because she was living one of her worst nightmares, trapped in a closed space in utter darkness. Panic had suffocated logic and reason.

She was lost, following blindly, clinging to his large hand as they proceeded slowly but unhindered through the taller horizontal passageway and thence into the inclined smaller one. There she had to let go of his hand and grope along behind.

She knew she could not continue holding his hand while traversing the small tunnel. One part of her mind—the small part still functioning—understood the necessity. But the rest was too chaotic to understand anything, and when she let go, she felt wretched and lost and alone.

Telling herself to stop being so childish, she followed as closely behind as possible, listening to his footsteps while she slid her hands along the passage walls. What seemed a very long time later, though she knew they could not have traveled many feet, he put his hand back, touching the front of her turban.

"We're at the shaft, I think," he said softly. "There's room for you to stand upright, at any rate. But stay a moment while I find the ladder."

Another long wait. Daphne heard rustling, then his familiar rumble, too low to understand. Then a degree more audibly he said, "You'd better let me carry you."

"Have the villains broken the ladder?" she said.

"No. Where the devil are you?" His voice was clipped and distant. One large hand found her forearm, the other her hip. "Where's your waist, confound it?"

Though the pyramid's interior was far from cool, she was acutely aware of a very different warmth where he touched her, and of a strength that the childish part of her wanted to lean into.

She retreated. "I can climb up the ladder without aid," she said. "I climbed down it, did I not?"

"As you wish, madam. Try not to step on the bodies."

"Bodies," she repeated.

"They're human, they haven't been dead for very long, and they've fallen or been flung onto the pile of stones near the ladder," he said.

"Good grief," she said.

"Don't faint," he said. "I've pushed them out of the way as much I could, but space is limited. If I can get you onto the third rung, you should be clear of them."

She quelled a shudder. If she gave way, she'd soon be trembling uncontrollably.

"Very well," she said. She groped in the darkness, about where she reckoned his shoulder must be. She found it, rock hard and warm. Only the thin linen of his shirt lay between her palm and his skin. Within her a welter of unnamable feelings stirred, a hurrying and a prickling and a piercing recollection of her youth and its not-quite-forgotten longings.

She beat them down and quickly worked her way from his shoulder to his hand. She grasped his hand and brought it to her waist. "Here I am," she said breathlessly.

Two big hands circled her waist. "What in blazes is that?" he said.

"My waist," she said.

"I mean the sash thing you've wound about it. Have you rocks in it?" He patted a place near her left hip.

"It is called a *hezam*," she said.

"Yes, but what *is* it?"

"A scarf girdling the waist," she said. "Useful for stowing things. Like my knives."

"Have you the least idea how to use them?" he said.

"I know that you hold it by the handle and the sharp end is the part you stick in," she whispered impatiently. "What else do I need to know?"

"Hold it with the sharp end aimed upward rather than downward," he said. "More control, better aim that way."

"Oh," she said. "Yes. I see."

"Good." He grasped her firmly about the waist—or the *hezam*, rather—and lifted her smoothly up. He held her until she had her feet firmly planted on the rung and her hands clutching the sides.

Then, "Don't move," he said in an undertone. "We don't know what's up there."

"I don't hear anything," she said.

"I'd better go first all the same," he said.

"There's only one ladder," she said, "and I'm on it."

"I'd rather not climb over the corpses," he said.

"No, no, of course not."

"I'll have to squeeze by you, then," he said.

"Will the ladder hold two persons?"

"We'll soon find out."

She felt his hand travel up her back and along her arm to where her hand grasped the ladder. She squeezed to one side, to leave room, but there was little room to leave. A moment later, she felt his hard torso against her back, then a long, muscular leg pressed against her thigh. She sucked in her breath. Flames raced up from the place of contact, and even the cold shame instantly following couldn't altogether douse them.

Then he was past, and she concentrated on getting out

of this beastly place and away from the horror a few inches away. She listened to him climb out, then to the muted sound of his boots moving away from the shaft. She became aware of her own breathing, too fast, and the matching tempo of her heartbeats. Her mind darted to the bodies nearby, then to unknown others, still alive, lying in wait for him.

Panic flooded in, and with it a mad grief. Finally, she heard his returning footsteps. Relief wiped out panic, and the wild grief sank back into whatever dark cave of her being it had come from.

"All's clear at the moment," he said.

The ladder was nearly perpendicular. Daphne all but ran up it. At the top rung, she paused and released her death grip to feel for the floor of the passage. Her searching hand found his knee.

Then strong fingers circled her wrist, and she grasped his in the same way. "Hold on," he said. "I'll steady you." His other hand slid down from her shoulder over her breast, then caught her firmly under her arm. If he lost his hold, her madly working mind told her, she'd fall to the bottom—or on top of the corpses. But his grip was firm, and in a moment she was clambering over the edge of the shaft and sinking onto her knees, while her heart raced and her breath came in racking gasps.

"Steady," he said. He did not let go of her.

She tried to steady herself, but her hands trembled, and she couldn't seem to catch her breath.

"Don't faint," he said.

"I. Never. Faint." Four heaving, irate syllables.

"The way seems clear as far as the portcullis," he said. "Beyond that is the first passage. I doubt anyone would lurk there, so near the entrance."

She directed her churning mind to practical rather than hysterical thoughts. "Twenty-two feet seven inches to the portcullis," she said. "The portcullis section itself is six feet eleven inches." But while her rational mind calculated the remaining distance, the other, darker part of her being was engulfed in physical awareness: the size and strength of his hands holding her steady . . . his nearness, a breath away in the small space . . . the musky scent of Male, mingled with faint traces of smoke and soap.

The thin shirt under her jacket clung damply to her skin. She was swimming in heat and confusion, and she longed, desperately, to be anywhere else, safe and clean, with her brother.

She was aware as well of a darker longing, one she'd rather not examine too closely. The two feelings tangled, and she understood only that she was weary and confused and desperately unhappy. She bowed her head and leaned toward the man who wasn't her brother or even her brother's trusted friend, until her turban touched his chest.

He grasped her shoulders. "No fainting," he said. "No weeping, either."

Her head shot up. "I was not weeping," she said.

"Oh," he said. "Were you finding me irresistible? Sorry." He tried to draw her back.

Daphne pulled his hands from her shoulders and retreated as far as she could in the small space. "You are impossible," she said.

"If you were not fainting or weeping or making an advance, what were you doing, then?" he said.

"Succumbing to despair," she said. It was true enough, if not the whole truth. "But it was momentary. I am fully recovered. Shall we proceed, and ought I do so with my knife drawn?"

"You'd better keep it where it is for the moment," he said. "Otherwise you might stab me to death accidentally."

"If I stab you to death," she said, "it will not be accidental."

AS IT HAPPENED, neither Mrs. Pembroke nor anyone else attempted murder or mayhem on the way out. Rupert emerged with her into the sunlight unscathed.

Then followed a chain of events with which he was more than familiar. A large body of men closed about them and, despite Mrs. Pembroke's furious protests in what seemed to be five different languages, arrested them.

• • •

GHAZI, WHO STOOD among the onlookers, found it amusing that Chephren's pyramid, which had not housed a corpse in thousands of years, now held two.

The police found the two guides, their throats slit, on the stones piled alongside the ladder. That was all they found. They could not discover who had screamed. No one in the vicinity had heard or seen anything.

This was because everyone had been gathered about and listening raptly to a Cairene's tale of the evil genie who lived on his neighbor's roof and played cruel tricks on passersby.

The Cairene was one of Ghazi's men.

Ghazi had sent another to the district police with a tale of a mad Englishman—the one who'd tried to kill a soldier the other day—bent on evildoing at Chephren's pyramid. Ghazi's associate had gone well-supplied with money, to encourage the police to act quickly.

Ghazi had had to improvise, and swiftly, because matters had not proceeded as planned.

Two of his men had hidden in Chephren's pyramid just before dawn. They'd been awaiting the Englishman, in order to help him have an accident.

No one was expecting the woman.

Luckily, Ghazi had not sent stupid men into the pyramid. They knew the Englishwoman was very important to Lord Noxley—the man they knew as the Golden Devil. The men knew they must not harm her. They also realized—as stupid men would not—that it was unwise to harm the Englishman while she was about. She would make a fuss—much as she did at present—and force the English consul general to make a fuss, too. This would annoy Muhammad Ali. When the pasha was annoyed, people's heads and necks went separate ways. Sometimes there was torture first. Occasionally, a disemboweling.

Consequently, Ghazi's men had reassessed the situation and killed the guides instead. No one would make a fuss about a couple of dead Egyptian peasants. But word of the incident would quickly travel, and other Egyptians would decide it was healthier to stay away from the English lady and her concerns.

This, Ghazi decided, was more than satisfactory. She would have no one to turn to but his master.

Meanwhile, Ghazi would look for another opportunity to get the man called Carsington out of his master's way.

MEANWHILE, IN BULAQ, Cairo's port, Miles Archdale's servant Akmed was applying for work on one of the finer Nile boats. Nearly as well known as the pasha's barge, the *Memnon* belonged to a foreigner who had lived in Egypt for several years.

The captain studied Akmed's bruised face for a long time. "A fighter?" he said at last.

"I had trouble with some soldiers," Akmed said. It was true enough, though not the cause of his injuries. The soldiers had been ready to give him trouble—though the tall Englishman who'd so bravely intervened got the worst of it. The English had been very good to Akmed. He wished he could repay them in some way. But for now all he could do was run away.

Yesterday, when the false policemen came, he'd recognized one of the voices. It belonged to one of the men who'd taken his master captive the day before. That was when Akmed remembered they'd looked for a papyrus among his master's belongings and had been furious when they couldn't find it. They'd beaten Akmed and left him for dead because he would not tell them where it was. They would have done the same had he told them. They wanted him dead. He was the only witness to the kidnapping. As soon as they discovered they hadn't killed him, they'd be after him—and any who tried to protect him would suffer.

He had to leave Cairo.

But he had no money and dare not seek help from his family or friends.

And so he'd come to Bulaq, to look for work on a boat, one that would take him far away from Cairo as quickly as possible.

This one promised to suit his purposes.

"We need fighters," the captain said. "Some brigands have taken an Englishman hostage. We go to hunt for him. My master, the owner of this boat, commands us to be ready to sail by daybreak tomorrow. It is dangerous work, and needs men of courage as well as skill."

Akmed's heart beat with joy. Silently he thanked his Maker for this chance to help his master. He told the captain he spoke English and a little French, and had waited upon English travelers before and knew their customs. He knew how to shave them, dress them, cook and sew for them.

"Regrettably, I have no letters of reference," Akmed said. "The soldiers destroyed all my belongings."

The captain smiled. "Anyone can forge a letter," he said. "My master judges by performance. Do well, and you'll be well. Do badly, and it will go badly with you."

And in this way, all unwitting, Akmed became an employee of the Golden Devil.

THE POLICE ESCORTED Rupert and Mrs. Pembroke to a guardhouse in Cairo, and it was late the following afternoon before Mr. Beechey was able to arrange for their release. By this time, Mrs. Pembroke was in a murderous rage, and Rupert had to take her firmly by the arm as they left the guardhouse, to prevent her doing an injury to one or several members of the police force.

They had immediately disarmed Rupert but had not even searched her. Having quickly perceived that his so-called Maltese translator was a she, not a he, they foolishly assumed she was harmless. They kept her separated from her alleged accomplice for reasons of propriety rather than any fear of the two "suspects" combining forces.

To make sure the police continued in ignorance, Rupert hustled her away from the place and whistled for transportation. Two donkey drivers with their beasts came running. Rupert picked her up and planted her on one donkey and swiftly mounted the other. She glared at him but gave the drivers the direction, and off they went, the men running ahead, the donkeys trotting behind through the crowded streets.

Her servants who, amazingly, had not run away when the police arrived at the pyramids, had returned to Cairo when their mistress was arrested. When she came home, they bustled into action. Fresh coffee and a large tray of un-English food appeared within a quarter hour of her arrival.

The mistress glowered at it, then yanked off her turban and threw it on the floor.

"I have let myself be made fool of!" she cried. "If I had listened to Lord Noxley, this never would have happened. But no, I had to go to Giza on a wild-goose chase with a man who is a known troublemaker. Had anyone seen fit to inform me of the number of times you've been arrested, I should have left you to rot in the dungeon! I might have found Miles by now, instead of wasting an entire day and more!"

Her hair tumbled about her shoulders. It was thick and wavy and gleamed like red gems where the light caught it. Ruby and garnet. And her eyes were like . . . No, they were not like emeralds. This was a different green.

Rupert dropped onto the divan and considered the various items in the small dishes. "You gave me to believe that Noxious wanted you to sit quietly at home while he went about Cairo interrogating his friends. You seemed unhappy about this method."

"That is not the point! The point is . . ." She trailed off and looked about the room. Her gaze settled upon the wooden Egyptians staring back mutely from the shelf.

"I should have gone mad, sitting at home, waiting," she said tautly.

"Instead, you went to Giza and came back with a clearer picture of your enemy," Rupert said.

The green gaze shifted to him. "I did?"

"Of course you did," Rupert said. "You're a trifle overset at the moment, else you'd realize how much you discovered."

She came up to the divan. Her remarkable face wore a guarded expression. "Such as?"

"Even I collected a few clues," he said. He held up his thumb. "First, we are not dealing with common miscreants but an organization." His index finger went up. "Second, the man in charge is clever: kidnapping, papyrus theft, and today's events—all neatly arranged. Recollect that it was two ordinary Egyptians who were killed at Giza. We were not harmed, except in our pride. Our man knows how far he can go."

"Egyptian life is held very cheap," she murmured, nodding.

Rupert continued to keep count with his fingers. "Third, he knows how to manipulate the police. Interesting, isn't it, how they were on the spot as we came out, how they arrested us first, then went looking for the bodies."

"Bribed," she said.

She began to pace, innocently unaware of the enticing way the thin trousers slid against her legs, the way they concealed then revealed the turn of ankle and calf and thigh, the way the fabric shifted with the sway of her hips.

He watched, not at all innocent or unaware. "Fourth." He paused briefly. "It grieves me to admit it, but Noxious was right about one thing: French or not, our villain has an impressive network of spies."

"How else would he have had time to arrange events at Giza?" she muttered, still pacing. "There cannot be many men in Cairo who meet these criteria. It must be someone who has lived here for some time. He is well connected to the local underworld. He probably moves freely in the European community. He may be a member of the pasha's court. Anyone close to Muhammad Ali has influence, power."

"How many people qualify?" Rupert said.

"I've no idea," she said. "Egypt attracts opportunists. People who would be considered disreputable in their native countries can achieve a degree of respectability here."

She stopped abruptly, glanced at him, then away again.

After a moment she came back to the divan and sank onto it with her usual quick grace. She sat much nearer to him than she'd previously done, not quite an arm's length away.

She poured coffee, her gaze abstracted. Two cups. Apparently, he was forgiven. For the moment.

Rupert took his cup and drank happily. There was nothing like Turkish coffee. Or Turkish trousers on an attractive Englishwoman. He wished the jacket were equally revealing. He imagined her draped in gauzy silks, her intriguing body stretched out upon the divan while he with hands and mouth ascertained her precise dimensions.

He looked up to find her gazing steadily at him.

It was unsettling. For a moment he believed she could see straight through into his brain. Not that there was much to see. Still, he doubted she'd feel more amiably toward him if, for instance, she could discern how vast an amount of mental space his fantasies of seduction occupied, compared to the cramped corner devoted to the problem of murdered guides and corrupt police.

"Before we go any further, I must say something," she said. "I have a temper."

"I noticed," he said. "It's quite exciting. I don't know what you were saying to the police at the guardhouse, but you didn't seem to be trying to win them over."

"You guessed correctly," she said. "I was pointing out how illogical it was for us to kill our guides and leave ourselves in utter darkness."

"Is that what you were telling them?" he said. "It sounded a great deal more complicated."

Her color rose. "I may have commented unfavorably on their intelligence and added one or two unflattering references to their parentage."

"That *is* exciting," he said. "It's a wonder they didn't behead us on the spot."

"I was not thinking clearly," she said. "I have never been arrested before. It was infuriating. The thickheadedness of the police was beyond anything I have ever before encountered, or even imagined."

"Yet somehow these thickheads penetrated your masterful disguise," he said.

She looked down at herself. Her eyes widened. She put her hand up to her head. "Good grief," she said. "I'd completely forgotten." She rose hastily. "I am not at all present-able."

Her idea of "presentable" was buttoned up, pinned up, and covered up, all in black. Rupert vastly preferred the disheveled and temperamental version—especially the tumbled hair, which begged his fingers to tangle in it.

"It's only me," he said, helping himself to a date. "I don't mind if you're a bit of a mess." He threw her a look of innocent inquiry. "Or were you were wishing to make yourself more attractive to me?"

She sat back down. "I was explaining about my temper—and perhaps I ought to mention your genius for setting it off." She shut her eyes, and after a moment opened them again.

Rupert wondered if she was counting to ten. People often did that when conversing with him.

"I wish to apologize," she said.

"That isn't nec—"

"It *is* necessary," she cut in. "I should have been wretched if you hadn't taken me to Giza. And we did learn something, as you said."

He didn't want or need an apology. He didn't mind her temper in the least. Liked it, actually. Still, it was sporting of her to apologize.

She'd displayed the same pluck in Giza. Since she did seem to have a morbid aversion to being shut up in dark places, she must have been sick with fear. Yet she'd gritted her teeth and kept on, emerging in fine fettle for battling the police.

Even a night's incarceration had not shaken her.

Meanwhile he, who'd abundant experience with jails, had not spent the most comfortable night. He'd told himself the police wouldn't harm her. They'd restrained themselves during her tirades, hadn't they? All the same, he'd spent the night sharply alert, listening for any indication that she was in distress.

He banished the puzzling recollection. She was a handful. He'd seen that from the start. Not a restful sort of female. She even obliged him to think from time to time.

He did so now, eager to put the apology behind them.

"Obviously, our villain is trying to delay and mislead you," he said. "That tells us your brother is unharmed and probably not far away."

She nodded, but her green gaze was abstracted, shifting from side to side.

Rupert returned to eating while he watched her think.

After a few minutes' hard cogitation, she said, "All our clues point to a clever, powerful, and dangerous person. Surely someone in Cairo would know who the most likely suspects are. Lord Noxley . . ." She shook her head. "No, we need to talk to someone who's made his home here, someone who knows everybody and everything."

She looked up at him, then past him at the row of inscrutable wooden figures on the shelf. "Good grief. The merchant."

Rupert looked that way, too.

"We bought most of those figures from the same man who sold Miles the papyrus," she said. "That's where we should have started, with Vanni Anaz. Who told him the story of the lost pharaoh's tomb? How many people did he tell? How many showed an interest in the papyrus?"

"Excellent point." Rupert swallowed the last of his coffee and rose. "Begin at the beginning. And we'd better do it sooner rather than later—before our villain guesses our next move."

"Now?" she said. Her hand went to her head, and she looked down at herself in dismay.

He picked up the turban she'd flung down. "I'll help you," he said.

Chapter 6

DAPHNE'S MIND WASN'T AT ITS SHARPEST. SHE'D lain awake last night straining to hear what was happening elsewhere in the guardhouse and berating herself for losing her temper with the police. If they beat or tortured Mr. Carsington, it would be her fault.

Her beastly, unwomanly temper. Five years of Virgil's gentle reproofs had not helped subdue it. On the contrary, the reproofs only made her angrier.

Mr. Carsington did not mind her temper at all. *Exciting,* he called it—though she might have got them both killed.

She looked up at him as he wrestled with her hair and the turban.

He was . . . very much alive.

She was acutely aware of the rise and fall of his chest, of his breath on her face, and of his dark gaze focused on her head. And of his hands, those capable hands . . . so reassuring during the long, dark journey through the pyramid. And so dangerous, making her want more, making her impatient . . . to be touched.

Her heart began to race.

She swatted his hands away. "Never mind," she said. "I'll wear a shawl."

She hurried out of the room and walked straight into Leena. Daphne glared at her and continued on. When they were out of earshot she said, "Have you been eavesdropping—listening at the door?"

"Yes," Leena said, not in the least abashed. "But his voice is so low, all I hear is a growl. Is he making love to you?"

Daphne hurried on. "Certainly not."

Leena followed. "But your hair is down."

"I had a temper fit and threw off my turban," Daphne said. "I need to change. I'm going to the *suq*."

"Now?" Leena said, baffled.

They entered Daphne's bedroom. She pulled a pair of women's Turkish trousers out of the cupboard and found a shirt. She tore off the clothes she'd been wearing since yesterday and threw them on the floor. "Burn them," she told the maid.

"I do not understand you," Leena said. "Why do you not send me to shop while you stay and let him take off your clothes? What is the good of being a great lady if you do the work of servants and take no pleasure?"

Daphne went to the washbasin. While hastily washing, she reminded Leena that this was no time for pleasure. Not to mention that she was the daughter of an English clergyman! And the widow of another!

"Yes, but they are dead, and you are alive," Leena said. She gave her mistress a towel. "And this man—*y'Allah*! You saw how he lifted big Wadid straight off the floor." She pressed her plump hands to her plumper bosom. "So strong. So handsome. I saw how you looked at him. You—"

"My brother is *missing*," Daphne cut in tightly. "People have been *murdered*."

"Yes, but you have not." Leena helped her into the loose shirt. "I would like to be in a dark place with such a man. I would not hurry out."

Leena's moral principles left a great deal to be desired. But she was intelligent, multilingual, and highly

efficient. While she lectured her mistress about missed
opportunities—and life's brevity and unpredictability—
the maid's hands worked as busily as her tongue.

In a very short time, Daphne returned to the *qa'a,*
Cairo's answer to an English drawing room or salon.

Mr. Carsington studied her for a good while, his dark
gaze traveling slowly from the head veil Leena had pinned
onto a cloth cap, down over the cloak that covered the thin
shirt and most of the trousers.

His hands might as well have made the journey.

She could imagine the touch, practically feel it. Her
skin came alive, and she could scarcely stand still.

He tipped his head one way, then the other. Then, "I
give up," he said. "Who are you this time?"

A mad, bad, wild girl.

No, a woman who knew how to subdue her worst impulses.

"It doesn't matter," she said. "Everyone will stare at
you. I'll simply blend into the background."

"I think not," he said.

She looked down at herself, at the body she'd never understood and had been taught not to trust. "I was trying not
to look foreign."

"It's more useful to look fetching," he said. "To dazzle
Anaz into revealing all his secrets."

"It doesn't matter how useful it would be," she said. "I
can't do it."

"Can you not?"

"No," she said firmly. "I am not that sort of—that—"
He regarded her steadily, his dark eyes unreadable. Her
heart pumped overfast. Her fogged mind thickened. "I'm
not like the women you've met in Society . . . and the other
places," she said. "I'm bookish."

"Reading improves the mind," he said, and there was no
mockery in his eyes.

"But not the personality," she said. "I'm not fascinating.
I'm tactless and cross and stubborn." And worse. What she
must admit embarrassed her. The battle within, which she
could never speak of aloud, shamed her more. She was

beastly hot in consequence, and her face, she knew, was scarlet.

But Daphne was nothing if not persevering. "It isn't at all the sort of thing men like," she said. "We must find another way of wringing Mr. Anaz's secrets from him."

"Certainly," he said. "I'll wring him if you wish." The oddly penetrating expression vanished as though it had never been, and he was once more the cheerful blockhead she'd first supposed him to be.

Her tension eased a very little bit.

She had grown so used to being ignored or, when she wasn't ignored, earning some man's disapproval or disappointment. She'd learnt how to steel herself against these reactions. They didn't hurt her anymore.

With him she was all at sea, and at the mercy of the storm within.

She drew the veil over her face. "We'd better go," she said. She turned to Leena, who stood in the doorway looking both disapproving and disappointed. "If anyone asks," Daphne told her, "we've gone to buy a rug."

VANNI ANAZ WAS a former mercenary of unknown origins—Armenian, Albanian, Syrian, Greek, no one could say for sure. But everyone knew he'd settled long ago in Egypt, where he conducted a profitable trade in rugs, drugs, and antiquities. His shop, Daphne told Mr. Carsington on the way, was more like those of Europe than the typical cupboard-sized *dukkan* of the main shopping quarters.

The typical shop, seven feet high at most and three or four feet wide, could hold no more than three customers at a time. They would sit and smoke and bargain half the day over a length of cloth or a copper pot. The shop floors stood two or three feet above street level, making them even with the stone bench built against the front for the inconvenience of passersby trying to squeeze through Cairo's narrow streets. These stone or brick obstructions were called *mastabas*, Daphne explained, and it was upon them that business was transacted.

Anaz's shop was more like a private house. One went inside to view the rugs, and negotiated with the merchant while seated upon the divan.

Not on view when they entered was Mr. Anaz's collection of articles from tombs he and his agents had plundered.

"He is regarded as a reputable merchant," Daphne whispered to Mr. Carsington while they waited for the rug dealer to appear. "But the word *reputable* is more elastic in Egypt than in England. I think it most disreputable to make up stories about hieroglyphic guides to a pharaoh's treasure."

"You said the papyrus contained royal symbols," Mr. Carsington said. "A pharaoh is at least mentioned, I take it?"

She nodded. "A king's name is enclosed in an oval called a cartouche. Miles's papyrus had two. The simpler contained a circle, a scarab beetle, three short vertical lines, and a shallow bowl or basket."

She frowned at the paneled door to the back rooms. "Is the man *never* coming? Dishonest persons might make off with half the shop while he dallies."

"Maybe he has a woman back there," Mr. Carsington said.

Daphne looked up at him. "Do you never think of anything else?"

"I try to put myself in the other fellow's shoes," he said. "I ask myself what I'd be doing. Or what I'd most *like* to be doing."

He looked down straight and deep into her eyes, and down that midnight gaze took her, into deep waters. She couldn't catch her breath or find her balance. Her mind went dark and her hand came up and she almost, almost caught hold of him.

A noise from the back of the shop broke the spell.

He looked away toward the sound. She did, too, sick with dismay. Lack of sleep was the trouble, she tried to tell herself. Fatigue sapped the will and the mental faculties. But a small, vicious, inner voice mocked her: *Sleep won't cure what's wrong with you.*

"Mr. Anaz," Mr. Carsington called out.

He did not shout, but his deep voice seemed to expand

and intensify. Such a voice, Daphne thought, might have easily commanded armies or instantly silenced the drunken masses gathered in Rome's Coliseum. It called her to the present and brought her sharply alert.

It did not bring the shopkeeper running, however.

Mr. Carsington's expression hardened. He moved to the inner door and pushed it open.

"Confound it," he said, and added with a warning gesture to Daphne, "don't move."

She ignored the warning and hurried to the door. He put up his arm, but she pushed it away and looked at what he tried to hide.

Vanni Anaz lay on the floor, staring wide-eyed up at them. A red line snaked across his throat, and a pool of blood spread under his head.

RUPERT DID NOT wait to find out whether she'd faint or not but drew his knife and moved swiftly across the room. He'd seen a door curtain flutter as he entered. The killer couldn't have gone far.

Rupert couldn't hear the lurker, but he sensed his presence, an awareness that grew stronger as he reached the curtained doorway. He pushed the curtain to one side—and promptly retreated.

A large stone figure crashed to the floor, exactly where he would have been had his instincts failed him.

He heard Mrs. Pembroke shout, "Don't!" as he leapt through the doorway and onto the retreating figure. His target went down, but twisted free, and started up onto his feet. He kicked Rupert, who grabbed his foot. His opponent tried to shake him off. With a hard yank, Rupert unbalanced him. The man tried rolling away, kicking and thrashing. Rupert slowed him with an elbow to the head, and soon had him pinned down, a knee pressing on the small of his back.

"Look out!" Mrs. Pembroke cried.

Rupert ducked, and the missile caught him near the temple. He saw stars. He saw, too, the other villain bearing down on him, knife upraised. Rupert flung himself at him.

They went down, grappling with each other while falling pottery crashed about them.

Another figure appeared from nowhere, and another voice called out in Arabic. While Rupert knocked away one assailant, he saw out of the corner of his eye Mrs. Pembroke pluck something from the floor and leap into the fray.

He couldn't tell what it was, hadn't time. But he heard a yelp, and one of the attackers stumbled away, turbanless, clutching his head. Holding a large object aloft, she went after him, and the fellow ran. Then something struck the back of Rupert's head. The world went black with flashing lights. The ground opened up under his feet, and down he went.

The lights went out.

THE LIGHT CAME back slowly. Rupert smelled frankincense and ambergris and something else his brain called *she*. A feminine-scented softness pillowed his head. A pulse beat later he realized it was a woman's bosom. The pleasant stroking against his cheek was a soft, smooth, lady's hand. *Hers.* The exotic fragrance was hers, too. Incense. Goddess scent.

"Mr. Carsington, you must speak to me," she said.

He'd rather not speak. He'd rather stay exactly where he was, pillowed against her soft bosom and inhaling her scent while she gently stroked his cheek.

"Mr. Carsington." The hand left off stroking to pat his cheek, with growing impatience.

Remembering the lady had a short temper, he knew the gentle pats would shortly escalate to slaps. He opened his eyes and met her green gaze, where anxiety mingled with vexation.

"Where am I?" he said, though he knew the answer perfectly well. It was a delaying tactic. Her bosom made a perfect pillow. He did not want to leave it.

"On the floor of Anaz's storeroom," she said. "You seem to have fainted."

"Fainted?" he echoed incredulously. "I was knocked in the head. I ought to know. It's happened often enough."

"That would explain a great deal," she said. She started to rise. Aware she would have no compunction about letting his poor, battered head thump to the floor, he quickly sat up.

He looked about him. Broken crockery and small human figures littered the floor. Near him lay a statue, about a foot tall, of a falcon. He picked it up, testing the weight. It was made of polished black stone, and it was heavy. With this she'd attacked the villain.

"The falcon is an incarnation of the god Horus," she said. "It was the nearest object at hand that would do any damage. Those little figures are sweet, but they're useless as weapons."

The painted wooden figures were like the ones on the shelf in her house. He picked one up. "What are they? Dolls? Sacred idols?"

"No one knows," she said. "These, along with broken bits of pottery and mummy, are what one most usually finds in the tombs. Robbers made off with the treasures eons ago."

"So many secrets," he said. He tucked the figure into the breast pocket of his coat and stood. "It seems Vanni Anaz will keep all of his until Judgment Day."

"Not all," Mrs. Pembroke said. "While you were blindly charging after villains—without the least idea how many of them there were—I stopped to ascertain whether the man was still alive. He was. Before expiring he said, '*Cherchez* Ramesses.' That, at least, is what I thought he said." Her voice was brittle.

It was then Rupert noticed the dark stains on her cloak. She'd probably knelt to help the dying man as she'd done Rupert. She hadn't swooned or shrieked or run away. She had burst into the storeroom, snatched up a weapon, and fought the villains alongside him.

It was a stupidly brave thing to do.

Strange things happened inside him—a sudden rush of feeling he hadn't a name for. Lust was involved, naturally, since he was a man, and it would want far more than a few bloodstains on her clothing to make *that* go away.

Lust, though, was a hanger-on, an old friend as natural as breathing. The thing it hung upon was as strange and puzzling as the wooden figure tucked inside his coat.

He didn't understand the feeling and didn't try to. He did understand that she was upset. She had reason.

"That was rather a lot of dead men in only two days," he said, starting toward her.

She held up a hand. The tremble was so slight he might have missed it had he not been so acutely riveted upon her.

"Don't," she said. "Don't even think of comforting me."

Even for him it was instinctive. He knew how to hold a woman and let her cry on his shoulder while he gritted his teeth and endured the weeping. He hated it, but he could do it. Not that he would hate holding her. It was the weeping he could do without.

"You've had a shock," he said. "You can't be in the habit of finding men with their throats cut."

"I don't want comforting," she said. "I want a bath. And a cup of tea. Those two, in any order. But first . . ." She closed her eyes, shook her head, opened her eyes again. "We'll have to notify the authorities."

"Have your wits wandered?" he said. "You've blood on your clothes. You pointed out, recollect, how fantastically stupid the local police are. They're bound to think we killed the rug merchant."

"Running away will appear a good deal more incriminating," she said.

Rupert, too, wanted a bath—and a drink of something stronger than tea. He did not want to go to the guardhouse again and watch her argue with brainless bullies. He couldn't calm anybody down or lighten the proceedings with humor, because he didn't know the language. And he most certainly did not want to spend another night separated from her in a jail, unable to protect her.

He didn't want Beechey to come to release them, and to decide that perhaps, after all, it was not such a good idea to assign Rupert Carsington to look after Miles Archdale's sister. Rupert did not want the secretary to suggest to Mr. Salt that perhaps it would be better, after all, to allow a civilian volunteer like Lord Noxley to assist the lady. Perhaps, after all, it would be wisest to banish Mr. Carsington to the desert, where, with any luck, a three-hundred-ton obelisk would fall on him.

Most of all, Rupert didn't want to reveal any of these thoughts to her.

He donned an amiably stupid expression and said, "As you wish, madam. You're in charge of thinking."

WITHIN AN HOUR, Mr. Beechey, the police, the district sheik, and a translator had gathered in the shop. At present they stood in the front room. This, apart from the blood-stains on the floor, appeared undamaged. The storerooms beyond, however, had been ransacked—perhaps, Rupert suggested, while one villain kept Anaz busy in front.

"Maybe they made too much noise," he theorized, "and when Anaz went to investigate, the first villain cut his throat."

When this was translated, the sheik frowned and moved away to examine the corpse. When he was done, the body was taken away.

Meanwhile Beechey quietly let Rupert know that the situation could become most unpleasant. Vanni Anaz was not one of hundreds of insignificant Egyptian merchants; he was an important foreigner who'd performed numerous services for Muhammad Ali and for whom the pasha had, consequently, a great affection. He was, moreover, the third person to get himself murdered in Mrs. Pembroke's and Mr. Carsington's vicinity in two days.

Fortunately, Sheik Salim proved to be a more thought-ful and logical character than the police. Having studied the body, he went on to examine the storerooms and question people in neighboring shops.

He came back to report that neighbors had seen men running from the rear of the shop, one runner bareheaded.

An adult non-European male not wearing a turban was as rare and strange a sight on the Cairo streets as an adult male wearing one would be on those of London.

The sheik concluded that all the evidence accorded with the explanation the "learned gentleman"—meaning Ru-pert!—had given.

It was Mrs. Pembroke who'd explained, to be sure of a correct translation. But when she spoke, the sheik looked at Rupert, not her, and answered Rupert, not her. She might as well have been in Northumberland.

Rupert was sure it vexed her—even he found it provoking—but whatever she felt, she hid it well. Or perhaps she was simply too weary or too shaken to care.

At least the sheik had paid attention. He told them they were free to go. He would have the police comb the metropolis for a man missing a turban and sporting a large lump on the side of his head.

"Tell them to look for a fellow showing symptoms of concussion," Rupert said. "Mrs. Pembroke gave him a healthy thump, and the statue was solid stone."

Beechey sent a dour look his way, but said nothing until later, when they set out. Night had long since fallen, and they were following Mrs. Pembroke's entourage of police and servants to her house.

The secretary slowed his pace and said, "I had thought I'd made it clear that Mrs. Pembroke was to be shielded from embarrassment and distress at all costs."

"She doesn't like being shielded," Rupert said. "She objects most strongly to being treated like a child."

"That is no excuse for you to treat her as you would one of your sporting cronies," said the secretary. "Did it not occur to you that other villains might have concealed themselves nearby, and that you should have summoned assistance immediately? While you were leaping headlong into an ambush you should have foreseen, she might have been attacked. She might have been killed or worse."

Rupert came to a halt. "What could be worse than her being killed, do you think?"

"I thought I had communicated to you Mr. Salt's opinions and wishes in the matter of Mr. Archdale's disappearance," Beechey said. "I thought I used easily comprehended terms."

"You did," Rupert said. "I told Mrs. Pembroke about it in much the same way."

"You told—" After a pause, Beechey went on, his voice strained, "You cannot have revealed our suspicions about the—ahem—places of dubious repute. This is one of your jokes, I daresay. Ha ha."

"She said her brother was not in a brothel or opium den and I was on no account to go to such places looking for him," Rupert said. "I obeyed, as I was obliged to do. You did tell me I wasn't to upset her, did you not?"

There followed the kind of furious silence with which Rupert was more than familiar.

It was not the first time he'd rendered a listener speechless, and it would not be the last. They walked on without talking while Rupert wondered how much time he had before Salt sent him out to the desert.

THOUGH THE LADY was more than amply protected, Rupert continued with the escort all the way to her house. He remained to watch the assigned guards position themselves at strategic spots about the place, then parted company with Beechey and set out on his own.

It was night, and Rupert was aware that sensible persons did not traverse the Cairo streets after dark. The safe way, however, had never been his favorite direction.

He followed the route he and Mrs. Pembroke had taken two days ago. Though it was night, he found Lord Noxley's house with no difficulty—apart from repeated halts en route to pacify suspicious policemen, military guardsmen, and porters.

The street was gated and the gate locked, but by now he'd memorized the secret password. The watchman said something foreign, to which Rupert answered, "*La ilaha ila-llah.*"

He might have to see about language lessons after all, he thought, like it or not. Looking on the bright side, learning Arabic from Mrs. Pembroke had to be pleasanter than learning Greek and Latin from droning schoolmasters.

Eventually, after he'd carefully enunciated the phrases "Message from Mr. Salt" and "British consul" several times, he was admitted to his lordship's house. This was against the rules, Rupert later discovered. He was in luck, however: his visit coincided with a jealous young woman's temper tantrum.

The dusky beauty he'd noticed during his previous visit was named Juman. She'd been storming about the portico when she heard him hail the porter. She had Rupert admitted and was soon confiding in him in prettily broken English enlivened with intricate hand motions.

Lord Noxley had bought her in the slave market. Eager to please the handsome foreigner who'd saved her from life with a much older and less attractive owner, she had painstakingly learnt English. Since she was exceedingly handsome as well, his lordship let her please him in other ways, too. As a result, she'd developed expectations—as women so often did, fanciful creatures that they were—of a permanent arrangement, preferably including nuptial rites.

Her hopes were shattered yesterday, when his lordship departed Cairo in search of the English lady's brother.

The abandoned Juman was still sulking. This was why she'd told the porter that the man from the consulate must be let into the house. This was why she told Rupert all her master's private business. And this was why she offered to demonstrate the other talents she possessed besides eavesdropping. She was exceedingly talented: it took all of Rupert's limited store of tact to disentangle himself.

Not until a long time after he'd left Lord Noxley's abode and was composing himself to sleep in his own lodgings did Rupert wonder why he'd been so unaccommodating. After all, dusky beauties did not fall into one's lap—literally—every day. When heaven bestowed such gifts, only a churl would decline them. While Rupert was by no means lacking in faults, churlishness was not among them.

It must be a touch of plague, he told himself. Then he turned over and fell asleep. He dreamt of angry green-eyed goddesses in turbans.

WHILE RUPERT WAS dreaming, Ghazi and his men were setting out into the Eastern Desert.

They had found two of the men who'd robbed Vanni Anaz, relieved them of the papyri and other artifacts they'd stolen, and beat them until they revealed what little they knew.

They were mere common thieves hired, Ghazi soon understood, to divert suspicion from Duval by making the previous papyrus theft appear to be one among several, an ordinary crime. Since the thieves knew almost nothing, Ghazi might have let them live. But they'd made a fatal error: they'd panicked and killed Vanni Anaz, a useful and valuable man. Ghazi garroted them.

Based on that interview, he soon found other informants. Within a few hours, Ghazi had all the information he needed.

The kidnappers had set out with their captive in a nondescript boat. The papyrus traveled separately by land. The rendezvous point was a village south of Minya, more than a hundred fifty miles upriver.

Ghazi divided his men accordingly: one group to pursue the kidnappers and another to follow the papyrus. He led the papyrus team. The kidnappers, clearly, were not the most intelligent or efficient of Duval's underlings. On the other hand, Faruq, who carried the papyrus, was as clear-eyed, cold-blooded, and sharp-witted as Ghazi himself.

Ghazi looked forward to their encounter.

Chapter 7

Friday 6 April

"GONE?" MRS. PEMBROKE SHOT UP FROM THE divan in a flurry of black silk, knocking aside the silver tray containing their breakfast.

The coffee sloshed in the cups, and the *fateerah* started sliding from its plate, but Rupert caught the tray in time, saving its precious cargo.

While she strode to the shelf of wooden figures, Rupert helped himself to a piece of the buttery pastry, doused it liberally with honey, and sank his teeth in with a quiet sigh of pleasure. *Fateerah* was so far his favorite Egyptian food. But that was only one part of the present moment's deliciousness.

Mrs. Pembroke was taking a fit. And every abrupt movement gave him a glimpse of her slim, stockinged feet and perfect ankles.

"Of all the presumptuous—" she began. "I can scarcely credit—" She broke off, and he lifted his gaze from her feet to her face, to watch her try to contain the tempest within . . . and fail, praise be.

Few sights stirred his senses as did that of Mrs. Pembroke flying into a passion. She glared green fire at the little Egyptians. Her fine bosom—whose perfect contours the

dull mourning could not completely camouflage—rose and
fell like a stormy sea.

"I daresay Noxious hadn't time for tender farewells,"
Rupert said. "He had a villain to lure out of hiding."

"He knew who it was," she said tightly.

"I said only that his servant mentioned a Frenchman
named Duval," Rupert said. He'd told her of the late-night
visit to Noxious's house, but not in unnecessary detail. The
word "servant" discreetly covered a multitude of scantily
clad dusky beauties.

"I spoke to Salt and Beechey about him this morning,"
he went on. "Their description fits our portrait of the villain. Duval is one of the French consul's dearest friends.
He despises the English. Salt says the man's still nursing a
grudge about the Rosetta Stone. Believes it properly be-
longs to France, it seems."

"Duval," she said. She paced for a short time, the black
silk whispering against her legs. "I met him once. A dinner
at the Swedish consulate. Medium height, dark, elegant—
or perhaps *sleek* is the apter word. Polished manners."

"Salt and Beechey say Duval's generally reckoned a
canny fellow," Rupert said. "But lately he'd suffered a series of reverses in the antiquities line."

"Setbacks seem to sour and deform some men," she
said. She turned toward him, her countenance clouded.
"They become angry, anxious, suspicious. They brood.
They lose their sense of proportion. They grow resentful of
others' accomplishments and happiness."

Rupert nodded. Her troubled countenance, as much as the
words and grim tone, told him she spoke from experience.

He'd already guessed that she was not mourning quite
so much as her costume declared.

She came back to the divan. "It is not a state of mind
that makes for clear thinking."

"This would help explain Duval's jumping to conclusions about your brother and the papyrus," Rupert said.
"There Duval was, seething about this and that. He certainly mistrusts the English. Easy enough, then, to believe
an English scholar knew more than he was telling."

She settled onto the divan, this time only an arm's

length away. "Three people are dead so far—that we know of. All innocent bystanders. The man must be mad."

"He's dangerous, at any rate," Rupert said. "I suppose that's why Noxious wasted no time. He set out in his boat yesterday morning. The *Memnon.* A grand vessel, distinctive and quite famous, I'm told. He made sure everyone at the port knew he was going to search for your brother. No doubt he meant to get the Frenchman's wind up. It worked. I stopped by Duval's house on my way here. It seems he left Cairo suddenly yesterday afternoon."

She said nothing.

Rupert poured her coffee. She took the cup and only stared at it.

"You do know it's best to have Duval out of Cairo, I hope?" Rupert said. *And Noxious, too,* he silently added. "You don't want to risk his taking you hostage. Your brother wouldn't dare try to escape then."

She looked up at him. "I understand that. The trouble is, now I know Miles is *not* in Cairo—and I cannot ask Lord Noxley where these horrible men might have taken my brother, because Lord Noxley is gone, too. I've been running about in circles, wasting time, when, given a little information, I might have made progress."

"That's hardly likely to occur to him," Rupert said. "He'd assume you were waiting safely and dutifully at home, with a great dumb ox from the consulate as bodyguard. Meanwhile, put yourself in Noxious's place: brilliant scheme—waste no time—solve the mystery, race to the rescue. Return with the brother and the valuable item to universal applause. The lady weeps with gratitude . . . and bestows her—um—heart upon the gallant knight."

She stiffened. "Another lady, perhaps," she said. "Not this one."

"Ah, I rather thought not," he said. He'd certainly hoped not. He'd hoped she was too intelligent and spirited to accept the passive role Noxious assigned her.

Rupert watched her tense for battle. She thought he, too, underestimated her.

"We're going after them, then, I take it?" he said.

She blinked once, and the tension was melting out of

her, and her mouth was shaping a crooked smile when she caught herself. She lifted her chin. "Of course we're going after them."

It was what he'd expected of her. All the same, his heart gave a mad leap, because it was what he'd most hoped for as well. And because he'd surprised and pleased her enough to make her almost smile.

"I thought so," he said coolly. "Well, then, what's your pleasure, madam: boat or camel?"

Sunday 8 April

TWO DAYS LATER, Daphne stood in the doorway of her boat's stern cabin, acutely aware of Mr. Carsington standing close behind her.

"Well?" he said.

"It's quite . . . spacious," she said. *It's too small,* she thought, *too crowded.*

The boat was a *dahabeeya,* the Nile version of a yacht. Mr. Carsington—surprising her by knowing something of ancient mythology—had named it the *Isis,* after the Egyptian goddess who'd searched the world for her husband's body.

The *Isis* was large and luxurious, boasting six cabins under an unusually tall roof. Sheik Salim had commandeered it for his learned (!!!) friend Mr. Carsington. The sheik did not want his tall English friend to get a stiff neck from constantly bending over.

Viewed from the landing place, it had seemed impressively large, especially compared to the other boats. Within, though, was another story.

Too late Daphne realized it was a limited space, which she'd be sharing with Mr. Carsington for an indefinite span of time.

She'd made a mistake, choosing a river journey.

By land she need only cope with sandstorms, temperamental camels, and marauding Bedouins. It was too late to change her mind, though, and reason told her this was the wiser choice. She would do Miles no good if she got killed, and desert travel was a good way for foreigners to get killed. A large, armed escort might make it a degree safer, but this would take far too long to arrange.

As it was, Mr. Carsington had accomplished miracles. Hiring and provisioning a boat ought to take weeks. He'd done it in two days, though Friday, when he'd begun, was the Mohammedan Sabbath, when it was impossible to get anything done.

Unless you happened to be a genie.

"The cupboards hold your books and notebooks," the genie was saying. "Leena's stowed most of your wardrobe and other necessaries in her cabin next door. The other trunks and boxes we've put in the cabin after. I hadn't guessed you'd need so many. Perhaps your collection of masterful disguises is more extensive than I imagined?"

"Miles and I were planning a trip to Thebes," she said. "We'd already packed for it: medicines, rugs, mats, mosquito net, umbrella, lantern, broom, and candles—the everyday needs. But the other trunks' contents are mainly his."

She turned carefully in the narrow passage and started back. She glanced into the maid's crowded cabin. Leena would sleep in Daphne's room. However, Daphne could not share one room with her or anyone else the rest of the time, day in and day out. Deprived of solitude, Daphne would turn into a caged beast. The two women could not wander about outdoors on deck all day, either. Both custom and the midday heat forbade it.

I'll work day and night, Daphne told herself. Hieroglyphs demanded one's total attention, blocking out troublesome feelings and urges. She would not make herself sick with worry about Miles. She would not fret about the time passing. And above all, she would acquire a suitable detachment regarding Mr. Carsington's . . . attributes.

She wished she could do it now, but the task was beyond mortal abilities.

Technically, he was fully dressed. However, he'd untied his neckcloth and undone his coat and waistcoat buttons. Her gaze kept straying to his throat and the V of bronzed skin below it. She remembered the heat and weight of his body against her back in the pyramid.

It was impossible to subdue her vibrating awareness of the tall figure standing inches away. It took all her concentrated will to keep her hands to herself. A step would bring her against that muscled frame.

She edged past him to the door of the cabin assigned to storage. "We'd planned to spend some time in Thebes, making a study of the monuments and tombs," she went on hurriedly. "These trunks hold Miles's sextant and artificial horizon, chronometer, large and small telescopes, siphon barometer, thermometer, and measuring tape. And his clothes. His kidnappers did not give him time to pack, recollect." Her voice shook a little at this last.

"We'll find him," Mr. Carsington said.

"Yes, yes, we must." Alive, she hoped.

"Duval has only a few days' head start of us," he said. "Do bear in mind, your brother is valuable."

"Until his captors find out the truth," she said.

"He's a *scholar,*" Mr. Carsington said. "Obviously he'll know how to keep them in the dark, to make them believe they must take good care of him if they want to find their treasure. If I were them, in fact, I'd play it safe and take him all the way to Thebes to help search for the tomb. He can talk a lot of incomprehensible scholarly jargon and lead them on for months, looking for it. Or he could set them digging at random. These excavations take many weeks. So you see, time is on our side."

The words lifted her mind from the depths into which it had so unexpectedly plummeted. Though he wasn't the scholar the world believed him to be, Miles was by no means a fool.

"Yes, I know that," she said. "Or ought to know it. It's simply . . ." She remembered the woman she'd been less than a week ago, her life entirely a life of the mind, all her flawed being safely engaged in solving an intellectual puzzle.

She looked up at him, into the dark eyes that she, who could read so many languages, found so hard to read and so easy to become lost in. "Unlike you, I am unaccustomed to having an exciting life," she said. "My mind is used to going at an even, orderly pace. Perhaps, in some ways, I have been like those women locked up in harems. They are ill-equipped for dealing with the outside world. I feel as though I am stumbling blindly about."

"Ah, is that all?" His mouth eased lazily into a smile. Threads of heat slid over her skin, as though his mouth were there . . . everywhere. "No need to fret," he said. "If you stumble, I'll catch you."

RUPERT STOOD SO near that she didn't need to stumble. She'd only to tip slightly in his direction and some part of her heavily camouflaged anatomy would touch his.

He loved this boat. It was a brilliant idea. Close quarters. Narrow, dim passage. And a shifting deck where she might easily lose her footing and need catching.

She edged away and started toward the front of the boat.

"This is my cabin," he said, indicating the door.

"I deduced as much," she said, and hurried past it to the front cabin.

He ducked under the frame and followed her inside. "This is the salon, as you see," he said. "Like the whatsit in the house. The room where you receive visitors."

"It is called the *qa'a*," she said.

"Say it again," he said.

While she did, he gravely studied her mouth. The lower lip was a trifle fuller than the upper, making a tempting hint of a pout.

"It isn't complicated," she said. "You can say it if you try."

"Kah," he said.

She pointed to her throat. "More syllables. You make the sound here, in the back of the throat."

He looked at her throat—the bit one could see, a tantalizing inch or two of creamy skin above the prim collar of her black dress. It would be so smooth against his tongue. And her skin would touch his face . . . and he would drink in her scent. He leant in.

The boat lurched. He fell against her, and she fell back, onto the divan.

For one glorious moment she lay under him, her magnificent bosom crushed against his chest. His heart leapt into a gallop and his privy councilor leapt to attention. He lifted his head and looked down at her. She looked up at him, eyes wide and dark as an evergreen forest. He felt her breath on his skin, and heard it, too, soft and hurried. Her lips parted. He lowered his head.

She shoved her fist against his chest, and "Get off!" she snapped. "Get off, you great lummox! Someone's coming!"

That was when he noticed the clamor of voices and footsteps outside. He scrambled to his feet and pulled her up to a sitting position. He left the cabin, closed the door behind him, and took a few calming breaths. Patience, he counseled himself. This wanted a slow siege, not a sudden assault. After giving his reproductive organs another moment to compose themselves, he went outside.

He found a smiling Sheik Salim awaiting him.

THE SHEIK HAD come to inspect the boat and wish them a safe journey. He'd brought two large cats—which Mr. Carsington promptly named Gog and Magog—for rat control. He'd brought other gifts as well as a feast. He was sorry to have to part from his learned (!!!) English friend, he said. To cheer his heart, he had decided to make a fête, which they would enjoy together until the *Isis* reached Old Cairo, where he must take his leave of them.

Daphne was surprised when the sheik invited her to the party, since women were usually excluded. However, someone had informed him that "the English custom is different," he explained. He behaved most graciously, including her in the conversation, and complimenting her Arabic.

This was no small gesture, Daphne well understood. Deeply touched, she decided upon a more munificent than usual farewell gift.

She had Mr. Carsington present Sheik Salim with a fine set of pistols.

He remained on deck after the sheik had disembarked. Daphne returned to the front cabin. Then she left it and went to her own cabin. Then she returned to the front cabin. She sat down. She got up. She sat down again.

She could not decide what to do.

Was it cowardly to spend the rest of the day and night hiding in her cabin?

She could not hide from him forever.

But she was hotly aware that at the first opportunity, she'd very nearly run amok.

You are a little impetuous, Daphne, I am afraid.

I'm sorry.

It is your youth. In time you will learn to govern your passions, I know.

She hadn't known until Virgil told her. No one before had told her they were unnatural, and must be strictly governed. No one could have guessed how ungovernable they'd prove to be, wicked things: the temper . . . the restlessness . . . the mad longing, as urgent as hunger or thirst.

For one terrible instant, the longing was more than she could withstand.

It had felt so good, that big, hard body on top of hers. It wasn't good, she knew. It was animal feeling, animal urges: every instinct poised to attack . . . her hands a mere pulse beat from reaching up and bringing his handsome face down to hers and—

The door flung open.

"You've done it," came the deep voice. "I'd thought I was unshockable, but you've done it."

Heat washed over her. A wave of cold shame instantly followed. "I—"

"Those were John Manton's work." Mr. Carsington dropped onto the divan beside her. "I nearly wept."

"You—Those—I don't—" She took a calming breath and ordered her brain back to work. "Who is John Manton?" she managed to get out.

His eyes opened very wide. The dappled sunlight trickling through the shutters softened his features. This and his incredulous expression combined to make him look for a moment like the innocent boy he must have been long ago. Very long ago.

"Who is Manton?" he repeated. "Who is *Manton?*"

"Ought I to know him?" she said.

He stared at her for a time. "You said you lived a quiet life," he said. "Was it in a cave, by chance? A monastery?"

She folded her hands in her lap. "I told you I was book-ish," she said. "I do not go about much."

"Have you ever been to London?"

"Yes, of course," she said. "The Rosetta Stone is in the British Museum, is it not? And the head of Young Memnon. Naturally I went often to London to attend lectures as well. That is how I met your cousin Miss Saunders."

He shook his head. "Your ignorance surpasseth all understanding. Even Cousin Tryphena knows that the brothers Manton of Dover Street are the finest gun makers in all of England, perhaps in all the world. I hope those weren't your brother's. He may disown you—and I shan't blame him a whit."

"Before we left England, we bought a great many gifts," she said. "Mr. Belzoni was quite clear on this point. One of his rivals, you know, lost his chance to obtain for France the head of Young Memnon because he'd insulted the local chief with a paltry gift of bottled anchovies."

Mr Carsington's expression became tragic. "It's a good distance from a bottle of anchovies to a pair of Manton's best."

"I know *that*," she said. "Miles did tell me the pistols were for persons who performed services above the common. Sheik Salim spared us a stay in a dungeon at the very least—and possibly a short trip to the headsman. He found this boat and moved heaven and earth to help you make it ready. Furthermore, it was most kind and gracious of him to invite me to the fête and actually converse with me."

He shrugged. "He would have talked to you from the first, but he thought it improper. Once he understood that English custom permitted him to talk to a lady, he was more than happy to do so. He said he'd never realized a woman's brain could be so large. I'd never realized it could have so many great, gaping holes in it."

"Really, such a fuss you make about a set of firearms," she said. "Could you not see how pleased he was?"

"Of course he was pleased. Who wouldn't be? Those are Manton's finest. I have coveted them this age."

"Then I should think you'd already have a pair. Or do you want more? How many pistols does a man need, exactly?"

He let out a sigh. "My finances haven't been flourishing lately."

"Oh," she said. She wanted to say a great deal more. Or ask, rather. She realized she knew next to nothing about him. But one did not discuss money, except with one's man of business. She looked down at her hands, hoping her vulgar curiosity didn't show.

"One of those dreaded summons to my father's study," he said. "He told me if I couldn't live within my means, I was welcome to live within a debtors' prison. He meant it. All the world knows Lord Hargate never utters idle threats. I thought debtors' prison might prove rather confining."

"So you learnt to economize," she said. "I wish I had some lessons. Miles, too. He is even worse than I. No notion of what's reasonable and what isn't. If he had any notion, we mightn't be in this fix."

Mr. Carsington was studying her again. "I see," he said, and she wondered uneasily what, exactly, he saw. "That explains. Everyone knows the local bigwigs prefer gifts of European firearms. It didn't occur to your brother that a merely serviceable weapon would do."

"Of course it didn't occur to him. If you knew Miles . . ." She blinked hard and swallowed.

"Tell me," Mr. Carsington said, "if it had been you that day, in Vanni Anaz's shop, would you have haggled?"

IT WAS A desperate attempt. Rupert didn't know whether it would provoke her or not, but she was on the verge of waterworks, and he needed a distraction. The question was the first to come to mind.

She blinked, wiping out the almost-tears shining in her green eyes.

"Would you?" Rupert pressed. "Would you think, 'This would make a lovely gift for Miles,' and say to Anaz, 'I'll take it,' and not stop to add up piastres and purses and such and convert them into pounds, shillings, and pence?"

She considered, her green eyes moving from side to side in that way she had, as though she read her own thoughts.

"Well . . . possibly . . ." She blushed. "Yes, probably. Very likely. It was splendid. Impossible to resist."

"It was artistic, you told me," he said. "Superior quality. The papyrus version of Manton's finest, in other words."

"Oh, it was," she said, and her voice grew wistful. "I wish you could have seen it. The colors. The figures. There is a handsome papyrus illustrated in color in the *Description de l'Egypte*, and it is not half so beautiful."

She went on to describe her papyrus—for it was hers, Rupert was sure, and every word she uttered only confirmed what he'd suspected when she knelt beside the table in the *qa'a* of her house in Cairo, when she'd discovered the theft.

She had the thing memorized, practically. She described the illustrations, some in large blocks, most in long lines across the top of columns of signs. She told him the names of the easily recognized gods and speculated about the others.

She must have realized she'd said too much, because she stopped midsentence to explain. "I made the copy for Miles," she said. "That is why I recall so many details."

"It sounds a great deal of work," Rupert said. "I vow, you must be the most devoted of sisters."

Telltale pink washed across her wide cheekbones. "His penmanship was never good and only grows worse. It is barely legible. He must have an amanuensis—and it gives me something useful to do. And of course one learns a great deal in the process."

If she'd gone about in Society more, Rupert thought, she'd know how to lie better. He wasn't sure why she lied. It was clear, though, that she'd insufficient practice. It hadn't occurred to her to conceal her books, or mix them with her brother's belongings, for instance.

One had only to glance at the collection in the cupboard to realize she'd mastered at least a dozen languages.

Rupert wondered if the same could be said of Miles Archdale.

Sunday night

WHAT COULD BE said of Miles Archdale was this: he sat on a thin, vermin-infested mattress in the dirty cabin of a shabby boat. He stared at the chain fastened to his ankles. He was calculating how many blows with how heavy an implement would shatter the rusty metal, and wondering how to do it without breaking any of his bones in the process.

The boat seemed to have stopped for the night, which meant a rat and mosquito invasion. A pity he couldn't train the rats to gnaw at the chain. Or to gnaw on his hosts.

One of them looked as though something had gnawed on him.

Butrus, the leader, apparently, was a square block of a brute. His battered and scarred face reminded Miles of the Sphinx's mutilated visage, especially the nose, for his was smashed flat. His right hand bore a stump where the little finger should be. While the half dozen or so men occupying the boat were not the most attractive lot of villains, Butrus was by far the ugliest.

Miles was allowed on deck to stretch his legs—in a manner of speaking—only after dark and only with an armed escort. On the first night out, he'd tried calling for help. Butrus struck him with the butt of a pistol, which stretched Miles out on the deck unconscious for a time.

When Miles came to upon the filthy mattress, Butrus advised him not to try such tricks again.

"We are not to kill you," Butrus told him that first night. "We must not cut out your tongue, because this organ is necessary. We must not cut off your hands. But an ear? A few toes? A foot?" He grinned, displaying a sparse collection of crooked brown teeth. "We must keep you alive. But we need not keep you complete in all your parts."

Miles had assumed they were holding him for ransom.

By the third day, as the boat continued upriver, he grew puzzled. The farther they traveled from Cairo, the more inconvenient the exchange of money for captive would be.

They'd been on the river for seven days now. Where in blazes were they taking him, and why?

The sun had set, and the slow nightfall had drained away the last traces of light in the cabin. He sat in the darkness, his mind moving from the problem of the leg shackles to his sister. By now she would know he was in trouble. By now, he hoped, she'd gone to Noxley for help.

The door opened, and a lantern shone, not very brightly, instantly inhabiting the space with shadows.

Butrus carried the lantern. Behind him came one of his shipmates, bearing the familiar wooden tray. Butrus remained, as he usually did, while Miles ate his supper. This, apparently, was to make sure the prisoner did not secret away the single eating utensil, a wooden spoon. No doubt they feared he'd use it later as a weapon or means of escape—perhaps by waving it about until his captors died laughing.

"Where are we?" Miles asked.

He asked the same question every night. Every night Butrus only laughed at him.

He laughed tonight, too.

Tonight, though, Miles was tired of the game. While Arabic did not trip from his tongue as smoothly and naturally as it did from Daphne's, his grasp of the language was more than adequate. Especially for dealing with common louts like this one.

"Shall I hazard a guess?" Miles said.

Butrus shrugged. "Who cares, *Ingleezi?*"

"We've traveled at a fairly steady clip since Monday," Miles said. "This tells me the wind's been favorable for the most part, and we're well provisioned." He calculated briefly. Then, "Minya," he said. "I estimate we're not far from Minya." The area had a bad reputation, if he remembered correctly.

Butrus nodded. "I have heard that you are a man of great learning," he said. "Your cleverness does not surprise me. Before too long we will take you to a quiet place.

There, if you are wise as well as learned, you will do what is asked of you."

"Ah, I'm to do something," Miles said.

Butrus shrugged. "Perhaps you will, perhaps you will not. Perhaps you will be unwise, and refuse. This will be better for me, because I have not yet tortured any *Ingleezi*, and I am interested to improve *my* learning in this way."

"A man of ambition, I see," Miles said. "Most commendable."

He'd been told the Arabs didn't understand irony or sarcasm. He couldn't tell whether Butrus did or not.

The brute merely shrugged and said, "Soon we come to the place where some *Feransa* await you. They have something for you to read."

Feransa. Not *Ferangi*—the all-encompassing Frank, applied to Europeans in general. *Feransa* was the word for the French.

"It is written in the old language of this country," Butrus went on. "A papyrus."

"Hmmmm," Miles said. He dared say no more until he'd collected his wits. It was a joke, he thought first. It had to be a joke. The trouble was, Butrus was not a joke.

Noxley had mentioned having difficulties with the French and their agents. Belzoni, too, had had several unfriendly encounters with them.

This went beyond the usual rivalry, as intense as it was. This was madness. Did the French truly believe that he—that anyone—could read a papyrus?

Butrus must have misunderstood.

Miles said cautiously, "It's going to be difficult without my notes."

"When I torture you, maybe you will remember what is in your notes. Perhaps you would like to hear how I will torture you?"

Miles wondered if it was possible to kill somebody with a wooden spoon, because clearly, he must do something and do it quickly—

Which was when the shouting started.

He heard heavy, hurried footsteps over the decks, and the clank of weapons. Butrus jumped up and started for the door. It flung open, just as the boat gave a lurch. Butrus fell backward. A man burst into the room, another behind him. Miles saw the glint of a blade before the lantern toppled. A figure came toward him. He thrust out his shackled feet, and the figure fell. A sword rose and came down. A scream began and stopped suddenly. The last thing he saw was the sheen of metal slicing through the air down toward him.

Chapter 8

THE SWORD STRUCK THE DIVAN CLOSE BY HIM, then rose again. The boat shuddered, and the attacker stumbled. Miles couldn't see what happened next, though he heard the ring of metal on metal. Then came a shriek, cut short. A grunt. The thud of a falling body—was it more than one? The cabin fell quiet. Outside, the fighting continued.

He felt about for a weapon. He found a knife. Cautiously he made his way out, trying to clank as little as possible and taking care not to trip over any bodies.

He was inching his way to the door when the vessel shuddered. He fell against the door, whacking his head. He heard wood cracking and groaning: they'd run aground.

The human noise outside swiftly abated. A few low voices, none familiar, all speaking Arabic. Splashing. Then no more voices. He waited a bit longer to be sure. He thought he heard footsteps, but that might be the boat breaking apart.

He headed outside anyway, and found the tilting deck nearly deserted. He made out two dark figures in a dinghy tied to the boat. Only those. No other moving figures.

The small landing boat offered his one chance of getting ashore alive. He couldn't swim; the chains would drag him down. He'd be a fool to wait for rescue. The people hereabouts weren't known for their charitable impulses. They were probably friends of his kidnappers. Whoever had attacked the boat must be a rival gang of brigands. Freebooters would soon come to steal what they could. Or perhaps had already come. Those two fellows in the dinghy, for instance.

If he didn't get their boat from them, he was a dead man.

Feet shackled, one small knife his only weapon—the odds for a direct assault didn't look good.

He would have to use his head.

He thought quickly.

Then he dragged his hands through his filthy hair, making it stand on end.

He let out a groan. The figures froze.

He began walking slowly toward them, loudly clanking his chains and reciting the "Tomorrow" speech from *Macbeth* in the wailing voice of a vengeful ghost.

Screaming, they dove over the side.

THE *ISIS* DIDN'T get far on Monday, because the wind turned against them. The *reis*—the captain—had the crew tow the vessel. This only stopped her traveling backward with the current. Forward, it seemed, was out of the question for the time being.

Despite Tom's and Leena's arguing about vocabulary, Rupert did manage to communicate with Reis Rashad, who proved helpful on several counts. Leaving Leena and Tom to quarrel about which winds were the most deadly, Rupert turned his mind to Mrs. Pembroke. She was not going to be happy about the delay.

According to Leena, the lady was awake. She hadn't joined him in the salon for breakfast, though, and he was impatient to see her.

He and Tom had retired many hours later than the women last night. Rupert had stayed on deck long after the crew was asleep, ostensibly to make sure the boat was properly guarded. Actually, he'd needed to cool off, though there was little the lower evening temperatures could do for the kind of heat he endured.

It was the wanting-to-get-her-naked kind of heat, the wanting-to-get-skin-close kind of heat, the fire-low-in-the-belly kind of heat.

And it plagued him partly because he'd fallen on top of her—well, maybe mostly because of that: the suppleness of the soft body under his, the luscious peach of a mouth with its tantalizing bit of pout, and the green eyes, ocean deep, and the way they'd looked at him.

It was not a "get off" look. It was the kind of look Helen of Troy must have given Paris, the kind Cleopatra must have given Mark Antony. Wars broke out because of looks like that.

But that wasn't all of it. When Sheik Salim admired her command of Arabic and marveled at her large brain, Rupert wanted to get her naked. When she talked about her papyrus and its beautiful little pictures and its columns of perfectly drawn signs, he wanted to get her naked. When he thought about those books in a dozen languages in her cupboard, he wanted to get her naked.

He didn't know and didn't really care why. All he understood was that she stirred him up amazingly.

So much that she kept him awake half the night.

He would have to rethink his plans for a slow siege, he decided as he made his way to the stern cabin.

He found her on her knees, sorting through the heaps of books she'd brought. She barely glanced up when he tapped on the doorframe.

"Is something wrong with the boat?" she said. "We've stopped, haven't we?"

"Something's wrong with the weather," he said. "A southern wind. If I understood correctly, it's called the *khamsin.*"

All the color drained from her face. Her shoulders sagged, and she sank back onto her heels. "Oh, no."

"It can't be helped," he said. "The wind is dead set against us."

"But the villains are days ahead of us—nearly a week."

"Reis Rashad says contrary winds are normal at this

time of year," Rupert said. "That means other boats on the Nile are stymied, too, on occasion. Which means your brother might be a week ahead but not many miles distant."

The color came back, enhanced with a faint wash of pink at the top of her cheekbones. "Oh, yes, why did I not consider that?" She shook her head. "I am not usually so emotional. Usually, my thinking is clear and rigorous. I do not allow myself to succumb to *moods*. Nor am I weepy." She rubbed at the outer corner of her eye. "In fact, I am a predictable, boring person. This—" She waved impatiently at her extraordinary face. "This isn't *me*."

"I know what the trouble is," he said. He eased down onto the divan, something less than an arm's length away. "The trouble is, you haven't enough brothers. The more you have, the easier it is to develop a certain detachment."

"Are your brothers in the habit of getting themselves kidnapped by madmen?" she said. "Is that the sort of thing one gets used to?"

"No, I think it's the variety of incidents," Rupert said. "With five of us, there's always been one crisis or another. Alistair, for instance, was in the habit of getting himself into expensive catastrophes with women. So when he went off to Derbyshire three years ago, we all more or less expected an expensive catastrophe, and went on about our business." He frowned. "Actually, it did turn out more calamitous than usual."

"Is this the one who was so badly injured at Waterloo?" she said. "Good grief, was that not enough? What befell him in Derbyshire?"

"He got himself engaged," Rupert said grimly. "To be married."

"Oh, dear. The woman was unsuitable, I take it."

"No, he became *engaged*," Rupert repeated more slowly and distinctly. "To be married."

She folded her arms and considered him. "I see," she said. "Marriage is the great catastrophe."

"Well, naturally you don't see it that way," he said. "He was a saint, I collect."

She looked baffled. "Your brother?"

Rupert gestured at the head-to-toe mourning she wore.

"All that black. He must have been remarkable, the—um—departed."

"Oh, you mean Virgil." Her voice was wintry. "He was a scholar. A respected theologian."

She became busy again, shoving back into the cupboard any which way the books he'd so carefully arranged.

"A shame he couldn't have lived to make this journey with you," Rupert said. "Egypt seems to be all the rage with scholars."

"Not with Virgil," she said several degrees more frostily.

So much for Virgil Pembroke. If the mourning had anything to do with the deceased, Rupert would eat his boots. The forbidding black was camouflage, just as he'd supposed.

"He would have taken me to the Holy Land," she said.

"I'm sure that's a worthy—"

"I know I ought to want to make the pilgrimage, but I don't care," she said. "If I'm to be hot and uncomfortable, if I'm to eat sand with every meal and look for snakes and scorpions before I put on my boots, there must be a compelling interest." She threw him a defiant glance and slammed the cupboard closed.

"Well, then, have you a compelling interest in some ruins?" Rupert said.

"Of course I do," she said irritably. *"Egyptian* ruins. That is why I am here, not in the Holy Land."

"Reis Rashad says we're very near Memphis," he said. "We can hire donkeys and ride out to the ruins. There's a broken bit of temple, and a pharaoh, I'm told. Not far from that is a great lot of pyramids. Maybe you can find a piece of stone with unreadable writing on it."

DAPHNE WASN'T SURE what she expected to find in Memphis. Recent events had banished all thoughts of exploring. To the extent she had thought about it, she'd vaguely pictured a desert plateau like Giza, containing monuments.

Even when they set out, her mind was not upon their destination.

She rode with Mr. Carsington along a causeway, scarcely aware of her surroundings, for a number of reasons. Watching him undress was one of them.

He'd started out well enough this morning, in a species of Eastern attire. He'd replaced his torso-hugging coat with a tunic, and exchanged his snug-fitting trousers for loose Turkish ones, which he tucked into his boots. But now, as they rode away from the river, he first cast off the handsome green tunic, then undid his neckcloth, then completely unbuttoned his pale yellow silk waistcoat, thus exposing nearly all of his shirt—his *underwear*—to public view.

Naturally she couldn't stop looking at him.

She ought to tell him, very firmly, that it was most improper: the Mohammedans were people of modesty, and he ought to respect their sensibilities, even if he had no regard for English standards of propriety. She ought to insist he put his clothes back on.

She'd always had more trouble than she ought with *oughts*.

Like the undisciplined girl she'd once been, she kept stealing glances. She noticed the way his upper garments stretched across his broad shoulders and the way at certain moments and at a certain angle the wind and sun turned the shirt into a billowing, translucent curtain. Through it she clearly discerned—and could hardly look away from—the silhouette of his muscled arms and torso, the latter tapering to a narrow waist.

She ought not look lower than that.

She did though, covertly studying the part of him resting on the saddle. The loose trousers couldn't completely disguise his narrow hips. His bottom was no doubt as taut and hard as the rest of him.

She felt suddenly overheated and faint.

And then Virgil intruded, his voice and image in her mind bringing a chill, as ghosts reputedly did.

A saint, Mr. Carsington had thought her spouse.

Oh, very saintly. In the course of her marriage, she'd never seen Virgil undressed.

Even when they made love, it happened in the dark, and

he wore his nightshirt and she a nightgown; and there were rules, so many rules—too many for her, at a time when she didn't want to be thinking.

She didn't want Virgil in her head again. She was still angry, out of all reason angry, and it had started the instant she uttered his name, earlier, on the boat.

She remembered the way he'd close his eyes when she mentioned Egypt, and the patient little smile he wore when he opened them again, and the patient tone he invariably adopted while patiently reminding her that all a lady needed to know of Egypt was writ down in Holy Writ, in the books of Genesis and Exodus.

But she was here, and she would not let Virgil spoil this journey, even if everything had gone wrong. At present, she could do nothing about Miles. Until the wind changed, she could either fret about the present and seethe about the past or make the best of matters.

She looked about her . . . and found the world had changed, utterly.

They had entered a forest of date palms. The tall, graceful trees rose from a carpet of vividly green grass dotted with flowers of pink and purple. They rode past glistening pools beside which goats watched over their frolicking kids. Above them, a bird burst into song, then another.

At last they came to a grassy hollow.

Here, by the side of a pool reflecting the green surroundings and the brilliant blue of the Egyptian sky, an immense stone pharaoh lay on his face, his mouth curved in a small, secret smile.

Captivated, Daphne slid from the saddle, barely aware of what she did, and walked to the statue's head, her fingers at her lips. "Oh," she murmured. "How beautiful."

Not until this moment did she fully grasp how little she knew of Egypt, how little she'd seen of it. Pictures in books were all very well, and they had captured her imagination, but mainly as mysteries to be solved once she solved the riddle of the ancient writing.

The pyramids were wondrous, an achievement impossible to grasp, quite. But they were dark and empty within, colossal heaps of stones without. They were tombs, grand monuments to the dead.

This, too, was grand: some forty feet long, even with the king's lower extremities missing. But it was more than a fine monument. It was art carried to near perfection. One knew it was stone, yet stone so finely carved as to appear to be flesh and blood. The smile, the secret hint of a smile, was magical.

She became aware of Mr. Carsington close behind her.

She fought her way out of the enchantment the place had cast over her and shifted into her pedantic mode, where she felt safest: with facts instead of the confusing clamor of feelings.

"If I recall aright, this was discovered only last year," she said. "According to Herodotus and Diodorus, this is Ramesses II, also known as Ramesses the Great. It is said to have stood before the temple of Vulcan, or Pthah, which is the Egyptian name. Statues of his queen and four of his sons were there, too."

She walked alongside the vast frame, and paused at the elbow. She bent and tipped her head to examine the markings on the girdle encircling his waist. "There is his cartouche," she said, pointing.

"I'm not sure it's decent for you to be looking at his cartouche," said Mr. Carsington.

She was aware of the remark, aware of the heat slithering up her neck, and a niggling anxiety that he'd caught her studying his anatomy before. The statue exerted a powerful pull, though, and all other concerns evaporated in the sweetness of that enigmatic smile.

"I told you what a cartouche was," she said, crouching for a better look at Ramesses's front side. "Ovals containing hieroglyphic writing. There on his girdle, you see. And on his wrist. Oh, and I see another on his breast and on his shoulder. There seem to be several, but I cannot be sure. Two seem predominant."

"Has he two names, then?" Mr. Carsington asked. "Or perhaps a name and a title. You know, like the king—His Majesty George Augustus Frederick IV. Then he has that other lot of names: Prince of this, Duke of that."

"Very possibly," she said absently, her mind as well as gaze riveted upon one of the cartouches. She crouched down for a better angle of view and a thrill coursed through her. "That is the sun sign, certainly. In Coptic, the word for sun is *ra*—or *re*—oh, what one would give for a proper vowel. But there are the three tails tied together, next to the hook shape. The same as in the cartouche for Thuthmoses. The combination must be *moses* or *meses*. Dr. Young was mistaken, as I had thought. This cartouche cannot possibly belong to Maenupthes, as he maintained. This statue's identity is beyond dispute. Everyone agrees it is Ramesses the Great. Ergo, the signs in the cartouche must read *Ra-mes-ses*," she concluded triumphantly.

"Fascinating," Mr. Carsington said.

Daphne slowly straightened, her heart racing. Caught up in the excitement of discovery, she hadn't realized she'd been thinking aloud. She'd said far too much, given herself away. But no, not to him. He was no scholar. To him, it must have been meaningless babble.

He stood watching her, arms folded over his big chest, his dark eyes uncomfortably penetrating. "It isn't so much what you say as how you say it," he said. "That first day, when you knew immediately that someone had disturbed the materials on the table. *You* had been working on the papyrus, you said."

"I told you. I assist Miles."

"You knew exactly where each item had been," he said.

"He has a system," she said.

He smiled and shook his head. "You give yourself away. When you are on sure ground—on *your* ground—your voice changes, and a wonderfully arrogant look comes into your eyes, and you hold your head in a certain way."

Did she? Was she so obvious? "I fail to see the relevance of the way I hold my head," she said.

"It says you *know*. And when you speak of a sign and a sound," he went on, "and when you know the Coptic word for *sun*, and when you coolly dispute the famous Dr. Young's interpretations, I can only conclude—"

"Miles—"

"I doubt it," he said. "You told me what your brother's trunks contained. You never mentioned his books. How odd that a language scholar should travel without books."

"Actually—"

"You, on the other hand, travel with a remarkable assortment," he said. "Greek. Latin. Hebrew. Persian. Arabic. Turkish. Coptic. Sanskrit. And the usual: German, French, Spanish, Italian. Did I miss anything?"

"Apparently not," she said tightly. "I missed a great deal. You are supposed to be a great, dumb ox."

"I am," he said. "I only seem so brilliantly insightful because I've a hieroglyph fanatic in the family. Cousin Tryphena is not like you, though, and it isn't simply that she's older. She's usually impossible to understand. You even I can follow, more or less. She's hardly ever interesting. You always are. You have so much *passion*."

Daphne winced at the word, at its myriad meanings, so many of them dangerous. "You don't know me in my normal state," she said. "I'm a great bore."

"I find you intriguing," he said. "It must be the air of mystery that comes of leading a double life."

"I have no choice!" Daphne burst out. "I am not mysterious. I am not a person drawn to intrigue. I am dull and bookish and content to spend hours alone memorizing a new vocabulary and grammar or staring at a single cartouche. But one can't work in isolation. Those who do end up repeating others' mistakes or wasting time on disproved theories." Like Virgil, who'd wasted decades. "My sex and circumstances isolated me," she went on. "I had a choice: either give up my work or practice deception. I could not give it up."

"Passions are beastly difficult to give up," he said.

"You would think I was trying to seduce men rather than coax prepositions from a piece of crumbling parchment," she said bitterly. "A common harlot could not meet with more disapproval, scorn, disgust." She laughed, but it was an angry sound. She was still fighting. It still hurt. She was so tired of fighting, pretending.

"Maybe you were associating with the wrong sort of people," he said.

"What other sort is there?" she demanded. "The sort who laugh at intellectual women instead?"

"There's the sort like *me*," he said.

He didn't move, but physical distance didn't matter. She'd let him get too close because she'd let emotion loosen her tongue, and her secrets had tumbled out into the open.

She took a step back, into Ramesses's stony forearm.

Mr. Carsington's mouth curved a very little, like that of the stone pharaoh, and he closed the distance she'd tried to make between them.

"You could probably coax a proposition from me," he said, "if you set your mind to it."

"Preposition," she said. "I said *prep*—"

He slid his hand to the back of her head, into her hair, and she froze, on the outside, that is. Inside, a ferocious hammering started, and the place where her brain used to be was now a wild whirl of dark fragments as elusive as the lost language she'd struggled to decipher.

He tilted his head a little to one side, studying her. "Ah, well, so much for slow sieges," he said. He leant in, and she was too slow to duck or draw back, and so his mouth fell upon hers, and the bottom dropped out of the world.

She lifted her hand—to push him away as she must. As she ought. But his mouth moved boldly over hers, firm and sure, and she clung instead, her fingers curling round his upper arm. It was as hard as the stone figure blocking her retreat, yet warm and alive, its heat electric. Her fingers tingled, and the current shot under the skin. Every particle of her being reacted, as though galvanized.

The dark fragments in her mind swirled into a haze, and the mad hammering wasn't simply in her heart, but beating through vein and muscle.

She tightened her grasp, holding on with both hands now, as though the very ground were giving way beneath her, just as everything within was giving way. One powerful arm slid round her waist and pulled her closer. She stiffened at the collision with that rock-hard body, but in the next heartbeat she was melting in its heat and molding herself to him. It wasn't enough. She dragged her hands up over the broad shoulders and up his hard jaw. The pulse in his neck beat against the edge of her hand. Cupping his face, she parted her lips, offering herself. He teased her first, his tongue playing over her lips, then he stole inside, and the world spun as the taste of him swirled inside her, strangely cool and sweet and infinitely immoral.

His hand slid further down, curving over her buttock and pressing her closer yet, until her belly was crushed against his pelvis. It was wrong, completely wrong, but she was wrong, too—born that way—lacking the will to break away. She yielded to the shattering physical awareness of *him*—the long, sinewy body and the pressure of his hardened rod against her belly. She surrendered to the simmering heat between them and the tempest of feeling within.

Deep-buried longings clawed their way out of hiding. They tangled about her heart and coiled and twisted in her belly. She couldn't name them. This wanted a new language, or no language at all. Meaning narrowed to the taste of his mouth and his skin and to the scent of him, dark and dangerous and so familiar that she ached, as though it were a cherished memory or a reawakened grief.

She should have battled her baser self and pulled free of the woman-trap he was. Instead she struggled to get closer, her hands tangling in his thick hair while her tongue tangled with his. So wrong. So lewd.

And so strange and exciting, like crawling through a pyramid in utter darkness.

He and what he awoke within her were far more dangerous. At this moment, though, she loved danger, and she would have gone on, straight to ruination. But his hand slid from her bottom and his mouth left hers, and with the broken contact, she became aware of the sun and the tall palms and birds singing and the stone giant against whose arm she had so stupidly lost control—along with her self-respect and any and all claims to virtue.

She pulled away. "Oh!" she said. And then, because she didn't know what else to say—hadn't a good reason to blame him or any plausible excuse for herself—she did what she'd used to do when she felt this way, when she and

Miles were children. She balled her hand into a fist, swung her arm, and hit him, backhanded, hard in the chest.

PANIC.

One black, ghastly moment. Rupert must say something—conceal, divert, distract—but it meant thinking, and his mind wasn't up to the job.

The blow settled everything handsomely—and about bloody time, too.

"Sorry," he said. "I got carried away."

That was too uncomfortably true.

"Carried away?" she repeated indignantly.

He could have said she was a fine one to wax indignant when she'd cooperated fully, thank you very much, rather too fully, in fact. Rather more than he was prepared for—or any man could be prepared for.

He still saw stars—and moons and planets, too. The whole universe was spinning. Dizzy, he started to look about for the large object—a stone falcon for instance—with which she must have thumped him in the head.

He caught himself in the nick of time.

There wasn't a weapon. *She* was the weapon. She'd struck with her softly wicked pouting peach of a mouth and her body, the curving miracle of a body the Devil himself had designed to drive men distracted.

And then there was the passion, ocean-deep and as wild as any sea storm.

Rupert had a strong suspicion what it was her husband had died of.

He gestured about him. "The . . . um . . . romantic scene. The woman of mystery." With the magnificent rump. And a raw, rare talent for kissing a man deaf, dumb, blind, and deranged. "The mood of the moment. And no one about."

That was to say, he hoped there had been no witnesses. He looked past her, over the gigantic Ramesses he'd assumed would shield them from prying eyes. Their guide and the handful of servants and crew members who'd come along had gathered a respectful distance away. They sat in the shade of a clump of palm trees, smoking their pipes and listening to Tom talking nine to the dozen. In the other direction, the donkey drivers remained with their beasts and talked in the same animated Egyptian manner.

"I am no mystery," she said crossly. "I told you—"

"Your mind is so intriguing," he said. "So filled with learning. And all those secrets, too. Complicated. Fascinating."

Her expression grew wary. "My mind?" she said. "You kissed me for my *mind?*"

"Don't be ridiculous," he said. "Do you want to see the pyramids?" He pointed. "They're that way."

Chapter 9

DAPHNE WANTED TO RUN BACK TO THE BOAT
and hide in her cabin, which was childish and silly, she
knew. When she did get back to the boat, she would give
herself a good talking-to. She could not revert to the heed-
less schoolgirl she'd once been, ruled by her passions.
Then she'd paid with a prison sentence of a marriage. Now
she would pay with her reputation, shaming Miles, who'd
made it possible for her to continue her work and to whom
she owed her sanity.

If your honor means nothing to you, she told herself, *at
least consider his.*

Aloud she said, with all the composure she could summon, that she would very much like to visit the pyramids—
as soon as she made copies of the cartouches.

Mr. Carsington unloaded her drawing supplies from her
saddlebags, then kept out of her way while she worked. It
did not take very long, and she was surprised, when she
was done, to look round and find him standing under a
palm tree, sketching.

"I didn't know you could draw," she said.

"It's one of my deep, dark secrets," he said. "Actually,
it's the only one. Not much of a secret, either. My father

believes a gentleman must know how to draw as well as fence and shoot. If I go home with no pictures, I'll never hear the end of it. There." He showed it to her.

The sketch was of the colossal Ramesses—and of her, seated on her stool, copying the signs on the stone pharaoh's wrist.

"It's very good," she said, surprised. She felt a surge of pleasure, too, because she was in the picture, and a chill of anxiety, because she was in the picture, and the portrayal struck her as . . . intimate. But that was ridiculous, emotion playing tricks on her reason. Who'd ever know it was Daphne Pembroke, that tiny figure next to the immense pharaoh who'd fallen on his face?

THE SAQQARA PYRAMIDS were reputedly older than those of Giza. They were still imposing structures, Daphne thought as they crossed the plain. The main one, the Pyramid of Steps, was their destination.

When they reached the pebbly sand slope leading to the pyramids' plateau, she and Mr. Carsington dismounted, to spare the donkeys.

Debris littered the way. He paused for a time, studying it, an odd expression on his face. She said nothing, simply watched, surprised, as his countenance hardened and he turned into someone she scarcely recognized. The cold mask reminded her of the change in his voice when he found the bodies in the pyramid. He'd sounded like a stranger then, so cold and detached.

She saw the same stranger now. Usually, even when he wasn't smiling outwardly, she'd felt the smile was there all the same. In his dark eyes she usually discerned a gleam of amusement, as though he knew a very good joke. That, no doubt, was why one was so easily deluded into believing him an amiable idiot.

The good humor was completely gone. He straightened and, without a word, walked quickly on, taking long, angry strides she couldn't hope to match.

Puzzled, Daphne squatted to look more closely at the rubbish covering the ground. Bits of marble and alabaster.

Pottery shards. Shiny blue and green slivers. Shreds of
dirty brown linen. Some odd bits of dark material. And
white . . . bones.

She rose and gazed about her.

The place was a pillaged burial ground. These were the
contents of graves. The pieces of dark material were what
remained of mummies. The linen was the remnants of their
winding sheets. The other bits must be the vestiges of burial objects.

"Oh, you poor things," she whispered. Her throat closed
and ached.

She rubbed her eyes and sharply told herself to stop being maudlin. Her collection of papyri had been plundered
from the graves of ancient Egyptians. The same was true
of her little wooden Egyptians.

"What an idiot—and a great hypocrite—you are, to
weep about them now," she chided herself. But she'd been
an idiot from the time she woke up this day, it seemed. She
rubbed her itching eyes and took a steadying breath, and
continued to the pyramid.

She found Mr. Carsington at an ominous-looking black
hole in the north face. The cold, hard look was gone, and
the gleam was back in his eyes. A European in Arab garb
stood with him. Mr. Carsington introduced the man as
Signor Segato. He was excavating the pyramid for the
Baron Minutoli, she learned.

"He tells me the interior is wonderfully complicated,"
Mr. Carsington said. "Makes Chephren's tomb look like
child's play, by the sounds of it. This is the way in."

Daphne ventured nearer the hole. It was much larger
than the entrance to Chephren's pyramid.

"The shaft is only eighteen feet deep," Mr. Carsington
said.

"It can't possibly be that easy to get inside," she said.

"No, that's the beginning," he said. "The burial chamber's about a hundred feet below, under the pyramid."

"A hundred feet," she repeated while her heart beat a
fearful *No, no! No, no! No, no!*

"It's gradual," he said. "Miles of descending passages

and stairs. Some pits and such. And a place where the stones are threatening to fall in. Are you game, Mrs Pembroke?"

She did not want to go down into that hole, be it ever so large. Every natural instinct recoiled, and common sense warned against it.

"There are hieroglyphic signs on a doorway," he said.

"Inside?" she said. *"Inside a pyramid?"* She'd never heard of anyone's finding hieroglyphs inside a pyramid. But this excavation was very recent. She turned her gaze to Signor Segato and fired a series of questions at him in Italian.

Yes, yes, he agreed with the *signora:* this was most unusual. He was greatly surprised when he found them: birds, snakes, insects, and the other little pictures. The chamber itself was decorated, very beautiful.

She swallowed. "Very well," she told Mr. Carsington. "I should like to see this inscription."

It was a beastly long and uncomfortable way to the chamber, and the heat so far below ground was sufficient to bake bricks. But once they'd amassed torches enough, and she stopped coughing from the smoke, she could appreciate the interesting labyrinth of passages and the complex of chambers, so unlike the simplicity of Chephren's pyramid at Giza. This one, too, was empty of treasure, which could surprise no one. In Egypt, plundering tombs had been not simply a fact of life but a profession since the time of Cheops at least.

She found treasure enough for her, though, deep in the bowels of the pyramid.

The chamber was all and more that Signor Segato had promised. Upon the dark blue painted ceiling gleamed golden stars. Turquoise-colored tiles covered the walls. But most wondrous of all was the doorframe. Above it and along the sides were hieroglyphs, beautifully cut in low relief.

A repeated motif adorned the sides. A falcon wearing the pharaoh's crown stood upon a rectangular pedestal divided into two squares. The top square contained three signs: at top, the hatchet that signified a god; beneath this, the almond shape she'd decided must be the *r* sound; and under it a sign less familiar: a rattle, insect, flower, or musical instrument, she couldn't be sure. Four vertical sections divided the bottom square. Did these signify pillars? she wondered. Doors?

"Is that the god Horus?" came Mr. Carsington's deep voice from behind her.

The voice went straight down her spine and up again. In self-defense, she adopted her pedantic mode. "So it appears," she said. "The sign below him is the one Dr. Young interprets to mean *god.* As you see, Horus wears a pharaoh's crown. The kings were believed to be gods. Perhaps this one was closely associated with Horus."

"The signora can read the ancient writing?" Signor Segato asked.

"Ah, no," Mr. Carsington said quickly. "She has read a little Greek, though."

"Herodotus," Daphne said quickly.

She really *must* learn to keep her hieroglyphic speculations to herself. As Noxley had remarked, the Egyptians loved to talk, and news traveled swiftly. If the explorer mentioned an Englishwoman who could read hieroglyphs, all of Egypt would soon hear of it . . . including the mad villains who'd kidnapped Miles—and who wouldn't hesitate to come after her.

"She uses a little Herodotus and a great deal of woman's intuition," Mr. Carsington said, in precisely the patronizing tone one would expect from a superior male.

Normally, the condescension would have had her seething. Now she almost laughed—with relief—at how adeptly he'd covered her blunder.

Ironic that she could trust *him* to keep her secret better than she could do.

She did not half understand him, she realized, and she apparently had a less than perfect understanding of herself.

It seemed she understood only her work. She gazed at the hieroglyphs, at the familiar cobra and vulture and bee and hatchet. She pondered the significance of the semicircles under most of the figures. Baskets, the larger ones with the round side down? What of the smaller ones, round side up? Sound or symbol? Thus questioning, speculating, theorizing, she swiftly forgot everything else.

o   o   •

GETTING MRS. PEMBROKE away from the confounded falcons and what-you-call-'ems took steady and patient coaxing.

This was not what Rupert wanted to be doing.

While he watched and listened to her, he wanted to get her naked.

There was the seeing-stars kiss, from which he still suffered aftereffects, something like the morning after a debauch—except that his head wasn't what ached.

There was whatever she was doing to him now, and he wasn't sure what that was.

She managed—just barely—to hide her learning from Segato. She couldn't conceal her excitement, though. It set the very air vibrating.

Since she couldn't run about the place, openly gesticulating and theorizing and talking six languages simultaneously, she stuck close to Rupert. And when she couldn't contain herself—which happened every few minutes—she'd clutch his arm and tug to bring his ear near her mouth, so that she could whisper.

He had to feel her breath on his ear and neck and cheek and be aware of how close her mouth was and how all he had to do was turn his head to taste it again—and see stars.

But he couldn't turn his head. He had to behave, because they weren't alone, which was why he had to endure the whisper torture.

Luckily for her, Segato was Italian. Assuming the whispers were romantic rather than pedantic, he kept a tactful distance.

This belief wouldn't do Mrs. Pembroke's reputation any good. Still, the alternative was worse.

It wasn't hard to guess what Duval and his underlings would do if they found out they'd kidnapped the wrong sibling. They'd come after her, and they'd murder whomever happened to be in the way: captain, crew members, Leena, and Tom.

If Mrs. Pembroke's secret got out, none of them would be safe.

Keeping the secret was going to be more difficult than Rupert could have foreseen. Every time she met a hieroglyph, she'd act like this: vibrating like a tuning fork, the gigantic brain bubbling over and spilling out its secrets: Greek and Latin and Coptic and names of scholars and who believed what and this alphabet versus that one and phonetic interpretations versus symbolic ones.

The day was waning when they finally climbed out of the pyramid. She was not waning in the least.

Several members of their party had come up from the plain to wait nearby. Though they carried food and water, the lady paid them no heed. A heap of stones a few feet away caught her eye. She wandered thither.

Tom trotted over to Rupert with the clothes he'd discarded en route. Though it was late afternoon, the air had not yet begun to cool. In any case, Rupert wanted to wash off the layer of sand and sweat first. Shaking his head at the boy, he turned away to watch Mrs. Pembroke.

Beside him, Segato watched her, too, remarking how unusual it was to find a woman who shared one's enthusiasm for exploration and who bore hardship so cheerfully.

There was an understatement.

She must be at least as hot, dirty, and tired as Rupert was. Like him, she'd had nothing to eat since morning. Yet instead of hurrying to the waiting servants who carried food and water, she crouched to peer at a slab of rock poking out of a pile of rubble.

She brushed it off, bent close, shook her head, and with an impatient twitch, knelt in the pebbly sand. She dug under, and after a moment, unearthed the two outer corners. She grabbed the edge and lifted it up. It seemed to be a tablet of some kind, for it was covered in writing.

Rupert saw that, and the shadowy form revealed when she rested it against the rubble heap. He saw the snake rear up, and his heart froze. She sank back on her knees, and, *"Don't move!"* he roared.

He was moving as he spoke. He grabbed the clothes from the boy, discarding all but the tunic while swiftly covering the few feet to where she remained immobile. The snake swayed in its place, still confused perhaps after the abrupt awakening, or not sure where the threat lay.

Mrs. Pembroke was leaning as far back over her heels as she could, balanced on one hand, her green gaze riveted upon the serpent.

"Don't move," Rupert repeated more quietly. He shook out the tunic, as a bullfighter would shake out his cape. The snake made a quick dart at it without moving farther away from her. The creature was still aware of her, a larger and more solid threat. She was still within its range, and it was fully alert now, waiting. If she moved, it would attack her.

While gently waving the tunic, to fix the snake's attention there, Rupert inched nearer to her. When he'd finally got the cloth between her and the snake, he said softly, "Now. Back away. Try to make as little disturbance as possible."

She did as he told her, but the snake must have sensed the movement. The striped head darted forward, and the fangs tore into the tunic.

In the instant the animal was occupied, she edged back quickly. When she'd moved well out of the snake's reach, Rupert said, "It's all right. You can get up now."

Though aware of her rising and moving out of danger, he stayed focused on the vexed serpent.

"There, there, my dear," he said soothingly. "You're safe now. The naughty lady's gone away. Sorry we disturbed you." He went on speaking gently to the creature as he gradually drew the tunic farther away from it.

When Rupert, too, was out of range, the snake began to settle down. Rupert gently let the tunic fall. The striped head sank down, and after a moment, the creature slithered with remarkable speed into the nearest crevice of the rubble heap.

Rupert watched until it was safely inside. Then he looked about for Mrs. Pembroke.

To his surprise, he found she hadn't run away and down the sand slope. She stood only a few yards away, looking from him to the hole into which the snake had disappeared.

"You want to be careful around piles of stones," he said, buttoning his waistcoat. For some reason he felt chilled.

"Yes." She brushed sand from her clothes. "How foolish of me. Thank you." She straightened her posture and started toward the others.

Rupert joined her.

It was then he became aware of the eerie quiet.

Egyptians were never quiet. In his experience, they did not stop talking from the time they woke up to the time they fell asleep.

He looked about. His and Segato's attendants had gathered nearby. Mute and motionless, they stood staring at him.

Segato broke the tableau, hurrying to Mrs. Pembroke. The signora was good? Not hurt?

She was quite unhurt, she told him.

He turned to Rupert. "Almost I cannot believe my eyes," he said. "It was so quick. My mouth is open, to warn the lady—but too late. I see it come up—like this." He snapped his fingers.

"Snakes dislike surprises," Rupert said. To Mrs. Pembroke he added, "You frightened her. She attacked because she thought she was in danger."

"Oh, you had time to discern that it was a female?" she said, her voice higher than usual.

"Might have been," he said. "She was pretty enough. Did you note the markings?"

"I know those marks," said Segato. He turned his gaze to the hole into which the snake had vanished. "I know that sound also. Everyone here knows this sound: the scraping it makes, like a saw. *La vipera delle piramidi.* What is the English word?"

"Viper?" Mrs. Pembroke said, her voice rising another half octave. "Of the pyramids?"

"*Si.* Very bad temper. And quick it moves, so quick. Very bad poison. Not simply is this the *vipera,* but of all snakes in the *Egitto* the most deadly."

Her face turned chalk-white, and she swayed, and Rupert said, "No, *don't!*"

But she folded up, and he was already reaching to catch her as she fainted dead away.

•   •   •

DAPHNE RECOVERED ALMOST immediately. Nonetheless, Mr. Carsington carried her down the sand slope, berating her all the way.

"How many times have I told you?" he said. *"No fainting."*

"I did not faint," she lied. "I was a little dizzy. You can put me down now."

He did not put her down, and she lacked the moral fiber to put up the struggle she ought. She had so little moral fiber that she was quite happy to be where she was.

He was so very big and so very strong and warm, so vibrantly *alive.* He was her genie, carrying her away, and she let herself be a child and believe in the fantasy. She let out a huff, as though defeated, then rested her head upon his shoulder.

His shirt was damp, and the skin of his jaw was gritty against her face. But he wasn't cold and rigid, lying upon the ground, as he might so easily have been. The snake could have turned on him. He could have been dead in an instant. That's what she'd seen in her mind's eye when Signor Segato spoke of the pyramid viper: Mr. Carsington stretched out dead on the debris-strewn ground. And then she'd heard the buzzing sound and seen the strange wash of bright color before the black wave dragged her down.

" 'I never faint,' " he said, mimicking her.

No, he was very much alive and not in the least subdued by the experience.

"I don't," she said against his neck.

"You did."

"I was dizzy for a moment."

"You collapsed into a heap, like a marionette when someone cuts the strings. I know fainting when I see it. You did it, after all the times I've warned you not to."

"Perhaps I fainted a little," she said. "But I didn't mean to."

He went on scolding her: she'd done everything possible to bring about a swoon, he claimed. She baked inside a pyramid for half the day. She let herself become overexcited about a lot of falcons wearing hats. She had nothing to eat and little to drink. When at last he and Segato got her

away from the confounded falcons, she did not stop talking
once, all the way through the miles of passages and stairs.
Then, when finally she came out into the air, did she stop to
rest and take a bit of refreshment like a sensible woman?
No. She went straight for a heap of rocks—and frightened
witless a snake who'd been peacefully napping, minding
its own business. Poor Mr. Segato. He'd so generously and
patiently shown her his wonderful discovery. In return,
she'd given him a shock from which his sensitive Italian
soul might never recover.

Daphne didn't argue. It was all true enough, she supposed. So much had happened this day. She wasn't used to
having an eventful life. She was dull. Her life was dull by
normal standards. Everything revolved around her work.
She was herself then, and in control, her passions—all of
them—focused on a lost language.

She wondered who she was now while Mr. Carsington
went on lecturing, striding down the sand slope nearly as
rapidly as he'd gone up it, though this time he carried a
full-grown and by no means feather-light woman. She
meant to ask if he was squeamish about the remains littered about, but she was too tired to interrupt the sermon.
She closed her eyes and listened to him criticize her. It
sounded like a lullaby.

RUPERT WAS HOPING her too-complicated mind
wouldn't erupt in a brain fever when her body relaxed in
his arms.

Devil take it, had she fainted again? Or had she sunk
into a coma? "No fainting," he growled. "No comas."

She mumbled something, her mouth grazing his neck,
and she shifted slightly in his arms.

Not comatose. Asleep.

"Well, I hope you're quite comfortable, madam," he
muttered. *"Asleep.* Really, you are like a child at times, a
complete child."

Well, not really. Far from it. He was aware of every diabolical curve of her body while he carried her down the

sand slope, bits and pieces of ancient Egyptians crunching underfoot.

It was easier once they reached the plain. He might have carried her all the way to the *Isis* if he wanted to completely stun the Egyptians with his prowess.

But holding a sleeping woman in his arms—one who, moreover, kept nuzzling his neck and murmuring unintelligibly in his ear—was asking too much of his limited store of self-restraint. He knew he wouldn't be getting her naked anytime soon. She'd built a wall of moral principles he must find a way to get round, along with other, harder-to-identify obstacles. No point in torturing himself.

He summoned the donkeys, woke her up, and planted her on one. Then, leaving it to the servants to make sure she didn't fall off, Rupert mounted his donkey and kept his mind off his frustrations by looking out for vipers and villains.

Chapter 10

AT SUNSET THE CONTRARY WIND DIED AWAY. BY this time, Daphne was aboard the *Isis*. She was clean, dressed in fresh garments, and trying not to bore her dining companion out of his wits. This was difficult for a dull scholar like her even in the best of circumstances. After such a day, it was impossible.

The Ramesses cartouches . . . the kiss . . . the stepped pyramid with its wonderful interior and fascinating falcon motif . . . the kiss . . . the tablet with its inscription . . . the snake lunging at her . . . death so near . . . the kiss . . . the strange, dreamlike time of being carried like a sleeping princess in a genie's arms . . . the kiss . . .

Avoiding the many improper or disturbing subjects on her mind limited her to the dullest of scholarly ones. Now, while they lingered over sweets and coffee, she babbled about the Coptic language, believed to be the modern version of ancient Egyptian. Though no longer in everyday use, she told him, it remained the Egyptian Christians' church language. It was written using a Greek alphabet with added symbols for sounds that didn't exist in Greek.

She explained how one might use it to decipher hieroglyphs.

Mr. Carsington frowned into his coffee cup.

She wondered what he was thinking. She knew it was not about Coptic, one of the world's most boring topics.

She wondered what she would have talked about if he hadn't found out her secret.

"I always go on far too long," she said. "Miles will cry out, 'Enough, Daphne! My head is about to explode!' If you do not speak up, Mr. Carsington, I shan't know when to stop. I tend to forget how few others, including scholars, find the Coptic language as engrossing as I do. Your cousin Miss Saunders is one of the few. She and I have carried on a most stimulating correspondence. It was she, in fact, who obtained for me several Coptic lexicons many years ago, when I began my study of hieroglyphs in earnest." Daphne paused and bit her lip. "Well, that is not very interesting, either."

"Yes, it is," he said. "Fascinating. It was my own Cousin Tryphena who obtained these books for you."

"As well as a number of papyri in my collection," she said.

"I suppose, being so devoted to theology, Mr. Pembroke hadn't time to hunt up lexicons and papyri for you," he said.

"Mr. Pembroke did not approve," she said, trying for a light tone, with mixed success.

"Of Egypt altogether?" Mr. Carsington's dark brows rose. "I can understand wanting to avoid the dangers of travel here, but where's the harm in studying the language?"

"Mr. Pembroke, like most of your sex, did not believe intellectual pursuits constituted a proper occupation for women," she said.

"Really," he said. "What evil did he see in it, I wonder? Or was it your devotion to scholarship he found so objectionable? Was he jealous? You did say it was a *passion,* when we were at the statue of Ramesses. Do you recall? It was moments before—"

She stood abruptly. "I can hardly keep my eyes open," she said. "I had better make an early bedtime. Good night." Face ablaze, she hurried from the front cabin into the passage. It was only a short way to her quarters.

Not nearly short enough. She heard his footsteps at the same moment she heard his deep voice close behind her.

"What a nodcock you are," he said. "We're on a boat. How far do you think you can run?"

"I am not running." She was, though she knew it was stupid and childish. She was not afraid of him.

It was herself she feared, the self she couldn't trust, the one who belonged in a room with books and documents, pens and pencils.

"You're not a coward," he said. "Why are you behaving in this cowardly way?"

She'd reached the door of her cabin. As her fingers closed over the door handle, he laid his palm against the door and rested his weight on it. The passage was narrow, and this was the end of it. His big frame, inches away from her, blocked any return to the front of the boat. His big hand held the door shut. He not only took up most of the space but most of the air, it seemed. She found it difficult to breathe, near impossible to think.

"You had your turn to talk about Coptic," he said. "Now it's my turn. I want to talk about . . . Ramesses."

She knew he hadn't followed her to discuss the pharaoh's cartouches. "That is quite unnecessary," she said. "You already apologized."

The passage's gloom veiled his expression, but she heard his smile when he said, "Did I? That's unusual. What on earth for, I wonder?"

"I know it is the merest trifle to you." She lowered her voice to an undertone while hoping that Leena, inside the cabin, did not have her ear pressed to the door. "However, many people believe it is highly improper to kiss a member of the opposite sex who is not a close relative."

"Oh, that kiss wasn't a trifle," he said. "I've had trifling ones, believe me, and that was another category altogether. That kiss was—"

"I think we had better pretend it never happened," she broke in desperately.

"That would be dishonest," he said.

The space was small, and growing smaller and warmer by the second. She was desperately aware of the large hand on the door. She remembered how easily he'd captured her, how gently yet firmly he'd grasped her head and held her while he claimed her mouth and made it his. She remembered his powerful hand on her backside, pressing her so close, and the pressure of his arousal against her belly. She was awash now in the mingled scents of Male: boot polish and shaving soap, pomade and, most intoxicating of all, the combination that was so absolutely and devastatingly *him*.

"It was an aberration, a momentary madness," she said.

"It was madly exciting," he said, his voice so low that she felt rather than heard it, on her neck, behind her ear, and deep, deep within, where the devil lurked and made her ache for wild and wicked things.

She said, her voice taut and a little too high, "But above all, it was *wrong*, Mr. Carsington."

She didn't see him move, but it felt as though he stood nearer, too near.

"Really," he said. "What was wrong with it? Which part? Should I have done this?" He laid the palm of his other hand upon the door, boxing her in. "And this?" He lowered his head and lightly kissed her forehead.

It was the gentlest of touches. The world slowed, and awareness narrowed to the light touch of his lips upon her skin. It was butterflies. Rose petals. The glisten of morning dew. The first note of birdsong. She had no words in any language for the sweetness she felt.

"And this?" He kissed her nose.

She was afraid to move, afraid the sweet feeling was a dream. If she moved, if she breathed, it would vanish, as so many dreams had done.

"And this?" His lips brushed her cheek.

"Oh," she said. "Oh, this is . . . Oh, I don't think . . ."

"Don't think." His lips touched hers, and then she was melting, everything within her dissolving into liquid.

She leant back against the door, her hands flat against it at her sides, keeping herself still, or trying to. Her knees weren't there anymore. She was dying of pleasure. It was wicked, but so sweet. The sweetness held her, made her give back in kind, and the pleasure deepened and darkened into longing.

She knew better than to long for any man, especially this kind. She knew the sweetness was seduction, not affection. This was not the youthful innocence it felt like. She knew this, in some safe, sober corner of her drunken mind.

Knowing all this, she should have turned away or pushed him away. She couldn't, wouldn't.

She had to have the feel of his mouth hard against hers. She needed the taste of him again as much as the *hashisheen* needed their drug. She could not get enough of the slow, wicked game he played with his tongue, and the tiny heat shivers he triggered in the back of her neck and in her belly. In some part of her clouded mind she knew she'd suffer for it, but that was far away, and he was near, and the scent and taste of him blocked out everything else. He took her into the darkness, and that, it seemed, was where she was meant to be.

RUPERT KEPT HIS hands on the door. He'd meant to hold back, to wait. He'd had enough torture this day, and pursuing her, touching her, was begging for more. Still, for the moment, torture was delicious.

It was only a kiss. Merely the longest kiss in the world, a thousand kisses blossoming from one. His mouth played upon hers, and hers upon his, and in no time at all she'd set the moons and planets and stars whirling.

He kept his hands on the door. For balance. For strength. And to stop it from ending. He mustn't move his hands, mustn't let them touch her, or she'd shy away.

He could drink her in, though. He could inhale the scent of her, a hint of incense carried on the desert wind. And he could savor the taste of her, a strange champagne, light and fresh even while it made fire trails in the veins.

He could let his mouth tease hers, playing over the hint of a pout. He could brush his face against hers, skin to skin, hers like silken velvet, a softness that stabbed him some-place within, and left him weak-kneed and half-laughing inside at how easily a woman could bring a great lummox to his knees.

He feathered kisses over her creamy, heart-shaped countenance and traced her beautiful cheekbones with his lips. He found the sensitive place behind her ear, and the pulse point in her throat. He felt its quickened beat under his mouth, and heard his heart hammer an eager answer.

His hands slid down the door, and they were not quite steady, either. He brought them to her shoulders, because he had to stop. Enough was enough. He was no saint. He could barely resist temptation at all, and he'd already tested his limits and beyond.

And then somehow his fingers were sliding up the smooth column of her neck and pushing into her silken hair. Then he needed more of her mouth and the strange champagne and her tongue playing a wicked game, enslaving his.

Then it was all too easy to forget what he'd meant to do. She was warm and soft and so passionate and for the moment completely his. Every perfect, curving inch of her was close at last, and she fit exactly as she should in his arms.

He brought his hands down over her straight back to her waist. She felt so right under his hands, and the rightness swept him along. He forgot about slow sieges and getting round obstacles and winning her by slow degrees. He forgot that it was too soon and he mustn't rush his fences or she'd be on her guard next time. It was too much to remember. He was drunk on her scent.

He was only distantly aware of the gasp that faded into a sigh as his questing hand moved over her breast. It was warm and soft and fit his hand as though made precisely for the purpose, bespoke for him from the beginning. And so it was the most natural thing in the world to need to touch skin and to reach for the bodice fastenings—

"Good grief!" She pushed him away, so hard that he stumbled backward. "What are you doing?"

"Taking off your clothes," he said.

"No," she said. "No, no, no." She yanked the door open, staggered inside, and slammed it behind her.

Breathing raggedly, he regarded the closed door with narrowed eyes.

"You knew this would happen," he told himself in an undertone, "and you did it anyway."

But she had said it was wrong, and she'd done it anyway, too.

And so he left the passage and went out onto the open deck, softly whistling all the while.

Zawyet el Amwat, opposite Minya

MILES HAD PLANNED to row to the nearer and more thinly populated eastern shore, rid himself of the shackles, find a hiding place where he could sleep for a few hours and gather his strength, then set out at first light. The dinghy held the tools and weapons he'd taken as well as a basket of Egyptian bread. This, along with lentils, had made up the crew's diet. It ought to hold him for a week, by the end of which—in a small boat, traveling by day, with the current carrying him—he should be back in Cairo.

All he needed—apart from getting rid of the curst shackles—was a disguise. It would be best not to attract anyone's attention. He couldn't play a ghost in the daytime, and he couldn't travel under cover of darkness and risk colliding with another boat or a sandbank. Even experienced Nile navigators had accidents, sometimes in broad day. The sand-laden desert winds constantly reshaped the riverbed, and navigation was most difficult at this time of year, when the Nile was reaching its lowest point.

He wished he'd thought of stealing clothes before he fled the sinking boat, but he would deal with that later.

It turned out to be later than he expected.

It took him all night to rid himself of the shackles. By then his head and hands were throbbing. A wave of nausea and dizziness drove him to his knees. He vomited, but the nausea only worsened. His head was on fire.

The sun was coming up, the fierce Egyptian sun, compared to which the English sun was a lantern in the fog.

He couldn't travel, sick with plague or whatever it was, under the baking sun. He could only conceal the boat as best he could, pack as much as he could carry, and drag his shaking, burning body across the narrow stretch of fertile land to the cliffs looming behind it.

Many hours later, when he woke up inside a tomb, he couldn't remember how he got there. He wondered if any-

one had seen him. He thought of Daphne, and hoped he'd
live to see her again. Those were his last coherent thoughts.
By nightfall he was delirious.

Wednesday 11 April

WHEN LORD NOXLEY'S *dahabeeyah* the *Memnon* arrived at Minya, Ghazi was at the landing place, waiting for
him, along with two men.

Neither of the two men was Miles Archdale, a circum-
stance which caused a small frown to mar his lordship's
angelic countenance. While the expression seemed mild
enough, those who knew him easily discerned the black
thundercloud forming above his head.

Ghazi discerned it. He had, in fact, expected it, which
was why he'd hurried to Minya as soon as he heard of the
debacle with the kidnappers. He let the two men tell the
master their story. It was short enough.

They were all that remained of the group Ghazi had
sent to recover the Englishman, the friend of the master,
they said. Everyone else was dead, including all of the
kidnappers.

Had these two men been a trifle more intelligent, they
would have pretended to be dead, too. Most certainly they
would not have lingered in Minya, waiting to give their
master bad news. But like many of those Lord Noxley employed, they had not been hired for their intellectual skills.
Like most of the others as well, they'd dealt with his lieu-
tenants, never with the Golden Devil directly.

"The kidnappers killed the Englishman?" said his lordship. "How odd. Why should they kill a valuable captive?"

The men were unable to explain this.

"I trust you recovered my friend's body, at least," his
lordship said.

They looked at each other. Then they told him about the
ghost who'd come after them when they were tying their
small boat to the larger one.

Lord Noxley said little during the ghost story, merely
nodding with what they took to be sympathy and under-

standing while the thundercloud they couldn't see grew blacker and thicker. He dismissed them, telling them to make themselves useful aboard the *Memnon*.

Then he set out with Ghazi to visit the *kashef*, the pasha's local representative.

On the way, Ghazi provided a less garbled account of events. "My men attack the boat. Someone cuts the mooring ropes and the boat drifts because everyone is fighting and no one steers. The boat strikes a sandbank. These men come last, a little after the others."

"And run away from a ghost, 'tall as a giant and pale as a shroud,'" his lordship quoted, shaking his head.

"It is your English friend, yes," said Ghazi. "He did not know who my men were—thieves, perhaps, from one of the villages, he thinks. He wished to flee. He needed the boat. It was most cleverly done."

"I should think so," said his lordship. "Archdale is a genius, you know."

"I came the instant I heard," Ghazi said. "Duval has followers to the south. This is where Faruq goes. By now they will hear of the ghost, and Faruq will know, too, who it is, because he is no fool. I came to find your friend before Duval's men do."

The thundercloud lightened a degree. "Very wise," said his lordship.

Encouraged, Ghazi went on, "This ghost is seen most often on the east bank, in places from the rock tombs near Zawyet el Amwat to those of Beni Hasan." He gestured toward the east bank of the Nile.

"A range of about fifteen miles," said Lord Noxley. He paused to gaze that way. "And the cliffs riddled with tombs throughout. Not to mention that most of the sightings have been imaginary. The Arabs are so credulous. One of them thinks he sees a ghost, and soon everyone sees armies of ghosts and ghouls. Doubtless Archdale will have appeared in several locations simultaneously. Finding him could take weeks."

"It is true they see him everywhere," Ghazi said. "But me, I think a clever man keeps away from the villages and stays close to the tombs. To find him is not impossible, especially if the *kashef* helps. He has many spies."

"Then all it wants is baksheesh," said Lord Noxley, walking again. "I'll see to it." He continued for a moment, thoughtful, then said, "I'd better leave finding Archdale to you. Faruq still needs to be caught."

"He knows we follow him, and so he will change his plans," Ghazi said. "I think he will not linger in Beni Hasan, to wait for Duval as they arranged. In his place, I would continue south. A large party of French is in Dendera. I think he will go there."

"I know what that party of French is after, curse them," said his lordship. "The brutes have got permission to carry away the magnificent zodiac ceiling from the Temple of Hathor. They shall not have the papyrus as well. I'll set out as soon as we've dealt with the *kashef*."

They walked on in silence. As they reached the official's residence, Ghazi said, "Those two men of mine, the cowards. What is your pleasure regarding them?"

"Find Archdale," said Lord Noxley. "Leave the cowards to me."

THE WIND, WHICH had died down completely the previous night, revived the next morning, this time in their favor. To Daphne's relief, it blew strong and steady, driving the *Isis* swiftly upriver. They made up much of the time lost previously, reaching Beni Suef in less than three days.

The sights beckoned, certainly. To the west of the village lay the remains of ancient Herakleopolis. On the east bank, a road through the desert led to the Coptic convents of Saints Anthony and Paul. It was impossible to pass the area without feeling at least a twinge of longing to explore.

It was no more than a twinge, though. Finding Miles was more important to her than any monument. After that they'd have all the time in the world to explore Egypt, together, as they'd planned, she told herself.

In the meantime, with a clear head if not conscience, she could pursue the discoveries she'd made recently. She needn't worry about distractions. Mr. Carsington had evidently decided to be "dishonest." He pretended, as Daphne had asked, that nothing of an intimate nature had occurred between them.

He reverted to the easygoing blockhead she'd first encountered. He stopped asking uncomfortably penetrating questions. He made no gesture or remark that in any way resembled an advance.

They had companionable dinners, during which they talked, much as she might have done with Miles, about the sights they glimpsed as the *Isis* flew along: the variety of birds, for instance, or the interesting rock formations, or the Egyptians' agricultural methods, which had not changed, apparently, since the time of the pharaohs.

Clearly Mr. Carsington had no trouble interpreting the meaning of "No, no, no," and a door slammed in his face. He had promptly and with amazing ease put their two embraces from his mind.

Daphne should have been pleased and relieved.

She was annoyed.

How easy it was for him, she brooded. To him she was merely one in a long line of forgettable women. At the next large town where they moored for the night, he'd probably go looking for dancing girls. It was all the same to him—except, perhaps, that dancing girls would not be as boring as she was, droning on about Coptic and cartouches and crowned falcons.

She knew that to men like him she was a freak, and a tiresome one at that. There were times when even she wished she hadn't been burdened with a brain, times when she wished Miles had inherited the famous Archdale intellect. It would have been easier on their parents, especially their father, who'd spent so many years in turmoil about what to do with her: treat her like a normal girl and ignore the gift heaven had bestowed, or educate her as her intellect required, though it was unnatural?

It would have been easier on Daphne, definitely, had she been a normal girl. She would not have had to listen to Virgil's constant *correcting*.

I am sure you meant to take into account . . .

No doubt you have overlooked . . .
Naturally, it did not occur to you . . .
Doubtless you were unaware of my wishes . . .

She could still hear his voice, so very gentle and patient and . . . infuriating.

He'd wanted a normal wife. She wasn't normal.

And she didn't want to be, not really, or she would have changed, as he wished.

She did not, really, want to be like other women. Her work intrigued and stimulated her and made her happy.

She knew men didn't understand her. They didn't like her, either, most of them. It was her well-rounded person, not her well-filled mind, that pleased them. This was true, certainly—and to her great shock and disappointment—of Virgil.

She knew Mr. Carsington's interest was purely physical. And temporary. She knew it was right and reasonable for him to cease attempting her virtue.

She knew it was illogical and wrong of her to miss the pleasure and heat she'd felt, the sense that this was as it should be: without rules, without shame.

It was disgraceful and stupid of her, but she longed for more. When he stood near—on the deck of the boat, for instance, while they gazed at the swiftly passing scenery—she wanted, with something like desperation, to press her face against his cheek and drink him in. She wanted, with the same mad urgency, to feel his body crushed to hers.

It was a purely animal desire, as deep and primitive as hunger or thirst. But those needs were rational: food and drink were essential to life. Intimacy with him was not only not essential but not good for her in a hundred ways.

She knew this. She knew she should be happy that he treated her like a sister. But she was wretched.

This morning, as the boat passed Beni Suef, she was still trying to subdue the wild creature within. Small wonder she'd made so little progress with the cartouche in front of her. It was one of those she'd copied from Ramesses' gigantic statue.

She gazed at the goddess with the feather on her head

and wondered if all women became featherbrained in Mr. Carsington's vicinity, or she alone.

A rap on the door and a familiar, impossibly deep voice called her out of the latest bout of self-flagellation.

She very nearly bade him enter. She was opening her mouth to do so, in fact, when she recollected the cabin's narrow dimensions. Given her deranged state, inviting him into a confined space with her was an exceedingly stupid idea.

She rose, went to the door, and opened it.

And suppressed a sigh.

There he was: tall, dark, far too handsome for anybody's good, and only half-dressed, as usual. Loose white Turkish trousers tucked into gleaming boots. An Arab-style shirt, called a *kamees,* with very full sleeves. Over this he wore a wine-colored English waistcoat, unbuttoned. He hadn't bothered with a neckcloth. The shirt had no buttons, merely a slit in the front. This left his neck and collarbone as well as a deep V of his powerful chest completely exposed. The Egyptian sun had turned his neck several degrees darker than the outer edge of the V. She wanted to draw her tongue along that paler edge of skin. She wanted to bury her face in his neck.

She wanted to bang her head against the wall.

She wiped the damp palms of her hands on her skirt and asked if anything was amiss.

"Far from it," he said. "Matters look to become a great deal more interesting. Reis Rashad tells me we're entering bandit territory."

Of course Mr. Carsington would find this "interesting." A chance to break heads, fire off pistols, and swing swords. A chance to play I Dare You with death. Daphne could almost comprehend his enthusiasm. She, too, would like an excuse to do violence.

"Apparently, the neighborhood from Beni Suef to Asyut is notorious," he went on. "Nearly two hundred miles of marauders. Leena says we must hire guards from the town at night, which will make the local sheik responsible for our safety. But we must have someone watch the guards, because they're worthless. Even in the daytime, we dare not turn our backs even for an instant. Otherwise"—he began to gesture in the theatrical way Leena did—"they will strip the boat down to a stick, and we will all be hacked to pieces. They are wicked and evil, and so ugly and dirty they make you sick."

He went on, mimicking the maid's overwrought style as he repeated her dire warnings.

The inner tumult abated, and Daphne felt a smile tugging at the corners of her mouth. She gave up and let it have its way.

"The prospect of certain death amuses you?" he said, smiling a little, too.

"You have caught her manner perfectly," she said. "You are aware, I hope, that Leena tends to exaggerate?"

"I've noticed," he said. "But Tom seems to agree in the essentials. He did a few of his pantomimes: a pickpocket, a thief creeping onto the boat. He did a good deal of it with one eye shut. Leena claims that most of the locals are hideously disfigured. A great many are blind in one eye. She assures us that the interior matches the unattractive exterior. In short, it appears we shall have to put those pistols of your brother's to work."

Daphne tried to pay attention to what he was saying, but her mind wouldn't cooperate. She wished he would not dress so provocatively. It was unfair to show so much skin, when she was haunted by memories of the scent and taste of that skin. She had only to draw a few inches nearer to inhale the provocative scent of Male. She had only to reach up and grasp the back of his neck and draw him down—

"Mrs. Pembroke?"

She heard laughter in his voice. Her face caught fire. "I'm sorry," she said. "You said . . ." What had he said?

"Your mind is elsewhere, it seems." His dark gaze went past her to the papers strewn about the divan. "Ah, of course. Ramesses. The cartouches. Have you worked out the lady with the feather on her head?"

"A goddess," she said.

"And the feather?"

"That would tell me which goddess she was," she said. "But at present I am altogether in the dark about her."

He bent nearer to look over her shoulder, and she caught a whiff of shaving soap.

"Light as a feather," he said. "Light-fingered. Light-headed. Lighthearted. Wait." He closed his eyes. "I saw it somewhere. That feather of hers on a scale. What was on the other side? Something weighed in the balance. A judgment scene of some kind, it looked like. You smell like a goddess, like incense."

He opened his eyes and gazed straight into hers.

She stared into those dark depths, wondering if she'd heard aright.

"I must have seen it in one of Tryphena's picture books. One of the French lot." He stepped back. "Where do I find the pistols?"

She was still reeling from the smell-like-a-goddess remark. It took her brain a moment to attend to the other revelation. Picture books. French lot. "The *Description de l'Egypte*?" she cried. *"You studied it?"*

"There is no need to become hysterical," he said. "It was wonderfully popular with the ladies, who liked to sit close and comment on the pictures." He shook his head. "Anyway, I don't remember where I saw the scene. Tryphena has countless books and drawings. Maybe the feather-headed goddess herself sat on one scale. Weighed against . . ." His brow knit. "I think a jar or vase stood on the other."

He was playing battledore and shuttlecock with Daphne's brain.

Still, habit and obsession soon reasserted control. She quickly thrust to the back of her mind his familiarity with Miss Saunders's Egyptian collection and its usefulness in luring women to his side.

"Scales like the scales of justice, you mean?" she said eagerly. She turned away, hurried to the divan, and snatched up one of her pictures. "The Egyptian goddess of justice, do you think?"

"No, Mrs. Pembroke," he said. "I don't think. You do. But I am happy to see you so . . . excited. If, however, I might have a moment—a mere moment—of your attention? The pistols? The fine Manton pistols?"

Chapter 11

A FEW MILES SOUTH OF MINYA, A ROW OF ROCK tombs had been carved into the Arabian hills on the Nile's eastern bank. Miles had taken refuge in the first one he reached. He'd expected to die there.

But three days after crawling in more than half dead, he was beginning to recover. He waited until the sun was setting before exploring his surroundings, though. Superstitious Egyptians, fearing ghosts and ghouls, avoided tombs and burial grounds after dark.

Most of the tombs, he found, were ill-preserved. Some were destroyed, the locals having carried away the stones for building elsewhere. He decided to move to one of the better ones, the next to last toward the south. Its walls contained scenes of agriculture, fishing, shipbuilding, and weapon-making.

By the time night fell, he was starved. The food scenes reminded him that he'd eaten almost nothing in the last few days. He'd nothing in the tomb to eat. Something had eaten his stale bread. He was down to his last mouthful of water.

And so, as the stars came out, Miles took up his basket and made his way in the moonlight to the river, to the place where he'd hidden the little boat.

It was gone.

No great surprise, really. The region was notorious. Why shouldn't someone steal his boat? He'd return the favor and steal someone else's. Tomorrow.

Tonight, though, he wanted a proper dinner.

He set about fashioning a fishing line.

IN THE EARLY morning hours, he sat in his tomb by his little fire, cleaning a sad assortment of very small fish. A faint sound made him look up.

A pair of beady eyes reflected the firelight.

"You'll have to fight me for them, friend Rat," Miles said.

The creature drew nearer. It was not a rat.

It had long, bushy grey fur and a black tail and reddish legs and feet.

Miles smiled. "A mongoose, by gad."

They could be pests, killing poultry and stealing eggs. On the other hand, they were also partial to rats, snakes, and other vermin. As a result, they were not unpopular. Some natives domesticated them. This appeared to be one of the tamer ones. It was small, a female or an adolescent perhaps. As it came closer, he noticed it limped.

"That had better not be an act," he said. "I had a dog once who used to do that whenever he'd done something deserving a scold."

The mongoose eyed the fish.

"No," Miles said firmly. "I worked hard for these. Go find yourself some rats. Lots of them about. Snakes, too."

He watched it warily. Mongooses were very quick. That was how they survived their battles with venomous snakes.

But this one couldn't be as quick as its fellows, given the wounded foot.

It looked at him. It looked at the fish.

"Rats," Miles said. "Lots of nice, tasty rats down by the river, I'll warrant. Oh, and big, delicious snakes."

The creature regarded him with sad, glistening eyes.

"I'll wager anything you're a female," Miles muttered.

He scooped up one of the uncleaned fish and tossed it to the mongoose. "The rest are for me," he said. "Big journey ahead. Fraught with peril. Need my strength."

He finished preparing the rest of the fish and cooked them. She ate hers and didn't beg for more. But she didn't leave, either. She was still there when he woke up the next morning, just as the sky was beginning to lighten.

But later in the day, when the men came for him, one of them kicked her, and she ran away.

Sunday night, 15 April

CONTRARY TO RUPERT'S hopes and Leena's predictions, the *Isis* and all aboard it passed the two nights after leaving Beni Suef without mishap. Thanks to a strong and steady north wind, they reached Minya on the third.

Darkness had already fallen by the time they moored, and stars winked in the deep blue sky. Yet in the west, a beam of light lingered on the horizon for an hour or more. Long after this light was altogether gone and the party had supped and gone to bed, Rupert lay awake.

He vowed he wouldn't do it again. Minya was a large town, the largest until they reached Asyut, nearly a hundred miles away. They must spend all of tomorrow here, replenishing supplies. While the others haggled in the marketplace and Mrs. Pembroke looked at rocks, he would go to one of the cafés where a man could find dancing girls and other women untroubled by morals.

A short celibacy wouldn't kill him, he knew, but he couldn't go on like this. He hadn't enjoyed a good night's sleep since the night he'd made the tactical mistake outside Mrs. Pembroke's door.

He was a man of the world who could tell when a woman wasn't ready. But once he got close enough to inhale her tantalizing fragrance, once he touched his lips to her skin, he didn't know what he knew anymore.

All the same, you'd think he'd have settled down by now. But no. It was worst at night, when he'd nothing else to do and no warm body to take his mind off hers. Six days had passed, and the restless nights were making him short-tempered and dull-witted.

First thing tomorrow, then, he'd find himself a warm, willing body, and get his humors back in balance.

He was trying to remember the Egyptian word for *dancing girl* when he heard the splash.

Instantly he was up, and in another moment he was out of the cabin, onto the deck, knife in hand. Something slammed into him, and he went down.

DAPHNE WAS AWAKE, too, sharply awake, her heart pounding because of the dream, so real that when she first woke, she thought she'd actually done it all, every forbidden, unwomanly act.

In the dream she wore only a transparent veil. She stood in the doorway of Mr. Carsington's cabin and smiled at him and let it drop to the floor.

He lay on his back on the divan, looking up at her, a light dancing in his dark eyes. He laughed a deep, wicked laugh and beckoned with his forefinger.

She went down on all fours and crawled to him, and over him. She bent and trailed her tongue along the bronzed skin near the opening of his shirt. She let her hands roam over his big chest. She undressed him. She kissed him everywhere, touched him everywhere. She used her tongue as boldly as she did her hands. She took him inside her and rode him until she collapsed, satisfied, exhausted.

She broke every single one of Virgil's rules.

She'd always hated those rules, because she wasn't like other women. She had a brain that belonged in a man's head, attached to a man's body. It put unfeminine ideas in her head, aggressive, animal ideas. It made her want to go after what she wanted instead of waiting for it to come to her. It made her want to crawl on top instead of lying quietly underneath. It made her want to *do* as well as be done to. It made desire a wildcat inside her instead of the sweet kitten Virgil wanted.

She lay there, eyes wide, staring into the darkness, her nerves taut as though she'd been caught doing what she'd dreamt.

She knew the wildness and wickedness were inside her. But it was like the experience in Saqqara: she knew there were snakes. She knew they sheltered from the burning sun in dark places. But that was an abstract idea, worlds away from the real thing appearing suddenly, fangs bared, carrying instant death.

She was supposed to have grown tamer, to have quieted with maturity and learnt to rule her passions instead of letting them rule her. But Mr. Carsington had come into her life, and then . . .

She'd thought he was the genie let out of the bottle, the dangerous force released. But she was the one set free. Discovering who and what she'd become was like lifting the rock and seeing the snake spring up.

She lay staring into the darkness, wide awake, painfully alert. That was why she noticed the splash, then the movement shortly thereafter—in a nearby cabin or the passage, she couldn't tell. But the sound brought her bolt upright. She grabbed her wrapper and shrugged into it.

She didn't waste time fumbling about in the dark, looking for a weapon, but snatched up one of her boots. She tiptoed past the sleeping Leena to the cabin door and slipped into the passage.

Even before Daphne reached the deck she heard the muffled grunts and thuds. The rational part of her brain told her to run the other way, back to her cabin. She almost did so. Then she noticed the door to Mr. Carsington's cabin was ajar. He was out there—in trouble, very likely.

She muttered a quick prayer and burst through the entryway onto the deck. A dark form came at her. Not his. She struck with the boot as hard as she could, and the man stumbled backward. Why hadn't she brought something heavier, deadlier? Where was Mr. Carsington? Not dead. Dear God, he could not be dead.

She was opening her mouth to call for him, when the man growled a curse and sprang at her again—

And let out a yelp and fell hard upon the deck. He did not get up.

The boat was stirring, men coming to life, sleepy voices calling to each other.

Out of the darkness came Mr. Carsington's deep voice, cool and calm: "Pray don't trouble yourselves, gentlemen. It is merely a villain come to cut our throats, rob our stores, and ravish our women. No need for alarm. Mrs. Pembroke has the matter in hand."

LATER, IN THE front cabin, while she picked splinters from Rupert's hand, Mrs. Pembroke told him the Egyptians didn't understand irony or sarcasm in any language.

"Perhaps not, but it made me feel better," he said. "I think you missed one." He didn't know or care how many splinters his collision with the deck had given him. He only wanted her to go on holding his hand and peering closely at it while he watched the lantern light make red-gold and garnet and ruby threads in her hair. It streamed over her shoulders, a fiery waterfall against the muslin nightclothes.

Her bedtime attire was plain and severe, the very antithesis of provocative.

So naturally he wanted to get her naked. Naturally his privy councilor swelled with hope.

"You should not have crept out onto the deck to investigate," she said, plying the tweezers again. "You should have made a stir. If I had not happened to be awake, I should never have heard—"

"You had a sleepless night?" Was he keeping her awake, then, the way she did him? What a tragic waste of nighttime! "I'm sorry to hear it. That is, I would be if you hadn't turned up at a crucial moment."

He couldn't believe he'd allowed a sullen oaf of a villain to take him by surprise. This was what came of too little sleep and too much celibacy: bodily humors horribly out of balance.

"I was not sleepless," she said. "I woke from a bad dream. That was when I heard the noise. Splashing. And other sounds that didn't seem right. Then I saw your door ajar, and guessed there was trouble."

She'd come to help him—to save him, darling girl. It was touching, really. And terrifying. She might have been raped, murdered.

"You should not have crept out onto the deck to investigate," he said, mimicking her. "You should have cried out and woken everybody. If I'd been an instant slower to recover my wits, the villain would have had you."

"In future, I shall keep a knife under my pillow," she said. "It hadn't occurred to me before to go to bed armed. Even now I can hardly believe a lone prowler tried to sneak onto a vessel containing so many people." She frowned. "But it would have been worse had several ruffians come. You had better teach me how to use a gun."

"Mrs. Pembroke, I'm not at all certain I want you shooting firearms in the dark. A pistol isn't like a boot. If you'd struck me, thinking I was the intruder—"

"Oh, I knew it was not you," she said. "He was too short and square, and the smell was completely wrong."

"The smell?"

"Dirty and wet. From the river."

She smelled wonderful. So clean . . . with a ghost of a fragrance hovering about her: smoke and herbs, like incense. Rupert leant in a hairsbreadth closer.

"I could have been wet," he said. "I might have had a whim for a midnight swim." Now he thought about it, a vigorous swim before bedtime would probably help calm him. Until he found a dancing girl, that is.

"You wouldn't be so idiotish as to go for a swim in the dead of night without warning anybody," she said. "You wouldn't want to throw the crew into an uproar."

"In case you hadn't noticed, we've manned our vessel with some of the world's soundest sleepers," he said.

"All the more reason for me to be better prepared for attack," she said. She gave him back his hand.

"A heavy candlestick would do," he said. "You might easily incapacitate an attacker while still giving him a chance of surviving the blow. On the other hand, if you put a ball through a man, he's likely to die. And the trouble with this is, you might put the ball through the wrong man."

"All the more reason," she said, "for you to teach me how to do it properly."

THE SECOND LOT of villains had proved more civilized than the first. Miles hadn't been sure, in fact, that they were villains. They came peaceably enough to the cave, weapons tucked into their girdles instead of in their hands.

Still, the leader Ghazi knew his name, and this put Miles on guard—for all the good it did, when he was outnumbered a dozen to one, and none of the others appeared to be convalescing from a bout of fever.

"This is not a fit abode for you, my learned friend," Ghazi said. "I have a fine tent and food and drink. You must accept my hospitality."

"Must I?" Miles said, uneasy at the "learned." Butrus had believed him "learned" enough to read papyri . . . and had spoken with happy anticipation of using torture to encourage Miles's brain.

Ghazi smiled. "I hold no knife to your throat, no rifle to your head. But in the village is the young widow who told us where to find you. If you refuse our hospitality, perhaps one of my men will take this as an insult. Perhaps he will kill the woman for sending us to be insulted. Then her baby will be an orphan. Perhaps it would be a mercy to kill the child as well. What is your opinion?"

"I believe I'd better do as I'm told," Miles said.

Ghazi smiled his approval. Unlike Butrus, he had all his teeth.

They traveled to an encampment a few miles distant. There they fed Miles a good meal and gave him fresh clothing. This was at least more kindly treatment than he'd received from Butrus's lot, who'd ransacked his belongings. What they'd expected to find he had no idea, but their grim expressions told him they hadn't found it. They'd left him only one shirt in addition to what he'd worn when they kidnapped him. Both shirts were filthy and ragged, and the one not on his back remained deep in the cave, with the incriminating remnants of his chains.

This new batch of cutthroats most politely invited him to mount a camel the following morning. He decided it was best to follow instructions lest one of Ghazi's sensitive minions be offended and avenge the insult on innocent bystanders.

They didn't tell Miles what their destination was. He only knew they traveled south, and he'd as soon have done so on a mode of transportation other than the camel.

The creatures bore heavy inanimate burdens calmly enough. But his showed a marked aversion to being ridden. The camel made insulting noises as Miles circled it, looking for a place to get on. The animal complained loudly and cursed him bitterly in camel language when he was finally seated. It snarled and growled and turned around to give him venomous looks. Then, as you'd expect, it flatly refused to obey him. When Miles tried to turn its head, it tried to bite his feet. When he snapped at the animal to behave, it promptly lay down. When at last the humor seized it to get up, it made sure to throw Miles back and forth violently in the process.

The journey was excruciating, though Miles's captors made allowances for his inexperience, traveling no more than eight hours at a stretch. Yet even at this pace, with long stops between for rest and refreshment, they left Minya farther behind more quickly than they could have done by water. Instead of following the bends of the Nile, they rode straight across the desert. Furthermore, they could and did travel by night, without worrying about colliding with boats, sandbanks, or rocks. The only concerns, as Ghazi explained on the first night when they stopped to eat, were bandits and sandstorms. The sandstorms were God's will. The bandits would quickly learn their mistake, he said cheerfully.

"I believe you," Miles said. "I only wonder what the great hurry is and where exactly we're going."

"I sent men to take you from the boat," Ghazi said. "They failed. This is why I had to come for you myself. But I have other matters to settle, to the south, and must go quickly to make up for the time I have lost."

"And if you don't?"

Ghazi laughed. "If I don't—" He drew a line across his throat with his index finger. "Like that, or maybe not so fast, and with more suffering, ha ha. The man who fails, my learned friend, is the man who dies."

Zawyet-el Amwat, Monday 16 April

THE DAY FOLLOWING their arrival found Daphne on the opposite side of the Nile from Minya. A ways to the north behind her, a small cluster of hovels signified a village. Nearer at hand a larger and more extensive cluster of chapels and domed tombs signified the district's burial ground.

She stood at a respectful distance from the cemetery proper, staring at a complicated arrangement of metal pieces whose operation Mr. Carsington was explaining.

He had one of the coveted Manton pistols in his hand and was telling her about breeches and priming pans and flints and cocks and such. She was beginning to understand how he felt when she talked about Coptic.

They had an audience. Nearby stood Udail/Tom, several crew members, and a pair of guards the *kashef*—the pasha's local representative—had sent to accompany them. As usual, the Egyptians were all talking excitedly. She couldn't follow their conversation. She had all she could do to follow Mr. Carsington's explanation.

"Do I need to know how it works?" she said finally. "Can't I just shoot it?"

"If you understand how it works, you're less likely to make mistakes," he said patiently. "If danger threatens, you will not have the leisure for trial and error or even for thinking."

Daphne became aware of laughter behind her.

She turned that way. Udail/Tom was pointing at the gun, at Mr. Carsington, and at her, and talking too low for her to understand. The men were shaking their heads and chuckling.

She must have looked as slow-witted as she felt.

She turned back to Mr. Carsington.

She told herself that if she could learn Coptic, she could learn this. But it was hard to concentrate. He stood so near, and spoke so earnestly and enthusiastically—nay, *lovingly*— of the wood and metal thing in his hand. He even took out a handkerchief and wiped his fingerprints from the polished handle.

"I'll load it for you the first time," he said.

"Please let me do it," she said. "I shall learn more quickly that way." She would have the weapon in her hand and be forced to pay attention to what she was doing, instead of to the angle of his jaw and the arch of his dark eyebrows and the delicacy with which those large, clever hands caressed the pistol.

He shrugged and gave her the pistol and the cartridge.

"Where is the powder you spoke of?" she said.

He briefly gazed heavenwards, then reverted to her. "In the cartridge," he said. "You have to open it first."

The cartridge was made of paper, with the metal ball at one end. She needed two hands to open it. She tried to hand him the pistol, but he shook his head.

"You tear it open with your teeth," he said. "Try not to swallow too much gunpowder in the process."

"Why? Is it poisonous?" Would she explode? But no. The gunpowder needed a spark. He had just explained all that. What was the matter with her?

"I daresay it's toxic," he said. "But the point is, if you swallow too much, you won't have enough left to fire the weapon."

She used her teeth, as he insisted, and definitely tasted powder, which was horrid. She spat it out, but the taste lingered.

Then she simply followed his directions, carefully tipping powder into the priming pan, closing the pan, tipping into the barrel the remaining powder, then the paper cartridge containing the ball. Then she rammed it all home, using the tool he gave her.

She became aware of silence behind her.

She glanced that way.

The men were gaping at her. An instant later, they turned

and ran back to the cemetery. She watched them take shelter behind one of the domed structures. Udail/Tom grinned and waved, then trotted after them.

"You were right, after all," Mr. Carsington said.

She turned back to meet his deep brown gaze, serious now. "About what?"

"About learning to take care of yourself," he said. "The Egyptians have been beaten down cruelly time and again. What reason have they to stand and fight to protect us—a lot of foreign invaders? It makes more sense to run away. You and I shall have to rely upon each other."

She could hardly believe her ears. He had been so reluctant to teach her how to shoot. But these were words used between equals, words of trust—in her judgment, her skill—from a *man*. Her heart leapt—with pleasure or fear, she wasn't sure. Perhaps both.

He pointed to a large mound some twenty yards away. There were many such mounds of rubble hereabouts.

"Don't I need a target?" she said.

"Choose a spot to aim at," he said. "For now, you mainly need to practice loading, aiming, and firing. Later we can work on your sharpshooting skills."

He showed her how to fully cock the weapon. He stood behind her, and holding his arm alongside hers, showed her how to aim. The weapon was heavy, and she was more than a little afraid of it. These weren't the only reasons her hand shook. She'd caught his scent. She was acutely aware of his nearness.

"Hold the pistol with both hands, if you need to," he said.

She did so, and it helped, but the shakiness went deeper than unsteady hands.

Then he moved away, and her head cleared.

"Fire when ready," he said.

She took a deep breath and pulled the trigger. There was a click and a little puff of smoke, then a blast so powerful that she nearly dropped the weapon.

"Excellent," he said. "You hit the mound."

The mound was the size of Bedford Square. Blindfolded, she could hardly miss it. Still, a wave of happiness surged through her. She wanted to jump up and down. She wanted to dance. She wanted to throw her arms about his neck and kiss him senseless—for teaching her how to *do* something, a useful thing that men knew how to do, a skill that even her indulgent brother hadn't taught her.

"Try it again," Mr. Carsington said. "This time, see if you can do it without any prompting from me."

This time she went through the preliminaries a degree more confidently, aimed, and fired. Again the ball struck somewhere in Bedford Square.

She fired several more times, and it seemed the ball struck nearer and nearer to the spot she aimed for.

"It is not so very difficult, after all," she said casually, while her heart pounded with happiness. "Now I should like to try the rifle."

Chapter 12

SHE WAS VASTLY PLEASED WITH HERSELF, flushed and smiling, her green eyes sparkling. For a not-beautiful woman, she was amazingly handsome at times, Rupert thought.

She'd been pale at first—frightened, no doubt, as people unused to firearms so often were. But she wouldn't let fear master her.

He'd noticed this about her the first time they met. She must have been frightened in the dungeon. It was dark, and it stank of death and decay—and those were the more agreeable odors. Yet she'd beaten back fear for her brother's sake.

Since then, Rupert had seen daily examples of her pluck. They all made him want to get her naked, naturally, but he had other feelings, too. He wasn't sure what they were: a sort of fondness, a kind of affection, something oddly like what he felt for his brothers.

He hadn't thought overmuch about it, though, and didn't do so now.

At present he was vastly entertained watching her: the fierce frown of concentration while she loaded the pistol, the grimly determined stance as she held the weapon with both hands, and the reasonably straight shots she got off in spite of a not-quite-steady grip.

It was great fun teaching her, too, especially the parts where it was necessary to stand quite close, touching a little now and then.

He looked down at the rifle he'd brought and smiled. This would be more entertaining than the pistol.

"I can learn that, too," she said, misinterpreting the smile. "It must operate according to the same basic principles."

He nodded. She gave him the pistol and picked up the rifle.

While he carefully put away the pistol, she tried the rifle's weight and studied the mechanism—quite as gravely and intently as she studied hatted falcons.

She had no trouble loading it, though at forty-five inches long, it was a good deal more awkward to handle.

It was also a good deal more weapon to manage. She'd soon find out how much more. That would be interesting.

When all was ready, he made his face very serious, and drew closer. "You rest the butt against your shoulder, so," he said. He explained about recoil, placed her hands, straightened the rifle, showed her how to sight, and so on. Then he moved behind her, made some final adjustments, and said, "Fire when you're ready."

She gave a little twitch of her backside as she sought a comfortable position. Then she fully cocked the weapon, shifted her stance slightly, and pulled the trigger.

There was a metallic snap, a puff of smoke, a brief delay, then the explosion and the recoil, driving her backward.

Though he'd warned her, she was not prepared for the recoil's force. The rifle fell from her hands, and she stumbled back into him. He was fully prepared, though, and caught her, his arms closing over her bosom, his crossed hands firmly upon her breasts. He might have regained his balance but didn't try. He simply gave way, and fell backward onto the sandy ground, taking her with him.

It was unnecessary and thoroughly improper—her breasts were in no danger of becoming dislodged—but he didn't care. She would probably plant him a facer in the next second or drive an elbow into him, but he didn't care.

Smiling happily, he lay under her, his hands upon her splendid bosom while he waited for the explosion.

A long moment passed.

Then she pushed his hands away, twisted sharply about, and raised herself up to glare at him.

He grinned at her. She gazed at him for a time, green eyes fierce. Finally, she opened her mouth, and he thought, *Here comes the tongue-lashing.*

She let out a huff of vexation . . .

. . . and her soft mouth came down on his.

She tasted like gunpowder.

Rupert grasped her waist and held on. It was like being shot from a cannon or thrown from a precipice. She had only to bring her mouth to his, and the world flew apart, and he rocketed to places he didn't recognize.

She pushed her fingers into his hair and held him—as though he was imbecile enough to try to get away—and dragged her mouth over his. The teasing hint of incense was everywhere, mingling with the taste and scent of gunpowder and the taste and scent and feel of her: the ripe peach of a mouth and silk velvet skin, the feathery tickle of her hair, the curving body shaped exactly for his hands.

He'd waited so very long. He'd been so patient—for him—and careful—for him. But she was so different. He'd never known a woman like her. He'd never had so many *feelings.* He might as well be a raw schoolboy. He became heated in an instant, like a boy.

Not that he cared who he was or how old he felt. Only her mouth mattered and the lure of her wicked tongue, drawing him deeper, and the strange champagne taste of her, sweet and tangy in his mouth and swirling through him to make a smoky haze in his brain. Only her body counted, moving sinuously over him, the delicious friction of her breasts against his chest.

The Egyptian sun beat down, but it was nighttime to him. The gritty sand under his head and back was silken sheets. He forgot where he was and why. Her mouth left his, and she rubbed her cheek against his jaw, and the touch was a jab to the heart. She pressed her lips to his neck and trailed kisses to the base of his throat, little lightning strikes to the skin. Everywhere her mouth touched caught fire and set off thunderbolts in his heart.

If he could have thought, he would have let her have her way, going at her own pace. There were all the obstacles, after all. He'd kept a distance, sure that time and proximity would wear down her resistance. He had known all this: what to do and what not to do and above all, *don't hurry her.*

But that was before she destroyed his mind. Now all he could do was feel, and the feelings all added up to *I want.* He was hot, and his mind was a black nothing, and she was close at hand, in his hands, and he had to have her. Now.

He dragged his hand down over her backside and pressed her hard against his throbbing cock. Ah, it felt good. But it could be better, much better. He dragged up her skirt and slid his hand over stocking and garter and up under the bunched-up skirts and petticoats over the back of her thigh.

She jerked away as though he'd shot her.

"Good God!" she cried. She rolled off him, tugging down her clothing. "Are you mad?"

He blinked and dragged in air. "Well, yes," he said thickly. "Lust does that to a man."

"You thought we would—you would—do . . . *that? In public?*"

"I wasn't thinking about where we were," he said.

Her eyes widened.

"I'm a man," he said with what he was sure must be, in the circumstances, saintly patience. "I can do one or the other. Lovemaking or thinking. But not both at the same time."

She stared at him for a moment. Then she drew up her knees and folded her arms upon them and buried her face in her folded arms.

She did not pick up the rifle and knock him on the head with it.

Perhaps all was not lost.

"Somewhere else, then?" he said hopefully.

•　•　•

DAPHNE LIFTED HER head and stared at him in blank wonder.

"Somewhere more private," he said.

"*No*," she said. "Not here. Not anywhere."

"But we like each other," he said.

"It is completely physical," she said.

"Isn't that the point?"

She stood and brushed sand from her clothes and tried to straighten her petticoats discreetly. She could still feel his hand on the back of her naked thigh. Within, she was still atremble, still felt excitement and need along with other sensations she couldn't name and didn't trust, shivering through her.

They had come so close, too close. And in public. In *public!*

"The point is finding my brother," she said, keeping her voice low and calm. It wasn't easy. "This is not a pleasure cruise. The *Isis* is not a seraglio. I am not your mistress, and I don't intend to become your mistress. I'm sorry I gave you reason to think so. I'm sorry I behaved badly."

Oh, but how was the wild girl inside her to resist?

If, like a proper woman, she'd scrambled away from him the instant they fell, she would have had a chance. But she wasn't proper, and it wasn't possible. A proper woman would have been outraged. But she was improper, and she'd wanted to laugh. At the way he'd so boldly clasped her breasts. At the way it felt: so good and pleasurable and *right*. She'd relished the pressure of his hands. She'd gloried in the feel of the long, powerful body under her . . . and most horribly improper of all, the feel of his arousal against her backside had thrilled her to the core.

How on earth was she to behave properly when primitive urges so easily conquered her moral principles?

She was not sure where or how she'd found the willpower to push his hands away. She'd wanted to stay there, trapped in his arms, sinfully aware of his desire for her. Somehow, though, she found the strength to break away and make herself turn and face him.

Then what was she to do when he lay there, grinning at her, quite unrepentant, a mischievous boy? Devilment danced in his dark eyes. It should have warned her off. But it called to the devil in her instead, and down she went to him, to claim his wicked mouth and make it hers. She'd no sooner touched her mouth to his, felt the smile against her lips, than she caught his scent, the diabolical woman-trap that sapped her reason, will, and morals.

Nonetheless, it was not his fault.

She couldn't blame him. He was a man, after all. It wasn't his fault that she was so sadly lacking in moral fiber or willpower or whatever normal women used in such situations.

"You have a remarkable animal magnetism," she went on into the taut silence. "I've had no practice with that sort of thing. I'm sorry for misleading you. I was taught moral principles. I ought to be capable of adhering to them. I shall do so in future, I promise you."

He walked a few steps away and came back. He kicked a pebble. He said something under his breath. He picked up the rifle and brushed off sand.

"This will want a thorough cleaning," he said. His voice was dry, detached. "Where the devil are the servants?"

He whistled, and Udail/Tom came running. Minutes later, Daphne found out what had kept the party engaged for so long after she'd stopped shooting.

One of the guards had them enthralled with a story—about a white-haired ghost who'd caused a boat to collide with a sandbank and sink near Minya a week ago.

THE GHOST, THE guard said, had a very small beard, even though it appeared as a full-grown male. It was tall—almost as tall as the English sir—and dressed like a foreigner. It was very pale and wearing chains. Several people had seen it, the guard said.

Some on shore had seen the apparition on the boat as it was sinking. They saw two men jump into the water and swim away in terror. The ghost appeared again upriver later the same night, floating toward the tombs, then again a few nights later, going to the river. Everyone avoided the tombs beyond the red hill now, because of him.

Ordinarily, Daphne would have simply smiled at the tale. Egyptians' lives were thickly populated with supernatural beings. But the "white" hair and small beard gave her pause, and she asked for a fuller account.

As she translated for Mr. Carsington, she saw the stiff, distant expression fade from his countenance and an arrested look come into his dark eyes. He, too, had guessed the ghost's identity. Like her, though, he was careful to show no more than a mild interest in the tale.

But when the guard was done and had rejoined the others, Mr. Carsington said in a low voice, "Your brother, I collect."

Her heart thrummed—with hope, anticipation, and fear, too. She composed herself, met his gaze, and nodded. "The guard says the boat broke apart when it stuck on a sandbank. Several corpses have turned up but no survivors, apparently. He must have escaped."

"He played a ghost to keep people away," Mr. Carsington said. "Very wise of him."

"Miles has a vivid imagination," she said. "When it comes to solving practical problems, he can be amazingly sharp and quick, often ingenious."

"That's good," Mr. Carsington said. "From all I've heard, Minya isn't a safe place for a solitary European."

In truth, even with a large, armed escort and Mr. Carsington towering over everybody, Daphne had been glad to leave the town behind.

Leena hadn't exaggerated about the people. Daphne had never before seen in one place so many one-eyed individuals or so many sickly and stunted children. She knew the eye disease opthalmia was one of Egypt's perils, and she'd brought sulphate of copper and citron ointment, the medicines recommended to treat it.

The Egyptians had no medicines and took no precautions against disease. Magic and superstition ruled. She'd seen too many small children—even helpless babies—with flies clustered upon their eyes. She'd seen a mother prevent a child from brushing them away. She'd also heard that some boys were deliberately mutilated to make them ineligible for conscription into Muhammad Ali's army.

The flies and scarred faces were reason enough to pass through the town quickly, even had it been friendly. It was not friendly. The people were sullen and evasive.

Miles, who'd been in charge of planning their journey, had told her about the two hundred miles of marauders. No wonder he'd done what he could to keep people away.

"The Egyptians believe in an immense variety of *jinn,* good and bad," she told Mr. Carsington. "Ghosts, ghouls, and *afreets*—demons—are species of *jinn.* They frequent graveyards and tombs."

"Well, he's not haunting the burial ground at the moment," Mr. Carsington said. "I daresay he only comes out at night."

"There are tombs a short distance southward," she said, pointing. "Near the red mound, the Kom el Ahmar."

"Then we'd better have a look," he said.

IT WAS DANGEROUSLY close to sunset before they found any sign of Archdale, and then it was clear they'd come too late.

As the day waned, their Egyptian entourage had grown increasingly reluctant to continue the search. At present, the guards waited outside the tomb. Most of the crew ventured only a few feet inside the entrance. Only Tom and another young servant, Yusef, carrying the torches, had bravely followed Rupert and Mrs. Pembroke into the interior.

Deep within the tomb they found the remains of a cooking fire and other signs of habitation. This was not unusual, Rupert knew. Foreign explorers often took up residence in tombs and temples, as did some natives.

But this tomb held pieces of chain, as well as the remnants of English clothing of high quality. While dirty and torn, it was royal raiment compared to what the average Egyptian peasant wore. No native tomb dweller would have left such riches behind, in plain sight.

At the moment, Tom and Yusef stood in a corner, talking in subdued tones.

Mrs. Pembroke had the ragged garments and pieces of chain in her hands. She was staring at them, her torch-lit countenance bleak.

The heartbroken look only added to the nasty stew of emotion Rupert was experiencing.

He'd rather not think about how he felt or she felt. He wanted to get out of here and on to the next thing. But he had to do something, say something. She'd started the search so eagerly and hopefully, and she was so bitterly disappointed.

Not to mention that Rupert was still disturbed about what had happened earlier.

While he wasn't a saint, he did have rules, simple sporting rules regarding what a gentleman did and did not do. A gentleman didn't bed an unmarried lady, for instance. He did bed unwed women who weren't ladies: actresses, ballet dancers, courtesans, and such. He might bed a married lady—but Rupert had always shied away from such liaisons, deeming them far too complicated. Widows, though, weren't complicated. Virginity breached, husbands permanently out of the picture, they were supposed to be fair game.

He was desperately in lust with this widow. She'd shown clear signs that she wasn't indifferent to him. She wasn't easy to seduce, and the challenge made her even more attractive.

Besides, she had the face and figure of a goddess and a gigantic brain. Everyone knew goddesses were more difficult and dangerous than the common run of females. Look at what happened in the Greek myths. You couldn't expect an extraordinary woman to behave like an ordinary one.

If she'd hit him with the rifle butt or bloodied his nose or at the very least given him a blistering scold earlier, he would have accepted the punishment cheerfully. He'd misbehaved, after all, using a minor accident as an excuse to take an outrageous liberty.

Instead, the baffling creature blamed herself and apologized to *him*, of all things! She was vexed with herself instead of with him. This made no sense. Worse, it made him feel all wrong inside.

He was experiencing the ghastly sensation he remembered from boyhood: conscience. It hadn't troubled him in years. Now it yowled at him and tied his innards in knots.

Because of a bit of a grope with a widow who'd said in plain English that she liked him physically!

"Well, we're a few days late, it seems," he said finally. "Still, looking on the bright side, we know we're on the right track: he isn't being held captive in Cairo. He's less than a week ahead of us."

"Or behind us," she said. "He might be trying to return to Cairo."

Or he might be dead. Or he might have moved on to another hiding place. The cliffs were riddled with tombs. It was a miracle they'd found any sign of Archdale after only half a day's search.

But she knew this as well as Rupert did, and if he didn't say something to rouse her spirits, she'd lose heart. Her face would get the dead-white, taut look that upset him almost as much as actual weeping.

"You'd think Noxious would have found him by now, then," Rupert said. "You'd think he'd be looking diligently. Everyone stops at Minya. Surely he'd have heard about the boat mishap, and put two and two together. It hardly takes a genius. After all, *I* worked it out."

She looked up, and he saw her come out of whatever dark place of her immense brain she'd gone into. Her countenance brightened. Even in the wavering torchlight Rupert could see her remarkable eyes shifting back and forth.

"Good grief, I'd forgotten about him," she said. "But there's been nothing to remind me. No one's mentioned him. Isn't that odd? His boat is distinctive, you said. He's been up and down the Nile several times. People would recognize his boat. The *kashef* would know him."

"Not so strange," Rupert said. "The locals aren't the most forthcoming lot of Egyptians we've ever encountered."

"Then we'll have to make them talk," she said. Clutching her brother's effects to her bosom, she hurried out.

AS THEY WERE returning to the landing place, Daphne was calculating her stores, debating whether she ought to sacrifice another set of the pistols or perhaps some of Miles's instruments as bribery. She was glad to have a plan of sorts, something productive to think about.

She had not realized how deeply—painfully so—she'd hoped, until the hope was dashed. She had not realized, truly, how much she missed Miles until she held his filthy shirt in her hands. Then to see the broken pieces of chain . . . and imagine what he'd endured, and feel so helpless . . . She'd told herself not to succumb to despair, to be grateful she had not found his body. She'd told herself not to weep. It would avail nothing.

But never had she wanted so much to sink to her knees and cry until she had no tears left.

She was recovered now, though, thanks to Mr. Carsington's mentioning Lord Noxley.

His lordship had pointed out how quickly news traveled here. It was odd that no one in Minya had said a word about him. His boat must have stopped there for supplies. Otherwise, they must wait until they reached Asyut, nearly a hundred miles away.

Calculating bribes and speculating about his lordship kept her mind occupied all the way back to the landing place. As they neared the water, a young woman pushed past the men and thrust a baby wrapped in dirty rags in Daphne's face.

"Help my child," the woman cried in anguished Arabic. "Give the babe your magic, English lady."

Some of the men tried to push the woman away.

Mr. Carsington's arm went around Daphne's shoulders.

"Her baby's sick," Daphne said.

"I can see that," he said. "But they're all sick, and I don't trust anybody. Tom, get a coin from my coat, and give it to her." He drew Daphne closer. "Come away."

Daphne started to go with him but glanced back. The woman was young, little more than a girl. She shook her head at Udail/Tom, who was holding out a coin. Tears streamed down her cheeks. "My baby," she cried. "Please, English lady."

Daphne glanced up at Mr. Carsington.

He wore a pained expression.

Then to the woman she said, "Come with us."

• • •

RUPERT COULD SEE that the mother was young, poor, and desperate. He didn't want to turn his back on her. But it might be a trap. Or it might lead to trouble. If the babe died—and it looked very near to drawing its last feeble breath—any of a number of things might happen, none of them good. Tom and Leena had agreed that blood feud was popular in the countryside.

Rupert had enough to do, protecting Mrs. Pembroke and her entourage from villains. What the *Isis* did not need was a lot of vengeful villagers in pursuit as well.

The sensible thing to do was give the girl a generous baksheesh and get away as quickly as possible.

He would have been sensible, would have carried away Mrs. Pembroke bodily if necessary—if the confounded Egyptian female had not commenced weeping.

As the first tears trickled down, he knew he hadn't a prayer.

He got everyone safely aboard and kept vigilant watch as they crossed to the *Isis*. There he spent his time on deck with the men. Occasionally, Leena would emerge from the middle cabin, which had been quickly transformed into the *Isis*'s infirmary. Her reports on the infant's progress were invariably pessimistic. The child suffered from a bilious fever, perhaps the typhus fever or something even worse. Fevers killed strong, healthy adults. They'd brought the consul general to death's door more than once, she'd heard, and he had proper doctors, not shamans and village hags. What hope was there for a weak, ill-fed baby who'd been treated with nothing but charms and magic spells for days? Now they would all catch the fever and die in one of the filthiest and ugliest places in all the world, and when they were all dead, the peasants would come and pillage the boat and throw their bodies in the river for the fish and the crocodiles to eat.

After Leena returned to her mistress—and certain death, by the sounds of it—Rupert could spend the next several hours cursing himself for once again falling victim to feminine tears.

He was an idiot. No, worse, he was a cliché.

Women wept. Easily and often. An adult male ought to be able to remain sane while they did so. Had he remained sane, Mrs. Pembroke would be in no danger—or no more than the usual danger—of contracting some unspeakable foreign disease.

They were miles from civilization and anything remotely resembling medical care. All she had was her medicine case, whose contents were shrinking, thanks to the crew members' frequent accidents. She'd treated with success someone's bruised foot, someone else's swollen thumb, and one case of sunstroke. Rupert had no idea how much she knew about treating fever. More than he did, beyond question. If she fell ill, he wouldn't have the first idea what to do.

From sunset until the last streak of light faded from the sky and the stars arranged themselves in the familiar constellations, Rupert paced the deck, growled when spoken to, and repeatedly waved away Tom's attempts to lure him into the front cabin to take some supper.

When he heard the footsteps behind him, he assumed it was Tom again, come to plague him.

"No, I don't want any supper," Rupert said. *"No.* Is that not clear? I thought you had mastered the English term. Clearly, I was wrong. What is the Egyptian word for no? How about *bokra?* Not today."

"No is *la,"* came an amused feminine voice. "The polite refusal would be *la shokran."*

He turned quickly, and his heart slammed into his rib cage. He managed to keep from reaching for her and pulling her into his arms. But he couldn't suppress the moronic smile or the laugh of pleasure that it turned into.

All this, at the sound of her voice.

But she sounded happy. He was relieved, naturally. The child wasn't dead. The prognosis must be hopeful, else he'd have heard the disappointment and sorrow in her voice.

"The babe?" he said. "It's well?"

"It's a *she,* amazingly enough," she said. "Girls are not very important and normally wouldn't be worth the trouble. But Sabah's mother deems her exceedingly valuable. The name means *morning,* you know. We got some liquids into her, which seemed to help. We gave her a cool bath, and she bore it well, unlike her mama, who was terrified. Then I tried a decoction of Peruvian bark. The fever seems to be declining. Quite rapidly, in fact."

Rupert let out the breath he hadn't realized he was holding. "I'm glad to hear it," he said.

"You can have no idea how relieved I am," she said.

Not nearly as relieved as he, he'd wager.

"I have no experience of children," she went on. "Still, I did care for my parents and Virgil, and must have absorbed some doctoring wisdom. It is little enough, but these people have none. A compress, a bath, a poultice—the simplest remedies are great miracles and magic to them. Good grief, what a world this is." Her voice caught.

"You've had a long and trying day," he said quickly. "Come inside and help me eat the supper Tom's so frantic about." He paused and added, "Dr. Pembroke."

She laughed at that, but he heard the strain in her voice.

"Come, I'm starved," he said. And then it was simple instinct to put a protective arm about her shoulders and lead her inside.

They had a quiet, companionable meal, and Rupert was reaching for his third helping of sweet pastry when Leena screamed.

Chapter 13

EVERYONE IRRUPTED INTO THE PASSAGE AT once: Daphne, Mr. Carsington with a piece of pastry in his hand, the mother Nafisah with the baby clutched to her bosom, and Leena, who slammed the door to Daphne's cabin shut behind her.

She ended the barrage of questions with the grim announcement, *"Mongoose."*

"Is that all?" said Mr. Carsington. He made his way through the gantlet of females and grasped the door handle. "I thought someone was cutting your throat."

"He showed his teeth at me," Leena said.

Mr. Carsington opened the door and smiled. "Gad, it's only a baby. Well, not fully grown at any rate." The smile faded. "But he's got—or is it a she? I think it's a she, actually."

"What's it got?" Daphne said. She edged round Nafisah and baby and past Leena and on tiptoe looked over Mr. Carsington's shoulder. "Oh, it's Miles's shirt."

The creature had a clump of sleeve in her teeth. She gazed balefully at the humans in the doorway.

"They're good with rats," Mr. Carsington said. "And snakes. She could come in handy, Mrs. Pembroke, when you're dismantling temples and pyramids." As he spoke, he turned to meet her gaze, his as black as midnight. His mouth was mere inches away, a smile teasing at the very corners. She wanted to bring her lips to that hint of a smile and kiss it away from him and into her. She needed the smile, the secret joke, the humor that was so much a part of his fierce *aliveness*.

She inched back and told herself to calm down. "We have two cats," she said.

"Killing venomous snakes is not their specialty," Mr. Carsington said. "Recollect, you do like to poke about places where short-tempered vipers like to sleep."

"I am not at all sure the cats will be happy about her," Daphne said. "Besides, she might be wild. Or rabid. I cannot think why any rational mongoose would wish to eat a dirty shirt. It is not as though there is any shortage of rats hereabouts."

"Yes, it's very interesting," said Mr. Carsington. "Such interesting things happen in your vicinity." His amused expression faded. He looked . . . puzzled? Lost?

But of course he could not be lost. The indecent embrace yesterday must have disarranged her mind as well as her morals.

The unusual expression quickly vanished, though, and his gaze returned to the mongoose. "I suppose you want me to take the shirt away from her."

The creature still watched them, garment in her teeth. Her fur bristled.

"I'm not sure that's wise," Daphne said. "She looks ready to fight about it."

By this time, Leena having apprised Nafisah of the situation, the young mother approached and asked if she might look.

Daphne and Mr. Carsington moved out of the way. Nafisah looked in. The baby pointed and said something in baby gibberish.

"I think this is my neighbor's mongoose," Nafisah said. "She is tame but lately she has become troublesome. One night, I catch her near my chickens. I chase her away with a stick. In a little while, my neighbor comes, and he is angry with me. He says I hurt her foot. Now she limps, he says, and she is worthless to kill snakes, because she is too slow. I think he was the one who hurt her. She came to steal my eggs because it is easier than killing snakes. But my husband is dead and I have no one here to stand up to this man. This makes him bold. See if she is lame," she urged. "He put her down to show me, and she ran away from him. I could see her foot pained her, and I felt sorry for her. Later I went out again to look for her, but I saw the ghost, and I was afraid. See if she is lame," she repeated.

The art of brevity was not highly prized in Egypt. Daphne was able to condense the tale to a few English sentences. When she was done, Mr. Carsington crouched down, held out his bit of pastry, and called to the animal, "Come, my dear. Wouldn't you rather a bit of sweet than that dirty old shirt?"

The creature stared at the pastry without moving.

"She's *Egyptian*," Daphne said. She crouched down beside him. *"Ta'ala heneh,"* she crooned. *Come here.*

The creature looked up at her and sniffed.

"Ta'ala heneh," Daphne repeated.

The mongoose advanced a few steps, dragging the shirt along. Then she stopped, chittered at them, and sat down on the garment, her teeth still firmly clamped on the sleeve. Those few steps showed her favoring the front left paw.

"That's the way Alistair walks," said Mr. Carsington.

"Your brother," she said. "The one who was injured at Waterloo."

He nodded. "Such a melting effect the limp had on women. They sighed. They swooned. They threw themselves at him. Maybe what I need is a limp." He shot her a glinting sidelong glance.

It was not merely a glance. It was purposeful and intimate. It conjured the taste of his mouth and the feel of his hands and his hard body and the rush of mad joy she'd experienced when she fired the pistol for the first time, and when she'd kissed him. Her knees softened first, then her muscles, then her head.

While Daphne struggled to reclaim what used to be her

brain, Nafisah said, "This is my neighbor's mongoose. I am sure of it."

Daphne's intellect sorted itself into order and her attention reverted to the girl and the crucial words she'd uttered moments ago. "You saw her the night you saw the ghost, Nafisah," she said. "Tell me about the ghost."

DAPHNE TRANSLATED FOR Mr. Carsington later, when they returned to the front cabin. He'd already got the gist of it from Leena, though.

Nafisah had seen the ghost last Thursday night. The next morning, she reported the sighting to her neighbor's wife. Before long, some of the *kashef*'s men came to her house and questioned her for a long time about the ghost. She described what she'd seen and where. They gave her money and went away. Later, she saw a group of men go out to the tombs. They were strangers and foreigners. They weren't from her village or from Minya, but most of the villagers seemed to know who they were, and they were afraid of these men.

"Shall we return to the *kashef*?" Daphne asked. "A large enough bribe will probably elicit the information we want."

"I'll deal with him, first thing tomorrow," Mr. Carsington said. "I'll take Tom."

"Tom's grasp of English is haphazard at best, and his vocabulary is exceedingly limited," Daphne said.

"That's all right," Mr. Carsington said. "I don't mean to do much talking."

"But—"

"You're not coming with me," he said. "I need you to take charge of the boat while I'm gone."

"Take charge?"

"I need someone here I can rely upon," he said. "You must persuade Nafisah to travel with us. It isn't safe for her to go back to her village. Her neighbor is one of the *kashef*'s spies, I don't doubt, and they all seem to be in league with our villains."

"But you—"

"If anyone attempts to board, shoot them," he said. "You're the only one I can count on to keep a cool head if there's trouble."

"But I don't shoot straight!" she cried.

"Hardly anyone does," he said. "However, men are struck cold with terror at the sight of you cocking a pistol. Just start shooting, and tell Reis Rashad to make sail."

"But you—"

"If Tom and I run into difficulties, we'll catch up with you later," he said.

THEY WOULD CATCH up if they survived the encounter with the *kashef,* that is. Rupert expected trouble. He was looking forward to it, actually. But he kept his expectations to himself.

The next morning, when he visited the fat liar, Rupert simply offered to teach him to fly. Then Rupert demonstrated his teaching method by picking up the largest of the guards and throwing him against a wall.

Several other guards started for Rupert then.

He told Tom to run, then stood, arms open in welcome, and grinned at the oncoming guards.

A fight was exactly what Rupert was hoping for.

He was not in a good mood.

He'd had a disturbing experience the previous evening, when his gaze had turned from the demented mongoose to the woman beside him. He'd looked into Mrs. Pembroke's remarkable green eyes and realized he hadn't endured a dull moment since the moment she'd entered the dungeon in Cairo.

He couldn't say why, but this made him uneasy.

He was never uneasy and didn't like the feeling.

Meanwhile, he was still horny and hadn't spied a single attractive female in this provoking town.

So he'd settle for the next best thing: a fight.

•   •   •

DAPHNE PACED THE deck, rifle in hand. Leena and Nafisah—the latter with naked baby astride her shoulder, Egyptian style—paced alongside her.

"He will return safely," Nafisah assured Daphne. "The mongoose is a good omen. Everyone recognizes this."

"The boy will say the wrong thing," Leena said. "The *kashef* will take offense and cut off his tongue, maybe his head. You should not have let your Englishman go this morning, mistress. You should have gone to his bed and taken off your clothes. If you had kept him happy in this way, he would not notice or care if the boat set sail. We might have departed this accursed place when the sun came up. What shall we do if the town turns against us and the wind fails? All the men will be killed, and we will be sold in the slave market. Or else they will rape us and leave us in the desert for the vultures and jackals to eat."

The wind showed no signs of failing. If anything, it had grown stronger in the course of the morning. If the town turned hostile, the *Isis* could be off at a moment's notice. Daphne and Mr. Carsington had consulted with Reis Rashad at daybreak. All was in readiness for a quick departure.

If the wind held.

"Be of good heart, lady," Nafisah told Daphne. "This boat is magical. You have healing magic, and the English master has power over snakes."

"No one fears snake charmers," Leena said scornfully.

"But in Saqqara he commanded a wild viper, not a tame snake with no fangs, like those in the snake charmers' baskets," Nafisah said. "Everyone here has heard of his magic at the Pyramid of Steps in Saqqara. Everyone has heard of his strength, like a genie. Why do you think only one man came to rob your boat the other night? The others feared the magic."

Daphne paused in her pacing. "Really? How disappointing for Mr. Carsington. He was so looking forward to fighting bandits."

"He is looking for a fight," Leena said grimly. "Anyone can see this." Lowering her voice she added in a still-audible aside to Nafisah, "They desire each other. But they are *En-*

glish, you see, and the English people have strange——"

A shout cut her off.

Daphne's attention swung back landward.

The man they spoke of was sauntering down toward the landing place, Tom behind him. Yusef, who'd gone ashore, was running to meet them.

Daphne was tempted to do the same.

The sun glinted on hair as black as a raven's wing. The wind whipped the *kamees*'s billowing shirtsleeves against Mr. Carsington's powerful arms and his loose Turkish trousers against his long legs.

Her heart felt wind-whipped, too, beating with a mad happiness against her ribs. He was *alive.* He looked toward Udail/Tom, who was talking, then laughed at whatever it was the boy said. Then Mr. Carsington's gaze came to her, and he grinned and waved, and she thought, *I'm lost.*

THE *ISIS* GOT under way the instant Mr. Carsington and his youthful devotees came aboard. By this time, Daphne had herself under control.

"You are alive," she said with wonderful composure. "In one piece. No visible bruises."

"That's Tom's fault," Mr. Carsington said. "Just as things were about to get interesting, he started jabbering. It went on forever. Something about *jinn* and *afreets,* I think. At any rate, the *kashef* turned pale and sent everyone away except his interpreter. Then, suddenly, His Honor began 'remembering' things."

A sound near their feet made him look down. The mongoose stood on her hind legs, peering up at him. The creature still held the shirt in its sharp little teeth.

The animal had had a dispute with the cats last night, but that was all. The cook, who had reason to fear for his chickens, had actually fed her. And the crew seemed to accept her. Everyone aboard—except the cats—seemed to view the mongoose as a good omen, as Nafisah said.

"Ah, still with us, I see," Mr. Carsington said.

Far more important, *he* was still with them. Alive. In

one piece. Only when she saw him strolling so casually to the landing place did Daphne realize how much anxiety she'd suppressed.

"It seems she means to stay," she said a little breathlessly. "Nafisah, too. No difficulty there. She wasn't at all eager to return to her late husband's village. Negotiations had begun, you see, to add her to her neighbor's collection of wives—the neighbor whose mongoose this was."

"She's ours now," Mr. Carsington said. "What shall we call her?"

"Nafisah," Daphne said. "Surely you can pronounce that."

"I meant the mongoose," he said.

"Oh." Daphne regarded the creature, who was still transfixed by Mr. Carsington. Could anybody resist him?

The cats, Gog and Magog. They were as majestically indifferent to him as they were to everyone else aboard.

If only I were a cat, Daphne thought.

"Marigold," he said. "What do you think of the name Marigold?"

"I think it's silly," Daphne said, "which fits her perfectly. She's the silliest mongoose I've ever heard of."

He crouched down. "Marigold?" he said.

The mongoose chewed on the bit of shirt in its mouth.

He rose. "She's thinking it over."

"While she does so, perhaps you would be so good as to tell me what the *kashef* remembered," Daphne said.

"Oh, that." He frowned. "Come inside. I'm perishing for coffee."

THE COFFEE CAME, and food, too. The tray, crammed with dishes, none of them remotely English, reminded Rupert he'd eaten nothing since his quick breakfast at daybreak. Between mouthfuls, he began giving Mrs. Pembroke a fuller account of his meeting with the *kashef* of Minya.

When Rupert described his initial diplomatic efforts— the flying demonstration—she stared at him, green eyes wide. Then the pale, stunned look reddened into anger.

"How could you be so irresponsible?" she said. "They

might have killed you—and Tom. Then where should we be? Did you forget we've several females aboard, one little more than a girl and another a baby?"

She stood up quickly, in a flurry of muslin. "But why do I ask? Of course you are irresponsible. If you were not, you would not have been in that dungeon in Cairo. If you were a responsible, thinking individual, Mr. Salt would not have jumped at the chance to be rid of you."

As you'd expect, her brain was in excellent working order: she was right on every count.

"Come, don't be cross," he said. "It was stupid, I admit. But I was in a foul temper and not thinking clearly."

"We cannot afford your indulging in ill humor," she said. "I cannot do this alone. I rely upon you, Mr. Carsington. I do not like to—to inhibit you. I know you are a man of action, who must find so much responsibility oppressive. But I must ask y-you . . ." Her voice wobbled.

"Oh, no," he said.

She held up her hand. "I am not going to weep," she said.

"Yes, you are," he said.

She came back to the divan and sat down. She bit her lip. He sighed. "Go ahead."

She shook her head.

"It's all right," he said. "I'd rather you hit me, but this punishment is much more painful. Exactly what I deserve."

She smiled crookedly. "I'll show mercy this time," she said. "But you must not do it again."

The crooked smile might as well have been a hook. It dug in sharply, into someplace deep inside, and he stared at her stupidly, like the fish he might as well be, caught on a crooked brink-of-tears smile.

"I will never, ever do it again," he said.

"Good." The smile smoothed out, and she settled back onto the divan, tucking her feet under her. "Tell me what you learnt from the *kashef*."

"Noxious's famous boat did stop here, not quite a week ago." Rupert focused on the story and the food, to keep from thinking about what she was doing to him. "It was a short visit, to load supplies. He came with another man to call on the *kashef*. The ghost was discussed. After Noxious left, the other fellow inquired in the area about the ghost. A day or so thereafter, he went with a group of men to the rock tombs to perform holy rituals to summon the ghost and make it vanish. And lo and behold, a genie came in a sandstorm and carried the ghost away into the desert. In other words, your brother is traveling across the desert at present in the company of unsavory characters of various tribes and nations. And these men are known to be in Noxious's employ."

Her green eyes widened. "Good grief."

"All the consuls in Egypt—including our own—employ disreputable persons on occasion," Rupert said. "Noxious is trying to recover your papyrus as well as your brother. The people who kidnapped your brother are cutthroats, literally. Much as I dislike defending him, I can well understand why his lordship should hire men of the same breed."

"Perhaps that's understandable," she said. "But leaving Miles in their care is not."

"Yes, well, matters are a bit more complicated than we thought," Rupert said. "There's a war in progress, apparently, and it isn't mere unfriendly competition for antiquities. This one seems to be personal, between Noxious and Duval—and it's more violent than the usual disputes."

"In other words, Miles has been caught in the middle," she said.

"So it seems." Rupert went on eating, occasionally glancing up now and again to watch her green eyes shift from side to side. He knew she was only thinking and it wasn't about seduction. She was working out the implications of what he'd said. He wondered why he found it so fascinating, watching her think.

"A war," she said finally. "And since Lord Noxley's men now have Miles, we can expect Duval's men to come after me."

"You'd be a valuable bargaining chip," Rupert said. He paused before adding, "If I understood correctly, they're all headed south. If you think it would be wise, at this point, knowing what we do, to—"

"Absolutely not," she said sharply. "I'm not turning

back. They can fight over the silly papyrus, if they want, but I am not leaving Miles in the hands of brigands and assassins, no matter who employs them. I'm not going back to Cairo without my brother. I did not come this far only to run away at the first difficulty."

"It's hardly the first difficulty," he said. "Have you forgotten we were trapped in a pyramid? Have the various corpses we stumbled over slipped your mind? We were arrested, recollect. There was the intimate encounter with a viper. And we've been invaded by a lunatic mongoose."

She dismissed this with an airy wave of her hand. "We knew early on that Duval might come after me to use me against my brother. The threat did not deter me then, and it will not deter me now."

"I rather thought not." Rupert grinned stupidly. He couldn't help it, any more than he could help feeling so stupidly pleased. He would have taken her back if she wished, though he wasn't at all ready to cut short their adventure.

She rose. "We shall continue as planned. Lord Noxley's men must meet up with their employer sooner or later. We'll retrieve Miles and let them proceed with their war without us. For the present, however, I need to collect my thoughts. In solitude." She opened the door, and the mongoose entered, shirt trailing. "Marigold will keep you company."

THE WIND GREW stronger with each passing mile. It subsided at sunset only to return with increased force when the sun rose the next day. Fortunately, it was in their favor, and it did give Daphne an excuse to remain cloistered in her cabin.

The wind-driven sand often kept the women inside, in cabins whose chinks were stuffed with rags. Leena spent a good deal of time with Nafisah and the baby, leaving Daphne to study her new cartouches in peace.

Except that she wasn't peaceful.

She couldn't concentrate. She wasn't at all easy in her mind about Miles, but that wasn't the whole trouble.

She knew she'd crossed a line on the day they left Minya. The outburst itself wasn't unreasonable in the circumstances, but what she'd said wasn't half of what she'd felt.

She'd become attached to him, which was the stupidest mistake, because he was not the sort of man who could become attached to anybody, and most especially not to a dull bookworm nearly thirty years old.

She was glaring with helpless incomprehension at a set of cartouches in her notebook when she heard footsteps in the passage, then a tap at her door.

She flung the notebook aside, went to the door, and opened it. And her heart opened up, too, and had a little party, with dancing.

Udail/Tom stood in the passage bearing the coffee tray. Behind him stood Mr. Carsington, in one of his Arabian Nights costumes. Deeply tanned, his black hair windblown, he looked more untamable than ever.

"Leena says you're cross," he said.

"I am not," Daphne lied. "I was working."

"No, you weren't," he said. "You haven't got ink all over you." He looked over her shoulder into the cabin. "Your papers and notebooks are not scattered about the divan."

"Arranged," she said. "My materials are carefully arranged. I told you, there must be order."

"Your idea of order looks like a muddle of books and papers to me," he said. "But then, I'm an idiot."

"Mr. Carsington."

"You need coffee and sweets to stimulate that immense brain of yours," he said. He patted Udail on the shoulder, and the boy carried the coffee tray into her cabin and set it down on the low stool near the divan.

Having completed his assignment, the boy departed.

The aroma of freshly brewed Turkish coffee filled the small cabin. Daphne settled onto the divan once more. Mr. Carsington set one broad shoulder against the doorframe and lounged there.

"Oh, come in," she said. "You know I cannot eat all this *fateerah* by myself. Not to mention how ridiculous it is to pretend you meant to go away directly when the tray is set for two."

"You're so clever," he said. "I did have an ulterior motive." From the folds of his shirt he withdrew a roll of heavy paper. "We need to look at the map and decide how many stops we ought to make before we come to Asyut, where we're obliged to stop."

While he spoke he came in and sat on the divan, folding up his long legs as easily and naturally as though he were the Arabian prince he so closely resembled.

"Asyut," she repeated, blank for a moment, then, "Oh, yes. The crew bakes bread there."

"We must give them the whole day," he said. He poured coffee for them both.

She would not let herself think about how intimate the gesture seemed, even with the door properly open. She would not let herself be stupid anymore.

"I can think of no reason to stop before then, except for the night," she said. "It's most unlikely anyone will give us information. One of the two warring sides will have bribed or terrified the locals to hold their tongues, and you cannot go into every single village and knock people about to encourage them to talk."

She took the map and turned a little away from him to unroll it and look for the place. "Ah, yes. Asyut will do very well. It is an important town. The caravans stop there. We can send the servants into the marketplace to collect gossip." She studied the map. "We have passed Beni Hasan, I don't doubt, at this rate."

"Long past," he said. "Reis Rashad expects to stop for the night at someplace unpronounceable. Some famous ruins nearby."

"West or east bank? Antinopolis is to the east."

"West."

"El-Ashmunein, then," she said. "The ruins of ancient Hermopolis are nearby. It was dedicated to Thoth, the Egyptian god of learning. He is the equivalent of the Greeks' Hermes and the Romans' Mercury. According to Plutarch, Thoth was represented by the ibis, and had one arm shorter than the other."

"I read Plutarch," Mr. Carsington said. "That's all we read. Greeks and Romans, Romans and Greeks."

She looked away from the map toward him. He was reaching for another piece of *fateerah,* the supply of which had noticeably dwindled in the last few minutes.

"You had a sound classical education, in other words," she said.

He ate his pastry, his black brows knit, as though she'd said something vastly puzzling.

She set aside the map and sipped her coffee, wondering what on earth could cause him to deliberate . . . about anything.

After a rather long time, he spoke. "I daresay my schooling was sound enough," he said, "but it was ghastly dull. The same authors and subjects are much more entertaining when you talk about them. I thought at first that was because you are so agreeable to look at."

It was nothing, a mere handful of words uttered in the most offhand way. He drank his coffee and scarcely looked at her.

She didn't know where to look. The idiotish dancing had recommenced in her heart.

She knew men liked her figure very well. Even Virgil. That, apparently, was all he'd liked.

She was aware that her face, while not pretty, was not repellent to men, either.

All the same, she was moved. Everything inside her seemed to open up, like fresh blossoms. "Oh," she said, aware of the blush simmering in her cheeks. "A compliment."

"It's a simple enough fact." His voice dropped lower, to a rumble that vibrated deep within her. "When I don't understand what you're talking about, I pretend I'm in a picture gallery and you are all the pictures."

She thought she must burst with pleasure. No one, *no one* had ever said anything like that to her before. It was more than a compliment. It was . . . it was . . . poetry, almost.

"But it isn't simply your looks," he went on, his gaze elsewhere, reflective. "It's the enthusiasm. The love of what you do. You make it interesting because you love it. You may talk of the driest stuff, yet I feel like Whatshisname, listening to Scheherazade."

His face changed then, darkened. If it had been any other man she would have thought he blushed.

But his dark gaze came back to her, and he shook his head, and laughed in his usual carefree way. "I am like a child, you see, easily entertained. Why do you think the fellow—the god, I mean—was misshapen?"

20 April

IT WAS NEAR daybreak.

Lord Noxley's *dahabeeya,* which had stopped at Girga overnight, set out well before the sun had cleared the horizon. A mile or two upriver, the *Memnon* approached a sandbank where half a dozen crocodiles slept. They were the first to be seen on the journey thus far, for the creatures had, over time, retreated from their haunts farther south.

Moments later, his lordship watched as the two men who'd run away from the "ghost" were bound and tossed into the water. At the first splash and scream, the reptiles woke and had breakfast.

Most of the company, accustomed to the Golden Devil's methods, watched as he did, with no evident emotion.

A few of the company, who were not accustomed, turned away.

One of these was Akmed.

Until now, he'd thought Lord Noxley a good man. Like Akmed's beloved master, this Englishman paid well, never shouted or abused those who served him, and did not permit beatings.

Now Akmed saw why the shouting and abuse were unnecessary and why everyone aboard worked diligently.

Now it dawned on him that he might have made a terrible mistake.

But it dawned on him, too, that his master needed him now more than ever.

Running away was out of the question.

Chapter 14

THE *ISIS* SAILED ON, THE WIND CONTINUING
true and strong, dying away at sunset only to return, fresh,
at dawn.

On the fourth day after leaving Minya, they reached
Asyut.

The bustling market town was the site of ancient Ly-
copolis, whose people worshiped the jackal or wolf. The
Description de l'Egypte contained cross sections and other
detailed illustrations of some of the more elaborate tombs
carved into the nearby hills.

It was nearly an hour's journey, over one of the Nile's
wider stretches of fertile land, then over a bridge, to the
mountain necropolis. The openings to the tombs and caves
were plainly visible from a distance. A modern cemetery
lay below.

The famous rock tombs were not Rupert and Mrs. Pembroke's destination, however. They'd decided to venture
into the hills and desert beyond, where people might feel
freer to answer their questions.

Accordingly, dressed in Arab style garments that would
not attract attention, Rupert and Mrs. Pembroke set out on

donkeys with Tom, Yusef, and a pair of guards from the town.

Rupert noticed the change in the wind as they reached the hillside. It had come up less fierce this morning, though still favorable, and he'd regretted the loss of time almost as much as Mrs. Pembroke had. But in the course of this morning's journey it had died away altogether.

Now, as they reached the edge of the desert plain, it was reviving. It had changed direction, though.

After a few miles, he was getting a bad feeling. The guards were dawdling far behind, and the lads looked uneasy.

Rupert met Tom's gaze. "*Simoom,*" the boy said. "*Simoom* comes, I think."

Yusef beside him nodded and went into a long spate of Arabic.

The wind was picking up, whirling sand.

Mrs. Pembroke said, "I think we'd better—"

Tom gave a shout and pointed southward. Rupert turned that way. A great yellow fog bank welled up from the horizon.

Another shout made him look behind him. The guards were galloping away.

Yusef cried, "*Hadeed ya mashoom!*"

"*Allahu akbar!*" Tom shouted.

Rupert knew that last one. *God is most great.* It was a charm to ward off evil. In Minya he'd found out that the Egyptians believed the *jinn* rode in the sandstorms.

Running for cover was definitely the best idea.

"Go!" he told the boys. "Follow the guards."

"Mrs. Pembroke," he called. He could hear the wind's roar, drawing closer.

"Yes, I—" The words slid into a shriek as her donkey reared and galloped away in the wrong direction.

Rupert spurred his animal after her. The fog swelled into a wave of sand, billowing toward them. An instant before Rupert reached them, her donkey came to a sudden halt, turned abruptly, and fell. Rupert dismounted and hurried to the fallen rider and mount.

But her donkey was already struggling up onto its feet.

Before he could grab it, the beast, freed of its burdens, fled. Rupert grabbed the bridle of his mount before it could follow.

Mrs. Pembroke struggled to rise, too, but fell down again. "Just my foot," she gasped as Rupert knelt beside her. "Silly ass fell on it."

The billowing sand was welling up, like a whirlpool upside down. It grew into a great swirling pillar of sand, and it was racing straight at them.

He caught her round the waist with one arm and lifted her up from the ground, his other hand still holding his anxious donkey's bridle. He dragged them both toward the jagged, stony slopes of the mountain necropolis.

The sand beat at his face, stung his eyes, filled his nose. The swirling pillar was nearly upon them.

He hauled woman and beast into the nearest crevice. He pulled off his cloak and sank down to the ground, taking Mrs. Pembroke with him. He pulled her between his bent legs and wrapped the cloak about them both. The donkey pressed close to the humans.

The sandstorm, shrieking and roaring, bore down on them.

THE MEN WHO were following the party abruptly reversed direction and raced back to Asyut. They waited out the *simoom* in a coffee shop near the southwest gate at the back of the town, facing the tombs. At this shop, one could obtain "white" or "black" coffee, the former laced with forbidden brandy. The men drank white coffee. They were all mercenaries who worked for a Frenchman named Duval. They had orders to capture the redheaded Englishwoman they'd been following recently. Today offered the prime opportunity. The woman had left most of her people behind. She traveled to the tombs with only a few servants and a pair of guards who could be counted on to run at the first sign of trouble. The large Englishman who accompanied her didn't worry them. One man stood no chance against ten experienced killers.

After several cups of white coffee, though, they began

arguing about the Englishman. They'd all heard he was the son of a great lord whose wealth far surpassed that of Muhammad Ali. Now some of them said he would be worth more alive than dead. With each succeeding cup of coffee, the debate grew louder. They woke from his nap the gatekeeper nearby, who left his post to demand silence. One of the men, Khareef, apologized and escorted him out of the shop. The instant they were out of onlookers' view, Khareef thrust a knife between the gatekeeper's ribs. He propped up the corpse in its usual place, where it remained undisturbed until the watch changed next morning, everyone who passed assuming the gatekeeper was sleeping as usual. Khareef found this highly amusing, and laughed from time to time, thinking about it.

RUPERT COULDN'T GUESS how long the sandstorm went on. It seemed an eternity.

The wind howled, and the sand lashed at them like an enraged monster. Small wonder the Arabs thought the *jinn* rode in the sandstorms.

In the cloak's shelter it was hot and dark. It smelled of donkey, too. But the rocks sheltered them from the worst of the storm's brutality, and the tightly woven cloth blocked the worst of the biting sand.

Mrs. Pembroke clung to him, mute and motionless, oh, and soft. He felt her breath, the quick inhale-exhale of fear, against his collarbone, where his shirt had fallen open. He was acutely aware of the hurried rise and fall of her bosom against his chest and of the soft pressure of her bottom against his thigh and groin.

He bent and pressed a reassuring kiss to the top of her head. Her hair was so soft, and fell in waves, like the rippling desert sand.

She'd lost her veil, he realized: the obnoxious veil he resented while aware of the protection if afforded against the Egyptian sun as well as prying male eyes. It wasn't black, he remembered, but he couldn't recall what color it was. She hadn't worn black in days, he realized. Since Minya?

"We'll be all right," he said. He could barely hear his own words over the whistle and wail of the sandstorm. He didn't know if she answered or not. He knew, though, that she held him tightly, her arms wrapped about his waist, as though she feared the storm would bear him away otherwise.

At moments he thought it might. The wind was unlike anything he'd ever experienced on dry land. It was more like an ocean storm, like being caught in a tearing sea of sand. Twice he thought it would rip them out from their crevice to throw them miles into the air, then drop them in so many broken pieces upon the Libyan hills.

But if so, it must take them both or none. He would not give her up to man or to force of nature, however great. He wrapped his arms more tightly about her, his fingers clutching at the robe to keep it closed while he prayed the storm would end soon, before they suffocated.

He didn't waste any more breath on reassurances she couldn't hear over the storm. He only pressed his lips to her head, again and again, hoping she'd understand: he'd take care of her. She would not come to harm so long as he was alive.

Some lifetimes later, the world began to quiet. The wind still blew strong, and the sand beat against them still, but not so ferociously. The juggernaut of whirling sand had moved on to sow destruction elsewhere.

He lifted his head. Gingerly he loosened his hold on the robe and peered out.

"I think it's safe to breathe," he said.

She let out a whoosh of breath, then coughed.

"Sorry," he said. He kissed her temple. "Sorry. I didn't mean to crush your ribs."

Her arms slid from his waist. She lifted her head. She eased her rump a few inches away from his crotch.

He wanted her back. He wanted her tucked into his arms, her soft hair tickling his chin. He wanted to feel her breathing against his collarbone, and the soft pressure of her breasts and her backside.

After a moment, she crawled farther away and spat out sand. "Good grief," she said. "Good grief."

"Are you all right?" he said. "Your foot?"

She turned her foot experimentally. "It seems to be functioning," she said. "My boots are filled with sand. My trousers are filled with sand. I am a walking sandbag. No, not walking. Not yet. Let me just . . . catch my breath."

She drew up her knees and folded her arms upon them and bowed her head upon her arms.

He looked about them. The wind had heaped a large mound of sand into the opening they'd entered.

He rose cautiously and looked to the southeast.

A fresh yellow tidal wave was building.

"Um," he said.

"Yes, I'll be up in a minute."

"I'm not sure we have a minute," he said. "And I don't fancy being buried here." He hauled her up and started pulling her and the donkey up the mountain.

BEING ABRUPTLY DRAGGED to her feet and yanked up a mountainside knocked out of Daphne the half a breath she'd managed to collect. She'd none to spare for commentary. Not that he would have listened—or needed to. He'd summed up their situation accurately, she soon saw.

A glance back showed her why he was so impatient to be moving. Sand had partly filled their shelter, and another sand funnel was hurtling toward them.

Fortunately, paths had been worn or cut into the hillside for access to the tombs. With Mr. Carsington to lean on, Daphne could get along well enough. She was thankful for her Turkish trousers, which allowed for easier movement than the usual layers of petticoats under not-very-wide skirts. The donkey experienced no difficulty at all, and came along agreeably enough.

Daphne wondered where her mount had got to, and whether the poor thing was alive. She looked for it without much hope. Visibility was uncertain at best. The sun was either a hellish red behind a veil of sand or disappeared altogether. Not that one could look in any direction for long. Eyes, ears, nose, and mouth filled with grit. One could scarcely breathe for the sand. Simply trying to protect herself from it exhausted her. Yet what she experienced at present, she now knew, was hardly the worst of the punishment the hot wind could bestow.

She made herself stop looking back at the deadly yellow thing racing toward them, and focused on her companion.

She recalled her moment of panic when her donkey had fallen, and she'd seen the monstrous sand tide rolling toward her. For an instant, blinded by the blowing sand, she'd felt alone, abandoned. But it was only for an instant, because in the next he was there.

As long as he was by, she could face anything. She'd followed him through the absolute darkness of the pyramid, squeezing past corpses on the way. She'd been arrested, and locked up in jail, like a common felon. She'd burst into a room filled with cutthroats, and attacked them. She'd knelt by the dying rug merchant and tried to comfort him as the last drops of blood trickled from his slit throat. She'd shot a pistol and a rifle, though firearms had always terrified her.

Even now she wasn't sure how she'd done any of these things. Perhaps she didn't really know herself after all. Perhaps, somehow, Mr. Carsington knew her better.

She'd survive this, she told herself. All she had to do was stick close, not let him get killed, and this difficulty, too, would soon be behind them.

He hauled her into the first tomb they reached. The donkey balked. It pulled back abruptly, tearing the bridle from his hand. Then it stood stock still in the doorway, braying.

"Hermione, get in here," he snapped.

The donkey brayed and pawed at the ground.

"Hermione, don't make me come after you," he said.

"Oh, for heaven's sake," Daphne said. "This is an *Egyptian* donkey. *Ta'ala heneh,*" she called sharply to the agitated animal. "*Ta'ala.*"

The donkey snorted, and tossed its head.

"*Ta'ala,*" Mr. Carsington said.

The donkey trotted inside and went directly to him and nuzzled his arm.

Naturally.

"She's afraid," Mr. Carsington said, stroking the creature's muzzle. "The smell, I daresay."

It was a smell Daphne was growing accustomed to: death. Not ordinary death but mummy death, the thousands-of-years-shriveled-and-petrified smell distinctive to Egypt.

"It's better than the sandstorm," Daphne said. "Can we move further inside?" Now that she was out of immediate danger, she was trembling. "I should like to sit down. But out of reach of the wind and sand." Without waiting for him, she started down the entrance passage.

It was much wider than the typical pyramid entrance. She could make out figures on the walls and what appeared to be a block of hieroglyphs further on. It quickly grew too dark to see, though, and she moved more slowly and cautiously, keeping close to one wall, testing the way ahead with her foot, to avoid tripping over or into something.

"This is far enough, Mrs. Pembroke," his deep voice came from behind her. "We're well out of reach of the sand, and Hermione is shaking like a leaf. Let's wait out the storm in a quiet, restful manner, shall we?"

REST, YES.

Rupert needed to catch his breath, collect his wits. He might have lost her in the sandstorm. He needed a moment to calm down, that was all.

He never meant to fall asleep.

He'd seen them all settled inside: the donkey's saddle-bags and—most important—the leather water bottle, stowed safely, a space cleared in the rubble, and Mrs. Pembroke seated on a mat. Then Rupert simply leant against the wall to rest and collect himself.

The next he knew he was waking up to utter darkness.

And to heat, of course, the heat that continued to surprise him, though by now he ought to be used to it.

In England, deep inside a cave like this would be cold and damp. But not here. It was like the pyramids. One expected, going down so deep under so many thousands of tons of rock, it would be cool.

But in Egypt, the rocks and mountains stored thousands of years of hot desert sun.

Along with thousands of bodies.

Whether it had been the long-dead Egyptians troubling Hermione, or some donkey superstition, she'd settled down. He could hear her steady breathing. If anyone else in the vicinity was breathing, Hermione drowned it out.

"Mrs. Pembroke," Rupert said. He reached toward where she'd been last time, on the mat he'd dug out from his saddlebag and laid on the ground for her. The mat was there. Her cloak was there. She wasn't there.

"Mrs. Pembroke," he said, a little louder.

Nothing.

"Mrs. Pembroke."

Hermione snorted, but no human voice responded.

"Confound it." Still groggy, Rupert stood. It took him a moment to recall which way was out and which way was in. He went toward the entrance first, recalling how she'd slowed there, captivated, as you'd expect, by the pictures on the walls.

The hot wind still blew, whirling sand and bits of rock within the passageway. A dull light penetrated, but not far. It was hard to guess what time of day it was. He could see, though, that she was nowhere in the outer passage of the tomb. He turned and made his way back.

"Mrs. Pembroke," he called. Not a trace of sleep clung to him now. He was acutely, painfully awake, his heart beating fast, heavy strokes. *"Mrs. Pembroke."*

Hermione said something in donkey talk as he went by, but that was the only sound he heard apart from his boots scraping along the tomb floor.

Rupert knew he couldn't run blindly into the interior. He might easily collide with a wall or trip over something, get concussed, and then be no good to anybody. He couldn't see his hand in front of his face or the ground beneath him. The tomb floor abounded in obstacles and pitfalls: gaps and cracks, chunks of stone, animal skeletons, and other debris he preferred not to think about.

He thought only of staying upright and finding her.

Alone, in the dark, she might kill herself in a hundred different ways. She might stumble into a burial shaft, and fall a hundred feet to end up unconscious—or dead—at the bottom.

"Mrs. Pembroke!" he roared.

A sound. A voice, at last. Distant, muffled.

"Mrs. Pembroke, where the devil are you?"

"Oh, the most wonderful place," she called. "Do come see."

He stumbled on, groping along the tomb walls, endlessly it seemed. He walked into dead ends and had to grope his way back out. He felt his way along the sides of a room until he found the doorway. He edged through a long passageway.

Then at last he saw the light flickering, and the outlines of a chamber.

THE BACK WALL of the chamber had three recesses. She was in the central one. On the rear wall, an ancient Egyptian fellow followed three women carrying flowers. The man appeared again elsewhere, presiding over a lot of people and performing what looked like rituals.

Rupert took all of this in without really seeing it. His attention was on her, alive and unhurt, occupied with her ancient men and women and never thinking of him, while he'd been half-mad with fear for her.

"Candles," he said tautly. "You didn't tell me you had candles."

"In my *hezam*—my girdle," she said, leaning in to study one of the figures. "That time when we were abandoned in Chephren's pyramid taught me to carry a tinderbox and some wax candles. Is it not beautiful?"

"You didn't tell me you were leaving," he said.

She must have heard the tension in his voice because she dragged her gaze from the figure and looked at him.

"You fell asleep," she said. "I was talking to you, and you answered with a snore."

"I never snore."

She shrugged. "It must have been Hermione, then."

Rupert wished he could deny he'd fallen asleep or

blame that on the donkey, too, but there was no getting out of it gracefully: he'd collapsed with fatigue.

Well, when was the last time he'd had a proper night's sleep? And what of today, when he'd towed her and the donkey up a mountain, struggling against wind and sand and fighting to drag a morsel of air into his lungs? All the while he'd been terrified he'd lose his hold, and the monstrous wind would tear her away and the sand would bury her so deeply that he'd never find her in time.

Even Hercules had his limits, and Rupert was not a demigod. He was a mortal man who could endure only so much. He'd needed a moment, at least, of respite.

Still, he couldn't believe he'd collapsed at her side, like a weakling.

Embarrassment did not improve his mood.

"You should have woken me," he said. "You should not have set out on your own. You might have fallen into a burial shaft."

"I had a candle," she said in an I'm-talking-to-an-idiot tone that only fueled his temper. "Furthermore, the burial shafts are easy enough to distinguish. If you'd paid proper attention to the diagrams and cross sections in the *Description de l'Egypte*, you would be aware that the shafts are located in the inmost depths of the tomb and do not appear willy-nilly underfoot. Burial is an elaborate matter, and burial places are laid out according to a careful system. A shaft would be marked with an entrance, actual or symbolic, like this recess. But of course you did not give the French illustrations your full attention. They were merely a means of attracting women to your side."

He was in no mood for lectures about diagrams or his morals or anything else.

"The point is, you should have stayed with me, instead of making me fumble about this infernal place looking for you," he said.

"I was bored," she said, less patiently. "Did you think I should be content merely to sit by your side in the dark, listening to you sleep?"

"I'd think you'd consider the possibility of snakes," he

growled. "And scorpions. And pitfalls and booby traps. But you've no notion of caution. When there's a hieroglyph in the vicinity, or a god with a beast's head, you take leave of your senses. You plunge headlong into danger—"

"I?" she said indignantly. "Talk of the pot calling the kettle—"

"What should I do if you were hurt?" he exploded. "What should I do if you were killed? Do you never think of *me?* No, why should you? I'm merely a great, dumb ox. I have no feelings, so why should you consider them?"

"Feelings?" she cried. "What do you know of feelings?"

"This," he said.

In the same breath he'd closed the space between them. In the next he'd pulled her into his arms. She didn't come easily. She tried to wriggle away, but he held on. And once he'd caught her firmly, she beat at his chest.

He pulled her hard against him and kissed her.

She stopped beating his chest.

Her mouth, taut with anger at first, yielded in the next instant. And then her hands were climbing up to his chest, pushing his shirt out of the way and sliding up, her bare palms against his skin, to his shoulders. She held on tightly, as he wanted her to, as though she needed him.

She kissed him back, and he tasted hunger like his own, laced with desperation and anger.

He didn't want to feel this way. He didn't know why he did, or when it had come upon him. A moment ago, he was aware mainly of a tumult of feelings, and they were dark to him, like snakes and scorpions lurking unseen in the shadows.

She turned the world dark and bewildering, but now he didn't care. She was in his arms, and the taste of her was a strange champagne, and her curving body was made to wrap with his. The alluring incense scent of her filled his nostrils, his consciousness. He forgot about his inner turmoil and about the deadly storm outside and about the ancient dust and death inside, underfoot as well as in the air they breathed.

Her hands moved over his skin, over his shoulders and down, pushing his shirt out of the way as she went. He longed to tear it off, but he didn't want to let go of her, either. He dragged his hands down her back to her waist and down, but the girdle was in the way, a long, wide scarf, folded and twisted and filled with who knew what. It was the work of an instant to untie it. Then down it slid, its contents making a muffled clatter when it hit the stony floor.

He clasped her waist. So little it seemed in his big hands, with all that baggage gone and no padded buckram corset to thicken it. In wonderful truth, there was nothing in the way but the long, snug-fitting vest and the thin crepe shirt underneath . . . and the waist of her trousers.

He was aware of all this, of the construction of clothing, in that problem-solving place in his mind, the place where a man stored the logistics of undressing women.

He was far more aware at present, though, of the supple curves under his hand and the way she moved when his hands moved over her. She moved like a cat, lithe and sinuous and unself-consciously demanding to be petted: *yes, here. Ah, yes, there. More of this. That again. Yes.*

Her mouth left his to make heat trails over his face and down his neck. Meanwhile her hands stroked down over his chest under his shirt. There was no hesitation, no unsureness: he was hers for the taking, and she knew it. He fell back against the wall, to brace himself, because she made him weak-kneed and because he wanted everything at once: he had to have her then and there that instant, yet he didn't want to move, to do anything to interrupt the sensations coursing through him. He had no names for what he felt. He might be dying, for all he knew. The pleasure was beyond anything. Let it kill him.

She was welcome to kill him with heat and pleasure or torture him. So long as she wanted him, she could take him any way she liked. He was strong; he could bear whatever she did to him, and happily, too. But he wanted her, too, and he couldn't wait forever.

He caught the back of her head and tangled his fingers in her hair, and drew her head back and kissed her. Not gently. She didn't answer gently, either. Her tongue twined about his, and her hands slid under his shirt, kneading the muscles of his back until he groaned against her mouth.

He pushed the vest from her shoulders, shoved the tight sleeves down her arms, tugged and wrestled with it until it was off at last. He flung it down. He unfastened the ties at the top of the shirt's opening and thrust the fabric back, exposing her beautiful breasts. Then he paused, in spite of heat and need and impatience to possess.

Her bosom was golden in the candlelight, and he felt like an ancient tomb robber who'd come upon a pharaoh's treasure. He bent and kissed the silken skin and heard her first startled gasp slide into a sigh. He brushed his thumb over one tautening nipple, then brought his mouth there. She gave a little cry. Then her fingers were dragging through his hair, holding him, pressing him to her, and the quiet pause ended.

Heat and need flooded back, demolishing thought, and he was tearing off his shirt, then hers, and pulling her against him, skin to skin. It wasn't close enough, not nearly.

He grasped her buttocks, crushing her against his groin, against his swollen cock, but that would never be enough. In a moment, he'd found the knot of her trouser string, and in the next it was undone, and the trousers were sliding over her hips, down her beautiful legs. He dragged his hands over her bottom and hips, over the swell of her thighs.

Her skin was hot velvet. She trembled under his caress. He stroked upward, to the feathery triangle between her legs. So soft here, so very delicate. Again, the wild storm of need paused. He took his time, took care, caressing gently, so gently, drawing his fingers lightly over the place.

"My God," she said. *"My God."*

He nuzzled her neck. Her mouth was soft against his ear, her voice a husky whisper: "Oh, it's . . . yes. Oh, *yes.*"

He stroked more deeply, while his thumb caressed the sensitive nub. He knew what to do. He knew how to please women. But she was hot and wet, and *"Yes,"* she said.

A storm swirled into his mind, and he couldn't remember anymore what ought to be done. Mindlessly he tore at his own trousers. The fabric fell away, and his rod sprang free. He caught her under the thigh, lifting her leg up. She wrapped her leg about his waist, and he thrust into her. She cried out, "*Oh*. Oh, my God."

He would have echoed her, but he was long past words.

He was lost in her and in the need for her. Desire was a raging thing like the sandstorm. It was a juggernaut, unstoppable. He thrust again and again, and heard her cry out and felt her body shudder to climax. But it wasn't enough. More. More. More. Hard, desperate strokes, as though he could get to the beginning and end of her, have all of her.

She held nothing back, riding him with the same ferocity, vibrating with one climax after another. Finally, she grasped his face and kissed him hard, and then it rushed through him, the flood of pleasure. And with it came a strange exaltation, like the pillar of light soaring up from the Egyptian horizon at sunset. It was only in the very last instant that awareness sparked, and he pulled from her. His seed spilled against her thigh, and release came, and the quiet darkness.

DAPHNE SAGGED AGAINST him, her naked leg sliding down along his. She stayed there, waiting for her heart to stop pounding and her breathing to steady. She let her head rest upon his big chest and listened to his heart gradually slow. She held onto him, her arms circling his taut waist. She didn't want it to end quite yet, and her uncertain heart gave a flutter when she felt his chin rest upon her head. She remembered how he'd kissed the top of her head during the sandstorm, and the swell of feeling within her at those light caresses, so terribly like affection.

She didn't want to think about the surge of feeling. It was more frightening than the sandstorm. She'd left his side a little while ago because it was the only way to keep from tucking herself into his arms while he slept, and burrowing against him, and pretending he was hers and she was his.

She'd taken refuge in the scenes adorning the tomb walls. She'd wondered who the ladies were and what their flowers signified, so there wouldn't be room in her head for thinking about him and how attached she'd become to him—though she'd known from the very beginning, perhaps from the moment she'd first heard his voice, that he was made to break women's hearts.

She'd worked so hard to keep from being hurt again.

Now look what she'd done.

He stroked her head, his long fingers sliding down to her neck. "No weeping," he rumbled.

Her head came up, and she would have pulled away, but he held her there, his hand gentle but firm against the base of her neck.

"I was not weeping," she said indignantly. "I am not a weepy sort of woman. I am not emotional. I am not . . ." To her dismay, a tear spilled from her eye.

"I knew it," he said.

"I am not weeping over *you*," she said. "Or over what happened . . . just now." She lifted her chin. "Apparently, it was inevitable, the result of prolonged proximity and excessive emotional upheaval. I have heard of such things, desperate acts after a close brush with death."

"Ah," he said. "That was a desperate act?"

"Yes," she said.

"Really."

"Yes." She brushed the tear away. "It means nothing. It is a kind of—of instinct, perhaps. A primitive reaction. Quite irrational."

He wrapped his arms about her and crushed her against him. "Don't be daft," he said. "It was nothing of the kind."

It took her a moment to collect her wits. They wanted to wander: to the hard chest against which her breasts were squashed, and to the agreeable sensations accompanying being squashed in that way, and to the humid awareness of the contact further down.

Oh, his body was magnificent. Godlike. She oughtn't think such impious thoughts, but they flooded in, along with the recollections. He might as well be a god, because he'd taken her to paradise and back half a dozen times. Those hands, those wicked, clever hands . . .

And then, "It wasn't?" she said. She drew her head back to look at him. Shadows flickered over his handsome face, impossible, as always, to read. But laughter seemed to gleam in the black eyes.

"You've been in lust with me since the moment we met," he said.

"That is not at all—"

"And finally, after behaving in the most deranged manner for this last age, you did the logical, rational thing." He slid his hand down her back and over her bottom.

Her completely bare bottom.

Daphne became aware, then, of her trousers, in a heap at her ankles. One trouser leg was still tied under her knee. She ought to be mortified. She wasn't in the least. On the contrary, she felt an almost overpowering urge to giggle.

"What happened was, you finally came to your senses," he said. "At long last, after deluding yourself with every sort of puritanical poppycock, you admitted the truth: I'm irresistibly attractive."

She was about to object to this conceited pronouncement when he clapped his hand over her mouth.

"Mmmph," she said.

"Hush. I hear something."

Chapter 15

WHAT THEY HEARD WAS THE DONKEY. SHE sounded agitated, though it was hard for Rupert to be sure. Sound carried oddly in here. Small wonder that Mrs. Pembroke, with her mind in ancient Egypt, hadn't heard him calling earlier.

"Something's frightened Hermione," he said. He did not want to let go of the woman in his arms, so soft and yielding. But he could not risk the donkey breaking loose and bolting. She'd provide transport if either of them became injured or sick. She'd provide food if the situation grew desperate.

Gently he set Mrs. Pembroke aside. "I'd better see what the trouble is." He bent and collected his trousers, pulled them up, and started out, tying the waist string as he went.

"Wait, wait," she said.

He turned. She was stumbling after him, naked from the waist up, tugging up her trousers with one hand, holding the candle in the other. "Take the candle. I've another."

By Zeus but she was a magnificent specimen of womanhood, he thought regretfully as he hurried out to the hysterical Hermione.

*   *   *

DAPHNE WAS NOT far behind him. She had her *kamees* on by the time she reached the first chamber, where Hermione was making a fearful row.

"I thought it was a snake," Mr. Carsington called over the braying. "But there's nothing moving that I can make out. No snakes, scorpions, or other alarming beasties."

Daphne crouched down and moved her candle slowly to examine the floor of the chamber. "I see nothing alive, either," she said. "Bits of rock and plaster. Rusks or dried reeds or dried animal dung or . . . oh."

Mr. Carsington was crooning to the donkey. "Come now, my dear, it's all right. We're here now. You were afraid of the dark, I daresay, poor girl. We abandoned you, and you started imagining there were monsters."

"I think it's this," Daphne said. She picked up a long, pear-shaped object, slightly mangled. It was composed of a familiar brown substance.

Hermione raised loud objections and tried to back out of the tomb, dragging Mr. Carsington with her. While he struggled with the donkey, Daphne retreated to the opposite end of the chamber.

Hermione quieted somewhat, though she was still restless, still complaining.

"What the devil is it?" Mr. Carsington demanded.

"I'm not sure," Daphne said. She dripped wax onto the stony floor and set her candle onto it. Then she squatted Egyptian style, to study the object in the light. "An animal or bird of some kind. They mummified cats, you know. And hereabouts, wolves and jackals."

"Mummy," he said. His voice was cold, distant. "I should have guessed. Are you sure it isn't human?"

"Reasonably so," she said. "It's still in the wrappings, but it's too small and the wrong shape for a human, even an infant. I collect Hermione stepped on it. Or sniffed it, looking for food. She is remarkably squeamish, is she not? You'd think an Egyptian donkey would be accustomed—"

"Perhaps you could put it somewhere," Mr. Carsington

said in the same cold voice. "At a distance. Where she can't smell it."

Daphne's mind flashed a recollection: Mr. Carsington gazing at the detritus on the ground near the Pyramid of Steps at Saqqara . . . the grim expression . . . the rapid ascent of the sand slope.

"Are you squeamish, too?" she said.

"Certainly not," he said.

"Amazing," she said. "I thought you were utterly fearless."

"I am not afraid of a lump of petrified matter," he said stiffly.

"Come here," she said.

"I'm trying to keep Hermione calm," he said.

"She's calm," Daphne said. "It's far enough away not to worry her. Don't you want to look? It's very interesting. I've never seen an animal mummy before, at least not in one piece . . . more or less. It's only a bit dented."

"Hermione is not as calm as she appears," he said. "We'd better not give her an excuse to bolt. If she runs away—"

"You're afraid," Daphne said.

"Don't be ridiculous," he said.

"Then come here," she said.

He petted the donkey.

"Come here," Daphne said.

He muttered something to Hermione about "silly females."

"Mr. Carsington," Daphne said, "come here."

He stroked the donkey's head and began to whistle softly.

"Rupert," Daphne said.

At last he turned to look at her.

"*Ta'ala heneh,*" she said.

TYPICAL, RUPERT THOUGHT. *Make love to a woman, and she thinks she owns you.*

Well, maybe she did.

Rupert, she said, unprompted. She called him by his

Christian name, and they were not even making love. Yet to
his ears it sounded like lovemaking: the way she crooned his
name, the way the foreign words sounded in her mouth. His
mind conjured harems and concubines and dancing girls and
she was all of them, it seemed, all the most alluring women
in the world in one.

Oh, he was in a bad way, a sad, sad way.

He went to her. Obediently he looked down at the thing
in her hand. His mind revolted, and his gaze shifted away,
to her bosom. It was mostly exposed, since she'd neglected
to fasten the neck of the crepe shirt.

Except for the obnoxious veils, Egyptians did know the
proper way to dress a woman.

"It disgusts you?" she said.

"Certainly not," he said.

She glanced down at herself, at her barely veiled bosom
shimmering gold in the candlelight. "I meant the mummy,"
she said. She did not attempt to cover the exposed flesh.

This lack of modesty was perfectly agreeable to him.
Still, it did not make it easier to think. He tried, though he
wasn't sure why.

"Not disgusting, exactly," he said at last.

"The mummies trouble you," she said. "I remarked it
before. They trouble me, too, especially when I find them
in pieces, after someone's torn them apart, looking for
amulets and such. But they enchant me as well." With her
index finger she lightly stroked the thing in her hand. "See
how beautifully it is wrapped, how lovingly preserved."

He tried to see the beauty she spoke of, but he couldn't.
Looking at the thing was too upsetting. He turned away.

There was a silence. He could *feel* her thinking, wondering.

"I saw a mummy unwrapped in London," he said
harshly into the silence. "A great entertainment, with a lot
of aristocrats gawking and a physician presiding over the
proceedings. It was a woman, naked, the poor creature,
once they'd removed her *lovingly* prepared wrappings.
They pretended it was a scientific inquiry, but most of the
audience was there for a sensation. It was all a show to
them, as though she'd never been a living woman, once,

like their wives and sisters and mothers and daughters."
His throat tightened at the recollection. He could say no
more. He'd choke.

"I see." She set down the mummy and rose.

He looked at her, and at the thing she'd set aside. He knew
she wanted it. He'd seen the longing in her eyes, the same
expression she wore when he found her studying the pictures
on the walls. Yet she set the little mummy aside for his sake.

His heart clenched and twisted.

"It's only a bird or a cat," he said. "Somebody's pet or sacred animal. You found it. You might as well keep it. The
next person to come along will trample it accidentally or tear
it apart on purpose, looking for treasure. At least you will
treat it kindly." He bent and picked it up. The smell made
him gag. He held his breath and offered the thing to her.

Her eyebrows went up.

"Yes, yes, take it," he choked out, resisting the urge to
throw it at her.

"Are you sure?" She took it from him though, the gods
be thanked.

He retreated a pace. "Of course. Didn't I tell you I'm
easy to manage? A lively bout of lovemaking makes me
mere putty in your hands. I vow, I am overflowing with
kindness and generosity."

. . . and with something else, something different from
the sense of well-being he usually experienced. There was
an ache, a something not quite right and not quite wrong.

"But it also makes me devilish hungry," he added
quickly. "As I recall, we've bread in the saddlebags."

IT MEANT NOTHING to him, that was clear to Daphne.
He'd spoken of feelings, but desire was all he meant. He'd
satisfied a bodily appetite, no different from hunger. That
was the way he saw it. He'd said so: she was in lust with
him, and the logical response was lovemaking. For hunger,
the logical response was eating.

In other words, the passionate interlude held no more
significance for him than did the simple meal of bread and
water they ate a short time later in a corner of the first

chamber, surrounded by images of the tomb's owner and his women and long columns of hieroglyphs.

Meanwhile, Daphne's world had come crashing down about her ears. She stared blindly at the hieroglyphs wobbling in the candlelight. She felt as though she'd spent her adulthood in a kind of darkness, translating at least one part of her life into the wrong language.

"Any idea what it says?" he said.

She dragged her gaze back to him. He had not put his shirt back on. The faint light glimmered on bronzed skin and traced the outlines of his muscled torso. His eyes were dark, unreadable.

Not that she could have read them easily, even in better light. Rupert Carsington's eyes were not windows into his soul, as Virgil's eyes had been. But then Rupert Carsington seemed to keep very little hidden. His words and actions were plain and direct. His anger, too. He didn't hide it behind a veneer of gentleness and saintly patience. He spoke his mind . . . instead of trying to dismantle hers.

"You know I don't," she said. "I have explained the difficulties of decipherment to you time and again."

"Yes, but now that you've relieved the terrible lust oppressing your mind, I thought you might have a burst of insight or inspiration," he said.

"I had an insight," she said, "but not about hieroglyphs. As to the lust . . ."

"Ah, yes. Not quite relieved, I daresay."

"That was not what I—"

"The trick with lust is, you can only eradicate it with steady application," he said. "Steady, *repeated* application. So, as soon as it begins to vex you again, be sure to let me know."

"That is not what I . . ." But it was part of what was on her mind, and so she said quickly, to get it over with, "Do you find me womanly?"

"Did the sandstorm dry up your brain?" he said. "Do you think I mistook you for a man?"

"I mean, do you find me *un*womanly?"

He bent closer and peered at her face, scarlet now, she'd no doubt. "Where?" he said. "In what way?"

"Not . . . feminine. Indelicate. Too . . ." She recalled Virgil's gentle admonitions, his infuriating *patience,* and anger burnt away embarrassment. "Too boisterous," she said tightly. "In lovemaking."

"A woman—too boisterous—in *lovemaking*?" Mr. Carsington said incredulously. "There's no such thing. Where did you get that fool notion? Never mind. Don't tell me. I can guess. You shouldn't have married an elderly man."

"Virgil was four and fifty when we wed," she said. "That is not exactly Methuselah."

"How old were you?"

"Nineteen and a half," she said.

"You'd have done better with two husbands of seven and twenty," he said. "As to the late lamented, he should have married a woman closer to his own age, whose animal spirits were of a similar strength. He might have lived longer. More important, he wouldn't have needed to cover up his lack of vigor by criticizing his handsome, passionate wife."

"His . . . lack . . . of vigor," Daphne repeated. "Was that—"

"Not that there's any excuse for him," Mr. Carsington went on indignantly. "To tell such hurtful lies—and he a clergyman! I hope you made him do without for a long, long time—a fortnight at least—to teach him a lesson. By gad, that was ungentlemanly—and you shackled for life to the brute. He made you feel unwomanly—you, of all women!—when it was he who was unmanly. It makes my blood boil. Come here."

"Ungentlemanly?" she said. "Unmanly?"

"He was a small man," he said, "else he wouldn't have tried to cut you down to size."

She stared at him, trying to take it in. He said she wasn't unwomanly—he, a man of vast experience.

"I must have the truth," she said. "You must not be tactful. This is important."

"Tactful?" he echoed. "I cannot believe that a woman of your intelligence could not see what he was about. It must be obvious to the slowest of dimwits that he was jealous of your brain, because he knew his wasn't as big. He was

afraid you'd accomplish something and put him in the
shade. That's why he forbade you to study ancient Egyptian writing. Obviously he was jealous of your passion and
energy, too. You were *too much woman* for him."

"Too much woman," she repeated, savoring the words.
Not too little. Not too much like a man. Hers wasn't a
man's brain. It was simply *her* brain, that was all.

"You may have noticed you are not too much for me."
His black eyes gleamed.

"You don't mind about my brain," she said.

"I'm not afraid of your brain," he said. "Come here.
Ta'ala henen." He pulled her into his arms and kissed her.

It was not polite or gentle. It was long and bold, sinfully
deep and lascivious, and it melted her muscles, along with
the remnants of her morals. She did not even pretend to
struggle. She sank back in his arms and let her hands rove
over the powerful contours of his chest and shoulders, his
arms, his back.

She was not sure she could ever get enough of touching
him. She didn't know how she'd managed to keep her
hands off him for as long as she had. He was warm and
strong and fiercely alive . . . oh, and he was beautifully
made, on the grand scale, and perfectly proportioned. Her
hands slid down to cup his buttocks, so smooth and taut,
and he groaned against her mouth, then drew away.

She opened her eyes, dismayed. She'd been too bold, disgusted him. But no, he'd told her she couldn't be too bold.

"I meant to please you before," he said. Growled.

"You did," she said. She'd never been so pleased in her
life. She'd never guessed it was possible to be so pleased—
and the word was grossly inadequate.

"But I was in a hurry," he said, "after waiting so confounded long for you to come to your senses."

"I was perfectly satisfied," she said. She'd thought she'd
die of pleasure and happiness. She'd thought she'd burst
from it, from the feelings, so immense.

"What do you know?" he said. "Your previous lover was
an *old man.*" He kissed the special place behind her ear. He
kissed her neck, the base of her throat.

She didn't argue. What did she know? Nothing, apparently, when it came to lovemaking.

This man did, though. He was writing mysterious messages in kisses upon her skin, along her collarbone and down, across her breasts, and down. He eased her out of his arms and onto the mat. Her clothing slid away from her body, and his mouth was there instead, the lightest of brushes, writing kisses over her skin.

His lips told a long and complicated tale upon her belly, and then the kisses moved lower, and his fingers were there, too, tracing the contours of the most secret of her places. It made an ache in the pit of her belly to be explored and known so, a sweet, killing ache.

She tangled her fingers in his hair because she must touch him, do something. The ache was everywhere, beating in her heart and making a strange current in her veins and thrumming over her skin. Oh, and there . . . the tiny flesh-bud, wicked thing . . . his thumb teasing . . . and then he took her in his mouth.

Oh, no, you mustn't. It's . . . indecent . . . lewd. Wrong, surely. We'll be damned for all eternity. . . . I don't care. Let me be damned. Don't stop. Don't ever stop.

Pleasure, almost unbearable, swept through her, wave upon wave of a dark joy. Again and again she trembled on the brink of ecstasy; again and again he carried her over. Until she could bear no more, not alone. She curled up, grasped his shoulders. "In me," she gasped. "Be *in* me."

He came up onto his knees. She dragged her hands over his chest, down over his taut belly, and down to his virile member, immensely erect and hot to the touch. She stroked it, longingly, lovingly, and he gave a strangled laugh. "Ah, well, then, don't be so shy," he said. He set his big hand on her chest and pushed her down, and remained so for a moment, looking at her.

She gazed up at him, and for that moment, in the darkness with its faint, flickering candlelight, it seemed she'd entered the underworld and this was no mere mortal who straddled her but a demigod.

He smiled and moved into her, so slowly, so deliberately. Ah, but deep, deep, where she needed him.

"Like this?" he said. "In you like this?"

"Yes," she said. She moved, taking him in deeper still. "And like this."

He moved inside her slowly this time, as though they had all eternity. Slowly she moved with him, relishing the heat and the rolling swell of pleasure. She was his and he hers for this time. She was in no hurry to reach the ending and the separation that must follow.

He bent and kissed the top of her cheekbone, so tenderly she thought her heart would break. But her heart beat on, harder and faster. The slow pleasure swelled into pulsing need, and then she was lost again in the storm. But now he was with her, and the tempest was rich and wild and wondrous. She plunged into it with him in the same way she'd plunged with him into pyramids, into danger. The world lit up in showers of gold, and it spilled through her and around her, a happiness like a glimpse of a perfect hereafter. He gave a low cry, and shuddered once, and a liquid heat filled her.

The storm slid away, and he sank down upon her, and she sank, too, into a welcoming quiet and peace.

THE INSTANT HE returned to himself, Rupert knew what he'd done.

This made twice he'd behaved like an adolescent with his first lover.

The first time, he'd made a great hurry of the business, as though it was the only and last chance he'd ever have and death was coming in the next breath.

The second time, he'd managed the bare essentials of pleasuring her, only to forget himself at the crucial moment.

He'd not only fallen on top of her, great clumsy oaf that he was—and she lying on a thin mat, on a stony floor—but he'd spilled his seed *inside her*.

Idiot, idiot. Great dumb ox.

What if—

Never mind. Worrying accomplished nothing.

He lifted himself off her and scooped her into his arms. He slid up to a sitting position and arranged her upon his lap. She laid her head upon his shoulder, and he felt her breath on his skin. He stroked her hair, glistening ruby and garnet in the candlelight. His gaze wandered lower, and he saw ruby and garnet there as well.

He smiled, forgetting his grievance with himself for the moment. That part had surprised her.

She was a woman of experience, yes, but not very much experience and that little not very good.

The thought restored his humor. It was like having all the benefits of a virgin without any of the drawbacks, he told himself.

And as to his mistake—well, the damage was done and couldn't be undone. He could only take care of her. This he was well-equipped to do. He relaxed, leant back against the wall, and promptly fell asleep.

"WAKE UP! WAKE up!"

A frantic whisper in the darkness. Someone shoving at him.

Rupert quickly shook off sleep. "What?" he said. "What?"

"Someone's out there and I—Hush!"

Rupert listened.

Voices. Men's voices. Their guards? He rose and started pulling on his clothes.

"There are a number of them," she whispered. "I went out to check on Hermione, because she was complaining again. I heard them outside. I don't know if they heard her. But I know they're looking for us."

"Well, it's about time somebody—"

Her hand clamped over his mouth. "I heard them because they were arguing—about whether to kill you or hold you for ransom. We have to hide."

Rupert pulled her hand away. He hurriedly wrapped the sash round his waist, found his pistol, and shoved it into the sash. "We can't hide," he said. "For one—"

"Don't talk, just listen," she said. "That rumble you think is a whisper carries." She pushed him. "Back. The inmost chamber."

He didn't know where "back" was. Either the candle had burnt out or she'd wisely extinguished it. The darkness was impenetrable. But she grabbed his hand and led, and she seemed to know what she was about.

It didn't take as long this time to get to the end.

The dead end.

"We're going to be trapped," he muttered. "Which is what I was trying to tell you. Unless you've discovered a secret passage."

"Not exactly," she said.

"Then what?" He felt the walls and found a recess.

Then he remembered: the French diagrams she'd lectured about earlier. *A shaft would be marked with an entrance, actual or symbolic, like this recess.*

She tugged on his arm. "Not the center recess. This way."

"We're going to hide in a burial shaft," he said. "That's your cunning plan."

"There's no other way out," she said. "I explored the entire chamber earlier, because I'd read that some of the Theban tombs are labyrinths. This isn't."

While she spoke, she was pulling him to the left. "Hurry," she said.

Rupert could hear the voices now, distorted, seemingly distant. But he knew they were not very far away. This was not like the interior of a pyramid. With torches or lanterns, the men would be here in minutes.

He wanted to stand and fight, and he would have done, if he'd had some idea of the odds. But there was no way of knowing how many men there were, or how dispersed. Three might come inside while another ten or twenty waited outside. And if they killed him, what would become of her?

"You'd better let me go first," he said, though reason rebelled at the prospect: a narrow burial shaft, a small space at the bottom with room for a coffin and not much else, most likely. Anyone who wished them dead would have no difficulty arranging it.

"No, let me," she said. "I know where it is. Oh, do hurry. I can hear them. Get down. It's safer to crawl. Someone's excavated . . . ah, here it is. Can you feel it?"

She caught his hand and curved it over the edge of an opening. "There," she said. "It's clear to the bottom. I checked earlier."

"I'm going first," he said.

THE SHAFT WAS steeply angled. Rupert went down backward, and half slid to the bottom. She followed closely, using the same method. The sepulchral chamber was surprisingly large. But the floor was covered with rubble, and a disagreeably familiar smell signaled ancient dead in the vicinity.

He'd no time to dwell on the dead, though. Mrs. Pembroke had hardly reached the bottom when he heard the voices. He pulled her back, well out of range of the shaft.

A light shone where they'd been standing a moment before, and voices called down in Arabic.

Rupert loaded his pistol.

A new voice spoke, in French with a thick accent this time. There was nothing to fear, the voice said. He and his friends had come to rescue the English lady and gentleman. Since sunset, when the wind died down, everyone in Asyut had been looking for them.

Rupert touched Mrs. Pembroke's lips, signaling silence, and by cautious inches drew her farther away from the shaft—until they came up against a corner of wall.

Nowhere else to go.

He moved to stand in front of her.

No sound for the longest time but his breathing and hers. The others, above, were listening, too, no doubt, for signs of life. But they must come a good deal closer to hear any.

At last someone spoke. Then someone else. They seemed to be arguing. Rupert caught the words: *Ingleezi, jinn,* and *afreet.*

Were they talking about him?

Tom had used tall tales about Rupert's supposed magical powers to persuade Minya's *kashef* to cooperate. The boy had greatly embellished various incidents that had occurred during the journey upriver, citing these as "evidence" of his master's close personal relationship with supernatural powers. Apparently, Rupert possessed as well a fearsome skill in administering "the eye"—the calling down of curses and calamities upon those who gave offense.

On the other hand, the men might merely be continuing the argument about whether to shoot him or cut off his head, or debating whether to sell the English lady into slavery or rape and kill her. They'd mentioned demons only because such beings were known to haunt burial chambers.

He turned and put his mouth close to Mrs. Pembroke's ear. "What are they saying?"

"The tomb is haunted," she whispered. "Why climb down when the demons or hunger will soon drive us out? says one school of thought. The other fears we'll find a way out. They seem—" She broke off because the row above them had ceased.

Rupert heard movement at the top of the shaft, a rustling and scraping. Someone had decided to risk demons, evidently. He cocked his pistol.

Even before he emerged into the chamber, the man was easy to see. He had a torch in his hand as well as being lit by the torches or lanterns above, but he hadn't yet spotted Rupert and Mrs. Pembroke in the shadows. From the sounds of it, another fellow was close behind him.

Rupert took aim.

Then something flew past him, and the man crumpled to the floor.

Mrs. Pembroke pressed a hard, irregular object against Rupert's side. A chunk of rubble.

She said nothing, but Rupert understood. He bent and picked up several chunks of rubble from the floor. When the villain's associate started into the chamber, Rupert threw as hard as he could. The man fell.

Someone called down.

While those above called to their unconscious comrades, Rupert hurried to one of the bodies, grabbed the feet, and dragged him deeper into the tomb. Mrs. Pembroke did the same without being told.

By gad, she was a wonderful female.

Rocks instead of firearms. Near-silent destruction.

Much more effective than shooting pistols—balls ricocheting off stone walls—and very possibly bringing the entire crumbling structure down upon their heads.

Those from above would hear at most the clatter of rocks—which could be falling rubble. They couldn't be sure what was below: their prey or hungry ghouls.

Now several voices called for Amin and Omar.

Under the noise, Rupert said, "If they come to—"

"Help me get these two into the sarcophagus," she whispered.

"The sarc—What?"

"I can't kill a man in cold blood," she said. "We've nothing strong enough to tie them with. It's right here. The lid's broken."

The men's torches lay where they'd dropped them, one still burning feebly. It illuminated very little. At first Rupert couldn't discern the sarcophagus. But she'd already started dragging one of the inert men. Rupert did likewise, guided by the sound of her panting.

Getting the men into the coffin was easy enough. Keeping them in was another matter. Rupert heaved a few pieces of the broken lid on top. That at least would slow them down.

He doubted they'd be considerate enough to remain unconscious until their friends gave up and went away.

He doubted the friends would give up and go away.

Maybe it was wiser to simply kill this pair now and improve the odds. A knife would do it quietly enough.

Rupert's entire being recoiled. He'd never yet killed anybody, and like her, found the notion of doing so in cold blood abhorrent.

Then she said, "I was wrong."

He looked toward the sound of her voice. He could barely make out her shape against the surrounding darkness.

"Behind the coffin," she said. "There's a hole."

Chapter 16

THE PASSAGE WAS SMALLER AND MORE IRREGU-
lar than the shaft to the burial chamber. At some points Rupert had to crawl on his belly. It was also a great deal
longer.

At one point during the interminable journey, he called
a halt for rest. "Are you all right?" he said.

"Don't waste breath being solicitous," she said crossly.
"We haven't enough air as it is. And I don't need to rest.
Can you not go faster?"

"Mrs. Pem—Dash it, I don't even know your given
name."

"Daphne," she said.

"Daphne," he repeated. "That's lovely."

"Ye gods, what does it matter? Will you please *move?*"

"You need to rest," he said. "You sound short of breath."

"I want to get out," she said. *"Now."*

It was then he remembered her morbid aversion to
closed spaces. He started crawling again, this time as fast
as he could. She was probably near hysteria, with good
reason. The tunnel was hot, and what air it held was stale
and foul. He wanted to be out of it, too.

He crawled on, hoping for fresh air at the end, if not

light. Above all, he hoped they hadn't leapt out of the pan into the fire.

AT THE TOP of the burial shaft, Khareef discovered that brandy did not always give men courage. None of the others was willing to follow Omar and Amin down the shaft.

It was too quiet down there, they said. Something bad was down there.

"This place is evil," said one coward. "The donkey is possessed."

A distance behind them, near the mouth of the tomb, the foreigners' donkey continued its wild braying.

"We made too much noise," said another. "The English heard us coming and ran away."

"Where can they go?" Khareef said. "There is but one way in and one way out."

"What about the thieves' hole?" another asked.

Khareef laughed. "If they've found it, they won't get far. It's falling in. They'll have to turn back."

"Perhaps it will fall on their heads."

"Then they will die."

"Duval will not be pleased."

"The woman was not to be harmed."

Khareef, like the others, was drunk. The mention of Duval sobered him. The woman was to be Duval's hostage. For what purpose Khareef neither knew nor cared.

He did know and care what would happen to him if he bungled this assignment.

He grabbed a torch from one of the men and started down the shaft.

The others squatted at the mouth of the shaft and waited.

After a moment, Khareef's voice wafted up, filling the air with curses. "Come down, you cowards," he called. "Come down and help your brothers."

One by one, the men began crawling down the shaft.

They found Khareef bending over a stone coffin. "See what the swine of an Englishman has done," he said.

It took two men to move the broken pieces of lid enough to get their battered and terrified friends out.

"Why didn't you call for help?" Khareef demanded. "These old women thought a ghoul had eaten you."

"Englishman," Omar gasped. "Demon. Rocks." He clutched his bloodied head.

"The woman," Amin said. "Fearless and fierce like a lion."

"She is only a woman," Khareef said scornfully. "She threw rocks at you, as naughty boys do. The man is only a man. But you will all see, when they come out of this hole." With his pistol he pointed at the thieves' tunnel.

He leant against the sarcophagus and waited.

DAPHNE WAS NOT fearless.

She was, in fact, on the brink of babbling in terror.

She'd not altogether willingly or happily traversed pyramid and tomb shafts. Those, however, were spacious promenades compared to this roughly hewn tunnel. She doubted it was part of a tomb complex. It was more likely the work of robbers.

They'd certainly done a great deal of work, because it seemed longer than any of the endless passages in the Pyramid of Steps at Saqqara.

But perhaps it seemed longer than it was. She had no idea how far they'd gone when Mr. Carsington stopped again abruptly. She had an unhappy suspicion why he'd stopped.

In the course of the last few yards, bits of debris and dirt had been falling on her head. Now the floor of the tunnel was rough with rubble.

"Is it bad?" she said.

"It isn't good," he said. "The way is blocked."

Judging by the sounds, he was shifting rocks.

"Looking on the bright side, it's loose," he said.

Bright side, indeed. The thing could cave in, burying them alive.

"On the other hand," he went on, "I can't tell how far the blockage extends."

If she had to go back the whole long, suffocating way she'd come, she'd go mad.

"The ancients dug into rock using primitive tools," she

said. "Surely we can make a way through loose rubble, using our hands and our knives?"

"We can try," he said. "But it could take a very long time, and it might be more densely packed farther on. Are you sure you don't want to turn back?"

"I have the greatest confidence that they'll be waiting for us," she said.

They would kill him. *Kill the man first,* one of the men had said. *Once he is dead, she will give us no trouble.*

But others said the Englishman was more valuable alive: they could hold him for ransom or make him into a eunuch and sell him as a slave. Someone brought up the difficulties of finding a suitable buyer; another pointed out how much easier it was to dispose of a corpse than to conceal a large, ferocious Englishman. And so on.

They had haggled about Mr. Carsington's life as they might have haggled over the price of a pipe bowl.

She would not let him fall into their hands.

"If I squeeze up alongside you," she said, "I can help move the debris out of the way. We've a better chance using two pairs of hands."

And if they were buried alive, she'd be close to him at the end at least.

"Say no more, m'dear," he said. "You had me convinced the instant you suggested squeezing your magnificent body alongside mine."

"You're impossible," she said. "I'm filthy. And I smell."

"Me, too," he said cheerfully. "Yet you offered anyway. I can't decide whether you're desperately brave or desperately infatuated. Perhaps both."

She squeezed up, forcing him to draw aside. "When we get out of this, if we get out of this, I shall box your ears," she said.

"We'll get out of it," he said.

"Stop talking," she said. "Start digging."

RUPERT STOPPED THINKING, too, and started pulling rocks out of the way. As in the tomb they'd escaped, the debris was mostly chunks of rubble. It might have been far worse, he told himself. The collapse must have happened fairly recently. It was not packed down. It wasn't sand. As soon as he shifted some of the rubble out of the way, he saw the tunnel was of wider dimensions here than previously. They must be near the end.

He said nothing of his hopes, though, but worked silently and steadily with her, hip to hip, he tackling one side, she the other. His mind worked, too, reviewing these last hours, this day that seemed to compass a lifetime: the sandstorm, his fear and rage about her, the lovemaking—ah, that was well worth remembering—her passion, her courage.

Daphne.

It was one of those Greek names. A goddess? A nymph?

"Which one was Daphne?" he said.

She paused in her work. He felt rather than saw her rub her face. "Which one what?" she said.

"In the Greek myths. Which one was she?"

"The daughter of the river god. She's the one who turned into a laurel tree to escape Apollo."

"Ah, yes, now I remember. Those Greek females were always doing that sort of thing. Turning into trees, flowers, echoes. Excessive, I always thought. What's wrong with 'I have a headache'? And what sort of missish creature runs away from Apollo, anyway? Wasn't he one of the good-looking ones?"

"I always thought she was a fool," Daphne muttered. "Apollo, of all gods. But there's no rhyme or reason to those myths. You have one woman accepting the attentions of a swan, another of a bull. On the other hand, there's . . . Mr. Carsington, what's that smell?"

"I was Rupert before," he complained. "Why am I Mr. Carsington now? Is it my fault our escape route's caved in? In any case, if I smell worse than before, it's on account of the digging and the fact that this place must be close to ninety degr—" Then he caught it: the distinctive odor of long-dead Egyptian.

It was very strong, stronger than anything he'd encountered before.

He dragged away stones faster now, despite the revulsion and dread.

The smell grew stronger still.

But the way was clear. He reached ahead, into emptiness. He set his hand down. Something cracked under it.

"I think we're at the end," he said.

He felt her move beside him, advancing into the space ahead.

"It definitely smells like a tomb," she said.

"I don't suppose you have any candle left," he said. "The floor seems to be . . . rather crowded."

He heard rustling. "I've a stub in my girdle," she said. "But I can't find my tinderbox."

He found his, and after several failures succeeded in lighting the bit of candle.

It did not produce much light. There was enough, though, to show him they'd entered a sepulchral chamber whose floor was covered with broken mummies.

HE MADE DAPHNE keep the candle lit until they'd found the opening to the shaft.

He didn't want to step on the mummies, he said.

They were hard *not* to step on. The sepulchral chamber had housed a large family. They'd been torn apart, limbs and skulls strewn about the floor. The search for treasure must have occurred fairly recently, Daphne guessed. Either that or someone else had tramped through here not long ago, because mummy dust still hung in the air. It clogged the nostrils and scratched the eyes.

But rock dust already coated her nose and eyes, providing a degree of insulation from the mummies' emanations.

At any rate, they didn't linger.

Thanks to recent excavations and plundering, the way out was clear, and it was a short way out. This tomb wasn't as deep as the one they'd left. Once they were away from dismembered mummies and well clear of the shaft, they put out the candle.

Moonlight showed the entrance not many yards distant. They hurried that way, past crudely hewn walls bare of decoration.

At the entrance they paused.

In Egypt the moon seemed to cast a deeper, more illuminating glow than it did in England. They looked out.

They had come out on the part of the mountain overlooking Asyut. The town stood in the middle of the fertile plain, its minarets snow-white in the moonlight. From it an earthen dike, built to contain the annual inundation, wound its way to the Nile, whose own windings were plainly visible over a great distance.

Clearly visible, too, was the little village of El-Hamra, the port of Asyut, crowded with boats. Among these it was impossible to distinguish the *Isis*.

The *dahabeeya* wasn't the first concern at the moment, though. Getting to the harbor alive was.

"Shall we chance going through the town?" she said. "If we go around, that could take hours."

"If all the gates are locked, we won't have a choice," he said. "But I'd rather try the town first. It's late, and most people will be indoors. With luck, we'll get through without attracting attention."

"Those men," she said. "They might have found the tunnel. Or maybe they know where it comes out."

"Then we'd better move quickly," he said.

NO ONE STOPPED them at the southwest gate. The gatekeeper appeared to be asleep, like the rest of the town. The men who wanted Mr. Carsington dead failed to appear. Daphne and he nearly made it through the place with no trouble. But as they approached the main gate, the one nearest the river, a Turkish soldier accosted them.

Luckily, it was only one, and he was drunk. When he started making difficulties, Daphne "accidentally" lost her grip on her veil. It fell away to reveal her almost fully exposed bosom. While the soldier gawked, Mr. Carsington withdrew his pistol from his girdle and struck the man in the back of the head. With a low groan, the soldier went down. She helped drag him into the nearest alley.

Then, "Run," Mr. Carsington said.

They ran.

They arrived, gasping for breath, at the main gate.

It was locked.

"This," Mr. Carsington said, "is the last straw."

He woke up the sleeping gatekeeper and demanded to be let out. The gatekeeper yawned and grumbled at him to go away.

Daphne tried making the request in Arabic.

The gatekeeper waved her away. They must stop their noise, he said. The gate would be opened at the proper time and not before. If they made trouble, they would go to the guardhouse.

Then from the shadows of the wall, a young, sleepy voice piped up. "Master?"

"Tom?" Mr. Carsington said.

The boy came running. "Oh, sir, oh, sir." He fell to the ground and commenced hugging his idol's knees. "I knew you were not dead." He jumped up. "Oh, lady, I rejoice to see you. The *jinn* of the sandstorm did not take you away."

Daphne grabbed the boy and hugged him. "And you are safe as well," she said in his tongue. "My heart is glad. And Yusef?"

"We hid in the big tomb, the one they call the Stable of Antar. When the sandstorm ended, we looked for you, all the day and into the night."

He turned to the gatekeeper. "Behold, here is the master and his *hareem*. I told you they would come. The sandstorm tried to eat them, but the master is powerful, and made the *jinn* spit them out. But he is angry at this place, because it holds evil men who wish him ill. Let him go away with his *hareem*, and let none out after him, until the proper time. I beg you to do this thing, before he casts the eye upon you."

The warning alone might not have had the desired effect, but the coins Tom held out did.

The gate opened as little as possible, and closed the instant they were out.

As they were hurrying down to the harbor, Daphne heard angry shouts.

The gate remained closed.

They reached the boat and found the crew awake. They

quickly hushed the cries of joy and thanksgiving. Minutes after they were aboard, the *Isis* slipped out of the harbor.

THEY'D HARDLY STEPPED upon the deck when the women came and bore Daphne away to her cabin.

Rupert had only the dimmest recollection of what happened thereafter. He bathed—or someone bathed him. He ate—or someone fed him. He wasn't at all sure. Once he'd got her safely aboard the boat, a profound weariness set in, and he went through the motions of bathing and eating like a sleepwalker. He did not remember returning to his cabin or falling asleep.

He remembered the dream, though.

He stood at the bottom of the mountain, at the cemetery, watching a hawk soar overhead. Then he saw her at the entrance to a large tomb. He called to her, but she appeared not to hear him. She entered the tomb. He hurried up after her and inside. He heard her voice coming from the depths of the tomb. He followed the sound, but it never grew any closer. He came to the sepulchral chamber and, heart pounding, went to the sarcophagus. It was open. He looked in. Empty.

He heard weeping and followed the sound, but again it was some cruel trick. No one. Nothing. Not even a mummy fragment. Only a dark, endless emptiness. Then from a distance came a mournful cry.

He woke to heat and bright sunlight streaming through the slits of the window shutters. From outside came the wailing that he recognized as Egyptian music. The sailors were singing, one of their number accompanying on the pipes and another on the earthen drum.

He sat up and looked about the cabin. His gaze met Tom's. The boy, who'd been squatting patiently by the door, now rose and brought the water ewer, bowl, and towel.

Rupert washed.

"Will you shave, sir?" Tom asked.

Rupert felt his face and grimaced. He hoped this was

overnight growth. He hoped he hadn't scraped Daphne's delicate skin with these deadly bristles.

Daphne, he thought. Her name was Daphne. It made him smile; he didn't know why.

"Sir?"

"Yes, yes. *Eywa.*"

He shaved and thought about her body, and the way she moved under his hands, and the way she tasted. He remembered her running after him, naked from the waist up, holding her billowing trousers up with one hand.

Unself-conscious, uninhibited, passionate . . .

. . . and now, he abruptly realized, out of reach.

They were no longer cut off from the world.

They occupied a large boat, but a precious small world. No one knew what had happened in the tomb above Asyut. But everyone would know everything that happened aboard the *Isis.*

Oh, this was not good, not good at all.

He'd never been good at resisting temptation. He was accustomed to doing as he pleased—within bounds, of course, albeit fairly wide ones. His father's tolerance had its limits, and Rupert was not fool enough to overstep them. He was not afraid of his father. Rupert was not afraid of snakes, either. That didn't mean he'd thrust his hand deliberately into a viper's nest.

Furthermore, even Rupert wouldn't dream of blackening a lady's reputation. This was far out of the bounds of gentlemanly behavior.

England was a world away, true. But it was not out of reach of letters. English travelers would pass on scandalous tidbits to their friends and family quite as enthusiastically here as at home. He would have to be discreet. He would have to keep away from her until . . .

Gad, who knew how long?

He told himself not to think about it. He had no solution, and fretting would only make him disagreeable company. He finished shaving. He dressed.

"I bring coffee now?" Tom said.

"Yes. No. I'll have it in the front cabin. Is the mistress awake?"

"Awake, yes," the boy said. After a pause he added, "Not good. Sick, sir. They showed the door to my face." He put his hand in front of his face.

Only then did Rupert notice how quiet the lad had been. Normally, Tom jabbered away at a ferocious rate in a bewildering mixture of Arabic and English. Belatedly, the words sank in.

"Sick?" Rupert repeated, his heart racing.

Yes, very sick. The women chased Tom away from the door because he made too much noise with crying. But he couldn't help it. The enraged *jinn* of the sandstorm had struck the mistress's heart because she escaped from him. She was a very good mistress, Tom said, a good mother to him. She would never allow him to be beaten, even when he broke things. She took care of him when he was sick. She brought back his uncle Akmed from the dead. The boy commenced bawling.

"Stop that row," Rupert snapped. "She isn't dying." All the same, he hurried from the cabin and down the cramped passage to the stern cabin. He tapped on the door.

Leena opened it a crack. "My mistress cannot come to amuse you," she whispered. "She is too sick."

"What is it?" he said. "What's wrong? She was well yesterday. Why didn't anyone wake me?"

"She does not wish to see you," Leena said. She started to close the door.

Rupert pulled it open.

Daphne lay curled up on the divan. Her face was taut and bone-white with pain.

His chest hurt as though he'd been running for miles.

"What is it?" Rupert said softly. "A bilious fever?" Had she caught it from the baby, after all? But he knew what to do. She'd told him. A cool bath. A decoction of . . . of what?

"Go away," she said. Her voice was taut as well.

He knelt beside the divan and laid his hand over her forehead. It was damp but not feverish.

"Go away," she said.

"You have to tell me what's wrong," he said. "Tom's bawling his head off. The instant the crew stop singing, they'll hear him, and everyone will be weeping and wailing."

He leant closer, dropping his voice still lower. "Daphne, you know how emotional these people are. They all love you because you mend their broken thumbs and sun-baked brains and bring their dying children back to life. You must not let us—them—imagine the worst. What's wrong? Tell me how I can help you."

"You can't help me." She turned a little to look at him. She winced. He winced, too, in sympathy.

"It's all right," she said. "I'm not dying. You've nothing to worry about. Really. *Nothing.*"

"But you're not well. Even a great, dumb ox can see that. Shall I make you some hot, strong tea? Or is there something you need from your medicine box? A decoction of—of something."

She turned more fully toward him then and managed a wan smile. "All I need is time," she said. "It's my monthly courses."

He sat back on his heels. "Oh."

"Perfectly normal," she said. "The pain is rather more unpleasant than usual, but it won't kill me. There's nothing one can do but wait for it to be over."

Nothing to worry about. He hadn't impregnated her. He was relieved, yes, of course he was. He needn't think about . . . complications. It was a female problem, not his fault and none of his business. The women would look after her. He should go away, let her have her privacy.

He did not like to leave her alone, suffering, even if it wasn't his fault and the only cure was time.

"For such a clever woman, you are woefully ignorant," he said. "There's a great deal one can do."

He had no idea what one could do. He had no sisters, and even if he had, they would have kept this secret from him as every other woman did. Even his mistresses had used a code phrase to signal that the time was not convenient. They had certainly not expected him to nurse them. He had not realized, in fact, that women were in need of nursing at such times. He'd never seen one laid so low on such an account.

To see her laid low—she, so bold and brave and brilliant . . .

It was very disturbing.

"What you need is . . . um . . . a cool cloth on your head," he improvised. "And your back rubbed. And I do not understand why you lie there suffering pain when you have a full stock of laudanum in your medicine box."

"It is for *acute* pain, for emergencies," she said. "It is ridiculous to take laudanum for a perfectly natural monthly event."

"If you cannot get up from bed, if you lie there clutching your belly and curled up like a baby, I reckon the pain qualifies as acute," he said. "And this isn't a perfectly natural monthly event. Consider what happened in Asyut. You were not only dragged through a sandstorm and up a mountain, but you had to dig your way out of a caved-in robbers' tunnel. Among other things." He gave her one of his impudent grins, though he was not feeling at all impudent.

He felt all at sea.

"When I am well again," she said, "I shall box your ears. In the meantime—" She winced. "Perhaps I will take a drop of laudanum. But only a drop. Now go away."

He didn't go away. He mixed the laudanum with honey and water and watched her drink it. He wet the cloths and wrung them out and laid them on her forehead. He rubbed her back. He distracted her with humorous family anecdotes. He did not leave until she fell asleep.

MILES'S CAMEL JOURNEY ended at Dendera, at the Temple of Hathor.

He'd heard of the place. He'd seen pictures in the *Description de l'Egypte*. He'd read travelers' tales. Daphne had talked about it as well. But as he and his captors entered the sand- and rubbish-filled space that constituted its courtyard, he was interested mainly in the shade it would offer deep within.

After nine days' journey across the desert on a hostile camel, after the sandstorms' repeated batterings, he only wanted to lie down and die someplace out of the sun and the hot, gritty wind.

The men led him inside, and he stumbled wearily along

with them. Now and again he glanced up at the massive columns. Daphne would be thrilled, he thought. The place was covered with hieroglyphs.

He wondered what she'd think of the famous Hathor, the Egyptian counterpart of Aphrodite. Miles found her singularly unattractive. She had a low forehead, close-set eyes, and wide, fat cheeks. Cow's ears stuck out from the sides of her head like jug handles. She looked more like a gargoyle than a goddess, he thought. But then, not being in the best of humors, he mightn't be able to appreciate her properly.

The men took him through a great vestibule, through a door into a smaller hall—though it was still immense— along whose sides he perceived narrow openings into dark chambers. His escort never paused. They led him on, straight ahead through more chambers, and at last into a narrow, enclosed, and profoundly dark space. Even the candles could illuminate no more than the lower portions of the relief-covered walls.

They had no difficulty illuminating the man within, however.

"Noxley?" Miles said, half-disbelieving what his eyes told him.

Lord Noxley came forward and clasped his hand. "My dear fellow, how relieved I am to see you!"

"Not half as relieved as I am to see you," Miles said. "Not to mention happily surprised. I had hoped my sister would go to you once she realized something had gone amiss with me, but I'd little hope of seeing you so soon."

"It was a near thing," Noxley said, releasing his surprisingly strong grip. "The consulate was inclined, as always, to drag its feet. But Mrs. Pembroke took matters into her own hands. As a result, I was able to set out after you not three days after you were captured. But we can talk at length later, when you have rested."

He addressed Ghazi. "Have you anything else for me?"

"Soon," Ghazi said. "A few days."

"Duval is not here," said Noxley. "None of his people are here."

Ghazi smiled. "Perhaps they heard it was not safe."

"We'll need to find him," said Noxley. "But the other thing first."

"The other thing first, yes," Ghazi said. "Unless you require me, I set out now."

"That would be best," said Noxley. He withdrew a small bag from his coat and gave it to Ghazi. The bag chinked.

The man took it with thanks, bade them farewell with his usual suave courtesy, and departed, taking his associates with him.

"You're shocked, I daresay, at my choice of employees," Noxley said. "In England that man would be a common criminal."

"Not at all common," Miles said. "His manners are beautiful, and he has a charming way of offering to kill innocent bystanders if one doesn't cooperate."

"Alas, without men like Ghazi, one can get nothing done in this barbaric place," Noxley said. "When in Rome, you know." He smiled disarmingly. "I could never have found you so quickly without those fellows' help."

"It's not their fault we didn't arrive sooner," Miles said. "We've been nine days coming from Minya, thanks to the sandstorms."

"Wretched for you, I don't doubt," Noxley said. "But otherwise you should have arrived here days ahead of me. The winds slowed those of us on the river as well."

He led the way out of the narrow chamber. "By gad, I am happy to see you," he said, lowering his voice. "This has turned out to be a nasty business, indeed. The curst French . . ." He paused and looked about the dark temple. "They are taking away the zodiac ceiling, the swine. The pasha has given leave, you see. They will carry it to Paris—and I can do nothing until this other wretched business is settled." He shook his head. "But never mind the French. You've had a filthy time of it in the desert. You're longing for a bath, I daresay, and clean clothes and proper food. And I—if I stay here much longer, I shall be tempted to do murder."

Chapter 17

THOUGH DAPHNE TOOK THE LAUDANUM IN small doses, it helped a great deal. She was grateful indeed to Mr. Carsington for insisting, as she told him at the first opportunity.

Privately, she marveled at his taking the trouble over her monthly misery. But then, he was a marvel to her. For the two days she spent in bed, she thought about him, and all the ways in which he surprised her.

Though the drug made her mind rather foggy, this much was clear: He was not at all the lout she'd first supposed him. Instead, he made other men seem loutish, especially Virgil. Her late husband had made her feel defective, even monstrous at times. He'd left her with a great fortune and very little self-confidence.

In the weeks she'd spent with Rupert Carsington, her confidence had steadily grown. That day and evening in Asyut, she'd lived through the fear and danger and passion and one trial of endurance after another. And never before had she felt so alive.

Despite the fogginess, she was well aware of his large, capable hands laying the cool, wet cloths on her forehead or gently rubbing her back. She was aware of his deep voice, tinged with laughter now and again as he told an amusing story.

She was also aware that, like laudanum, he could easily become a dangerous habit.

By the morning of the third day the violent spasms of pain had faded to an occasional twinge. She was able to sit up and take note of the world about her and puzzle over how sick she'd been. It could not have been her menses alone, she decided. It always made her tired and cross, and was often painful, but never so much as this. Never before had it so completely incapacitated her.

But then, her life had never been so tumultuous before.

She decided that dyspepsia or some other stomach ailment had aggravated matters.

Whatever it was seemed to be gone because she woke with an appetite. It was Nafisah who brought the ewer and basin as soon as Daphne was sitting up.

"You feel better," Nafisah said, smiling. "I see it in your face."

"Much better," Daphne said. After washing, she noticed the baby was nowhere about. "Where is Sabah?"

"In the front room with the master and the boy Tom," Nafisah said.

"His name is Udail," Daphne said automatically.

"He wishes to be Tom," Nafisah said. "He says he is the slave of the master and will go with him wherever he goes because the master has saved your life."

"I was not dying," Daphne said. "You know the ailment isn't fatal."

"He saved you from the sandstorm as well. I, too, gladly serve such a master, who shows such kindness to his *hareem*, and waits upon her like a slave."

The word *hareem* made Daphne Mr. Carsington's property: a woman who belonged to him, who was part of his household. She squirmed at the term yet saw how unwise it would be to correct Nafisah. The girl would not understand. In her view, all women belonged to one man or another. In any event, it was unwise to encourage the servants to speculate too much about the relationship between the "master" and their mistress.

The relationship between European men and their women baffled many Egyptians anyway, although the majority accepted it philosophically. Practices Egyptians normally regarded as improprieties they often explained and excused with "It is their custom."

The crew and servants were well aware that Daphne's maid shared her cabin, that Tom shared the "master's," and that the cabin Nafisah and Sabah now shared with various domestic supplies stood between the two.

If this arrangement changed, everyone aboard would know. Daphne had no idea whether the men would think less of her or would disregard it as an alien custom. She had no doubt, however, that Miles would eventually hear of it. Depending on how talkative her people were, gossip and speculation might travel up and down the Nile.

In England she lived a reclusive life, and others' opinion of her mattered not at all. She had never made a scandal, though. Miles was all the family she had left. She could not disgrace him.

What had happened in Asyut must be the beginning and the end of all intimacy with Mr. Carsington, she told herself as she dressed. For a time they had been cut off from the world and its rules. They were back in the world now, and must live by the rules. And she must return to reality, to facts, not fantasies.

She and Mr. Carsington had no future together. This was for the best. Circumstances had thrown together two people who could not have less in common.

To emphasize her resolve to keep him at a distance, she donned her widow's garb. She looked down at herself and recalled the expression on Mr. Carsington's face when he'd gazed at her naked breasts. She remembered snuggling, naked, in his arms. She felt a pang.

Telling herself to be sensible, she went out to the front cabin.

The Egyptians therein welcomed her in the usual extravagant fashion: Tom launched into a long speech of rejoicing, his hand on his heart. The baby managed a few staggering steps in her direction before collapsing on the rug, laughing and clapping her hands. Even the mongoose darted in from wherever she'd been, and ran around Daphne's ankles, sniffing.

Mr. Carsington said nothing, only gave her a slow survey, head to toes and up again.

Her face grew hot, and she was well aware of heat further down, coiling in the pit of her belly.

She directed her gaze at the mongoose. "Marigold has grown lively while I was ill," she said composedly. "And friendlier." Had he won over the mongoose, too? Was there anyone or anything able to resist him? "What's happened to her precious shirt?"

"She hides it," Mr. Carsington said. "Today it's under the divan. You'll see her check at intervals, to make sure it's still there. She's vastly entertaining, now her paw has healed. I hadn't realized what busy, curious creatures they are. She's constantly running in and out, to and fro, investigating."

She left Daphne to run about the divan. The mongoose ran up Mr. Carsington as though he were a tree, sat on his shoulder for a moment, sniffing his neck, then ran down again and out of the cabin.

The baby found this highly amusing. She let out squeals of laughter. She stood up, fell down, and squealed some more.

Nafisah came in, scooped her up, and bore her away, to allow the mistress to enjoy her breakfast in peace.

Daphne settled onto the divan at a decorous distance from Mr. Carsington.

Leena entered then, bearing a large tray heaped with breakfast pastries and fruits. "Well, why do you stand there like a stone?" she cried to Tom. "Where is the coffee for your mistress?"

"I forget because my heart is so full," he said. "We are all well now, and safe. This boat is filled with happiness. The baby who was dying laughs and claps her hands. My master who was swallowed by the sandstorm came back to us. He brought back our mistress and made her well again when death tried to take her. He will find our master—our other master—and take him from the foreign devils who carried him into the desert. There are twelve of them, but Yusef and I will fight by his side, and we will fight like a hundred demons and devils."

"What's he on about now?" Mr. Carsington asked Daphne. She quickly translated. Tom went on with his rant.

"Hold on," said Mr. Carsington. He held up his hand. "Wait. Stop."

The boy paused.

"Foreign devils?" Mr. Carsington said. "Twelve of them? How do you know this?"

"But everyone knows," Leena said. "We heard it in the marketplace. The caravans come to Asyut. They see these men, one or two Egyptians, but most are foreigners— Syrian, Greek, Armenian, Turkish. They keep close watch over a tall, fair man who speaks very strange Arabic and whose camel quarrels with him. Did no one tell you?"

She turned a reproachful look upon Tom. "Did you not tell him? Of the talk in Asyut?"

"Oh, yes," said Tom. "I told you, sir, when you came on the boat. Everyone told you. Everyone heard of it in the *suq*."

"Did you tell him in English?" Daphne said.

The boy considered. Then he lifted his shoulders and hands. "In your tongue, in our tongue, I cannot say. My joy to see you was so great. Tears filled my eyes. So full were our hearts, who can say what words we spoke?"

"Leena, sit," Mr. Carsington ordered. "Tom, sit. Now, one at a time, slowly, tell us everything you heard in Asyut."

WITH LEENA AND Tom interrupting each other, and the usual excess verbiage, the report went on for some time, and to Rupert seemed to grow increasingly melodramatic. Daphne's translation reduced the endless saga to a few bald facts.

Archdale had been seen, alive, only a few days ago, en route to Dendera. If this was true, the *Isis* was not so many days behind him as they'd feared. Sandstorms had slowed the kidnappers' progress through the desert. The *Isis* was not far behind Noxious, either. His *dahabeeya* had stopped at Asyut earlier in the week.

At this point, the tale took the dramatic turn.

The *Memnon* was well known in Asyut, the servants reported. As soon as it was spotted, a number of people fled the town and went into hiding, not emerging until the boat was long gone.

"They call this man the Golden Devil," Tom said, "because his hair is the color of gold. He is English, like you. But he is a devil with an army of men like demons. The people of Upper Egypt have less fear of Muhammad Ali and his soldiers."

The Golden Devil had become a legend, apparently. When children misbehaved, their mothers told them the Golden Devil would come after them.

Tom went on for some time about the Golden Devil. Daphne provided her usual, concise English version.

She offered it calmly enough.

After Tom left to fetch the coffee and Leena to bring the maps Rupert asked for, he said, "These revelations about Noxious don't seem to have shocked you."

Her gaze was distant, abstracted. "After what I have discovered about my late husband, I doubt anything more I learn about any man could shock me. This voyage—or mission—or whatever one calls it—has been highly educational. No wonder Miles said I was naïve and unworldly."

"He's your brother," Rupert said. "Brothers can take the oddest views of their siblings. Perhaps because I'm not your brother, I see you altogether differently. From the first you struck me as levelheaded and clear-eyed."

"You've only known me in unusual circumstances," she said.

"Maybe unusual circumstances show us what we're truly made of," he said. "Maybe your life before didn't give you room enough to be yourself."

"I don't know," she said. "I haven't sorted myself out yet. Lord Noxley is easier. His activities at least fit a pattern. We knew he was at war with Duval, competing for antiquities. As to his lordship's army of demons and devils, Belzoni said much the same of his rivals' agents. He said they were lawless men. European 'renegadoes, desperadoes. and exiles,' he called them."

"It's wonderful," Rupert said.

Her green gaze shot to him.

"Your mind," he said. "The way you collect evidence, sort it out, and come to the logical conclusion. It's amazing, considering how much you've got in there."

She smiled faintly. "It's the one thing I can do."

"It isn't all you can do," Rupert said.

The faint thread of pink over her cheekbones spread and deepened into rose.

"That wasn't what I meant," he said. "That is, it wasn't all I meant, although you're brilliant at lovemaking as well, and I do wish—"

Leena bustled in with the maps. She was no sooner gone than Tom entered with the coffee.

Rupert waited until the boy had departed and Daphne had poured the coffee.

He said, "I know why you've donned your weeds again. You didn't need to warn me off. I know we're obliged to observe the proprieties. That's why I wish we were elsewhere."

"It doesn't matter where we are," she said. "This isn't the *Arabian Nights*. It was exciting, once—twice—to be carried away—"

"Was that all?" he said, and something stabbed inside, making him hot and cold at the same time. "You were carried away?"

"What do you want me to say?"

He didn't have an answer.

The silence lengthened while he looked for words and couldn't find any, found only feelings for which he had no names, either.

"I don't know," he said at last. "But you must say something more than that. You're the genius, not I."

"The matter doesn't require cleverness," she said. "What we experienced was lust, pure and simple—well, not pure—"

"It isn't simple for me," he cut in, stabbed again. "This must be Egyptian lust, because it isn't at all what I'm used to. I have . . . *feelings*."

• • •

DAPHNE LONGED TO ask, naturally, what kind of feelings they were. She wanted to probe, as she would a subtlety of grammar or vocabulary.

She wanted, in short, to grasp at any straw.

But that was emotion, not reason.

Reason reminded her that in normal circumstances she was bookish and reclusive while he was a man who hungered for excitement. He was dashing; she was boring. They came from different worlds. The world of fashionable aristocratic society was far more alien to her than Egypt was.

She didn't need to know what these feelings of his were. She knew they were fleeting, because he was not the sort of man whose interest in any woman could last. She knew she could not trust her heart to his feelings, and that was all she really needed to know.

"It's Egypt," she said. "It's the excitement. It's the narrow escapes from death. These make us feel more than we would do otherwise. That's what I meant about the *Arabian Nights*. We're living a romantic adventure. But it's only temporary. Once we find Miles—"

"It will be over," he finished for her.

"Yes," she said.

"What a pity." He shrugged and unrolled a map. "Your brother is headed to Dendera. Is that near Thebes?"

What a pity. That was all. He accepted her decision. Why should he not? What had she expected him to do: plead with her?

She turned her attention to the map. "There is Qena," she said, pointing.

"Three or four days from here, it looks like, if the wind holds," he said.

"There is Dendera, you see, across the river near the site of ancient Tentyris," she went on. "The famous Temple of Hathor is there. She is the Egyptian goddess of . . . love." She added quickly, "Thebes is forty or fifty miles upriver, if I recall aright."

"Another few days, then," he said without looking up from the map. "That's supposedly Noxious's stronghold at present. What do you wager he'll head that way rather than turn back to Cairo?"

She stared at the map while possibilities chased one another through her mind.

"You said the papyrus was reputed to describe a Theban tomb," he said. "Perhaps Noxious would like to help your brother find it."

IT WAS TYPICAL of Faruq to hide right under his enemy's nose, in Lord Noxley's own domain.

The remains of ancient Thebes sprawled over both banks of the Nile. On the west bank, close by the river, lay the ruins of the village of Qurna, destroyed some years earlier by the Mamelukes. Rather than rebuild their huts, the Qurnans decided it was more efficient to live where they worked, in the Theban tombs. They did not, like other Egyptian peasants, get their living from agriculture. They got it from excavating tombs and selling papyri and other *"anteekahs"* they'd stripped from mummies.

They were reputed to be the most independent people in all of Egypt, with the possible exception of the Bedouins. One army after another had come to subdue the Qurnans . . . and failed. They did succeed, however, in reducing the population from some three thousand to about three hundred.

The survivors had hidden in the distant Theban hills, which contained thousands of tombs and an intricate network of passages connecting them. Here Faruq had taken refuge.

Unluckily for him, Ghazi had a way with tomb robbers. He set fire to the nearer tombs, where the old women resided, shot their vicious watchdogs, and killed their cows, sheep, and goats. Had he been after one of their own, this method would have failed. But the Qurnans were disinclined to sacrifice their mothers, grandmothers, and livestock to protect a foreigner.

This was how Ghazi located Faruq so quickly, within

days of leaving Lord Noxley. The Qurnans, who knew all the best hiding places, also helped him find the dispatch bag under a heap of ransacked mummy parts. Once Ghazi had made sure the objects he wanted were inside, he rewarded the Qurnans generously, as his master would wish. He also rewarded Faruq as the master would wish, by beheading Duval's chief agent before a large audience of Qurnans.

25 April

WHEN LORD NOXLEY and his friend disembarked from the *Memnon* at Luxor, they found Ghazi awaiting them. He proudly produced not only the papyrus and the interesting copy with its numerous notes but also—in a basket rather than a dispatch bag—Faruq's head.

Lord Noxley's face lit at the sight of these offerings, and he felt as sunny within as he appeared without.

Miles Archdale's face was ashen.

"You must develop a stronger stomach," Lord Noxley told him. "These people respect only force, especially the Qurnans. Now they will think twice before harboring any more of Duval's friends."

Ghazi had other news, which he conveyed privately to his master as they set out for the house: Archdale's sister was not waiting quietly in Cairo, as everyone had assumed. Despite Ghazi's best efforts, the authorities had failed to charge Hargate's moron son with either the murder of the two men in the pyramid or that of Vanni Anaz. Consequently, Carsington was at large and at present taking Mrs. Pembroke up the Nile in search of her brother.

"By the time these things happened, I was far from Cairo," Ghazi said. "Even if I had known—"

"You couldn't turn back then." Lord Noxley slowed his pace, so they might lag behind the rest of the party. He considered for a time, then his expression brightened. "Perhaps it's for the best," he said. "We're here now. Why should she not be? Do go fetch her. As to Carsington, I should like it very much if you would make him go away."

•   •   •

SEEING FARUQ'S HEAD gave Miles his first inkling of something being not quite right with Noxley's.

In Dendera, Noxley had mentioned a "nasty business." Until it was settled, he told Miles on the way to the boat, Miles would be safer in Thebes, where Noxley could rely upon the loyalty of the Turkish soldiers stationed there. The French kept clear of Thebes at present.

It was not as though Miles had any choice but to go where his friend chose. Once the *Memnon* set sail, though, Noxley explained the "nasty business."

By "the French" his lordship meant, it turned out, a man named Duval, whom Miles vaguely recalled meeting at a consulate affair. Noxley said this was the man who'd hired the kidnappers. When they ransacked Miles's belongings, they were looking for the papyrus. The next day, others of Duval's henchmen went to the house and took both the papyrus and the copy.

In other words, Duval believed not only the story about the treasure-filled pharaoh's tomb but also that Miles could read hieroglyphic writing.

So far, to Miles's relief, no one had discovered the truth about Daphne. He preferred to keep it that way. She was vulnerable enough as it was.

Had she not been out at the time of the theft, she might have been taken, too, as a hostage, to make Miles cooperate with the French lunatic. But she'd been at the consulate, trying to make them do something, which, as everyone knew, they never did, unless the something involved getting ancient artifacts on the cheap. The theft sent her to Noxley, who had promptly set out to recover both Miles and the papyrus.

Clearly his lordship had succeeded on both counts.

Clearly Duval was a dangerous man.

Still, the business of the head . . .

It was all well and good to say, "When in Rome . . ." But the English had stopped cutting off people's heads and displaying them for the edification of the masses some years ago, and Miles saw no reason for recommencing a barbaric practice merely because one was among barbarians.

Preoccupied with making sense of his friend's behavior, he took little note of his surroundings beyond observing that the present-day Egyptians had built their houses in, around, and on the ancient temple of Luxor. Where the pharaoh and his high priests must have once performed sacred rituals, the peasants had built pigeon towers.

Noxley's house, which occupied a corner of the southern end of the temple, was not the most imposing structure. No doubt it would easily fit in the entrance hall of his lordship's ancestral home in Leicestershire. By Luxor standards, though, it was spacious and elegant, boasting upper and lower floors, the former airy and ideal for summer sleeping quarters.

At the house, Noxley suggested locking up the papyrus and the copy in a strongbox. Miles agreed, though he wondered who'd have the temerity to try to steal anything from anybody with Ghazi about.

Miles retired to his assigned chamber, bathed, and collapsed on the divan. He slept until a servant woke him for dinner.

When he rejoined Noxley in the comfortably appointed *qa'a,* Miles found he hadn't any stomach for dinner.

"My poor fellow, pray forgive me," Noxley said. "You must be sick to death of native fare. Let me tell Cook—"

"It isn't the food but Faruq," Miles said. "That head preys on my mind. Are you quite sure it's wise to encourage persons like Ghazi in these barbaric practices?"

"Why is it any more barbaric than hanging a man at Tyburn?" Noxley said. "I should say it was more merciful. It can take a good while to die on the end of a rope, you know. As to keeping the head for display, this is the only way to make sure the word spreads. We want to leave Duval in no doubt of his chief henchman's demise. Then he'll know he's lost the papyrus as well as you." Noxley smiled. "He'll be frothing at the mouth, like the mad dog he is."

"I only met him the once, and he seemed sane enough to me," Miles said. "Yet he cannot be, to believe that anyone has deciphered hieroglyphs yet. He must be madder still to act as he has, upon such a delusion."

"It is a delusion, beyond question?" Noxley looked up from his plate, his expression oddly childlike.

"The papyrus contains royal names," Miles said. "That's all any scholar can ascertain at present."

"You didn't buy it because you believed it described a royal tomb, as Vanni Anaz claimed?" Noxley said, still watching him with that childlike expression. "Nothing about it told you it might be a treasure map of some kind?"

Miles shook his head. He'd bought it for Daphne. Because it was beautiful, in near-perfect condition. Because she had nothing half so fine in her collection. Because he knew her eyes would light up as they used to do, a long time ago, before she wed Pembroke. Her eyes had lit, and Miles had never seen her happier than when she set to work on it. To him, this made the thing worth ten times what he'd paid.

"I heard the French consul general, Drovetti, offered Belzoni ten thousand pounds for the alabaster sarcophagus he found," Miles said. "I thought the papyrus, another rare specimen of great artistry, was of proportional value."

"Perhaps you've explained Duval's problem, then," said Noxley. He signaled a servant to take away the dinner tray.

When the servant had gone, he said, "Duval has always believed the French 'discovered' Egypt, because of the scientific expedition and the *Description de l'Egypte*. He hates the English partly because we beat them but mostly because we took the Rosetta Stone as spoils of war."

"Good gad, that was twenty years ago," Miles said. "It isn't as though the French never took valuable items from nations they conquered. I haven't noticed them giving any of it back."

"Try telling that to Duval," Noxley said. "Still, he was no worse than any of the other antiquities hunters until recent years."

Since you came and took men like Ghazi into your employ? Miles wondered. But the recollection of Faruq's head made him cautious. "Any idea why?" he said.

"Belzoni," Noxley said. "Duval has been in Egypt for more than twenty years. Belzoni was here for less than five, and now he's famous around the world. Duval had excavated in the Biban el Muluk, the Valley of the Tombs of Kings. He never found a royal tomb, but Belzoni did—a magnificent one, containing a rare alabaster sarcophagus. Neither Duval nor Drovetti could find the entrance to Chephren's pyramid, but Belzoni did. The French couldn't find a way to move the head of Young Memnon, but Belzoni did, and now it's in England."

"Twenty years of work and nothing to show for it," Miles said. *Rather like Virgil Pembroke's case,* he thought. "He must have been mad with jealousy." Again, like Pembroke, so jealous of Daphne's gift for languages.

"Imagine what he felt when he heard about the papyrus Anaz had sold you," Noxley said.

"The last straw," Miles said.

Noxley smiled. "I'll admit I felt a twinge of jealousy, too. Anaz must have taken a liking to you. He's dead, by the way, poor fellow."

Chapter 18

RUPERT SAW HIS FIRST CROCODILES ABOVE Girga, half a dozen of them basking on a sandbank.

The river had grown shallow, and sandbanks formed a maze of obstructions through which the *Isis* must pass. Previously he'd gazed at flocks of pelicans and wild ducks gathered upon them. That was to say, his eyes had been turned in that direction. His mind had been elsewhere.

On her.

On getting off the boat and finding someplace private. They were drawing closer to Thebes by the hour. Time was running out. Once they found her brother, nothing could be as it was.

Rupert told himself he ought to be planning how to get her brother out of the villains' clutches. He ought to be planning how to protect the women and children.

Instead, his mind was busily devising and discarding schemes for slaking his lust on Daphne Pembroke's magnificent body.

Even now, gazing at the crocodiles, he was wondering how they might help him get her naked.

All his brain produced was an excuse to see her. He left

the deck and went inside, where she'd lately been spending
the hottest part of the day. He found her not in the front
cabin but in her own. The door stood open for ventilation.

Spread out upon the divan was a familiar document
bearing three kinds of writing. It was a copy of the Rosetta
Stone. Her lap held a notebook.

He tapped on the open door. She looked up. A flush
overspread her creamy countenance.

He wanted to kiss all that rosy skin. And all the paler
parts. Then work his way down.

"Crocodiles," he said.

"Really?" She set the notebook aside. "Where?"

He found an umbrella and led her out to the deck. He
held it over her while she gazed raptly at the strange creatures. It was a long time before she spoke.

He didn't need to say anything. It was enough to be near
her, to watch her surprise and pleasure transform everything he looked upon. The crocodiles somehow became
more exotic and miraculous. With her, one always felt as
though one gazed upon marvels.

"I can scarcely believe they're real," she said at last.
"Look, one slithers into the water. It is like a dream."

Rupert became aware of two boyish voices nearby,
quarreling, by the sounds of it. He sent a quelling look in
their direction.

Tom hurried to him. "Please, sir, I must speak to you."

But he could not speak in front of the lady, the boy said.
This was talk for men. With a shrug and a smile, Daphne
went back inside, out of the baking sun.

"This had better be important," Rupert told the boy.

"Oh, yes, sir. Yusef is very sick."

Rupert studied the other lad, who hung back, looking
abashed. His turban was all askew and his clothes hung
crooked.

"Illness is the lady's department," Rupert said. "I'm not
the doctor here."

"He is sick with love, sir," Tom said. "This is why he
has no care for his clothes."

"Love?"

"Yes, sir. For Nafisah. His suffering is very great. I told him that you are our father now, and you will arrange for his happiness, but he does not believe me."

Rupert looked again at Yusef, whose expression had become pathetically hopeful.

Rupert reverted to Tom. "Since when am I your father?"

Tom explained. The plague had taken most of his family. His uncle Akmed had disappeared. Yusef had no family, either. Muhammad Ali's soldiers had burnt his village to the ground two years ago and killed everybody.

"Now we belong to you," the boy concluded. "You are our master and our father."

At that moment, the baby began to cry.

Rupert looked about him. A baby. Women. A pair of adolescent boys.

He *was* the father.

DAPHNE STARED DOGGEDLY at the cartouches, but it was no use. She couldn't concentrate. She couldn't remember what she'd been thinking before she heard the tap and saw Mr. Carsington in the doorway.

She remembered the way he'd trapped her against that door on the evening after their visit to Memphis.

The kiss, the magical kiss. The tenderness and playfulness of it and the strange discovery it was, as though no one had ever kissed before in all the world.

Then all the memories she'd tried to shut away came flooding back and left her sick with longing.

She could have borne the ache more easily if he'd been the lout he'd pretended to be. But no lout could have restored her confidence as he had done, and made her feel fully normal—even likable—for the first time since her girlhood. A lout would not stand beside her holding an umbrella to shield her from the sun. A lout would not play with the baby, or sit up late at night telling the boys stories, or let a mongoose use him for a playground. A lout would not be able to make everyone about him love him.

Including me, she thought. *Including stupid me.*

"Daphne."

She looked up, expecting to see nothing, because she was only wishing, and the deep voice she heard came from her imagination.

But no, he stood in the doorway again, head tipped to one side, because the space was a few inches too short for him. The north wind had made a tangle of his thick, dark hair. His eyes glinted with humor. She remembered how he'd whistled in the darkness of the dungeon, laughing at danger, as though it had been made purposely to amuse him.

Now she saw that he'd been driving away her own darkness, day by day. And day by day, she'd changed. Because of him, she'd become more than she'd been—or perhaps more truly herself. Because of him, she'd learnt to like and trust herself again. Because of him, desire had become a pleasure, not a shame.

I love you, she thought.

He gazed at her for a long moment. Then his mouth curved lazily upward. "Ah," he said. "That's better."

"What's better?"

He came inside the cabin. He closed the door.

"You know," he said.

"You should not close the door," she said, while her heart thrummed, wicked thing, in anticipation.

"You look at me in that *t'ala heneh* way," he said.

"I do not," she lied. The need beat in her heart and hummed in her veins: *T'ala heneh. Come here.*

"Then why do I forget why I came?" he said. He sank onto the divan beside her. "It was vastly important. But the expression on your face made me forget everything." He took up the notebook that had slid from her hand when she saw him. "Perhaps it will come to me by and by. What occupies you today? Or should I say whom? For here is a pair of those pesky cartouches."

"Not a pair," she said tautly. The space was too small. They were too isolated. Outside the crew launched into a love song. "They come from separate places."

As she and he did, she reminded herself. Separate worlds. She needed to stay in hers, to keep her distance. She knew this.

Yet she drew closer and pointed at the page while she

spoke, though it was unnecessary. He could see well enough. The matter wasn't complicated. "The one on top is Ptolemy's, from the Rosetta Stone. The one below is Cleopatra's, from Mr. Bankes's obelisk." She was too close. His scent was in her nostrils and seeping into her brain and making a haze there.

His gaze lifted from the notebook to her face. She should look away, focus her mind, or else he'd read in her countenance what she wanted, every reckless thought, every mad feeling. She couldn't look away. She wanted to trace the angle of his jaw with her fingertips. She wanted to lay her cheek against his.

"You've written letters over the signs," he said.

"Guessing games," she said. "Count the letters. Compare the letters. To keep my mind occupied."

"Is it working?" he said.

Think of Miles, she told herself. *Think of all he's done for you. Will you make him pay for your weakness and folly? Say, "Yes, it's working."*

"No," she said. "It isn't."

"Nothing works for me," he said. "It was stupid to come in here and close the door. Everything in here is yours. The goddess scent of incense. The scent of your skin. The smell of books and parchment and ink." He stroked his hand over the few inches of divan between them. "This is where you sleep. I sleep all the world away. That's how it feels. I miss you."

She came up onto her knees and laid her fingers over his lips. She mustn't let him say another sweet word. She would start believing things that couldn't be true. Then, afterward, it would hurt even more. Men would say anything, do anything. Even Virgil had changed his tune with her when he felt amorous.

Outside, the sailors sang of love. One voice rose above the others in a wail of longing.

> *Love troubles my heart;*
> *Sleep will not close my eyes;*
> *This agony tears my vitals;*
> *I weep endless tears.*

Alas, if only we were together,
I would not sigh, I would not weep.

He brought his hand up and stroked down over the fingers covering his lips, down over the back of her hand. He clasped her wrist. She let her hand slide down and curl into his. Their fingers twined. He brought their joined hands to his chest and pressed them over his heart.

"Miss you," he said. It was the barest murmur, scarcely a sound.

She missed him, too, missed the freedom they'd had in their tomb in Asyut: to touch, to kiss, to give and take pleasure, to hold each other. To be whatever it was they were when they were in each other's arms.

She bent toward him and touched her lips to his. He answered with a gentleness that made her ache. She slid her hand from his clasp so that she could hold him with both hands, cupping his beautiful face and looking into those eyes, those dark, laughing eyes.

Even now the wicked spirit lurked there, a glint of mischief in the darkness of heat and desire. It made her smile, and she brought her smile to his mouth and gave it to him. "Miss you," she whispered. "So much."

She should move away, but it was too late. She'd breathed the scent of his skin, and got the taste of him on her lips, and felt the warmth and strength of his hands. She pressed her mouth to his once more, and all the longing she'd tried to stifle spilled from her in the kiss she ought to have held back. Her hands slid to his shoulders, and she clung when she knew she ought to let go. Later it would only be harder.

But later was so far away. Now all her world was him, and the long, tender kiss that turned fierce in a moment. His arm went round her waist, and he pulled her against his hard torso. She shifted into his lap, and pulled up her skirts, and wrapped her legs around his hips. She was shameless. With him she could be. She could do as she pleased. No rules. Only to please and be pleased. She caught at his shirt, tugged it up, and broke the kiss only long enough to pull the garment over his head. She dragged her hands over his shoulders, his back, his chest. He was as smooth and hard as marble but warm and vibrantly alive. She'd never known anyone so fully alive as he.

Outside the men sang:

> *My heart is wrapped in fire.*
> *Who burns as I do?*
> *Is there no remedy?*

He caught the back of her head and pushed his long fingers into her hair. He held her away and looked at her. No words. Only the heat in his eyes and the glint of wickedness and the hint of a smile. Then his hands slid downward, and he undid the bodice fastenings, watching her face all the while. She remembered the first time he'd tried to undress her, against the door.

What are you doing? she'd said, like an idiot.

Taking off your clothes, he'd answered, clearly amazed at the stupidity of the question.

Now she laughed silently, recalling. He grinned, and she knew he remembered, too.

The bodice fell away, and his hands were upon her skin, and her brain slowed and thickened.

She pressed her fist to her mouth to keep from making any sound. She had craved his touch, his strong, clever hands tracing the curves of her breasts, her waist and belly and hips. She hadn't understood how desperate it was, the ache, until now, when it swept over her like a sandstorm, blotting out everything but the piercing need for him.

He pushed her skirts up further and loosened the waist of his full trousers. She trembled when the garments slid away, leaving them skin to skin. She wrapped her arms about his shoulders and pressed her mouth against his neck to keep from crying out when his hands moved up her thighs. She drank in his scent, hot and male and his alone. At the first intimate touch she screamed silently. If she could have done, she'd have cried out her pleasure, her torment, and impossible, contradictory demands. *More. No. Stop. Don't stop. There. No, there. Oh, don't. Oh, yes, please.*

Laughter bubbled inside her along with a sorrow all but unbearable.

Madness.

Wonderful madness.

Her teeth dug into his shoulder, her nails into his back while his wonderful, dangerous hands found every pleasure point, and streams of sensation, violently sweet and hot, coursed through her.

The sailors' drum was a distant echo, their aching song a counterpoint to the ache within. She longed for him. To be his. To be together. To be one.

She slid her hand down over his belly, and took his rod in her hand to guide it into her. He made a choked sound and pushed her hand away. He shifted her on his lap, and before she could tell him she couldn't wait any longer, he thrust into her. His mouth covered hers before she could cry out. *Yes, oh, yes. Like this. At last.*

Outside, the sailors sang:

> *O first and only one of my heart*
> *Show at last your favor to me*
> *I am thy slave eternally.*
> *Thou art my lord and master. . . .*

Outside was the wail of the pipes and the beat of the earthen drum.

Inside was an all-consuming need to be joined, completely and forever.

She took him deep inside her, wrapped herself about him, her hands moving over him, to have as much of him as she could, though it could never be enough.

She rocked with him, silently, to the music and beat only they two heard. Feelings swelled, dark and ungovernable, and she let them take her. With him, she would go anywhere. With him she feared nothing. With him she was finally, truly alive.

She held onto him as she'd done during the sandstorm. She let the pleasure rage around her and inside her and between them until it shattered them both. It brought release, and a quiet like peace.

•   •   •

"WHAT ARE THEY singing?" Rupert said later, when he could breathe again, think again. They'd sunk down against the cushions and lay there for a long time without moving. He held her still, close to him, and she held him.

He ought to help her get her clothes back on. Not a great deal to do. Put her bodice back together. Straighten her skirts. Nothing else. No corset. No petticoats. No drawers. He grinned.

"Love songs," she said. "What's so amusing?"

"You," he said. "You weren't wearing any underthings. I collect you were expecting me."

"I haven't worn underthings in days," she said. "It's too hot. We need to get dressed. It's getting late. We'll be stopping soon for the night."

"Love songs," he said. Then he remembered. The reason he'd come. The excuse. "Yusef is sick with love for Nafisah."

"That would explain the choice of song," she said. "All the burning vitals and misery and 'alas' this and that." She started to untangle herself from him.

He drew her back.

"We need to be sensible," she said. "*I* need to be sensible."

"Another moment," he said.

"Mr. Carsington."

"Rupert," he said.

"I need to keep a distance," she said.

"It's a bit late for that," he said.

"I know it is hypocritical," she said, "but I must try to maintain an appearance of decorum. For Miles's sake."

He kissed her forehead. "If he finds out, will he have my liver on a spit? Will he insist upon pistols at twenty paces?"

She pulled away and sat up. "Good grief! A duel? Over me? If he even contemplated anything so deranged—But no, he would not be so idiotish." She wrestled her bodice back into position, and turned her back to him. "Do me up, please," she said. "I can hardly call for Leena."

Reluctantly Rupert sat up. Reluctantly, he fastened the garment.

"Have you spoken to Nafisah?" she said.

"Can we talk about Nafisah later?" he said. "We're not done talking about us."

She turned back to him. "Please don't," she said. "We can't continue this. I don't regret what I've done. But the rest of the world will never understand, and the rest of the world is what Miles must contend with. I cannot embarrass him. I could not live with myself if I did. You can have no idea what he's done for me. Without him, I should have gone mad."

"He's taken care of you," Rupert said.

"Far beyond what most brothers would do for their sisters."

"Then I shouldn't wish to injure him for the world," Rupert said. He pulled on his shirt. He wished wisdom were a garment, that he might put it on so easily. He'd been so happy for a time. Now he was unhappy and growing unhappier by the minute. He had to leave. He would have to sleep alone this night.

He was not a monster. He did have self-control. He didn't wish to disgrace her. He didn't wish to shame the brother she loved, the brother who'd protected her from who knew what.

It shouldn't be so hard to leave. It shouldn't be so hard to tell himself they'd find her brother in the next few days. They'd rescue him or die trying. And if they died, it would be over. And if they succeeded, it would all be over between Daphne Pembroke and Rupert Carsington.

He'd never expected matters to end any differently, and he'd never had any trouble with endings.

He'd had other women.

When it was time to go, he went.

Whether it was his decision or—on the very rare occasion—hers, he said good-bye graciously and kindly. With gratitude, perhaps. Never with regret.

He told himself this day had brought more than he'd dared hope for. He'd come to the cabin on family business.

He'd come on behalf of the lovesick boy who'd looked at him with that pathetically hopeful expression.

"I'd better settle the matter I came to settle," Rupert

said. "Otherwise it will be obvious to everyone what we were doing here with the door closed."

"Yusef wishes to marry Nafisah, it appears," she said, rising up on her knees and twitching her skirts back into place.

"Yes, but he's very young. Fourteen, I think."

"Most Egyptian boys his age have a wife," she said. "I believe his countrymen employ the principle that it's better to marry than to burn. Fathers usually provide wives for their sons by puberty."

Rupert frowned. He'd never thought of marriage in that way. Well, he didn't need to, did he? The English didn't keep their women hidden behind veils or shut up in harems.

"It's easy enough to do, if she's agreeable," Daphne said. "A maiden's marriage is as elaborate an affair as the family can afford. For widows and divorced women, the business is much simpler. I made some notes on the subject. I intend to write a paper on several aspects of modern Egyptian culture."

She pushed the cushion they'd lain upon back against the cabin wall. She crawled over the divan and rummaged in a small chest in a corner of the cabin. While she searched, he gazed at her handsomely rounded backside. He suppressed a sigh.

She took out a notebook like the one in which she'd drawn the cartouches. She flipped through the pages. "Here it is. Quite simple. The woman says to the man, 'I give myself up to thee.' This is usually done before witnesses, but they are not necessary. The dowry is a fraction of that for a virgin. Naturally, I should provide a generous dowry, so that is not an issue." She looked up from the notebook. "It only remains for the girl to agree."

"That's all?" he said. " 'I give myself up to thee'? No banns? No license? No parson?"

"We might give them a fête," Daphne said. "It's a good excuse for a celebration."

He rose. "Yes, well, I'd better find out what Nafisah thinks of the prospective bridegroom, then."

"Send her to me," Daphne said.

"No, no, I'll use Tom as interpreter," he said. "They want me to do it. I'm the father."

"The father?"

He gave a distracted nod and went out.

HE RETURNED FIVE minutes later.

Daphne had not had time to put her feelings in order. She'd barely had time to wash herself. She hastily dabbed her face with the towel so that he wouldn't know the wet was from tears.

Making love with him again had only made everything worse. She knew it had to be the last time, but she wasn't done with him. She wasn't ready for it to be over.

She was acting like a romantic, emotional schoolgirl. It was as though the ten years since her first blind infatuation had never happened.

But it had, and she needed to remember what had happened every miserable detail, all the consequences of trusting feelings.

Thus she counseled herself, but when he was near, it was very difficult to be logical and sensible.

He stood in the doorway, his head tipped to one side.

"We could marry," he said.

She took the towel away from her face and clutched it to her stomach. She said nothing. She couldn't have heard aright.

"We could marry," he said. "The way you said. You're a widow."

Her heart was a great pickaxe inside her chest: one heavy blow after another. Something would break, something vital.

"Marry?" she said. "Did you hit your head on the way out?"

He smiled. "You see? That's one of the things I like about you. Your sense of humor."

"I have no sense of humor," she said.

"Maybe you don't notice because your mind is so taken up with scholarly matters," he said.

"No, the trouble is, you don't know the real Daphne,"

she said. "You think I'm dashing and interesting, but I'm not. Circumstances have forced me to behave differently. But as soon as everything returns to normal, I shall revert to the unamusing and unamiable person I really am."

"You believed you were unwomanly, recollect," he said. "You can't judge yourself by a fussy old man's standards."

"You don't understand!" she cried. "I have no hobbies. I have no other interests. I eat, drink, and breathe lost languages. My idea of a grand time is counting the number of hieroglyphic signs on the Rosetta Stone. One thousand four hundred nineteen. The corresponding Greek text has four hundred eighty-six words. Would you like to hear the conclusion I draw from these figures?"

"Of course," he said. "I love to listen to you talk."

"Even when you don't understand it."

"Is it necessary?" he said. "Do you understand cricket? The finer points of boxing?"

"Of course not," she said.

"My mother has said that it's often better for a husband and wife not to understand each other too well," he said. "A little mystery keeps a marriage more interesting, she says."

"With you and me it is more than a *little* mystery," Daphne said. "We have nothing in common."

His dark eyebrows went up.

"Lust doesn't count," she said. "It is no basis for a union that must last a lifetime. We are not Egyptians. We cannot divorce with a handful of words, and without disgrace. I can't, at any rate."

He appeared to think this over. Then, "You're telling me the answer is no, in other words," he said.

"It's for the best," she said. She tried desperately to remember what one ought to say in such circumstances. She must have read about it somewhere. "I fear we should not suit . . . over the long term. But thank you for making the offer. It was . . . kind."

"Kind," he repeated. He gave a short laugh and left.

o   o   o

BY NIGHTFALL, DAPHNE had herself in hand. It was not as though she had any choice. The wedding business quickly occupied everybody.

Not long after Mr. Carsington left, Leena and Nafisah hurried in with the happy news. Nafisah had agreed to have Yusef. She was very pleased. She wished to have more babies. Yusef was young and strong and would give her many children. He was handsome, too, and kind. She kissed Daphne's hand repeatedly, thanking her.

"What have I to do with it?" Daphne said. "It was you who stole his heart."

"If you had left me in my village," the girl said, "my Sabah would be dead, and I would be the fourth wife of an ill-tempered man."

Like Virgil, Daphne thought. He'd looked so saintly and serene, but it was a mask, and it had fooled her. She'd thought she was at fault and hadn't realized she was at the mercy of a moody, discontented man.

But she'd been so young then, older than Nafisah in years, but much younger in experience. She'd no experience of the outside world. Girls, even very clever girls, didn't go to public school. They didn't go to university. She'd studied at home, with her father. She'd lived a quiet, cloistered existence.

Were her feelings never to be trusted simply because they'd fooled her all that long time ago?

Was her judgment about men fatally flawed, or had she simply made a youthful error?

She was not sure, and she hadn't time this day to work out the riddle. Though the wedding was a simple affair, it ought to be a festive occasion. She busied herself with arranging it. By the time the boat moored for the night, the meal was in preparation and the bride dressed in a set of Daphne's Arab garments.

The bride-to-be was applying kohl to the baby's eyes when the mongoose raced into the room, chittering excitedly.

"What on earth is the matter with . . ." Daphne trailed off as she became aware of unfamiliar voices outside.

Leena peered through the shutters. "Officials, from the

town," she grumbled. "They will steal all our food, and call
it a boat tax."

Marigold dashed out again. Daphne nudged Leena
away from the shuttered window. The mongoose ran out
onto the deck and instantly went up on her hind legs, fur
bristling as though she'd spotted a cobra.

Daphne went to the chest where she kept the pistols,
took them out, and loaded them, her hands shaking.

The voices outside sounded calm, but she didn't trust
the calm. If she'd had fur, it would have bristled, too. She
didn't know what was wrong, only that she was absolutely
certain something was.

"Find knives, whatever weapons you can," she whispered to the women. "If anyone tries to get in here, attack
first, ask questions after."

For once, Leena did not launch into a prophecy of
calamities to come. She only nodded.

Daphne quickly wrapped a shawl about her waist and
tucked one pistol into it. The other she carried in her hand.
She went out into the passage. At the door that opened onto
the deck, she paused and listened.

The matter was quite simple, one of the strangers was
saying. The Englishman was invited to accompany them to
the house of the local sheik.

Rupert answered that he was honored by the invitation,
but he had made other plans for the evening.

The man said he feared that the sheik would be deeply
offended. In this case, every member of the crew must be
bastinadoed, to soothe the sheik's wounded feelings.

"I must invite you to leave," Rupert said. "We're having
a wedding, you see. We've just cleaned the boat, and you
don't want to be spilling a lot of blood on it, do you?"

The man muttered something to somebody nearby. The
second man grabbed the nearest sailor and started beating
him with a stick.

Then several things happened very quickly.

The mongoose leapt at the leader and sank her sharp
teeth into his leg. He shrieked. A rifle went off. Rupert had
an oar in his hands and was swinging it at the two men
rushing at him. A man fell overboard. A lantern fell onto

the deck. Daphne cocked the pistol, opened the door a little wider, aimed, and fired at one of Rupert's attackers. The villain screamed and went down, clutching his leg.

After that it was hard to sort anything out. The crew had picked up oars and tools and cookware and were using them to fight. She was pulling out the second pistol and cocking it when a hand closed round her wrist like a vise, forcing her to drop the weapon. Her assailant dragged her away from the door. She kicked it closed behind her, then kicked out at him. Her boot connected with a limb. He swore but didn't let go. He was dragging her to the back of the boat, away from the fray at the front. She swung the first pistol at his head. He knocked it away, grabbed both her hands, and pinned them behind her.

"Rupert!" she cried. "Tom! Yusef! Somebody!"

She thought she heard Rupert shout back. She looked toward the sound of his voice. There was a flash that lit his face in the instant before he clutched his chest and stumbled backward . . . and over the side.

"Rupert!" she screamed.

"You come, your people live," said the man who held her. "You fight, they die. All."

She went.

Chapter 19

MONSIEUR DUVAL WAS IN ABYDOS, SOME SIXTY
miles downriver from Dendera. The site lay well inland, in
the Libyan Desert at the edge of the mountain range.

With him were several of his countrymen and local allies, who'd hastily retreated from Dendera when word
reached them that the *Memnon* was headed that way. Their
numbers being small and Lord Noxley's feelings about the
zodiac ceiling being well known, they decided to play least
in sight until he'd moved on to Thebes.

When the man Jabbar arrived, Duval was inside an immense edifice that Strabo and Pliny had called the Memno-
nium. While his companions made the best of matters by
trying to dig the building out from under centuries of accu-
mulated sand and rubble, Duval spent his time staring at a
wall in a small inner apartment. Carved into the wall were
three long rows of cartouches, a list of kings.

There should have been twenty-six ovals in each row,
but the wall was damaged, and a number of names were
lost. None of those remaining resembled the one he remembered from the papyrus, the simpler of the two cartouches it had contained.

Now the papyrus was in Noxley's hands.

The news had come late last night: Faruq was dead. Noxley had both Archdale and the papyrus, and they were in Thebes, beyond Duval's reach, thanks to the Golden Devil's reign of terror.

Still, all was not lost, Duval had thought.

He'd sent a large party downriver to intercept the *Isis* and capture Archdale's sister. He planned to trade her for the papyrus and Archdale's key to deciphering the hieroglyphs.

Then Jean-Claude Duval might still achieve the triumph he'd dreamt of: he would discover an untouched royal tomb, filled with treasure. The discovery would make him famous, more famous than Belzoni. The bulk of the treasure would go to the Louvre, not the British Museum. He would win honors. Medals would be struck in his name. And at last France would be avenged for the theft of the Rosetta Stone.

That was the dream, the ideal. He knew matters might not turn out quite that way. The papyrus might lead him to a royal tomb as empty of treasure as the others found so far. He knew it might take many years to find the tomb. He knew it was possible he'd never find it.

Still, even in the worst of cases, he would have the papyrus, which would go to the Louvre. And he—and therefore France—would have the key to decipherment, which was far more valuable, for it was a key to unlocking the secrets of the ancients.

No, all was not lost, he'd thought . . . until now.

Heart sinking, he gazed at Jabbar's haggard face and said, "What has happened?"

"A slaughter," Jabbar said. "The Golden Devil's men were waiting for us. Most of our men are dead. A few escaped into the hills. Ghazi has the woman."

"What, again we lose her?" Duval said. "First, the men in Asyut let her slip through their hands when she was unguarded, practically alone."

"Drunken fools," Jabbar said bitterly. "We took care, but our enemy had word of our doings. Sometimes I think even the jackals and snakes and vultures spy for the Golden Devil, for he knows everything."

Lost, Duval thought. His last chance lost.

What now?

He didn't know. Yet. But he would find a way.
He could not let the English fiend win.

DAPHNE'S CAPTORS HAD kept their word. They'd stopped fighting her people. As soon as she was aboard their boat, they cut the *Isis*'s mooring ropes and let the swift current carry the *dahabeeya* downstream.

It would be a while, probably, before her crew had the boat under control. Meanwhile, the *Isis* might collide with a sandbank or another boat. Still, those aboard were far more likely to survive such mishaps than a battle with these villains. With Rupert dead, who could stop them from slaughtering everyone aboard and sinking the *dahabeeya*?

Rupert dead.

She ought to feel something, but she was numb.

After a short time on the river, her captors took her overland on horseback. Wherever they were going, they were going swiftly, with only the shortest possible pauses to rest and refresh the animals and themselves. Still, they treated her well enough, allowing her privacy to deal with nature's needs and a small tent of her own to rest in. She didn't know if she rested or not or ate or not. Food didn't matter. Sleep didn't matter.

She didn't care how they treated her or what would become of her.

Time had stopped for her. The scene in her mind's eye was clearer to her than the passing landscape: the flash of fire from the pistol aimed at Rupert's heart . . . the surprised expression on his face . . . his hand clutching his chest while the impact knocked him backward . . . and over . . . the splash as his body hit the water.

She couldn't weep. She felt frozen, the way she'd felt six months into her marriage, when she'd fully understood how immense and serious a mistake she'd made.

She'd been a prisoner then, too.

She'd trained herself not to think about the hurt, to concentrate instead on her work and how to hide it from Virgil and how to communicate with the scholarly world outside. The rage and despair remained, but she kept them locked inside. She couldn't live the rest of her life in open hostility with her husband. She could only build a wall around herself, and make a world inside it where she could live.

She had no work now to distract her, and she wasn't the girl she'd been then. She wasn't even the same woman she'd been a few weeks ago.

And in this new woman, the one she'd become, the rage and despair grew, hour by hour, until there was no more room for it inside.

It was the second evening of her captivity, and Ghazi had brought her food. He smiled and spoke so smoothly, and all she could think of was Rupert's smile, and the sound of his deep voice . . . and his hands, his large, capable hands.

She looked at Ghazi's hands, holding the bowl, and at her own as she reached to take it from him. Her right hand balled into a fist, and she knocked the bowl away, and the rage and despair poured out in a stream of Arabic invective.

The other men, gathered about the fire, all turned and stared at her, eyes wide and mouths open. They remained that way, like statues, during the short, deadly silence that followed.

Then Ghazi laughed. "Your Arabic is very pretty," he said. "You know all the curses. My men, I know, would like to teach you love words. I myself would like so much to teach you some manners. But we must leave all the lessons to the master. He will tame you soon enough."

"If your master Duval is foolish enough to try to tame a viper, let him try," she said.

"Duval?" Ghazi laughed. "Ah, no wonder you are so fierce, little viper. You have mistaken us. Duval is not our master. Can you not see where we go, angry serpent? South, to Thebes, where your brother is, and where the Golden Devil rules. And so, you see, you are safe, and have nothing to fear."

She knew she wasn't safe. But she had nothing to lose now, and so, nothing to fear.

THE LADY ARRIVED in Luxor on Sunday night, having made the last leg of the journey on the river. Lord Noxley was at the landing place to meet her. Though the moon hadn't yet risen, and the torches only dimly illuminated the scene, he could see that all was far from well. She was stiff and formal. He heard no pleasure or even relief in her voice when she returned his greeting. She declined his arm.

"My brother," she said, drawing away from him. "These brutes of yours said Miles was here."

Brutes of yours. A very bad sign. Something had gone wrong. Someone had bungled.

Lord Noxley concealed his displeasure. His face showed only puzzlement. Still, those who knew him saw the thundercloud forming as clearly as if it had been broad day and a storm truly threatened.

"Archdale is quite safe," he said. "Merely indisposed at the moment, else he'd be here."

"Sick?" she said.

"No, no. I wish you would not distress yourself. Come, let us postpone discussion until you've had time to rest. You must be weary and wishing—"

"What's wrong with him?" she cut in.

"A trifle too much to drink," Noxley said. Dead drunk was more like it. "I hadn't expected you before tomorrow. He will be so—"

"One of your men killed Rupert Carsington," she said.

The thundercloud swelled and darkened. "Surely not," Lord Noxley said. "I cannot conceive how—"

"I saw it," she said. "Pray do not tell me I must have imagined it. I will not be humored or patronized. I am not a child."

"No, certainly not."

"I shall insist upon a full report to the authorities," she said. "I shall wish to make a statement. Tomorrow, as soon as may be. In the meantime, I want to see my brother, indisposed or not. Then I want a bath. And a bed."

"Yes, yes, of course. Perhaps—"

"And I want to be left alone. In peace."

"Certainly. A terrible shock. I am so sorry."

He would most certainly make someone else sorry, too, very sorry.

He gave Mrs. Pembroke into the care of a maidservant,

who took her to see the unconscious Archdale, then helped her bathe and put her to bed.

While his future bride sank into exhausted sleep upon her divan, his lordship listened to Ghazi's report.

The thundercloud had grown black by now. The lady was supposed to be warm with gratitude to her rescuer and hero, Asheton Noxley. Instead, she was cold and angry.

She was supposed to love him. At present, she seemed to hate him. Now he must spend days—perhaps weeks—winning her over.

He was very unhappy, which boded ill for somebody, perhaps several somebodies.

"I told you I wanted Carsington out of the way," he said. "Did I not point out that the simplest method was to have him taken to the nearest guardhouse for questioning?" Once Carsington was in someone else's custody, it would be easy enough to arrange for him to disappear or die of "natural causes." It was perfectly natural to die, for instance, if a pillow got stuck on your face or poison got into your food or a viper got into your bed.

Instead, a man Mrs. Pembroke knew was in Lord Noxley's employ had killed Carsington. While she watched.

"I can scarcely believe my ears," his lordship said, shaking his head. "You are supposed to be men of experience. But a mongoose nips you in the leg, and all your discipline is thrown to pieces. You knew we needed to be careful with him. You knew the matter required the utmost discretion. Now, thanks to your carelessness, I am tainted with the murder of an English nobleman's son."

The nobleman in question was not one with whom his lordship cared to cross swords.

"I agree, lord," Ghazi said. "It was all very stupid. But if I may explain one matter for which we were not prepared."

"You didn't expect the mongoose attack," Lord Noxley said. "On its hind legs I daresay it came all the way up to your knee. Ah, but their teeth are very sharp, and once they take hold, they don't let go. Terrifying monsters, indeed."

"I do not know how it was," Ghazi said stolidly, "but

the Egyptians took courage from the mongoose, I think. They fought us. Common Egyptians—they rose up and fought us."

Lord Noxley frowned at him. No one could have been prepared for that. Egyptians—common Egyptians, that is, not members of the military—cowered, hid, or ran away. They didn't fight.

"If they had not fought, we might have taken the Englishman away with no difficulty," said Ghazi. "We had only to beat the others a little, and soon he must yield. A big man, but with a heart soft like those of so many of your people. I agree there is no excuse for the killing. It was needless and stupid."

Lord Noxley considered. After a moment, he said, "The killer must be brought to justice."

Ghazi piously agreed.

"You had better turn him over to the Turkish soldiers," Lord Noxley said.

Forty Turkish soldiers were stationed in Luxor, for it was a town of some importance. Torturing the murderer would amuse them, and keeping the soldiers entertained was one way to insure their loyalty. Paying them—which the pasha often failed to do—was another. But that presented no problems.

Once he wed Virgil Pembroke's wealthy widow, Lord Noxley could afford to be very generous, indeed.

Monday 30 April

"DEVIL TAKE IT," Miles said. "You were supposed to be safe in Cairo."

It wasn't the most affectionate greeting for a sister he hadn't seen in a month, but he wasn't feeling affectionate at the moment. His head pounded, a fire raged behind his eyeballs, and his mouth tasted like camel's breath.

He'd dreamt of her last night, or thought it was a dream. She said she'd come in to see him, to make sure he was really there.

Now *she* was really there—here—in his room, sitting

on the edge of the divan, and there was no imagining it was a dream.

"You didn't know I was coming?" she said. "Your friend didn't tell you he'd sent men to collect me?"

"I think he likes surprises," Miles said. *Like heads in baskets.* He sat up fully, dragging his hand through his hair.

"You look frightful," she said.

"So do you," he said. It wasn't because she was dressed like an Egyptian man, minus turban. Her face was dead white, and shadows ringed her eyes.

She glanced down at her clothes. "I hadn't time to pack."

"I don't mean your clothes," he said. "What's happened to you?"

"They killed Rupert Carsington," she said.

"Say again?"

She repeated the sentence. Then she told him how she'd occupied herself during the last month.

Miles lay down again, clutching his head and trying to take it in. His bookish, reclusive sister had set out—with Rupert Carsington!—Lord Hargate's hellion son!—to find Miles. He could hardly follow the rest of her adventures, when his mind couldn't compass the first simple facts.

Quiet, studious Daphne. Chasing up the Nile. With Rupert Carsington!

"You should not have drunk so much," she said. "I have never known you to get into that state. You are developing very bad habits. I hope it isn't Noxley's influence."

He dragged himself up again. "It's the curst papyrus," he said. "He takes it out every night and wants to talk about it. I think he thinks I know something I don't."

"Well, you don't know anything about it," she said.

"I mean, I think he thinks what the French lunatic thinks."

"That you can read it," she said.

"I've told him no one can read it. I've told him I went to Giza to study the entrance to Chephren's pyramid, to try to discern the clues Belzoni saw, the ones that told him where the entrance was. Something about the way the rubble lay. I thought, if I could see what Belzoni saw, I could apply the knowledge in Thebes, the way Belzoni did, and find a royal tomb. I told him the papyrus got me itching to find another one. But Noxley keeps picking at my brain, as though he thinks I'm keeping secrets from him."

"You are," she said. "My secret."

"He thinks it's the key to decipherment. I drink because his delicate probing is driving me mad."

"Well, then, we shall have to clarify matters," she said. "He's asked us to join him in the *qa'a*. Shall I go ahead or wait for you?"

"Wait," he said. "I'd rather not leave you alone with him."

She gave a short laugh.

"What's so amusing?" he said.

"I've looked a viper in the eye before," she said.

He didn't understand. She was behaving strangely. This wasn't the Daphne he knew. It must be the shock, he thought. She'd seen a man killed, and she'd traveled across the desert with Ghazi and his band of merry murderers. Not to mention the river journey. With Rupert Carsington!

She rose. "I'll wait for you in my room," she said. "I have a fine view."

It was only after she left that he became aware of the distant sound. A screech or shriek. Some sort of bird, perhaps.

HE LOOKED SO innocent, Daphne thought. Golden curls and clear blue eyes. He was dressed Arab style though minus the turban and beard and all in white instead of the bright colors the locals favored.

All in white, like an angel.

Smiling, all sunshine, as though all were right with the world.

She smiled, too, because she did not plan to make anything easy for him. She settled onto the divan and said, yes, she'd slept well, thank you. And no, she had no objections to native food, and yes, coffee would be just the thing— very strong, please, as Miles needed a stimulant.

Miles sat next to her, protective, though he was so ill and weak, he could scarcely sit upright. He'd never had a head for drinking.

Noxley apologized for her limited wardrobe. "I cannot think why the men failed to collect your belongings," he said.

"They were too busy killing people," she said.

"Daph," Miles murmured, giving her a nudge.

She ignored him. "Speaking of which—"

"Daph, could we postpone unpleasant subjects until after I've swallowed some coffee?" Miles said. "Good gad, what's that horrible noise?" He clutched his head.

Even without an aching head, she, too, found it disturbing. She'd heard it earlier, but faintly. She'd thought it some exotic bird or animal. Or maybe peacocks.

"The screaming, you mean?" said Noxley.

"It's *human?*" Miles said.

"Oh, yes," Noxley said. "It appears the Turkish soldiers are interrogating the man who shot Mr. Carsington." He brought his innocent blue gaze back to Daphne. "Naturally, as soon as you informed me, I questioned my men and ordered the culprit brought to justice."

"It sounds as though they're torturing him," she said.

"The Turks' notions of justice are different from ours," he said. "If the noise troubles you, I'll request they remove him out of earshot. It will not go on very much longer, at any rate. They must take him back to Cairo. Muhammad Ali will want the English consul general to witness the execution. Doubtless the assassin's head will be sent to Lord Hargate."

"Gad, another one," Miles muttered. "In a basket, I don't doubt."

A servant glided in, bearing an enormous tray. He set it down upon the elaborately carved stool near the divan and glided away.

"You had wanted the matter dealt with promptly," said Lord Noxley. "I wished to spare you the ordeal of reliving the experience."

As though she could ever stop reliving it.

He looked down for a moment, at his hands, then up at her again, all blue-eyed innocence. "I cannot apologize enough," he said. "My men were obliged to act in haste, for they'd word that Duval's people were coming for you. The

trouble is, thinking is not what they do best. In their eager-
ness to protect you, they were impatient, clumsy, and stupid. They are unaccustomed to defiance from the common
people. It gave them a shock that disordered their lamenta-
bly limited wits."

"I see," she said. "I had wondered why I had to be
forcibly removed from my boat. I should have thought an
armed escort would have sufficed as protection. But your
men were not thinking clearly—or at all."

He bowed his head again and pressed two fingers to the
place between his eyebrows. "I do see your point. It is so
difficult to explain the way of things here."

"Suppose you don't," she said. "Suppose you say
plainly that you are the Golden Devil, the terror of Upper
Egypt, and you want us here for a particular reason, not
necessarily altruistic."

She heard Miles suck in his breath.

Noxley winced and shut his eyes.

"Daph," Miles said, touching her arm.

She shook him off. "What is it, my lord?" she pressed.
"The papyrus? It does have a curious effect on men. Poi-
sons their judgment. Makes them see things that aren't
there. Royal tombs, heaped with treasure. People who can
read hieroglyphic writing. My papyrus could be an account
of a battle or a proclamation—no more to do with treasure
than the Rosetta Stone. But men see the pair of cartouches,
and their imaginations run away with them. You are such
romantic creatures."

Lord Noxley's head came up. *"Your* papyrus," he repeated. "You said—"

"It's mine," she said. "Miles bought it for me. Because
I'm the one. He is the famous scholar Miles Archdale, but I
am his brain."

AT SUNSET SHE stood at the window of her room, looking out over the river.

Like London, Thebes was built on both sides of the
river. There the resemblance ended. This was truly another
world. Here, above the fertile plain of the eastern bank rose

the immense temples, obelisks, and pylons of Luxor and Karnak. On the plain of the western bank the Colossi of Memnon sat upon on their thrones. Behind them loomed the vast necropolis, with its temples and tombs. The latter, cut into the flanks of the Libyan hills, honeycombed the eastern slope. She gazed at the mountains that concealed the Biban el Muluk and its royal tombs.

"Is your mind poisoned, too? Have you completely taken leave of your senses?"

She turned toward the door, where her brother stood. "Has the sun boiled away your brain, Daph?" he said. He came in, slamming the door behind him. "We can't stay here," he said. "He is—he is—" With his forefinger Miles made a circular motion near his temple.

"I don't care what he is," she said, turning back to the window. "We have no pressing reason to return to Cairo, as he pointed out. He's most eager to accommodate us. He's promised to send to Cairo for my books and materials. There may be a difficulty in replacing my Coptic lexicons—they were aboard the *Isis*—but he's promised to make inquiries at the Coptic monasteries."

"Daph, you must have heard how his fellows 'make inquiries,'" Miles said. "They beat the soles of a man's feet with a stick. For hours. And that's the mildest sort of interrogation."

"I'll ask him not to abuse the monks," she said. "He wants to keep me happy."

"Of course he wants to keep you happy," Miles said. "You're filthy rich. With your backing, he could excavate the entire valley. He could make himself king of Thebes. You're like the goose that lays the golden eggs: an endless supply of money."

Virgil's conscience money, she thought. It had been easier for him to leave her everything after he was dead than to treat her with respect and kindness while he lived.

"We shall be able to explore all of Thebes unhindered," she said. "All the royal tombs, including the one Belzoni found. I'll have hundreds upon hundreds of samples of hieroglyphic writing. It is a great opportunity. And I shan't have to pretend to be someone I am not."

"And he'll be able to make either of us do whatever he wants simply by threatening the other," Miles said.

"Then it would be wise not to provoke him to use threats," she said.

"He's got it in his head to marry you," Miles said. "Can't you see? He must be master of everything: of you, of your money. And mad or not, Golden Devil or not, he looks at you the same way other men do."

She remembered the way Rupert looked at her, the glint of laughter in his eyes. She remembered that last afternoon on the *Isis*.

We could marry.

Her throat started to close up. She bowed her head and willed the grief back. If she gave in, she'd sink and never find her way out again. She would be lost. She couldn't afford grief. She had to be strong and hard if she hoped to survive this and find a way out.

"Use your head," she said, her voice harsh. "Your friend won't let us go. We have to make the best of matters."

"The way you made the best of Pembroke?" Miles said. "Do you think I want to see you suffer again?"

She made herself look at him. She smiled crookedly. "If I could survive Virgil, I can survive anything," she said. "We'll get out of this somehow. But it will take time and thought and care—and you must learn to have more confidence in me."

ON TUESDAY AND Wednesday they toured Luxor, which, as she'd already discerned, was a grander spectacle when viewed from a distance, from the other side of the river or when tidied by the artists of the *Description de l'Egypte*. The reality, at close quarters, depressed her spirits, although that may have simply been her state of mind.

The place seemed to close in on her: the hovels squeezed into every corner and crevice, the squalor, the pigeons, the refuse, the mounds of sand and rubbish choking obelisks, pylons, columns.

Still, she made herself view it with a scholar's eyes. On Wednesday she borrowed a notebook from Lord Noxley and began copying inscriptions.

On Thursday, they went to Karnak. It was no great distance away: less than two miles. They rode their donkeys along the Avenue of Sphinxes, or what was left of it. At present, most of the sphinxes were destroyed, and the southern part of the avenue was covered with soil and rubbish.

Yet this destruction failed to diminish the place. Neither did the monuments' being half buried make them any the less overwhelming. The vast pylons, the giant forests of columns, the obelisks, colossi, and sphinxes—it was all as the *Description de l'Egypte* had illustrated, at length and in detail. Nonetheless, the reality far exceeded anything Daphne could have imagined.

As they made their way along the principal avenue in the hypostyle hall, she gazed up at the avenue of twelve immense columns—the largest in any Egyptian building, Noxley said—and wondered what Rupert would have made of it.

In her mind's eye she saw him looking up at one of the lotus-shaped capitals much as he'd gazed at Chephren's pyramid: fists on his hips, the breeze ruffling his black hair. She could almost hear the deep voice saying, "It's big."

And she smiled, but her lips wobbled, and her throat ached, and tears blurred her vision.

She closed her eyes and willed back the tears. She must keep working, employ her intellect instead of her emotions. Her work had given her strength before and would again. Her mind was the one ally she could always rely upon. In time, it would show her the way out.

THAT NIGHT DAPHNE dreamt of a pharaoh's tomb.

She descended sixteen steps into an entrance passage. At the end of it was a chamber crowded with various objects: boxes, baskets, jars, and articles of furniture shaped like animals. Her gaze was drawn to the right, to two figures guarding a door. She passed the two figures and stepped through the doorway into a dark chamber.

A faint light showed her a pair of doors. She opened them. An immense golden sarcophagus stood within. Goddesses stood at its corners, their wings spread out, protecting what lay within.

Daphne climbed a set of steps and looked down into the sarcophagus.

There lay Rupert Carsington, as though asleep, wearing a small, sweet smile like the one on the statue of Ramesses the Great at Memphis.

He wore a kilt of gold cloth and lay with his arms crossed over his naked chest. In the soft light, the muscled planes of his torso gleamed a darker gold.

She reached down and touched his face.

"Miss you," she whispered.

Tears trickled down her face and onto his.

He said, "Daphne, wake up."

No. She didn't want to leave the dream. She would never see him again except in dreams.

"Daphne, wake up."

She tried to say no, but nothing came out.

She opened her eyes to darkness. A hand covered her mouth. It wasn't her hand. It was big, and . . . familiar.

There was the scent. Man-scent. *His.*

A deep voice growled, "No screaming. No weeping. No fainting."

She choked out the three words on a sob, as her arms went round his neck: "I. Never. Faint."

Chapter 20

UNDER THE THIN BLANKET, SHE WAS SOFT AND wondrously curved and practically naked. As he pulled her tight against him, Rupert discovered that there was almost nothing in the way: a scrap of thin fabric, her *kamees,* bunched up at her waist. All the rest was skin, clean and silken-smooth and . . . strange.

Something was missing.

He buried his face in her neck and sniffed.

He raised his head. "What have they done to you?" he whispered. "Something's missing. The goddess scent."

"What have they done to me? To *me?* I thought you were dead."

"I know. I thought I was, too, at first."

"I saw you shot," she said. "You clutched your chest and went over. You didn't come up again."

"The ball grazed me, just under my arm," he said. "A scratch. But I tripped. Lost my balance and went over. And, as usual, I hit my head. I came to my senses a good ways downriver, clinging to a piece of boarding plank. It was deuced embarrassing."

"Embarrassing."

"The boys look up to me," he said. "I'm a hero. Heroes

don't trip. Heroes don't knock their heads on the way down. I must have looked a complete clodpate."

She pulled his face to hers and kissed him. So gently and sweetly at first. He tasted tears. He should have said, *No weeping* again, but he couldn't. The tender kiss started a queer ache inside him, not quite happy and not quite sad. It was the thing she did to him: stirring up feelings he had no names for.

He'd been wild, half-mad, when he finally caught up with the *Isis* and clambered aboard, wet and bruised but scarcely bleeding at all, though you'd never know it to hear everyone carrying on. It had taken him most of the five days' journey to Thebes to calm down, collect his wits, and realize how lucky his clumsiness was.

If the villains hadn't believed he was dead, they would have made sure of it.

Now they wouldn't be expecting him. They wouldn't be looking for him.

He had to make the most of the opportunity.

In a minute.

Right now, he was starved for the taste of her, the feel of her, the warmth and willingness and wickedness of her. He slid his hands down her smooth back, and brought them down to enclose the delicious inward turn of her waist. He grasped her wonderfully naked backside and crushed her against his groin.

"I missed you," she murmured against his mouth. She rubbed her cheek against his, in that way she had, and something opened up inside him, deep and dark. He didn't know what it was or why.

But he remembered the emptiness. He remembered how he'd see a strange bird and turn to point it out to her, and then remember she wasn't there.

He remembered looking into her cabin, where they'd made slow, silent love. He couldn't stop himself from picking up a cushion and pressing it to his face, hungrily seeking her scent . . . running his fingers over the covers and spines of her books . . . staring into the pages of her notebooks at the neat script and the words he didn't understand and the sketches: the little figures and signs, all incomprehensible.

"I missed you, too," he said. He'd missed her terribly, beyond anything he could have imagined.

He wanted to capture her mouth again, and everything else, and claim her in the most primitive of ways.

There wasn't time.

He drew away. "Well then, we'd best be going," he said.

"Going?" she said in a dazed voice. "We're going?"

"Yes. Now. You. Me. The window." He sat up, silently ordering his privy councilor to settle down. "Where are your clothes? Never mind. A cloak will do. You've clothes on the boat."

"I don't think—"

"You haven't time to think," he said. "We need to leave before the guards begin to sober—or someone smells the hashish and gets suspicious," he said.

She rubbed her face. "Hashish?"

"Remember your drugged doorkeeper? So cheerfully useless? How else do you think I could climb up the side of the house without setting off an uproar?"

"I can't leave Miles," she said.

"I know, but he's not conveniently situated at the moment," Rupert said. "I can't get to his window, and I can't go through the house. We couldn't drug everybody, and there are a great lot of people in the way. A maidservant sleeping outside your door. Other servants elsewhere, everywhere, underfoot. And then there are the guards prowling the passages."

"How do you—"

"Leena's been spying for us," he said. "Made friends with a talkative servant girl. Can we go into the details later? We can't dawdle."

"I cannot leave Miles," she said. "If I disappear, he'll pay."

"No, he won't. He's too valuable for them to harm. We'll devise a cunning plan to get him out. By tomorrow. I promise." He rose from the divan. "Where's your cloak?"

She rose slowly. "He isn't valuable," she said.

"You know that and I know that," he said, "but—"

"Noxley knows my secret," she said.

• • •

THERE WAS A short, taut pause. Then, "Yes, of course," he said, "I should have known this would be complicated."

"I told him," she said. "I had to. Miles could never keep up the pretense, living under the same roof, day in, day out. He started drinking to avoid answering difficult questions, and he has no head for liquor."

"I understand," he said. "I assumed it couldn't be helped. We'll deal with the problem. In the meantime—"

"Miles believes Noxley's insane," she said. "I'm not sure of that. I am very sure *he* won't do anything to Miles. Noxley likes to appear noble and kind." Another fraud, like Virgil. "He has others do the dirty work for him: torturing, maiming, killing people."

"Daphne—"

"Shhhh." She laid her fingers over his mouth.

Sounds. Footsteps. Voices. Outside the door.

He looked that way. He heard it, too.

She pushed him toward the window. "Go."

"Not without you."

She didn't want him to go without her, either, but they had no choice. And no time to argue.

She made a fist and hit him backhanded in the chest. "You're alive," she said. "Stay alive, or I'll never get out of this. *Go.*"

The sounds grew louder.

Daphne hurried back to the divan. *Go,* she begged silently. *Please go.*

She felt rather than heard him move away.

There was a quick, impatient rap at the door. A maidservant's voice called softly: was all well with the lady?

Daphne lay down and drew up her thin blanket. The door flew open.

She sat up hastily and looked about her, in the manner of one abruptly awakened.

A maidservant stood in the doorway, holding an oil lamp. Behind her a tall, bulky figure loomed.

"The guard heard sounds," the servant said, holding the lamp aloft. "Voices, he says."

"Did he?" Daphne said. "I must have been talking in my sleep. I had very strange dreams."

4 May

DAPHNE WENT WITH Noxley and Miles to Karnak again on Friday. It was amazing how glorious the place seemed, now the black weight had lifted from her heart. She soon filled her notebook, and Lord Noxley sent a servant to Luxor for another. She spent the latter part of the day in a small room called the Chamber of Kings. Under the various pharaohs' sculpted images were their hieroglyphic names, which she copied.

"You will not be bored, I think, if we return tomorrow?" Lord Noxley asked her as they started back to Luxor at sunset.

"I believe I could spend a month and never grow bored," she said. "But another day will suffice, if you have other plans."

"We can always return," Noxley said. "But perhaps if you made a general survey of Thebes, you might then choose the places of greatest use to your studies. I thought we might make a tour of the western bank next week. I do suspect you will find that area even more fascinating, Mrs. Pembroke. There one may study not only temples and palaces but the tombs as well. Equally important, the Tombs of the Nobles will supply you amply with papyri."

He went on to denounce the inhabitants of western Thebes, the Qurnans, who destroyed the tombs, tore mummies to pieces, and burnt beautifully decorated mummy cases for firewood.

"It was their ancestors who stripped bare the kings' tombs in the Biban el Muluk, you may be sure," his lordship said. "The whole greedy, thieving tribe should have been eradicated long ago, but the Turkish authorities will not bestir themselves. The trouble is, no one here considers tomb robbing an important crime. The Turks are diligent only in collecting taxes and bribes and bullying the peasants. They are barbarians who do not understand or care about bygone civilizations. They dismantle ancient temples to build factories."

"We're not so different," Daphne said. "We of supposedly enlightened nations plunder and destroy, too. It cannot be right to violate the dead, to tear mummies to pieces to find jewelry and papyri. But without the papyri, how are we scholars to understand the past? Is it right to leave the monuments here, at risk of destruction? Or is it right to take them away to our palaces and museums and mansions abroad? I don't know what the answer is. I only know that my papyrus came from one of those tombs—courtesy of the Qurnans."

Noxley shook his head. "Yours came from no ordinary Theban tomb," he said. "It came from a *king's* tomb, from the Biban el Muluk."

"That's what Anaz claimed," Miles said.

"Now that I've had an opportunity to study it closely, and compare it to a host of others, I am more inclined to believe him," Noxley said. "The cartouches, for instance. I've seen any number in royal tombs and on temples and other monuments, but never on a papyrus. Still, most papyri are written in the script, you know, not the picture signs, so I may have seen royal names without realizing."

Daphne had not seen enough papyri to make any such generalizations. "How many other papyri have you studied?" she said.

"I should never presume to say I've studied them, not as you have," he said. "I'm an explorer, not a scholar. But I've seen a great many—and at present I have at least two score."

"That is a great many," she said. More than twice as many as she owned.

"You are welcome to make use of them," he said. "I know your visit to Thebes started off on the wrong foot, but I am determined to make it right. Let me begin fresh by speaking frankly and honestly, as you clearly prefer. I should dearly love to discover a royal tomb. And you, I know, wish to unlock the secrets of the hieroglyphs. Working together, as allies—I shall not presume to speak of anything more, at present—but as allies, as a team, we are more likely to realize our ambitions, do you not think?"

"And Miles?" Daphne asked. "What is his role?"

Noxley turned a sweet smile upon her brother. "Archdale, you deceived me dreadfully. I was furious at first, to think what a fool you'd made of me. But you only did so on this lady's behalf. And so I forgive you. I am sure you'd rather try to discover a royal tomb than spend your time learning Coptic and solving word puzzles. You had some ideas, I believe, about locating tomb entrances. Perhaps we might put our heads together?"

"Certainly," Miles said. "Much more agreeable than having it cut off."

Lord Noxley laughed, as though it were a joke, and went on to talk about Belzoni's tomb and the likelihood of there being others even more impressive.

The conversation lagged as they reached Luxor and had to make their way through its narrow byways. Shortly before they reached the house, an old woman accosted Daphne and offered to tell her fortune.

Noxley gave her a coin and told her to come another time: the lady was weary today. The crone took the coin and offered to give the lady a charm for good fortune. Noxley shrugged.

The fortune teller took Daphne's hand and muttered, too low for anyone but Daphne to hear, "He comes with fire. Be ready."

THOUGH SHE WAS his sister, Miles had always understood that men turned into drooling idiots on account of Daphne's figure.

That was natural enough.

What he didn't understand was why those who managed to get close to her must be queer in the attic.

The poetically handsome Pembroke, with his sweet, gentle ways, had turned out to be a pious hypocrite of a tyrant. He was possessive, madly jealous of other men, and even more madly jealous of Daphne's superior intellect.

Noxley was another one with a beautiful exterior and charming ways and a black heart. And he was a fine one to speak of Miles's deceiving him, considering how he had completely taken in Miles.

Like Pembroke, Noxley was possessive to an extreme. This was a man, after all, who thought all of Thebes belonged to him. He was also a torturer and killer by proxy. And when someone presented him with a man's head in a basket, he lit up like a child who'd got a new hobbyhorse or a set of toy soldiers.

The closest he came to a redeeming quality was his lack of jealousy of Daphne's mind. But then, he believed her mind would eventually lead him to a great discovery, if not a great treasure. Noxley wanted fame and power, but he wasn't averse to increasing his wealth, either.

But Daphne said they had to go along, and she was right. They were prisoners in Thebes. They were watched constantly. They couldn't get away without help, and everyone here was either too corrupted or too terrified to take such a risk.

At the moment, you'd think Noxley was the dearest, sweetest fellow in the world.

They'd had their dinner and as he'd done before when only Miles was here, Noxley brought out the papyrus. This evening, though, he had several others brought in, and he was laying them out carefully on the carpet for her perusal.

Daphne knelt beside him, her attention completely on the documents. Noxley's attention was completely on her, especially her bosom, as she launched into one of her stunningly boring lectures on Dr. Young's work and where she agreed and disagreed with him, and why.

Perhaps because his mind was elsewhere, it did not put Noxley to sleep as you'd expect. Still, he did eventually acquire the vacant, dazed expression with which Miles was more than familiar. Those who could stay awake always looked that way after listening to Daphne for a time.

Boring, studious Daphne. If she didn't have her nose in a book, she had it smudged with ink, while she drew her little charts and her rows and columns of alphabets, signs, words. Shy, reclusive, logical Daphne.

The same woman who'd set out—with Rupert Carsington! Hargate's Hellion!—on a mad scheme to rescue her brother.

This wasn't the sister Miles thought he knew. Yet this was Daphne, beyond question, droning on about Coptic and other brain-strangling arcana.

"The sun sign, for instance," she was saying, pointing to a cartouche. "Here it stands alone, and I am quite sure it is *ra* or *re*, the Coptic for sun, whereas Dr. Young puts it in combination with a pillar symbol and gives the god the name *Phre—*"

A bloodcurdling scream cut her off. Another followed, then shouting.

Lord Noxley leapt up.

The noise intensified. From nearby came the patter of bare feet at a run. A servant shrieked, and others called on God to preserve them.

Miles made out the word "fire." He quickly rose, too. Daphne came up more slowly.

Noxley ran out of the room. Miles started after him. Daphne grabbed his arm. "Wait," she said quietly.

She gathered up an armful of papyri and looked about her expectantly.

A cloaked and hooded figure appeared in the doorway. "Trouble outside," he said in thickly accented English. "This way. Come."

"Who are you?" Miles demanded. "What kind of trouble? Let me see your face."

Daphne pushed him, hard, toward the door. "Don't ask questions," she said.

"But he might be one of Duval's—"

"He isn't!" she snapped. "Stop talking. Start running."

ONCE HE'D GOT them out of the main room and into the less well-lighted passage, Rupert had to throw back his hood, so he could see.

He heard Archdale whisper, "Who *is* he?"

"Rupert Carsington," Rupert said.

"But you're dead."

"Not anymore," Rupert said. They'd reached the stairway. He paused, withdrew the pistols from his girdle, and handed them out.

The brother said, "Better give her a knife. Daphne doesn't—"

"Is it loaded?" Daphne said.

"Yes. Be careful."

"But Daphne doesn't—"

"Yes, she does," Rupert said. He unhooked the rope from his sash. "Your room," he told Daphne. "I've people waiting below your window." He sent Archdale up after her, and followed, listening for signs of pursuit.

The boys had started a conflagration at the front door, where it would cause the most spectacle and confusion. But they could hardly haul a load of firewood, even if Egypt could supply such a thing. Straw and dung fueled the fire, and it would soon be seen for what it was.

Rupert had mere minutes.

LORD NOXLEY HAD reacted instinctively: he was under attack—Duval, no doubt—and he must organize his forces.

He'd grabbed a rifle and was nearly at the front door—after having to fight his way past panicked servants—when he realized his mistake. An open attack wasn't in Duval's style.

This was a diversion.

Lord Noxley hurried back into the *qa'a*.

They were gone, and most of the papyri with them.

He ran out of the room, shouting for Ghazi, then raced up the stairway to the large bedchamber he'd planned to transform into a bridal suite before too much time had passed.

She wasn't there.

But *he* was.

When Lord Noxley burst in, the tall figure was at the window. He turned.

Carsington.

The dead man.

Not dead enough.

Lord Noxley cocked the rifle, aimed, and pulled the trigger.

• • •

RUPERT DOVE FOR the floor, rolled, and grabbed Noxley's legs, bringing him down. The weapon discharged, and the ball pinged against the wall.

Rupert grabbed Noxley's wrist and banged it on the stony floor. The man let go of the rifle—then shoved his elbow into Rupert's gut, broke free, and scrambled onto his feet. He ran toward the window, but Rupert was quickly up again and close behind. He grabbed Noxley and flung him against the wall. Noxley bounced back, and came at him fist first. He thrust it into Rupert's jaw with surprising force.

Rupert drove his fist into Noxley's gut.

It was a harder gut than you'd think, and the man only grunted instead of crumpling in a heap as men usually did when Rupert hit them. In a flash, Noxley struck again. So did Rupert, and he was not gentle.

But Noxley went on, furiously giving back blow for blow, though he soon began to weaken.

"Give it up," Rupert gasped. "You're good, but I've got stamina."

"She's *mine*," Noxley said. His hand moved, and something glinted there.

And Rupert thought *knife*, an instant before it thrust into him.

DAPHNE WAS AWARE of her brother, below, calling to her, but she went on climbing back up. She'd heard the gun go off, and waited, holding her breath, for Rupert to come out.

He didn't.

But it wasn't over, she realized a moment later. She heard thuds and thumps, the clatter of broken crockery. They were still fighting.

It wasn't a great many men. Three at most. Perhaps only two.

She had to help Rupert before any more came, and he was outnumbered.

She found a place for her foot, and was looking for the

next foothold to get her back to the window when something flew over her head. It made a small arc, then, as she watched, horrified, dropped to the rocks below. A body. It was human.

"Rupert!" she cried.

"Coming," said an impossibly deep voice from over her head.

She looked up. Rupert leant out the window. "Don't dawdle," he said. "We haven't got all night."

THEY HAD NEARLY reached the landing place when they heard the shouts. Daphne glanced back. Men seemed to be coming from every direction. Some carried torches, in whose light she saw weapons gleaming. She saw a pair of figures pause at the body, before Rupert grabbed her arm and turned her about. "Run!" he said. "Archdale, get her to the boat."

"No!" She drew her pistol. "You're not facing them alone."

A shot rang out. Men were running at them. She cocked her weapon and fired.

After that was chaos. Shouting, the clash of swords, the occasional blast of a firearm. Men started running toward them from the other side, from the river. She thought she recognized voices. The *Isis*'s crew had joined the fray.

She saw two men tackle Miles and bring him down. She ran to them and started beating the men with the butt end of her weapon.

It was a while before she noticed the noise subsiding.

Then a familiar voice called out. "Cease, lady, or the big *Ingleezi* dies, truly, this time."

She turned, and saw everyone was looking the same way. Rupert was clutching his side. A dark stain was spreading outward from the place he held. Ghazi held a pistol to Rupert's head.

The last of the fighting stopped.

"The master is dead," Ghazi said. "I am master now."

Daphne thought quickly.

She remembered what Noxley had said about his men: *thinking is not what they do best.*

"Very well," she said in Arabic. "Congratulations. You're welcome to be master. I'm sure you'll make a fine one. But what has it to do with us? It was the Golden Devil who wanted me—for a bride. It was the Golden Devil who wanted my brother—to help read the ancient writing. Surely you can find your own brides? You don't need to steal them." She fervently hoped Noxley hadn't told anybody how much his future spouse was worth in pounds, shillings, and pence. "But do you truly wish to devote your life to digging in the sand to find holes in the ground with painted walls? Did you want to be a leader of diggers and scavengers or a leader of—um—the most feared assassins in all the Ottoman Empire?"

While she spoke, Ghazi's expression took on a troubled and confused expression. He glanced about him. His men were looking troubled, too. He quickly regained his composure. "This is foolish talk," he said. "The big *Ingleezi* has killed the Golden Devil. You have shot one of my men. And it is not the first time. You will not go free." With his free hand, he signaled to his men. "Take her. And the other man."

Rupert sagged. "Oops," he said. "Sorry."

He folded up and sank to the ground.

"No!" Daphne cried. She ran toward him, pushing the astonished Ghazi aside, and sinking to her knees beside Rupert. "He's no danger to you, you great bully," she cried. "Can't you see he's hurt?"

"I will put him out of his misery." Ghazi aimed the pistol at Rupert. Daphne threw herself on top of Rupert.

"As you wish," said Ghazi. "I kill two at once."

"Fire your weapon," Miles called out, "and pharaoh's treasure goes up in smoke."

During the momentary distraction, he'd grabbed somebody's torch. He held a papyrus close to the flame. "This is what the Golden Devil wanted," Miles said. "This is what Duval wants. Worth a king's ransom. Everybody play nice, or it's ashes."

Some of the men were muttering, "What's he saying?"

because Miles made the speech in English. But Ghazi had no trouble comprehending.

Thinking wasn't what he did best. This, however, was simple enough to comprehend. He knew the papyrus was valuable. He knew Duval wanted it. And he knew that these old, crumbly *anteekahs* took fire easily.

Still, once he had the papyrus, he'd no reason to let them get away, Daphne thought.

"Let them go," someone called from the crowd. "The Turkish soldiers are coming. Remember what they did to the one they thought had killed the big Englishman?"

Ghazi threw down his pistol and advanced toward Miles.

Miles looked at Daphne.

"Give it to him," she said.

Miles gave Ghazi the papyrus. Ghazi unrolled it a bit, gave it a glance, then quickly tucked it into his girdle. He moved away, snatched up his pistol—

And kept on walking, away from them.

His men turned away and followed him.

All but one, the one who'd warned about the Turkish soldiers.

He came forward.

"Let me help you, mistress," he said. In English.

She had turned away, to attend to Rupert, who was showing signs of consciousness. But the English words and something in the man's voice made her look up again.

She gazed into a familiar face, one she hadn't seen in more than a month.

"Akmed?" she said.

"This man saved my life," he said. "I will help you save his."

Chapter 21

DAPHNE DID AN ADMIRABLE JOB OF PATCHING
Rupert up, scolding him all the while she picked out bits of
cloth from the knife wound. It was thanks to those thick
layers of cloth—the Arab-style sash he'd worn and the
lethal objects it contained—that Rupert was alive.

The wound was rather more than the "scratch" he'd la-
beled it and was rather more uncomfortable than he'd expected. Nonetheless, she seemed to think he'd live. Her
main concern, she said, was infection. She did not think
that leaving shreds of dirty cloth in the wound would aid
his recovery.

He lay upon the divan of his cabin, occasionally peering
down to see what she was doing but mainly watching her
face in the lantern light. He would never grow tired of
looking at her wonderful face. He was quite pleased he'd
live to do so.

He'd truly thought the wound no more than a scratch, at
first. It hadn't hurt at all. But he'd probably been too furious at the time to feel anything. They'd been having a fair
enough fight, fists only, he told Daphne. But then, when
Noxley realized he was losing, he *cheated.*

"I cannot believe you so addlepated as to imagine Noxley would fight fair," Daphne said, when Rupert waxed indignant on this point, calling it "deuced unsporting."

"But it isn't *done*," Rupert said. "Ask your brother. Ask anybody. I did not draw my pistol. I did not draw my knife. I had never killed anybody, and I did hope it would not be necessary."

He was a great deal more upset than he let on. He hadn't meant to throw Noxley out the window. At least Rupert hoped he hadn't. At such times, though, a man was not truly capable of thinking. It was all instinct. Noxley had stabbed him. Rupert had yanked out the blade and thrown it aside—and the next thing he knew, Noxley was sailing out of the window.

Having got the wound as clean as she could, Daphne quickly and neatly stitched it up and bandaged it.

"Pray do not distress yourself about Noxley," she said, quite as though she'd spent the last few minutes reading his mind. "He would have killed you without a second thought, certainly with no qualms. He had no conscience whatsoever. A moral vacuum. He must have what he wanted. Anyone who stood in the way must be annihilated."

She turned away to the medicine case that stood on the floor nearby. Rupert couldn't see what she was doing. After a moment, she turned back, a small glass in hand.

"I had not realized he wanted me until his men dropped a hint," she said.

"I told you he wanted you," he said. "It was obvious in the way he looked at you. He might have been mad for power and fame, but he wasn't blind."

"Power and fame can be costly," she said. "He was not in lust with my person alone. He doted equally upon my fortune."

It took a moment for Rupert to fully grasp what she was saying, and these mental exertions must have shown in his face because she said, frowning, "You did know Virgil left me heaps and heaps of money, did you not? All the world knew, I thought."

"Heaps and heaps?" he said. "Well, it was the least he could do, the lying swine. Not that I imagined you were a pauper, when you saw nothing out of the way in your brother's spending thousands for one of those brown, rolled-up thingums."

"*Papyri*," she said crisply, almost as she'd done that first day, in the dungeon. But he heard the note of amusement.

"I know," he said. "I knew. I was only trying to provoke you that day. I knew you had a temper. I could *feel* it, when you were twenty feet away. It was like standing on the edge of a storm. Very . . . stimulating."

"You've had sufficient stimulation for the present," she said. She came close then, raised Rupert's head, pressed it to her delicious bosom, and held the glass to his lips. "Here, drink this."

He'd had an unpleasant feeling the glass was for him, but the conversation had diverted his attention. The warm femininity he rested upon was an even greater distraction. "What is it?"

"A little laudanum mixed with wine."

He carefully turned his head away from the glass without endangering his agreeable position on her soft endowments. "I don't want any."

"You will drink it," she said, "or I shall summon Akmed and tell him to gather the largest men aboard. They will hold you down while I pour it down your throat. Will you submit gracefully, or would you rather be embarrassed in front of the boys?"

"I don't need any laudanum," he muttered, but he turned back and drank.

When he was done, she set down the glass and gently but firmly transferred his head from her bosom to the pillow. "The wound is sure to become a great deal more painful as the shock wears off," she said. "This way, you will get some rest."

"I wish you might rest with me," he said, letting his hand slide to her thigh. She was dressed like an Arab man, but no man with working eyesight would ever mistake her for a member of his sex.

"That would not be restful," she said. "And kindly remember that my brother is now aboard."

Rupert sighed. The brother. Yes, of course. But the brother was not Akmed, with whom she'd threatened Rupert a moment ago. Who was Akmed?

Oh, yes, the fellow who spoke up, just as matters had promised to grow very interesting, indeed.

What had he said? He'd spoken in English first, then reverted to Arabic.

"What did he say?" Rupert said. "The Akmed fellow? He called you 'mistress.' "

"That was Akmed," she said, unenlighteningly.

"That's what I said," he said patiently. Really, there were times when he wondered whether that immense brain of hers contained an empty chamber or two. "He said something, just before I . . . um . . . dozed a bit."

"You fainted," she said. "Several times."

"I was a little sleepy," he said. "I hadn't slept since they took you. I was . . . tired. I did not faint."

Her delicate snort sufficiently expressed her views on the subject.

"I wish you wouldn't keep turning the subject," he said. "Who is Akmed and what was he saying?"

"He said you saved his life."

Rupert thought about this. "He must have confused me with someone else," he said.

"On the bridge outside Cairo," she said. "He'd been badly beaten. A Turkish soldier tried to finish the job. But you stepped in the way."

After a period of cogitation, which went even more slowly than usual, Rupert realized who she was talking about: the dirty cripple on the bridge. "Oh, *that* fellow."

"That was why you ended up in the dungeon," she said accusingly. "You risked your life on behalf of a miserable native you didn't know from Adam."

"It wasn't a fair fight," Rupert said.

She gazed at him for a good long while. Then she stroked his cheek briefly. "No, it wasn't," she murmured. "But only you would care." More distinctly she added, "Akmed is the servant who went with Miles to Giza. What you saw was the results of the beating the so-called police gave him—the ones who kidnapped Miles. Akmed is the servant who ran away when the men came to my house and stole the papyrus."

"He's the servant who didn't come back," Rupert said. "Tom's uncle. The fellow on the bridge. One and the same. And he turned up here? Extraordinary."

"Not really," she said. "Akmed knew he wasn't safe in Cairo and being there might endanger his family as well as me. So he went to Bulaq, to get work on a boat. There he heard Lord Noxley was going to look for Miles. Akmed had no trouble getting hired. He speaks English and a little French, and he is intelligent and hardworking. He thought Noxley was a fine man. Akmed had no doubts about this until the fine man fed a few followers to the crocodiles—very possibly the same ones you and I saw above Girga."

"But Akmed didn't run away then?" The lantern light was growing fuzzy—or was that Rupert's brain? He seemed to be drifting . . . on a river . . . no, a cloud.

"He stayed on because he was determined to find Miles," she said. "Then, when Noxley's men found my brother, Akmed stayed to look after him and protect him as best he could while avoiding discovery. He'd grown out his beard, and Miles didn't recognize him. Akmed decided not to enlighten him until he could arrange for an escape for both of them. Then I turned up and complicated matters."

She went on, but Rupert lost track of what she was saying. Her voice became a distant music, sweet and familiar. And then by degrees the sound, too, drifted away, and he slept.

Saturday 5 May

CARSINGTON DID NOT wake until midafternoon. Sun streamed through the cabin window, and Miles, sitting upon the far end of the divan, had been trying to while away the time reading a book.

He gave up the effort when Carsington pushed up to a sitting position.

"I'm not sure you're allowed to sit up," Miles said.

Under lifted eyebrows, the coal-black eyes regarded him steadily.

Miles remembered that the patient was not to be agitated, either. "On the other hand," he added, "I'm not sure who could stop you. Daphne, maybe, but I finally persuaded her to get some sleep. She sat up all night with you. Worried about a fever, she said."

"Not very likely," Carsington said. "How should I look them in the face, I ask you, was I to get infected and feverish and such—over a bit of a cut? They'd laugh themselves sick, the lot of them."

"The lot of whom?" Miles said.

"Family," Carsington said. "My brothers. Alistair was at Waterloo, you know."

"I know."

All the world knew. Alistair Carsington was a famous Waterloo hero. Why couldn't *he* be the Carsington in Egypt? Or any other one of them? Why did it have to be this one?

"They shot three horses out from under him, sliced him up with sabers, and stuck him with lances," Carsington said. "Some cavalry rode over him and a couple of soldiers died on him. Did *he* get infected and feverish?"

"Did he not?" Miles said.

"Well, not very much," Carsington said. "He lived, didn't he? If he could live through that, I can jolly well live through a nick in the belly."

"I hope so," Miles said. "I think Daphne would take it very ill, were you to require planting."

He couldn't imagine what she'd endured when she believed Carsington dead. He felt like a fool for not realizing she'd become attached. But she had concealed it so well.

Besides, Daphne never noticed men—or if she did, it was to regard them with mistrust. Why should Miles think Carsington's case any different? Why should he, of all men, turn out to be the one she'd risk her life for? Miles could scarcely believe his bookish sister had risked her life on his own account, and he was her *brother.*

Belatedly he recollected the instructions and explanations she'd given before departing the cabin. "I'm to offer you a glass of water," he said. "Daphne said she'd given you some laudanum, and you might wake up feeling dry."

"I feel as though someone moved the Arabian Desert into

my mouth while I was sleeping," Carsington said. "Along with the camels. Am I allowed to have a wash and a shave and clean my teeth at least? But never mind what she allows. She's asleep. What she doesn't know won't hurt her."

"Yes, but you really must move as little as possible," Miles said. "To avoid putting pressure on the wound. You will not want all her work to go for naught?"

Carsington instantly stilled. "No, of course not. She was picking out bits of cloth—the merest threads—for hours, it seemed. What a beast I should be, to undo all her efforts."

Miles blinked, once, twice. He was not sure what he'd expected. He knew Carsington was unmanageable. Everyone in the world knew it. Even his formidable father appeared to have given up the case as hopeless.

Miles did not wonder at his lordship's sending his fourth son to Egypt. He only wondered at the earl's not sending the son to China, or Tierra del Fuego, or the Antipodes.

"I'll valet you," Miles offered. He collected the bowl, ewer, and towel. He found Carsington's toothbrush and shaving kit, and placed all within easy reach.

While he was playing manservant, the mongoose ran into the room. She rose up on her hind legs and watched the proceedings.

When Miles had settled back into his place, she crawled into his lap and watched from there. "I heard her name is Marigold," Miles said.

"She's in love with your shirt," Carsington said.

Miles had already heard the story, and put two and two together. While Carsington set about his toilette, Miles told of his adventures in Minya and the limping mongoose he'd fed.

"Obviously it's the same one," Carsington said. "What a wicked deceiver she is. I thought she was fond of me. Yet I've never seen her sit still for so long. She usually grows bored with my shaving in a minute or two. I now realize she was only using me to while away the interval until she saw you again. You're the one she truly loves."

Miles stroked the creature. "You seem to have collected several strays on the way upriver," he said.

"Marigold collected us," he said. "The rest is Daph— Mrs. Pembroke's doing."

At that moment, Miles silently bore what he hoped was the last of the shocks. Daphne had not simply formed an attachment. She had formed an *intimate* attachment.

With Rupert Carsington, Lord Hargate's famously wild and famously untamable scapegrace son.

Still, Miles reminded himself, there were worse men in the world. Noxley, for instance. Pembroke.

Meanwhile this man had beyond doubt won the affection and loyalty of the crew and servants. They had nothing but praise for him. They'd fought for him. The mongoose liked him, too.

Even the cats had wandered in once this afternoon and deigned to sit at the foot of the divan and stare at him while he slept.

When the toilette was done, Miles helped him into a fresh Arab-style shirt, of the style that came nearly to the ankles. It was not elegant, but it was cool. The long front opening allowed easy access to his wound.

When he was dressed, and Miles had helped prop him up with another pillow, Carsington made him feel a little better by saying, "That was wonderfully quick thinking on your part last night: the torch and the papyrus."

"That curst papyrus," Miles said. "I should be glad to be rid of it, if not for Daphne. She had done so much work, and it was a fine manuscript, superior even to the immensely long one illustrated in the *Description de l'Egypte*. Now the French will have this one as well, plague take them."

"She still has the copy," Carsington said. "It isn't so beautiful, of course, and lacks the illustrations. But she'll persevere. She's dauntless. I've never known a woman like her, not remotely like her. Did you see her last night, when those fellows were coming at us, that great lot of ruffians? She turned and cocked her pistol and fired, just as sure as you please. Got the fellow in the leg, too. Not that I was surprised, when I've seen her courage again and again. From the very start."

He launched into the story: how Daphne had gone down into a dungeon of the Citadel to get him when no one else would help her . . . the murders in the second pyramid and the pluck she'd displayed then . . . the tour of the Pyramid of Steps at Saqqara, which had involved miles of narrow passages and during which she'd uttered no complaint—quite the opposite.

"I vow, she might have been at the Egyptian Hall in Piccadilly or making a tour of Stourhead," Carsington said. "If she was uncomfortable, she took no notice—and you ought to know it was ninety degrees at least inside that pyramid, and the air thick with smoke and dust."

"Daphne?" Miles said. "But she has a deep fear of small, closed spaces. Her voice goes up to a squeak, and she jabbers endlessly. It is very irritating."

"She did not squeak with me," Carsington said. "I saw she had a morbid aversion to such places, but she will not let the fear hold her back. I wish you had seen her when we were stuck in that caved-in robber's tunnel in the tomb in Asyut."

He went on to tell that tale while Miles listened, wondering if he'd got drunk again without realizing, because it could not be his sister Daphne of whom Carsington spoke with so much enthusiasm. And admiration. As though . . . as though—

"You're in love with her," Miles said. Then, "Er," he said. Because he hadn't meant to say it *aloud*. He stared hard at the mongoose. She licked his hand.

"In love?" Carsington repeated. "In *love?*"

"Er, no. Sorry. Don't know what I was thinking. The heat. The shock. Couldn't believe it was my sister you were talking about. Brave and dashing and and all that."

Carsington's countenance darkened.

"Not but what I expect she'd rise to the occasion," Miles added hastily. He was not afraid of Carsington, exactly. Yet he had to admit the glare was a trifle daunting. In any event, it wasn't good for the man to become overwrought. Daphne had said so. "My sister is a plucky creature, of course—continuing her work in spite of all the discouragement, and so forth."

"You've got it backwards," Carsington said. "It wasn't her rising to the occasion. It's the occasion rising to *her.* Egypt and this business with you and the papyrus have finally given her the chance to show what she truly is.

She's—she's a goddess. But human. A real goddess, not make-believe. She's beautiful and brave and wise. And fascinating. And dangerous. As goddesses are, as you know, in all the best stories."

"I'll be hanged," Miles said. "You really *are* in love with her."

The black eyes regarded him steadily. Then they regarded the cabin ceiling. Then the window. Then they came back to him.

"Do you know," Carsington said mildly, "I've been wondering what it was."

DAPHNE CAME AT sunset, accompanied by Nafisah. The *Isis* was still traveling upriver and would not moor until darkness made it too dangerous to proceed. The Nile was very low. Even in broad day, navigation wanted every iota of the helmsman's attention.

Archdale had thought they might make it to Isna before night fell.

Rupert didn't care where they were or where they would moor. He saw that Nafisah's tray held utensils for two. Daphne intended to dine with him. Alone.

Perfect.

Nafisah set the tray on the stool and left. Marigold ran in, stood up and sniffed at the tray, and ran out again.

Ignoring both the mongoose's antics and Rupert's not very convincing protests, Daphne arranged cushions behind him. Only when she'd settled him to her satisfaction did she settle herself.

Rupert didn't mind. She had donned a particularly fetching Arab-style ensemble comprising full but wickedly thin Turkish trousers, a thin crepe shirt, a silk sash draped provocatively over her hips, and a flowing silk overgarment. The faint scent of incense wafted about him.

This was all highly encouraging.

"That is a horrid temptation to put before a man who is forbidden to make vigorous movements," he said.

"Is it really?" she said. "No wonder Miles did not approve. He looked daggers at me."

"Maybe his face froze that way," Rupert said. "He was looking daggers at me a few hours ago. Do you think he suspects?"

"I think he *knows*," she said.

"I'm glad I don't have a sister," he said. "I should have to get over my aversion to killing people."

She turned her attention to the tray. "If I remember my physic correctly, you need to strengthen the blood. You must take some lamb stew. Red wine, of course. The rice is cooked in chicken broth with onions. Some bread and cheese. Some fruit. A little—"

"I can't eat just yet," he said. "I am too—too—" He frowned. "Too something. Feelings."

Her green gaze met his. "Feelings," she repeated.

"I meant to wait," he said. "Until I was better. Because I didn't want pity to influence you."

"Pity," she said.

"On account of my wound," he said.

"Don't be absurd," she said. "I shouldn't pity you on account of a nick in the belly."

"In any event, I can't wait," he said. "And I had better warn you that I don't mean to be in the least sporting. If I have to go on my knees, and start bleeding again—"

"I can think of no reason for you to go on your knees," she said severely.

"Then you're not thinking clearly," he said. "It's the usual way these things are done."

"These things," she said, a degree less severely.

"I should have done it that way the first time, but I hardly knew what I was doing," he said. "You said it was better to marry than to burn, and I was in a state of eternal conflagration, it seemed—but that wasn't what it was at all."

She shifted up onto her knees. "Perhaps you ought to take some wine," she said.

"My strength is up to this," he said. "I only hope my brain is, too. I want to explain first. Because you aren't to think it's completely on account of lust. Lust is a part, yes. A large part."

She sank back onto her heels and regarded her hands.

"But I liked you from the moment I first heard your

voice," he said, "when I had no idea what you looked like. I thought it delicious, the way you bargained for me, as though I were an old rug. Then I loved the way you looked at me. Then I loved the way you ordered me about. I loved your patient and impatient ways of explaining things to me. I love the sound of your voice and the way you move. I love your courage and your kindness and your generosity and your obstinacy and your passion." He paused. "You're the genius. What do you think that means?"

She threw him a sidelong glance. "I think you're insane," she said. "Perhaps you have developed an infection which has gone directly to your head."

"I am not insane," he said. "A woman of your highly advanced intellect ought to be able to perceive that I am in love. With you. I wish you had told me. It was deuced embarrassing to find it out from your *brother.*"

Her gaze swung toward him, green eyes wide and flashing. "Miles?" she said. "Did he get into a snit about my honor and insist—"

"Don't be ridiculous," he said. "He has not lived the life of a recluse, as you have. You may be sure he knows all about me. I've no doubt I'm the last man on earth he'd want near his sister. Well, maybe I'm second to last. After Noxley. But never mind them. This is between us, Daphne. I love you with all my heart. Will you be so good as to marry me?"

"Yes," she said. "Yes, of course. I should never have said no the first time. I have bitterly regretted the error, believe me. I could live without you, but that would only be breathing. It would not be *living.*"

He opened his arms, and she crawled toward him on her hands and knees and came into them. "I missed you," she said. "I missed you so much." She lay her head upon his shoulder. "Can we be married right away? I hate sleeping in my own cabin."

"We can be married now," he said, nuzzling her soft hair. "Remember?"

"Yes. But you must have a dowry." She reached down and untied the silken sash. "This will have to do."

He took it from her. It was quite heavy, even for a large

piece of silk. "What have you got twisted up in this?" he said. "Rocks?"

"Five purses," she said. "About thirty-five pounds."

"You came prepared."

"Of course I did," she said. "When I want something, I will stop at nothing. Look at what I'm wearing."

"I like what you're not wearing, too," he said.

"I am even so shameless as to take advantage of you when you are weak and wounded."

"I'm not that weak," he said. He dropped the sash onto the divan and put his hands to better use, roving over her shapely body. "We'd better get married *right away,*" he said.

"Yes," she said.

Her hands weren't idle, either. But her mouth, that soft mouth was even more dangerous, gliding over his neck and collarbone.

He raised her head and brought her mouth to his. She tasted cool and sweet, like Turkish sherbet. She tasted hot and dark like brandy held over a flame. She tasted mysterious, like a goddess, and her power over him would have terrified a lesser man.

But he wasn't a lesser man, and a strong woman was exactly what he wanted. A strong, wondrously curved woman who fit perfectly in his arms. He dipped his head and drew his tongue down the opening of her *kamees* and along the fragrant path between her breasts. She sighed and dragged her fingers through his hair.

He slid his hand over the beautiful swell of her bottom. She moved under his touch, shifting closer. He grasped that magnificent derrière and brought her sex firmly against his. And stifled a groan.

"You'll hurt yourself," she murmured against his mouth.

"That wasn't a groan of pain," he said.

He was aware of the wound. Every movement caused a twinge. He didn't care. She was all soft woman and in his arms, and in his mouth and his nostrils and he was drunk with the taste and scent of her . . . and she'd said she couldn't live properly without him. She'd said yes.

"We mustn't tear the stitches," she said.

"Then we'd better not move very much."

"Is that possible?"

"Yes." He stroked down her belly, over the thin fabric. He loosened the waist string of her trousers and pushed them down. He stroked over the feathery curls and the soft flesh, so warm and wet, so ready and willing. She sighed and moved against his hand. She pushed his shirt up to his waist. His rod sprang up in cheerful welcome, as usual. With a soft laugh, she grasped it and drew her slim fingers down its length. Then she shifted herself, bringing her leg up high on his thigh, and guided him in, and the jolt of pleasure in that joining took his breath away.

They scarcely moved at all. Awareness became all the more intense. He was aware each time her muscles tensed about him and eased, and of the very slight motion of her hip that sent waves of pleasure coursing through him. He was aware of her hands, gliding over him, and making long trails of sparks over his skin.

He opened his eyes and looked at her, and they smiled at each other in silent, wicked amusement, the devil in him recognizing the devil in her. And so they lay, watching each other, making secret love, while from outside came the familiar sounds of footsteps on the deck, voices calling out as they prepared to land.

A long sweet while of rippling pleasure ensued, like the Nile rippling beneath them, and then he was caught in a rushing current. She grasped him tightly, holding him still, while she moved upon him. The world went dark and wild, and he fell into it, into her, and all he knew was feeling beyond any words, a vast, mad happiness.

Then came her voice in his ear: "I give myself to thee. I give myself to thee. I give myself to thee."

And at last she sank onto him, and he wrapped his arms about her and savored the delicious peace. The stray, funny thought came: *we're married,* and he laughed out loud.

Epilogue

IN LATE JULY, FOLLOWING A LONG AND STORM-tossed voyage from Egypt, two representatives of Muhammad Ali arrived at Hargate House and presented his lordship with the news of his fourth son's untimely demise, along with a handsome chest containing the skull of his killer.

The rest of the family being in the country at the time, Lord Hargate was obliged to bear the news with silent and exceedingly lonely dignity.

Not wishing all the world to know before his wife did, his lordship mentioned the matter to nobody. He simply set out a few hours later for Derbyshire, to break the news in person.

He stopped only to allow the horses to be changed. He never slept. He had taken the chest containing the skull with him. He did not know why. This was one of the rare occasions of the earl's life when he was lost, quite lost.

He arrived at the house at the moment Benedict was leaving. The eldest son took one look at his parent's face and turned around and went back in with him.

Lord Hargate led his wife out into the garden and told her in a few broken words.

She said only, "No," and folded her hands tightly at her waist, and turned away and stared dry-eyed into the distance.

Benedict asked to see the letter. His father gave it to him, then put his arm about his wife's shoulders.

Benedict left them and went inside to read the letter. The house was strangely quiet, as though the servants, who'd not yet been informed, sensed a catastrophe.

It reminded him of the oppressive silence in his own house after his wife's death two years ago. He'd felt numb, then, too.

Hearing carriage wheels and hoofbeats coming up the drive—at a gallop by the sounds of it—Benedict went to the window. It was a handsome traveling chariot.

Waving the servants aside, he went out to intercept it. His parents were not in a state to receive visitors. Still, Lord Hargate might be wanted on urgent government business—and anyway Benedict needed something to do.

He arrived at the front of the house a moment after the carriage clattered to a stop.

Before he could start toward it, the door flung open, and a man leapt out . . . and grinned at him.

His brother.

His dead brother.

Rupert.

Benedict blinked once. This, from him, was a sign of overpowering emotion.

"You're not dead," he said as Rupert strode toward him.

"Certainly not," Rupert said, giving him one of his enthusiastic brotherly hugs.

Benedict, still in the grip of strong feeling, patted him on the shoulder.

"Whatever gave you the idea I was dead?" Rupert said when these first transports were over.

Benedict explained about the two emissaries from Muhammad Ali and the condolence letter from the English consul general and the chest with the head in it.

Rupert brushed this aside. "They are ridiculously slow about everything. I daresay the emissaries came to London after visiting all the brothels between Alexandria and Portsmouth. My letter to Father is probably coming by way of Patagonia. But never mind. His lordship will cheer up wonderfully when he sees what I've brought him."

"No exotic animals, I hope," said Benedict. "He will tell you his family is menagerie enough."

"It isn't an exotic animal," Rupert said.

"No mummies," said Benedict. "Mother dislikes the smell."

"As do I," Rupert said. "It isn't a mummy."

"I refuse to play guessing games," Benedict said. "You may tell me or not at your leisure. I, meanwhile, had better go in ahead and prepare our parents for your resurrection." He turned away.

"It's a wife," Rupert said.

Benedict turned back. "Whose wife?" he said.

Rupert had never, to his knowledge, made off with anyone's wife before, but there was no predicting what Rupert would do, especially in a foreign country where wives usually came in the plural rather than the singular. Rupert might think this sheik or that bey could spare one.

"She's mine," Rupert said. Dropping his voice, he added, "I've got her in the carriage."

Benedict had forgotten everything else in his astonishment at seeing his supposedly dead brother. Now, directing his attention to the carriage, he observed an occupant. A woman, bent over a book.

He turned back to Rupert. "She's reading," Benedict said. "A book."

"Yes, she reads heaps of them," Rupert said. "Most aren't even in English. She's a brilliant scholar."

"A *what?*"

"Her brain is simply enormous," Rupert confided. "But Father won't care about her intelligence."

"Beyond being amazed that any woman who had any would marry you," Benedict said.

"Yes, it is amazing," Rupert said. "But that isn't the funniest part." He lowered his voice to a whisper. "She's an *heiress.*"

Once more, Benedict blinked. He was aware that his father had told Alistair, his third son, and Darius, the fifth, to find well-dowered brides, because he refused to keep them forever. But Rupert, who came between them, was excused, on grounds that no rational person would give a fortune into his keeping.

"An heiress," Benedict said. "Well, I am very glad for you."

"Oh, I don't care about it," Rupert said. "You know I've no notion of money. But I can't wait to see Father's face when I tell him."

SOME HOURS LATER, after the bride and groom had retired to their assigned apartments, their eldest son joined Lord and Lady Hargate once more in the garden.

"Well, well," said his lordship. "It appears some unfortunate assassin got his head cut off for nothing."

"And the prodigal son returns triumphant," said Benedict. "Married. To Cousin Tryphena's brilliant and handsome young widow friend. The one with the handsome fortune." He smiled a very little. Smiles had never come as easily to him as to Rupert, and less easily still in the last two years.

"Tryphena will be delighted," said her ladyship.

"I had wondered why you sent him to Egypt, of all places," Benedict said.

His father merely lifted an eyebrow.

"Well, I am happy for him," Benedict said. "They suit each other very well, and naturally, the end justifies the means. At any rate, he's settled at last. Now you may give your full attention to Darius."

With that he took his usual distant leave.

His parents stood looking after him.

"Not Darius, I think," said Lady Hargate.

"No," said his lordship. "Not Darius."

Postscript

In August, Jean-Claude Duval boarded a ship bound for France. He took with him seventy-five cases of antiquities he'd collected in recent years. Since he failed to include the troublesome papyrus (and certain other objects) on the list provided to the customs officials at Alexandria, no one could be sure whether in fact he had finally obtained it. It was known only that the papyrus did not find a home in the Louvre, and the ship carrying him and his collection was lost in a storm off the coast of Malta.

New York Times bestselling author
Loretta Chase
Miss Wonderful

Alistair Carsington really, really wishes he didn't love women quite so much. To escape his worst impulses, he sets out for a place far from civilization: Derbyshire—in winter! But this noble aim drops him straight into opposition with Miss Mirabel Oldridge, a woman every bit as intelligent, obstinate, and devious as he—and maddeningly irresistible.

**"*Wickedly witty,
simply wonderful!*"
—Stephanie Laurens**

0-425-19483-3

b982